FLIGHT OF THE GOOSE

a story of the far north

*When all is well, Sila sends no message to
humankind...as long as we do not abuse life
but act with reverence toward our daily food*

NAJAGNEQ (INUPIAQ SHAMAN)

The author acknowledges the following publishers for the use of their copyrighted materials:

Poem excerpts by Yeats are reprinted with the permission of Scribner, an imprint of Simon & Schuster Adult Publishing Group, from the THE COLLECTED WORKS OF W.B. YEATS, VOLUME 1: THE POEMS, REVISED, edited by Richard J. Finnegan. (New York: Scribner, ©1997);

Viking poem excerpts reprinted with the permission of University of Pennsylvania Press, from the POEMS OF THE ELDER EDDA, REVISED EDITION, translated by Patricia Terry, ©1990;

Inuit poem excerpts reprinted with the permission of University of Alaska Press, Classic Reprint Series from ACROSS ARCTIC AMERICA: NARRATIVE OF THE FIFTH THULE EXPEDITION by Knud Rasmussen, ©1999;

Inuit poem excerpts from BEYOND THE HIGH HILLS, translated by Knud Rasmussen, The World Publishing Company, ©1961

Flight of the Goose: a story of the far north - First Edition.

ISBN 0-9678842-1-7

Cover design by Eric Oberg

in memory of Andrea

TABLE OF CONTENTS

AUTHOR'S NOTE

Itiak is a fictitious village, although it is resembles Inupiat villages of the Norton Sound and Bering Strait regions of Northwest Alaska. These villages are diverse and distinct, as are the individuals living in them. No particular village was my model for Inupiat culture, nor was any one person. Any resemblance to actual events, individuals or village is coincidental, or, if real, they are used fictitiously to lend authenticity. Any errors, omissions or misunderstandings are entirely my own. In 1971 "Eskimo" was commonly used by Inupiat people to describe themselves, as it is today; "Inuit" was not used. I am not Inupiaq but was partly raised by Inupiat elders, and have been intimately exposed to the traditions through my relatives and in-laws, and growing up in rural Northwest Alaska.

The titles of the seven "Books" are borrowed from nineteenth century shamans across the Arctic. Epigraphs are excerpts of poems, hymns or prophecies from many ancient cultures (I am sorry that I could not include *all* cultures). These are the words of mystics, shamans, witches, seers and healers. If the author is known to be a woman I point it out, since the role of women is of such importance in the novel. My method of finding and choosing excerpts was mostly serendipitous.

This story was long in the making, and without the encouragement of many allies, benefactors, teachers and guardian spirits in this mortal plane and in the other realms, it never would have flown. My gratitude goes to all the people in Western Alaskan villages, Kotzebue and Nome who shared their lives and the knowledge of their elders with me, and to David Mason, Nancy and Perry Mendenhall, Sue Nevins, Dolly Spencer and all my brothers and sisters-in-law for help in my research. Appreciation for my readers Barbara Bell, Jean L. Briggs, Nelda Danz (and Fritz for watching the kids while she read), Mary Alice Kier, Nancy Mendenhall, Michelle Merklin, Eric Oberg, and Mary Kay Seales. My husband Eric, mother Nancy, daughter Shannon and grandmother Jean helped me immensely with their understanding of a writer's funny ways. Special thanks to Jean L. Briggs, whose *Never in Anger* inspired me as a child living in an Inupiat village. And special acknowledgment to the late George Aghupuk, whose drawings of the old life stirred my soul before I could read.

Two geese made an appearance in a marsh in Seattle in the darkest hour of writing; thanks to them too.

PROLOGUE

My life will be too long on this earth
and I will never get beyond
the footprints that I leave behind me

QERNERTOQ (WIDOW, UMINGMAQTORTIUT)

How can anyone know
what is possible for those in love?

(ANCIENT NORSE, NALUAGMIUT)

ONCE IN TAIMMANI, *in long ago times, a hunter wandered into a village that kindly took him in. He married the headman's daughter. But as always in these stories, he did not stay. After he left the village and looked back he saw that they were really birds. He had been living with birds and even making love with one, yet he had not known. This old story reminds us that we are not so different from the other creatures and that we must take care of their feelings. But it also tells us that we can live in a society, a family, and never know who they truly are or who we ourselves are until we leave and look back.*

Let me tell another story of looking back as winter sets in. The birds have left us. The womanly sun is dying while the force of the hunter moon grows stronger. He follows his old path and we feel fear. At sea a mighty storm is gathering but no one knows when it will strike nor how long it will last. The seals or spirits may know, but who can ask them; who speaks their language now? Things have grown unfamiliar and we wonder what we did wrong. The warmth of summer is strange and long. The great ice is disappearing, the fish are leaving us and the skies are dark with smoke. The birds do not find their way back in spring; what has happened to them? The bears and walrus and seals have no place to nurse their young. The animals are sickening and we are told to not eat them, nor nurse our own babies. Soon we must leave our home, retreating from the rising waves. We will join the saddened animals and wander, hoping for mercy from strangers. We remember our grand-mothers and grandfathers who were born into a world that was changing, and doubt we can be so brave.

Let me tell a story to cast light on the dark world and the darkening heart. Read it as if you are listening in the old way, without interrupting. Don't ask why we felt the way we did. Don't say we should have felt differ-ently, or say it was impossible or complain that there should be more adven-tures of man against nature and man against man. Men have told so many of those old stories. I am not sure they help us anymore.

But this is not a tale just for women, that men must turn away. It is about men of not so long ago, when scientists believed digging for oil - not the burning of it in distant lands - was the worst danger to the animals and so to our way of life. It was a time when much was hidden, before outsiders came on bended knee to learn from us. Outsiders came, but it was to change us. There was a war and a university, an oil company and a small village, all run by men. There was a young man who hunted geese to feed his family and another who studied geese to save them. There was a young woman who flew into the world of spirits to save herself. And as I draw breath to tell this tale a bird flies into my mind, long-necked and brown with black bars on its feathers. Its harsh cry diminishes overhead.

Let me tell what happened, and don't ask at the end what the message is. Whatever is already in us at birth, we find again in stories. We see it in the face of the moon, in the face of our lover, in our own death, in the flight of the goose.

BOOK ONE

"Things Will Not Be Familiar"

But as the unconscious years wore by,
the Creator watched the unlit dawn of man wistfully
as the flight of a bird in the sunset beyond the marsh...
and dreamed he saw again those far-gone days
when he watched the Bird toiling under the moonless night
to make safe the bounds of the world

YORUBA HIGH PRIEST (ANCIENT AFRICAN)

Then wilt wish in tears and murmurs,
that as smoke thy soul had risen...
as a bird thou canst not wander
from thy nest to circle homeward...
thou must search for hidden wisdom
in the minds of perch and salmon,
in the mouths of ocean whiting,
gather wisdom from the cuckoo,
canst not learn it from thy mother...
where were born the human instincts,
where were born the minds of heroes
whence arose the maiden's beauty,
why all life revives in spring-time

KALEVALA BRIDE'S FAREWELL (ANCIENT FINNISH)

Seeing that I was longing for it
I gave it a name, the spirit

(PIUVLIQ SONG)

CHAPTER 1

Knowest thou thyself?
So little knowest of thyself
while dawn gives place to dawn
and spring is upon the village
ORPINGALIK (NETSILIK SHAMAN)

WHO AM I TO TELL a story? My hair is getting white and I have reached the age when men all across the North once respected and feared a woman, if they had not before. It is the age of witches and storytellers. I have visited the Outside to see in the flesh what I once saw in spirit. I have words now that give a different kind of power than what I once sought. I can barter using the past, its sense of loss and mystery. Maybe it is a tale to be told in the winter, for winter ruled in the north and they used to tell the stories then. But let me start in the spring. Spring was the time of beginnings.

We were coming back across the inlet in late May of 1971. The open skiff ran low, loaded down with us and the last of the whitefish we had chopped out of the storage pits on the bank of the Igaluk. In the fall we had picked them from the net and tossed them still twitching into the earth freezer. Abe and Flo had brought their two older grandchildren, who could boat in the cold without whining.

Their son, Willy, gazed steadfastly across the narrow peninsula to the sea. Surely he wished to be hunting seal instead of hauling dogfood, but he'd lent his boat out and he needed these fish. He was low on cash, lacking even cornmeal to feed his huskies. Abe's old mother came too, hunched in the bow. Though getting blind and crippled she went on outings to listen to birdsong. Maybe it reminded her of when she was a girl.

And there was me.

It was a fair day, the lagoon dark blue and clear of ice. I liked the feel of the wind grabbing my ribs through my thin cotton *kaspaq.* Though only just above freezing, compared to eighty below with windchill factor it was balmy. I craved the smells of saltwater and melting snow, of mud and grass springing up thick. Tiny flowers shook on the bare hills, in lowlands and along creeks, wind-tattered bits of color that made me smile. I loved the sun that traveled the ring of the world and dipped under near midnight. The sunset lasted for hours, fire turning into soft gray, and the children and birds couldn't rest.

And I was glad for the birds. Thousands were returning, led first by the little eider ducks, the messengers of spring. The sky, land and water was noisy with them. From all over the world they flew, so many kinds I had no name for some in any language. The region around our village was famous for that abundance. They came for the bugs wriggling in ponds and marshes or the small fish in the opening ice leads. They came to raise families. I think they also liked how they could see and hear so far, with no trees to block the views or their calls. They could look in a full circle and admire all the other birds dancing, or get jealous. And they could see a fox coming. The geese were my favorite even then, before they became such a force in my life. Watching their swift black arrows, I could forget I was a human bound to this earth, and a village. Their voices called urgently high above, *Come with us! Come with us!* And for a time I would, until the choir faded.

Of course, I liked to eat them too, in a rich oily goose soup.

We reached the choppy water where tide surged through the channel with a stiff wind. When the boat started to buck Abe's mother nearly fell from her seat. Spray hit us in the face to numb our cheeks and we ducked our heads, but Abe just squinted forward. Without looking in my direction he shouted over the shrill engine, the gusts, "Kayuqtuq, you change places with Aka."

Abe spoke the rest in English, as he did to his grandchildren. And that was how I felt, like he was commanding a child. I was cramped against a pile of fish-filled gunnysacks, hardly comfortable, yet I didn't move. Abe's hand that clenched the rudder was as leathery as an old walrus flipper and cracked from years of cold and saltwater. "*Ki,*" he said. Go on.

"Let one of the kids do that," I said under my breath. I was tired from chopping the rock-hard ground all day and there were grandchildren in the boat, I was grown - why should I be the one to jump? Because I had lost my sunglasses, it was hard to hide my resentment. I tried to relax my mouth, which would sometimes tighten like I was trying to bite off thread; others made sure to point it out to me. If you're going to resist, mad, it's better do it without expression and pretend nothing is happening. It's their imagination. You are innocent.

With a look, Abe appealed to Flo for help. Her spring *kaspaq* hurt the eyes in its brilliance of pink flowers and zig-zag borders. She couldn't be seen in warm weather without a bold, new print. Although she wore dark glasses I knew she was watching me. Her shoulders rose in a heavy, exaggerated sigh - *Adiii,* how troublesome I was. As we crested a wave and slammed down, Aka slid forward in the bow, her back hunched over. Ahead, little plovers skittered through the ripples of the shoal. I fixed my sight on them as Aka righted herself and tried to turn her old neck to scold.

In the corner of my vision I saw how Willy looked from Aka to me, then to his parents. Let him help his own grandmother! She was kind to him, so admiring of the game he brought in, ever since he laid his first ptarmigan at her outstretched feet. And he would sit listening to her wandering memories - she used to talk endlessly then and show him magic string animals that moved and changed into other things. They were a mutual admiration society.

But Willy didn't interfere with Abe's authority. Look at how he was, eager to spring up when the old man tipped his chin. If Abe wanted a gun or knife it was already there. Willy always wore a good smile, never mean, and his black eyes danced. He melted hard feelings with those eyes. If that didn't work he would look goofy, ready with a joke to ease matters. He really fit in, as if life was a well-made parka he could just slip on and look great. People admired his strong jaw and brow and his wide shoulders. If they noticed that his shiny black hair grew sneakily longer every season, they ignored it.

Willy was tough. When Abe trained him over the long years it took to create a good hunter, he held Willy's hands in frigid creeks and made him jog for miles on the tundra or walk over the rough ice holding his breath. Though Abe himself smoked, he was grieved when his son started, for he worried it would harm Willy's perfect lungs. On days when Willy was a clumsy shot the old man had silently brought him back to mull in the company of women about how *kuangazuk* he was, and regret the years he had lost while at boarding school learning useless things. Abe would never praise him - maybe worried he'd turn into a disrespectful boaster - yet Willy was always humble.

He proved many times over his courage and strength while hunting. Really, his only imperfection was his laugh, how sometimes it was too shrill like a seagull's cry and made us wince. Why shouldn't he be happy, the favored adopted son, complete opposite of me? I was not anyone's daughter, not even adopted. I never held it against him, though, because the good humor he spread over our home and over Itiak often landed on me as well, without prejudice.

When I caught Willy's eye under his dark shades, his half-grin lengthened until I saw molars. It was sympathetic, but a little teasing. The skiff bucked a sudden high wave, making Aka bounce and crash onto the seat. "*Vaaa!*" she cried, as if amused. Suddenly Abe cut the throttle so we were floating on the current, turning sideways. We heard the rush of water and the sad calls of plover over the wind. The grandchildren looked on, wide-eyed. The old man made the sound of disbelief, a soft raven-like call back in the throat. A noise we feared, it said, *I can't believe you would do this*. Especially in a boat at sea.

He said to Flo in Inupiaq, "Some people."

"Arnie," called Flo shrilly in English, "You climb up and sit in Aka's place. And Betsy help her come back there!" The grandchildren scrambled to obey. When everyone was resettled Abe pushed back his cap and with a backward lunge jerked the cord to open the throttle. The Evinrude roared and the skiff bucked and shot spray as it swung toward the border of white tents pitched on the inlet shore of the peninsula. We passed the flurry of birds in the marsh.

"Crazy like a fox," muttered Abe. I couldn't hear him over the engine - I read his lips. He was gazing past the stern but it was clear who he meant, and I imagined myself staggering and dripping foam as I circled the village to get at the tethered dogs. Boys chased me with Ski-Doos until I dropped on my haunches, snarling. Then they flattened me, with shouts of laughter. That is what boys did to foxes. Old people disapproved but looked the other way, for children had to grow into humanity slowly, like into a hand-me-down.

But *crazy like a fox* was a whiteman saying. In the old stories a fox was a cunning troublemaker, it stole, it tricked and lied, yet was not out of its mind. I wondered at Abe; surely he did not know I begged fox's spirit to be my *turnaq*, or that it had agreed. Not the white fox who trailed after polar bears on the pack, but the red *kayuqtuq*. In the last few years more had wandered from the Interior. They were outsider foxes. One was the red star, which I knew was Mars. One had bounded straight into my dream as I lay asleep on the tundra one summer. And Kayuqtuq was my Eskimo name.

Abe's furrowed eyes scanned the far shoreline and sky. Always searching, the old hunter. Did he really dislike me so much? Maybe he took pleasure in my ways because they made life interesting. Flo was scrutinizing the shore as well, probably looking for new groves of plants or the amount of *ugzruk* meat hanging on other women's drying racks. It was Flo who had taken me in years before. Without her I would be pushed off the boat like the Orphan, the Woman, and everyone would beat at my clinging fingers with the oar and I would sink to the bottom of the sea to live with crabs.

With a shudder I cleared my mind and took deep breaths of the clean air. Sometimes, if I let it, my imagination could fall like a dead fish into a steep pit from which even the spring sun couldn't lift me. Now we were in the sparkling shoal, where sandpipers raced on invisible legs. Abe swung the skiff and drove it into the shallows then cut the motor and tipped it up. In the sudden quiet the lapping waves sounded musical. Willy and I jumped out to drag the boat in, its aluminum bottom rumbling on gravel. Freezing water worked in through the cracks of my boots. Willy always got the hip-waders.

We were at the halfway-camp on the inlet side. It was still too early for fishcamp, but nobody wanted to be in the village with its stink of thawing dog manure, rotten skins, outhouses and garbage mounds. If people felt like it, they would overnight here in our big white canvas tent. Abe and Willy brought the big bearded seals through the channel for Flo and me to butcher at this camp. Our driftwood drying rack was already strung with *ugzruk* turning to black jerky in the wind. Their six-foot skins were stretched and staked, ready for us women to scrape. Stacked on the cache were pokes we made of the inflated skins of smaller spotted or ringed seals, into which we stuffed the blubber and dried meat. Maq, a dog staked there to keep away robbing gulls and jaegers, yapped and fawned in her silly way as we came near, and in futility threw herself to the end of her chain.

The grandchildren jumped out of the boat and raced around chasing birds and leaping over ponds. Beyond fetching water, they were too young to do much work. When they were tired or hungry they could run back into town to any relative's house, and grab stew and doze on the floor on reindeer hides. There was never darkness, few dangers, and school was nearly out. I envied their carefree life. I had never had one, even when so small.

We left Flo with the kids and pushed the boat out again, heading for the coast side of the peninsula. There, we'd throw the dogfood into another pit closer to home. As we were plowing through the channel, making slow headway through the incoming tide, an engine droned up in the eastern sky. It was the little mail Cessna that flew up from Nome every week. I craned to make it out in the blue. There it was, white and winking. It banked and headed toward the landing strip north of the village. The engine made a falling, disappointed noise, *Aaahh.*

Abe followed my gaze, a lit cigarette stuck in the corner of his mouth. Now that we were heading to sea without his mother he looked more relaxed. "Another scientist coming in," he shouted. "That's what they say."

"Just what I always wanted," Willy said. I kept looking at the plane, sensing its importance. It carried something out of the ordinary that was linked with me. A letter? That would be the day. Abe laughed at Willy's sarcasm, or maybe at my odd interest.

"Kayuqtuq, *uvva*! I can't smoke like this!" Abe turned the rudder over to me and switched seats. He was nimble for an old man with arthritis. He squinted against wind, scanning for the black dot of a seal's head, enjoying his Lucky that streamed smoke and sparks. He seemed to also enjoy watching me steer the boat - usually he didn't let me. Maybe he was sorry for his gruffness earlier.

"What kind of weather tomorrow, I wonder?" he asked suddenly. Was he asking Willy? He would not - it was a test and Willy was past any testing, a hunter in his prime. I studied the southern sky, where white clouds massed up. North was clear. A few snipe hung above the boat, their long tails fluttering. On the mainland the mountains loomed black with jagged white streaks. A strong southwesterly might rise and drive the pack-ice north along with the seals, but I didn't say so. Of course Abe knew what conditions were coming and he did not test girls. Some of us took birds and hares but we were not supposed to hunt at sea. Just by our blood we could bring bad luck or offend the animals. Abe didn't ever want me along, I didn't want to go, so why should he test me?

Some people - especially the old men - couldn't be read very well. They had built up a lot of protection over the years of mission school and close quarters and struggles with other men and hunting dangerous prey, until it was as thick as sea-ice. Abe's soul was like the tower the government built in Nome for missile detection. It stood on a mountaintop guarded by soldiers, and if anyone was caught snooping he would be shot.

His face was impassive. Still, when his narrowed gaze landed on mine for a split second before traveling on, I caught its mean little glint. Was that also a ray of fear shooting out? Nothing in this world scared that old hunter, only what came from the Devil. Like alcohol, and some kinds of whitemen. Then I saw the guilty quirk on Willy's mouth. He had told! That Willy - I could give away *his* secrets, then he'd know the old man's ridicule, the chilly anger waiting like pack-ice to close in. If Flo found out, the warrior of the church would be after me too.

Back then the women saw ghosts and could sense when people were in trouble. They knew their thoughts could help the men hunt or a baby to heal. Flo even used me to find the hiding places of her awls or hair clasps. But it was not considered evil, it wasn't powers, it was normal. This was different, it was from the world that young people had no name for and that no one spoke of anymore. It was buried deep and left alone like the artifacts along the cliffs where the village used to be.

"Does someone think she can make good weather, like those priest villages who dance to Satan?" Abe asked Willy. "Or she can make a south wind, move the ice in so we can't hunt? Maybe if all my prayers can't help, I better come to someone *else* about it, ah?" He chuckled, a hollow sound. Cutting it off short, he muttered something in Inupiaq about *itkiliq*.

Indians.

Willy covered his mouth with his hand and looked shocked at what he'd started. I wondered if he agreed with the old man, that I might try to harm them. He was careful to not look at me while Abe used him in his battle, the words of indirection that missed the heart but still wounded.

Abe said to him in English, "For rebellion is as the sin of witchcraft."

I had pored enough through Abe's Old Testament to send my answer back to him silently through the waves: *Is it nothing to you? Behold and see if there be any sorrow like unto my sorrow, which is done unto me?*

We heard the plane land.

YOU MIGHT MISUNDERSTAND. I did not want to bring back the terrors and sorrows I'd heard something about. People in the old days had ingenious ways to survive, but nature was ingenious too, in tricking you. If you did one little thing wrong it doomed you and maybe your family.

I didn't want the hunger, the animals suddenly taking offense and leaving, wolverines stealing everything in your caches, storms so long the food was gone, and fathers who went out day after day but caught nothing while mothers told the children not to cry. Or taking your children and wandering far in search of food and having to leave your *aka* behind, hoping she will not cry, or being that *aka*. Or having to eat your children.

Or living underground in dark, smoky huts following a hundred rules to protect the hunters and keep the animals and spirits from wrath, sewing and sewing tiny stitches by a tiny flame until you were bent and blind with teeth worn down to the jawbone from chewing skins - if you were lucky enough to get that old. Or having no skins to sew and no oil to feed that flame and no way to contact those you loved and missed who lived far away, and huddling in the fearful black, dying of thirst, dying in childbirth, dying of the sicknesses brought by the *naluagmiut*. I did not want to bring back *angutkoq* who reached a long arm into the dark tunnels and took your father's heart for revenge over some slight, or took *you* in payment. Or being killed by war parties, taken as a slave, sold to a man in a distant country, or traded to a familiar man that all the women hated.

I did not want the women's boat you had to row on high seas, and rain all summer on your skin tent, clouds of mosquitoes but no repellent, worms inside you, broken bones that never set. Or walking hundreds of miles under heavy packs, pulling boats up rivers, facing raging beasts with only a spear or knife, caught in storms, trapped in mush-ice, marooned on pack-ice and rushing away from land with no Search and Rescue. I did not want to wait for my family to arrive from a journey who never did arrive. I did not want to be a lost hunter who covered his face in his hood and cried while his family waited and waited, never knowing what became of him. The old ones could remind me of more if they were alive.

Things were still hard. The men still went out on the treacherous ice and took their skiffs through perilous currents. They lost their feet and fingers, fell off cliffs, got drowned in rivers, covered in avalanches or crushed by walls of *ivu* ice while they slept, lost in whiteouts, snowblind, frozen, mauled, killed and stripped to their bones by animals, and accidentally shot. Maybe the women's lives had changed the most in our comforts, though there was still so much drudgery for us. My life had not changed enough in some regards.

I didn't want to harm others - not really. I wanted to bring back a feeling I could not explain, that in spite of the danger and sadness or because of it, life in the old times was more joyful. People had a place in the world, and maybe they felt more alive. Or so I imagined. It seemed in modern times the old fears and hunger had just been replaced by new ones that kept me awake at night without any faith like the parents had to soothe me, and I asked myself, *Is this all there is?* Why was I even born? Why do the birds fly all the way here from across the world if this is *all there is?*

I didn't know if the grandparents had wondered that too. They weren't talking. And the birds, they had never changed.

CHAPTER 2

Nor shall your presence, how so ere it mar
The loveliness of Nature, prove a bar
To the Mind's gaining that prophetic sense
Of future change, that point of vision whence
May be discovered in soul ye are

WORDSWORTH (NALUAGMIUT)

I STILL HAVE the journal, salvaged from the last birdcamp. I still read it on
dark winter nights when I can't sleep for thoughts of the future, when no one
else is awake. It helps to make the tears fall, it makes the heart pliable like
chewing a stiff hide. It is better if they fall, for someone once so proud of her
lack of tears. I smile when I read it it too - I laugh out loud. She is far in the
past now, that girl, but the feelings remain. And I understand the journal
now - I understand him.

When I was young the writing was as outlandish to me as that on litter
washed in from the foreign ships. His handwriting was almost unreadable too,
if his fingers had been cold. Maybe to understand was what drew me Outside, later. Like me, he was a gatherer of ideas; he beachcombed for ideas,
searching far and wide to feed a great hunger, and was also misunderstood in
his searching.

ENTRY. 32 DEGREES, slush. If their psychologists read this it could be proof I've gone
to the birds and am unsuitable for search-and-destroy missions. I will quote from forefathers
demented by industrialization: "Each outcry from the hunted hare, a fibre from the brain doth
tear", etc. But of course they'd find a repressed Green Beret. My subconscious drew me to a
land of hunters, I live alone in the wilds: obviously a killer.

I'll try to describe Gyulnyev Peninsula. It was named by Tsarist explorers in the
1700's. It dangles down the coast like an arm throwing a rock, the fist being my research
zone and the stone a sandspit across the channel. From the sky it looked cellular surrounded
by its membrane of rotted land-fast ice. The pack has broken off it and is far out to sea but

there was an awesome, loose jumble of wildly varying floes, pans and bergs drifting by in the dark blue water like molecules, white blood cells in the interstitial fluid.

Gyulnyev lies beneath the Flyway, the most headspinning parade of diversity on Earth. A lot of stopover in the ponds, marsh and shoals here. My running tally: Canada, brant, snow, harlequin, eider, oldsquaw, merganser, pintail, scaup, scoter, whimbrel, curlew, yellow-legs, plover, sandpiper, godwit, loon, sandhill crane (and resident ptarmigan and raven). Gull, tern, kittiwake and passerine insanity. I had no idea there were so many songbirds here. What I thought was a line of strangely silent geese was really cormorants, shadowy and cool, heading toward some rookery island.

Seen from the air, Itiak is a thin wisp of settlement in a nearly scary expanse of tundra and whitecapped sea. It's just a smudge of shack a quarter mile long with a ribbon of mud down the middle and a green, fertilized perimeter. An airstrip controller named Ivan met me at the strip, middle-aged, taciturn. "Welcome to Itiak. You can stay at my house, room and board." I told him I had to camp near Elliraq Channel. "Windy place..." he remarked. He eyed my beard and hair, unkempt, probably, from this fierce wind. He's straight, with an overgrown military buzz that makes his hair stick up like black sealskin. Maybe I should hide my barbaric length under one of those ubiquitous duckbills. When I said I'd be waiting for a bird to show up there, "What bird?" he asked, as if I meant a singular bird, and he looked askance.

"A species. A kind of bird...a flock."

"Birdman, ah?" Ivan muttered to himself. "More birds somewhere else, maybe mainland."

A strong hint, although Master assured me Iliak's Council okayed the petition. Ivan may be just unhappy to lose rent. I explained the channel site was good because of the low marsh, ripe for destruction if an oil rig broke up on the Shelf. He looked at the empty sea, unimpressed. He had a point, if I read his body language right: there was no oil rig out there, so why invent catastrophes? I told him that also near the channel was where Tallin's goose was sighted last, but refrained from whipping out my field guide and interviewing him. The Company doesn't buy "anecdotes" anyway; it isn't data they can manipulate. And "primitive" observations would bring a sneer. When Ivan still looked courteously doubtful I said, "You know, kill two birds with one stone." He uttered a faint drawn-out sound, bird-like. Guess it means "You're pretty strange."

He offered to bring my gear down the coast in his boat. To my thanks he nodded and said nothing more. Ivan's as tall as me and gangly, which surprised me in my ignorance of the diversity of local physiognomy. Great upper body strength, enviable. We loaded his WWII flatbed, the mail truck. Children were everywhere, gawking and getting into my stuff, moving in packs like the unchained puppies. They were surprised I didn't hand out candy in the way of a Yank rolling through a bombed-out village. They crowded onto the flatbed with me, gig-gling and falling off as we went bumpety-bump over hummocks, mud and permafrost upthrust. They kept swinging on my arm and shouting questions but I couldn't understand a lot. They say "ah?" after nearly every sentence. Or "is it?" They tease and then cry "I jokes!" or "I fool", and everything about me is "funny" but I'm pretty sure they mean weird. Nearly every verb is prefixed with "always" and "play": Always play be funny. And they interchange "he" and "she": a cross-over from Inupiak?

A white steeple dominates the end of the row of shacks. Remember to avoid the north end, ah? Ivan drove at a breakneck speed onto the beach and loaded the gear into an out-board there for immediate transport south so I didn't get a good look at the hamlet, but I have to go in eventually to pick up word from the Man. Hard to imagine an office in that frail line of huts on the sea edge of a thousand miles of tundra.

I want to stay out of people's way. When we were flying here my bush pilot said I might not be too popular because of the Fish and Wildlife crackdown on migratory bird hunt-ing. All biologists are suspect. Was I under Fish and Game? Pilot Bob asked. I said no, under old ladies in boots. He didn't get it so I explained about the Audubon part of the grant. He lectured on merrily, screaming over the engine, pointing below at a reindeer, a wolf on the run. But little other mammalian life. I withheld my opinions on Alaskan subsistence or wildlife management. They have a more immediate effect on birds than potential oil spills. I don't think pollution and direct ecological disaster has even entered the argument here. Yet.

But Bob said Eskimos were well aware that something evil is going on "Down South" where the birds winter. In the old pre-state treaty being reincarnated, Natives can't shoot geese in nesting season, though traditionally geese warded off famine, when foul weather pre-vented seal hunts and stores had been used up. They're also not supposed to collect eggs, another spring staple. But a hunter in Barrow who studied under MLK had started a protest in '61 and the resistance spread. Federal agents have been shot at as they fly over fowling country; Bob was mistaken for one once.

A bush pilot, so erudite on conservation politics! I thought maybe he was a member of the sport-hunter lobby that tries to pass the blame of species depletion onto Natives. Then he told me his wife was Yupik. He admitted to "a sympathy", though he thought they overkilled with "all their high-power rifles." Maybe he wants them to return to bolas? And for molting season, nets and clubs?

"If an animal shows itself", Bob yelled, "they'll always take a shot at it. Any time, any kind of animal, because they eat anything, they even think the animal wants them to do it. And they have thirteen kids to feed; it ain't like the good old days when they killed the girl babies, keep things cool." He went on to blame Natives with guns for the loss of caribou. "And the Eskimos blame telegraph wires and the Gold Rush, by golly!" Fish and Wildlife chartered Bob to fly skeptical Natives over a herd so they could see for themselves the paucity. The Natives had said the biologists were lying; now they're accusing outdoorsman companies of using up all the geese in down products. "You can't tell them it's from farm geese. Maybe they can't imagine rows of geese inside pens. And paranoid! But they have their own agenda, keeping meat on the table. I can't say as I like a game warden either. And biologists are a bunch of egomaniac fairies!"

Bob apologized a minute later, seeming to recall who I was, and offered a lit reefer. I turned it down, thinking it a bad idea to land in a village stoned (or to fly a plane). Just out of Nome we'd been flying over barren volcanic mountains only two-three thousand in altitude. On the flats, mostly still brown, a radiant chartreuse of grass and sedge rings millions of glittering ponds. But the highlands are still winterbound with snow angling down their black basalt flanks, stark and forbidding. Spooky, the Kiglualik range. Ahead was a flat peak with horn-like escarpments on it, "Troll Mountain" (Norse prospector?). We banked and veered to get around it. The high gales often force planes to turn back from coastal villages.

"As for anthropologists," my pilot said, "the Natives think they're in the enemy camp too, passing on information to the government agencies." Bob's wife had asked him once what they were studying all the time. Why were they so interested in Eskimos? Nobody knew. "Do you like 'em?" he asked.

"Who?" I asked, confused.

"Anthropologists!"

When I said not at all, he gave me a sharp look as if he knew what my aborted major was before biology, then he cackled. "I see every white coming through these villages. You wouldn't fucking believe it: scientists, businessmen, artists, teachers, the church, election year politicians throwing bubble gum, everyone with an angle on the Eskimo. It's gotten worse since this Native Land Claims business, which is another story I don't want to go into, though my wife has an ancestral thing going with a piece of marsh."

Bob wanted to discuss it after all: he thinks it's a scam, a bribe so tricky in design the "stone-age mentality" won't understand it until it's too late, when all the aboriginal land is in corporate shares and lost due to mismanagement. And the barons can start up pipeline construction again right away; Nixon's pen is poised and he is meeting with the emperor of Japan in Anchorage to discuss tankers. Oil will save America. The pesky delay drives them nuts so they'll devise this treaty, "Just another fucking red blanket!".

I thought of the compromises offered the environmentalists: those underpasses for the caribou. Are the thinktanks snickering behind their hands at the primitive innocence of ecologists? Bob was screaming on about government scientists thick as mosquitoes in the Bush. "The Natives don't ask questions though, maybe because that's all anyone remembers, an endless string of gassaks with different stories. But I visited my wife's folk down in Unalakleet, and what the heck but there's an anthropologist living with them. No kidding, just like that old joke, who's in an Eskimo family? And what do you know but next day, who shows up but a Fish and Game biologist to live with them too!"

"You're pulling my leg, man."

Bob laughed wildly. "Nope! Hell no! About as much fun as shacking up with the CIA and FBI together! I told her folks, look, you should ask questions of these jerks, find out exactly what they're studying about you: your mating customs or your relationship with plankton!"

I attempted to chuckle. He warned me I might be shocked, that the village would seem "squalid", the children and dogs filthy and undisciplined and "piles of crap and junk, but not as bad as an Indian reservation, by gum." I kept a slow burn off my face, and held my breath against his terrible B.O. I'm not ashamed but I don't spill to strange Anglos. Until two years ago it was illegal for my parents to be married or, I guess, for me to be born. That tells you something. So, I "pass". Bob meandered into the topic of alcohol and drunken Natives, his style - and apparent sympathies - like the insanely winding rivers below. I don't know the complexities of human life here, though I have my own sympathies, by golly, first formed in the Puget Sound, where Indians and Norwegians battle over salmon rights as that god-fish nears the brink. But the vast untampered-with scenery was smiting me with awe, and I sighted more and more flocks as we neared the coast, so I didn't care to argue.

Bob seemed to want to make up too. We soared past Troll mountain, and there was the sea, the barrier beach and what had to be the Igaluk below, a golden curling thread. Oxbow lakes and sloughs like jewels broken off the strand. And at last the mosaic and famed dendritic creeks running through it in a tangled network: the arctic salt-marsh-goose system heretofore only seen, in photos. The entire sere, laid out in a glorious map. What a shot of adrenaline.

"Now's the time," Bob said, switching on a big old tape recorder, battery-op. He made me don earphones: I heard climactic violins, etc. Just then I sighted a flock of white on a lake. Snow geese aren't lake dwellers; it had to be swans. I estimated the flock at twenty; a lot for a bird that nearly vanished a decade ago. "Moldau!" Bob shouted, then ripped the phones off me for himself, going into a private rapture. His eyes were half-closed, tracking the Igaluk.

Maybe it takes this kind of character to be a bush pilot.

But back to Gyulnyev. A local visited me right away. He was out scoping for seals in the channel and had been lazily passing in and out of the inlet. He beached and sauntered into camp. Young, muscular with longish hair and headband, a wispy moustache, kind of debonair but a Cheshire cat grin. He asked for a smoke, and when I had none pretended to be sad in a droll way, all the while surveying the camp. Something amused him about my use of beach salvage, some rusted oil-drums. There are hundreds; from the air I took them for a walrus herd. My visitor noted my crate of books, then studied my rolls of corrugated sheet metal with inscrutable reaction.

"Ravens" he said, nodding to a couple crafty ones lurking nearby with heads cocked. As if I didn't know what they were. I wanted to tell him, Look man, I'm an ornithologist. He said, "They can be good luck if you treat them right." I asked how you treat them right. "I don't know..." he shrugged. "They're like people." He said at the channel a boy had been carried off by a giant eagle from the sea, an orphan boy. Was I going to write that down? (Just joshing maybe, but didactic too, implying I'm...an idiot?).

I asked if he wanted coffee. "Nope." His toothsome grin. "Well, see ya later, mister scientist. Adios!" And he strode to his boat like the prince of the world. Right after, he left the channel, chugging north. This was definitely a reconnaissance, a test. Did I pass?

It's two o'clock a.m., the squall recedes. A lemony yellow in the south promises a good bird day: "the great morning of the world, when first God dawned on Chaos". Tent survived, but my tarp billows with demonic ferocity across the tundra. Better run save it then to sleep, start the experiment upon waking. The coins fell in the "Already Fording the Great River", so I can't stop now.

CHAPTER 3

Alien they seemed to be,
No mortal eye could see
The intimate welding of their later history
Or sign that they were bent
By paths coincident,
Or being twin halves of one august evening

HARDY (*NALUAGMIUT*)

THE UNEXPECTED SPRING storm had moved on, leaving shreds of clouds in the sky and pieces of roof on the ground. It also left the old body of a whale near the village and we had to burn it, but it took forever and the sky was black with the oily smoke. We were glad when the wind changed.

Abe and Willy wanted to take the boats on another hunt, then we'd leave for fishcamp for the summer. Flo and I were busy repairing our nets before the men returned with another huge seal for us to put by and another skin to deal with. I didn't like splicing and tying nets either. Happily, Flo got the urge to eat greens and sent me out to pick *surra,* the new willow leaves. I had a secret grove near the channel I loved to visit - it was far out of town so no one could watch me, I could act however I liked, and many little animals and birds were busy there. It smelled sweet.

At the south end of the village stood the lonely cabin of Tuguk. His little daughter was in the dogyard teasing a puppy with a stick. It looked near death. As I passed by, the way the girl crouched like she might have to run for it reminded me of myself at that age, long before Flo had taken me in. Following Itiak custom, I would enter a house and stand inside the door to watch that family's business. People indulged other children in this - it was a way to learn about life - but they drove me out. I stopped trying at seven, the age when you wake up, as the elders said. That is when I started warming up at the schoolhouse. I also tried to hide there overnight under the hamster table but the teacher found me and sent me home. She didn't realize.

Tuguk's daughter warily studied me while picking *kakik* from her nose. She had a skin rash and her clothes were ragged and many sizes too big. Her father had no hunting partners and her mother had no one to borrow from. People didn't talk about it but I knew the family was shunned for Tuguk's bad temper. It seemed to me a self-fulfilling prophecy, to become what your enemies already thought you were. The little girl's future didn't seem too good.

"Hi, Paulette," I said kindly.

She grinned. "You know what? *Naluagmiu,* she...she play count bird *anaq!*" She giggled with her hand over her mouth, then pantomimed a whiteman stooping to peer at the ground. She straightened to scribble something in an imaginary book, and nodded wisely before collapsing in titters. What *naluagmiu* did she mean? It had to be the scientist at the marsh. Kids wouldn't go down there to watch and *papak* in his things if he was the scary kind. But why would he want to count little piles of green poop unless he had a mental problem? I wanted to see such a sight, this funny bird landed on our sandspit.

Other things were on my mind though. First I had to check on Maq at the halfway camp, and it was a good thing I did, because she had tangled her line and nearly choked. Sometimes when I looked into her crazy pale blue eyes I knew why the old people said dogs had no souls. All the other animals had souls except for murres, because there was too many of them. I held Maq's furry head in my hands before she got nervous and tore loose to bow her head to her paws in an apology. She had a soul, alright, but she was a slave and other animals were free. When I patted her and told her she was good, she was happy on her lonely chain. That was the difference between us.

I hiked out to my special ravine, where, hidden from view, I picked leaves and thought about my secret passion. Blind old Isaiah had introduced me to it when I was small. He allowed me to sit in a corner and listen while he told the *unipkaaq* - the long epic stories no one else told. He knew children barely understood the language, so he kept it simple or made his son Calvin translate, and chided him when the jealous boy threw mukluks at me. Through Isaiah's stories I learned the *angutkoq* had been heroes who performed miracles. The other elders, those who still knew such things firsthand, would only go so far before they pulled back. You couldn't ask how the world had been made, if not by God's hand, and on the subject of *angutkoq* they grew as vague as at the mention of the Great Death. Their faces would tighten and they would clap their mouths shut as if remembering a promise.

I heard a different side from Abe, who liked to rant about things. With *angutkoq* stories, though, he would drop his voice low in case one might be listening from the grave. His family had greatly feared and despised them. They were always evil and power mad, they had not helped the poor and they hated Christians. They used their powers to get wealthy while others suffered. Abe's mother had been born into the famine when even berries and fish disappeared during one of their wizard battles. They were murderers and so were murdered. People once had relied on them to learn why the animals were angry or caused bad luck or sickness, but those desperate days were over. Guns, outboard motors and snowmachines, hospitals, stores, government checks and Jesus helped us survive now. The *angutkoq* were gone forever, and good riddance.

As for Isaiah, said Abe, he was just a "bone doctor" who massaged sore joints and forecast the weather and threw seal knuckles to learn the whereabouts of game. It is true if I was there Isaiah would not play the drum hanging on his cabin wall, and no songs but hymns passed his lips. But it slowly dawned on me that Isaiah was *angutkoq*. He was hiding it. He was teaching Calvin how to be one. That was the true reason why Flo forbade me to go near their house. Calvin is a bad boy, she warned, a conceited boy with no friends whose mother had run off. Don't talk to him, she said, even though it was too late.

Isaiah never minded my visits to their little cabin. But as we grew older, he taught his son a special language to use whenever they didn't want me to listen in, and it was like having the door slammed in my face. Calvin hoarded the knowledge, and doled out scraps like I was one of the stray puppies that ran around the village. He said when his *ataata* died, he would learn the most secret of secrets not meant for anyone else. His powers, his *qilya*, would be far greater than mine. Recently he had gone Outside for a year of college to study "religion". He came back even stranger and more secretive.

While he was gone, I found a different source. I had gone with Polly to the school so she could get advice on the radio about splinting a hunter's broken leg, a compound fracture. Polly was the new health aide and Willy's older sister. She was young with cute dimples, and so nervous her first few times on the radio she made me go with her. She was afraid the teachers would try to listen in and boss her around. The new teachers were different, but the *eskuulkti* used to try to be doctors and run the trading post and everyone's lives, and we were still used to that.

While she was busy, I visited the teacher quarters. Itiak "visiting" was not what outsiders expected, since talking wasn't necessary, nor an invitation. Sometimes a visit was just to warm up while learning useful gossip. I went in and was looking at all the books in the teacher's living room. Like Isaiah, and other *eskuulkti* before her, Dolores had made me into a special project. She seemed to think I was good material, and reminded me of Flo when she eyeballed a high quality skin to decide how to cut it. I was a lost cause, already the age when it should be my kid the teacher wanted. But Dolores still had hope. That day, when she came into the room and found me looking with great interest in a book on her shelf, she offered to lend it. Usually she was stingy. Important old men could visit Dolores for hours and never be served anything, though their wives had presented gifts, and the *eskuulkti* were rich. Yet she gave me the book with delighted exclamations.

It was hard to find a way to read it, since people were always around, and Flo didn't want kerosene to be wasted reading late. So I hid the book at Willy's and read there sneakily, gulping ideas like a hungry thief. *Shamans of the Greenland Eskimo*. The author had that white style: "The Eskimos think this, they do that, although strange to *us*..." It was the old days in another country but the people described in those pages felt familiar: loners, outcasts, poor orphans, cripples. Or women. You had to go out alone into the hills to discover the truth. You didn't need an old man; it was the spirits - the *inua* - who taught you the dark arts. Even whites could experience the "fantastical journeys under the charismatic influence of the wizard", which the author himself had done, he kept assuring me.

I looked up *ecstatic* in my old dictionary. *Transcendent, seance, trance-state...Epileptic* I already knew. It was amazing - looking up words had been a chore at school that was forced on me, and now it was my will. The words hypnotized me. Some troubled me - *schizophrenic, legerdemain, hoodwink, arctic hysteria.* I didn't need to look up *quack.* I thought it meant the sounds the *angutkoq* made, mimicking a duck. I thought I knew *irony* too, and here it was: that white explorers long dead would help me when no one else would. The past was a mystery as thick as sea ice and the book cracked it a little more. A lead was opening up in my mind and rushing in with black water. And I couldn't stop.

Next I took *The History of Seward Peninsula* from the teacher. Nobody was around, so I stuck it in my *kaspaq's* large stomach pocket and ran to Willy's. Through the whole sunlit night I read. It was the Great Death! Almost everyone had died from epidemics. There weren't enough hunters so survivors starved, while dogs ate corpses and people too weak to fight them off. The *angutkoq* had been old and the first to die, without their magic saving them or anyone else. People scattered to far places, begging from distant relatives, sometimes forced to eat animal droppings, or worse. Then missionaries swarmed in and took over, followed by the *eskuulkti,* or one and the same. They raised the orphans and tried to make them white. People burned the drums and knocked down the *kazhgi,* the men's clubs where the *angutkoq* had led the seances. Women could enter these giant houses only to bring dinner or for a ceremony, but that men had lived apart sounded fine. Women must have invented the *kazhgi.* And if a woman became a shaman she didn't sew for one whole year - even finer!

But I kept dwelling on those orphans. Is that what Abe's mother meant when she said, "*poor, poor little thing*" if she told of her own childhood? And she would not give any detail of the dying. Every elder was one of those children who had seen the growing piles of dead, the world turned on end. And I did the math: even Abe and Flo were alive in 1919, when the flu took out whole villages. They did not mention it. I studied the brown old photographs, the unsmiling *naluagmiut* in hats. I had never seen pictures of the Inupiat grandparents; all along they were in these books that their families never saw. They stood rigidly in their skin clothes, lip plugs and braids. Their expressions struck me as forlorn or mad, but it may have been the photography back then, because the whites also looked that way.

After reading the book I couldn't breathe right, like I was dying of diphtheria or smallpox too. I rushed to the schoolhouse to get another book. It was strange to deliberately cause myself pain. Dolores started when I entered her quarters without knocking. She tried to make conversation, but as always, she talked while I just listened. Her eyes were mottled like green soapstone and I couldn't look in them even if she wanted me to. If I looked, I saw envy, as if the teacher thought my life was better than hers. Whites didn't know they insulted you by dredging your eyes for feelings, in the way they dug for gold and oil. It invaded your privacy. At last I said I wanted another book. The teacher laced her white fingers together.

"Oh...well, Gretchen, these books are very valuable and belong to Bill." That was her husband, the principal. Didn't he share with her? I knew she knew I still had her two books. But they are mine, I thought, or Itiak's, anyway. I did not intend to return them. "You can read anything you like *here*," Dolores said at last. "It's great you want to read..."

I tried not make her mad. Whites seemed thin skinned, at least the few I saw close up. Sloppy, like skin balls sewn so badly the stuffing could come out. Maybe they could afford to be careless. It was hard not to make teachers mad, for the more polite you were, the more upset they got. They thought we were angry, when it was *they* who were angry. They seemed to prefer rudeness in the beginning, before they were trained. It was crazy-making for most people, and *eskuulkti* usually left after one winter - gone crazy too - and we started over.

While Dolores hovered I studied her bookshelf. Above it hung an old polar bear spear and a *tunghat* mask with wall eyes and little fangs. Tunghat was the keeper of the animals up on the moon, the game manager of the spiritworld. You never saw such masks in any other home in Itiak, where people tacked up photos of their sons in uniform, babies, daughters in bridal veils and pictures of Jesus surrounded by kids. Maybe Dolores preferred the twisted faces of *inua* to those of her family. Maybe she prayed to them. She'd better be careful: a mask had raped a woman once, further north.

She had no idea with all her artifacts and literature that she was in the presence of a shaman.

After awhile the *eskuulkti* wanted to drink tea herself so she asked if I wanted some and I said no, and left. It was that night I began to teach myself in earnest, away from the village where only the birds could witness.

MY BUCKET WAS FULL. I was thirsty and looking in vain for a good drinking pond. There were dozens of ponds but all were scummy and alive with wriggling pond-worms, the baby mosquitoes. A man's boot print indented the bottom of one, and finger tracks like he'd scooped up mud to eat.

I found the nest of a phalarope in the grass and was going to suck all the little warm eggs but the mother charged me desperately. That meant the chicks were already formed so I had mercy. At last I drank from a dirty pond and ate *surra* but it wasn't a good dinner and my stomach still complained. I climbed to the top of a frost heave where the lichen was dry and lay down. The spice of Labrador tea filled my nose, the racket of birds my ears. The reindeer moss was springy, inviting, and the sun warmed me for the first time in ten months. It was the best time of year to lie outside if you found a dry place, before all the bugs grew wings.

I was waiting for the spiraling and the rushing-wing noises of the Otherworld, the plane where humans and animals and spirits became each other. *Angutkoq* used to travel through it hunting secret knowledge. It could be a dangerous place, Isaiah had warned Calvin and me; if you forgot and ate any berries there or killed the wrong creature, you had to stay there forever. I wasn't frightened. Even when my *turnaq* fox flitted ahead to guide me, I had never fully entered that world. I would reach the portal of black stone and could only peep in as if through a hole in a frosted window, like the orphan I had been in the mortal world, wandering a dark village, gazing into cabins where families shared food in the warm light. Once I found out how to enter, the *inua* would be like kind parents. They would teach me and protect me. I'd be home. Or so I imagined.

That evening I couldn't even reach the threshold, and my *turnaq* refused to come. It was fickle. Calvin instructed me to look for the signs of a new ally: "Watch their ears; if she lays them back and growls, then no way, but if she puts them forward to listen, she's yours." But only the fox had offered to help. You couldn't make a *turnaq* be friends or obey, you couldn't force yourself into the Otherworld. The universe took you when it wanted, and that day it didn't want. Calvin said I needed a drum anyway, and only *old* women had played drums...and how was I to make a drum or play it undiscovered? And the singing, *that* kind translated by whites: "*O mighty nameless one, an earth-dweller calls upon thee to bite my enemies, to slay them!*" I couldn't do it without laughing even if I found privacy, and what language could I use? Did the spirits even know English? A secret, silent *angutkoq* - that would be me.

At times the whole idea seemed stupid and made-up like playing with dolls, no better than church. A tiredness fell over me. I felt as waterlogged as an old stalk at the bottom of a pond that had never been stirred. And I fell asleep and soon was dreaming.

IN MY DREAM I traveled to a distant island with trees, where I knew my true mother waited. She made baskets there. She had woven a pattern into the grass which I could make out from afar: a string of geese in the heavens, and below, a solitary man looking up. With great skill she had made the simple human shape emit a strong feeling, but a mysterious feeling I couldn't name. The man held his arms up and bent his knees like he might fall to them in prayer. My mother nodded silently, aware that I saw. She would never speak to explain things.

Then a shadow passed over my face, blocking out the sun like a huge goose had flown by. My dream changed and I was being swept along by a riptide into choppy waters. The island grew strange and threatening and I no longer wanted to go there but I could not stop. With a gasp that sounded like a sob I woke. I couldn't breathe. A dark form had reared up on its hind legs before me in silhouette. The sun was behind it, blinding me. *Aklak!* my mind screamed. Brown bear were so rare I had only seen one skin in my life; their ancestors had been killed off by goldminers. Maybe it came off the mainland for revenge, irritable at the end of its hibernation. They ran very fast after anything that ran. Should I plead for my life in the old way? These thoughts spasmed all at once in my mind as I prepared to die. My limbs would not move, and I felt my will drain out of me.

"Oops, sorry," said the bear, "Didn't mean to sneak up on you." He held out his paws, but they were clawless, human hands. In fact, one hand held a notebook with a pencil stuck in the spirals. Just as fast as it had rushed out, now the blood flooded back into my head. How stupid to mistake a man for a bear! But in the next instant, as I looked from his hands to his face, I registered that he was a stranger, and not even Eskimo. A *naluagmiu*.

I was alone with him on the tundra, and he had been staring at me while I slept!

Imagine looking down on me, napping spread-eagled on a hill. Flo had sewn my *kaspaq* five years before, when I'd stopped growing, and it was fraying and patched, the green flowers faded. She had given me cloth to make a better *kaspaq* but I hated to sew. My knee bones poked through the jeans - that was before the fashion reached my part of the world, so the holes were just cold reminders of my poverty. No sunglasses. My knee-high black rubber boots with red tops were for kids, and patches were peeling off the toes. My hair fanned out tangled and minkish-black, not as thick as that of Itiak girls who could put both hands around their ponytails and fill the space. There is one photo from my young adulthood; it used to be pinned on Willy's cabin wall, the only picture he put there. I am balanced on the runners of his dogsled in a ski-cap with my head thrown back and mouth so wide open you can look down my throat. Maybe in a fake laugh. It is obvious even in winter clothes that I am skinny and flat. My old sunglasses disguise my eyes but not my narrow give-away nose. My teeth are sharp like I spent each evening filing them. Other girls complained that I turned as dark as a *taqsivak* from staying out in the sun, and no one ever said I was pretty.

But such things are unimportant to a man intent on raping.

There is a long history of assault on the tundra, as long as any in the world. It started when Moon raped his sister the Sun, and Tulunigraq the Raven-man raped a virgin at the beginning of time. In the grandmothers' days you had to be escorted when berry-picking, for a strange hunter might carry you off, and if you had no male kin or witch aunts to avenge you, a man from your own village might throw you down and take you. Once you got your tattoos, you had to marry fast or become a target. You were scarce, you were at risk, so you trained to run as swiftly as caribou to outrun a man, if not a bear. Contests were held to demonstrate this fleetness: starting from the seal butchering posture, bent double at the waist, you had to leap up and hit the ground running. Modern times had not solved the problem. There were a few bad men in every village and more men who turned bad when drunk, and every schoolgirl knew to be careful of strange *naluagmiut* Outside, where we had no protection at all. They planned to get us drunk and drive us in trucks to a far, lonely place. A girl had to find her way back on foot, if lucky. And there could be no vengeance against a whiteman.

Flo never cautioned me not to go out alone and fall asleep on hills. Maybe she figured I could take care of myself, or it was too late to worry. I could run very fast back then. When I scrambled to my feet to start doing it, the strange man stepped back from me.

"It's okay," he said. He smiled quickly to reassure me but he looked startled and embarrassed. The notebook, binoculars around his neck...oh, it was the bird scientist! This kind of whiteman did no harm, physically anyway, so little kids could visit their camps to stare at them all day. The do-good type. Immediately I relaxed, though my knees shook violently from their previous orders to run, and I hid my shaking hands up in my sleeves.

In some ways the scientist did resemble *aklak,* or a man who was turning into one. He was tall with long arms. He was black-bearded and his bearish-brown hair really needed cutting, many months ago. He seemed young; it was hard to tell with them. His coat was stupid for the Arctic: the wind could cut through the beat-up wool jacket with buttons. I was confused. We heard about longhairs and teased Willy that he wanted to be one, but could a scientist be a hippie? While I napped he had stood over me; maybe he even took notes in that book like I was a nesting bird. He had invaded my secret *surra-nakk*ing ground and caught me scared.

"Who are *you?*" I asked. My voice impressed me in its harshness. Other village girls would not dare to be so mean to a man - a whiteman, no less. They would have giggled and hid their teeth behind their hands. The bird-man passed the notebook from one hand to the other.

"Uh...I'm a biologist. Lay-if trigger son. Didn't they tell people I was here?"

I didn't smile. I never smiled enough, which got me into trouble, for then people thought I was mad. The trouble is, I *was* mad all the time, a mad *itki-liq*. What did I have to lose? You were not supposed to stare at fellow villagers - it gave them the idea you were harboring bad thoughts - but what else could you do with outsiders. They gawked at us too, and took pictures of us. In Nome a tour bus had crawled behind me on the mud street, the pale faces pressed to the glass viewing me until I ducked behind a building. *Naluagmiut* all over the place; why didn't they just go home? Thinking of those history books had already put me in a critical mood. I stared at the scientist rudely while he looked around like a bashful young bear. He looked at my bucket.

The low sun caught his eyes just as they met mine for an instant. The pupils were as plain as ink etched in the light brown so you could read them. An aspect of his eyes - or maybe the thoughts behind them - made him seem not exactly a whiteman. He took care of his whiskers; they weren't overgrown, but neat. And he was maybe good-looking. He was waiting for me to speak, strange in a *naluagmiu*. Strange in a man! I just kept staring at him. It bothered me when he leaned to see inside my pail for something to do while waiting for me to talk. He seemed curious about my leaves and was probably taking mental notes: *Eskimo women pick willow*.

"Nobody told me about no *naluagmiu* out here," I said finally. "This is *my* land."

He looked at me doubtfully. His narrow black eyebrows dove together like two camp-robbers flying after one garbage. "This area belongs to *you*?"

"You don't own the whole world."

He considered my answer. "I didn't think I did."

Maybe I was still in a dream, influenced by my books, to be so openly belligerent with a white. I had answered teachers' questions but had not conversed with any *naluagmiu*, not on equal terms, and was surprised I could, that one would respond, give and take. He took me seriously. It was pleasant throwing him and his plans off balance. But really I did it because I saw he wouldn't fight back. How far could I go? "You're trespassing. You have to leave."

He opened his mouth, closed it. "But I got permission from Itiak Council to be out here."

"Council, ah? Those old men? They think they're the boss of everyone, but they never pick *surra*!"

He smiled a little. "My research won't hurt any willows. I'm studying birds in the marsh."

Now he was noticing the unraveling trim on my worn-out *kaspaq*, and I was glad he wouldn't know it was out of style too. "So, you hurt birds," I said.

"No, I try to help them."

I thought about saying, *Help them, ah? Like a missionary?* But for half my life I had lived with Flo, who was so famous for diplomacy. I muttered, "I didn't say you could study birds here."

"Well..." He glanced at my childish boots and there was a shadow of another smile, to himself. Maybe he knew I was just a nobody, a girl not even Eskimo. But then he looked indecisive so I moved in fast.

"These are my ancestors' *surra* grounds. You stepped on some, and a nest. I get my subsistence out here."

He drew himself up; I didn't like how he loomed nearly a head taller than me. "Look, I'm sorry, but I cleared it with your authorities. I have it in writing."

"I am sorry too but I *am* the authorities here. I'll put it in writing too. Give me that book and pencil."

The biologist looked mad a second - if he had feathers, they'd be ruffled - but he hid it okay for a whiteman. I had on a stone face, my hands hanging straight down at my sides, but I was enjoying myself and the leftovers of my fear were utterly gone. He looked at the beach again like he had something going on down there. A gust of wind blew hair into his eyes and he brushed it away impatiently.

"Okay," he said, "Where precisely does your ancestral *surra* tract begin and end? Because I'm going to pitch my tent south of it."

I could have said, Clear to the channel, everywhere you see, but I blurted out, "I'm *angutkoq* of this place."

"Pardon?" I didn't say anything. He wouldn't know what an *angutkoq* was, but why did I tell him? No one but Calvin really knew how serious it was - Willy had no idea how far it went. I must have looked upset, because like a movie cowboy in surrender, the biologist held up his hands. "Hey, it's cool, man. I'll do what you want." He spoke soothingly, like I was three years old having a tantrum. I looked out to sea then inland toward the lagoon, pretending to ponder for a long time. Funny how he called me a man; the high schoolers were starting to call everyone *man* too, even their grandmothers. The *naluagmiu* shifted on his feet as he squinted against the evening sun, watching my face.

"You can stay here," I said.

He laughed shortly. "Thanks, man. I appreciate it, it's a real drag moving camp, and I'm sorry I ran into you like that if that's why you're upset."

"You might still have to move if I change my mind," I said. It was very bad manners to point out my bad mood. "And don't trample the willows. And watch out for my *siksik* traps. My squirrel traps, don't step in them."

"Right on." His grin was happy and seemed to be a peace offering; it lit him up and his teeth flashed white in the black beard. "So...uh...if this is a legal transaction, what's your name?"

I waited a space certain to be uncomfortable for him. The wind snatched a loose page from his notebook and he chased it. Even tall like he was, the scientist was lithe. As it circled in my direction I trapped it with my boot and tried to read some while he came back, but it was only numbers and scribbles and foreign words. *Halophytic...peat...alkali.* He snatched it from me and crammed it in his pocket like it was a private love letter; I imagined later he would carefully smooth it out. He shook the hair out of his eyes and flashed his smile again.

"Thanks! It always does that, like the wind doesn't want me to take notes, like it's in league with the oil company. Or maybe *you*," he added with a sly glance that caused my stomach to leap up and settle again, confused.

Other young women laughed at everything a strange young man said, for they were so rare, strangers. I just stared at him in a style antagonistic to all animals and people...and maybe whitemen too. I didn't know. He dabbed his nostrils with his sleeve - the stiff coastal wind made the noses of outsiders run - and the gesture seemed so humble I thought of letting him off the hook. "You got anything to eat?" I asked.

"What?" The birdman looked startled; he let his uncertainty show. Maybe he knew you had to share food, share everything without protest, but he was wondering about my motive. He was smart, I decided, perceptive. And it was fun to tease a scientist, forcing him to do things and be polite. After he'd thought about it far too long, he said, "Um...why don't you join me for dinner? Though I'm sure you'll find it awful."

I raised my eyebrows. Back of him, two noisy yellowlegs kept climbing high and falling straight down, vibrating their wings. They were in a contest. I kept lifting but he didn't understand; they couldn't read eyebrows. Finally I gave up and said, "Sure, where's camp?" though of course I knew where it was.

The biologist seemed unhappy that I agreed to his offer. Field scientists were anti-social; they did not keep our company because they were not studying *us*. They were annoyed by human life; it distracted them. He regarded me thoughtfully then shrugged a little, pointing south with a tilt of his head. "That way."

And he took off toward the beach, fast with a long stride, leaping easily over hummocks and tussocks. I would have to jog to keep up. Judging from the line of his back, he was mad, alright. It only hit me after he had reached the sand and driftwood up ahead and he stumbled as his ankle turned on a rock. He was the man woven into the basket! My mother had tried to tell me about him, or maybe warn me. Stopping short, I watched him recede, wondering what to do. Of what use were dreams if they didn't tell you what to do next?

Of course there are always such stealthy messages and hints wherever one looks in the world. They *are* telling you what to do, but it requires long study. The teacher can hardly be yourself at twenty.

CHAPTER 4

Sir, you speak a language
that I understand not.
My life stands in the level of my dreams,
which I'll lay down

SHAKESPEARE (*NALUAGMIUT*)

I WAS A FOOL to go with a strange man I had angered. Abe's favorite kind of tale from the old days went like this: an outsider wanders into Itiak land and meets a group of hunters. The stranger has a funny look but the hunters agree to eat with him at his camp. When their backs are turned he murders them all. Then he eats them. Abe always ended the story, "Too bad they didn't see he was Indian."

My book had told me a different story, that when hunters found a stranger on their land, *they* killed *him.*

The scientist was a longhair. It was only to his shoulders but even that much disturbed the old men. I knew hippies were being shot by the government while they picked flowers, and in Fairbanks their heads were bashed in by other whitemen just for walking down the road. It was like they were Indians. It was like they were trying to turn into women so men would want to beat them up. Abe said if they cut their hair they wouldn't be harmed, because they were white after all; they were stupid to make everyone hate them, when just five minutes of scissors and life would be easy again. I understood wanting to defy the old men, though.

I decided I was glad I had come. The birdman's locks made me feel safer, like I was going to the camp of a woman. All I could see of him now from where I sat on a driftwood log was that hair, whipping behind the duckblind he used for a windbreak as he fixed dinner. My plan was to scare him with *angutkoq* techniques as an experiment of my own. He wouldn't even suspect, for biologists did not believe in *qilya.* He was alone and unconnected, he would not tell, no one would find out. To crack a scientist would be as good as

42

overpowering another shaman, or a Lutheran minister. Calvin said the spiritworld would test me if it wanted me, I shouldn't go looking, but I was tired of waiting. I could try the "x-ray vision" described in my book. This was an ability - something like Superman's - to see through creatures down to their bones and life lines. I thought it meant knowing things as they actually were, to see the underlying spirit. Delving into an animal's secret heart had once been the job of *angutkoq* back when animals decided your fate.

I had practiced on Maq and other dogs - they were easy - but it was humans I needed to understand in modern times. It was difficult to practice on Itiak people. Just looking a second too long at Abe and "Someone sure has the evil eye", he would say with a nervous laugh. With the biologist I could try the look Isaiah once showed me: you face the opponent with narrowed eyes and suddenly shoot them wide. It alarmed people. Never try it on anyone, the old man cautioned, even to play. Calvin said there was an even more powerful *angutkoq* look that could make an enemy fall over dead. I didn't know that one. I didn't want to harm the scientist, anyway; he was hospitable when I was inhospitable, and even mad, he showed me respect. Few had done that; why a *naluagmiu*?

Respect. I frowned as I waited for dinner, my thoughts running down a well-worn path. No one considered me a real adult, and I was stuck in a low position. Because I had no relatives to put me up if I moved away, I was stuck in Itiak too. Hunters were honored but only men hunted. To become an elder everyone had to listen to took a very long time, at least fifty years. A job could gain me a certain kind of respect, because people liked money no matter what they said about the eye of the needle, but there weren't any jobs and I didn't like sewing yo-yos for the tourists. As a last resort I could become a mother...but that would take a man - at least for a night - and I seemed to scare off the ones I halfway liked. Or they scared me.

But a baby scared me more. I knew all about them from helping Flo with three grandchildren. I hauled the water or melted ice, heated it and scrubbed their diapers, hung them to freeze, shook off the ice crystals, rehung them inside and hemmed them, so many times I wondered why we favored cloth over the old disposable kind of moss. All that, while *amaq*-ing babies on my back. I butchered, prepared hides, rendered seal oil, packed for hunters, loaded and unloaded the caches, sewed, mended, hauled and chopped drift-wood, trimmed wicks, poured and pumped fuel, shoveled snow, fed and trained Willy's dogs, burned trash, emptied honeybuckets, plucked, cooked, cleaned, washed laundry for six adults and the kids, ran errands, cared for Aka, and lugged food to Abe's relatives. Not to mention summer foraging and the bustle of fishcamp. The grandkids' mother was in Nome and Polly never helped; she was too precious, and busy as the village's only health aide. I had overheard Flo say to the mother: *I can take them. Kayuqtuq will help.*

There was hardly time to do anything else. You never heard stories of *angutkoq* having to do chores or *amaq* babies. A baby would cry if I tried to read my secret books or fall into a trance. No, motherhood was the worst idea.

I hunched in the wind, moping, and eyed the biologist's hair blowing up behind the duckblind like frayed ropes, like long *umingmaq* fur. What an easy life *he* had, just watching birds. He didn't even have to hunt. He was taking his time and didn't offer tea for warming up. He had a radio but it was turned off so we heard only birds, wind and surf. Nearby were crates of food with exotic labels, making my stomach rumble at the idea of a meal.

I forgot about my plan and wandered around the camp, looking. Under a tarp lean-to held down with driftwood were mason jars filled with pond water and red mud, and bugs wriggling in different stages. *Larvae*...a word I knew from highschool. One jar contained weeds, another had fresh goose poops. A crate held old nests, feathers, and every kind of marsh plant flat-tened and dried under plastic and labeled with tiny bug-like writing. The odd-shaped metal gadgets, tools and finger-shaped bottles made no sense. Green outsider raingear with the name "Helly Hansen". No rifles - the shells in the gravel were from Willy's duck hunts.

Make yourself at home, the birdman had said, and I did, crawling into his tent. It was no bigger than an emergency snow cave, an impossible place to live. His sleeping bag was goose down, pretty miserable if it got wet. The fancy new equipment scattered around made me think he was rich: black cameras with long snouts, a radio, tape recorder, kerosene lamp, microscope and slide with a *larva* on it. I tried on a pair of aviator sunglasses. They were amber with gold-wire frames and highly desirable in Itiak, where you couldn't find any even if you had the cash. A Blazo crate made a shelf for books, but there were no cigarettes, bootleg whiskey or bad magazines such as littered bachelor cabins. That strangely gratified me.

Three pennies were laid in a mysterious row, and books splayed out on his bed with bird illustrations, poetry, and prehistoric Eskimos. I considered taking the last book in my pail but it was too risky. Funny how obsessed they were with Eskimos - they could not think of their own wisdom but had to rob it from others' dead. After they had tried so hard to destroy the old ways, now they were attracted. If I was really Inupiaq I could be complimented. I saw an official-looking envelope addressed to *Mr Leif Trygvesen* that was somehow scary; I didn't touch it.

When I discovered his journal, I had to strain over the bug-writing. In more elegant cursive leaped out, "*Thou wast not born for death, immortal Bird.*" I gave up. There were easier ways of figuring people out. As I held the notebook I could tell the owner had a problem besides birds. There was a loneliness, a frustration...and a growing feeling of...

Suddenly I felt he was looking for me outside. He must think I wanted to *papak* in his personal affairs. When I crawled out of the tent he was peeking from behind the windblock with a harassed expression. Which he immediately lost when he saw me. "It's taking a while!" he called. "It doesn't want to rehydrate!"

Dinner didn't sound very good. "You got a funny tent," I remarked. I thought of Flo's white-walled tent that could fit two families. But he had no family, not even a poop-counting partner. "Green is a bad color. Nobody can see it," I said, sitting on my log again.

The birdman said something about "camouflage" but a gust snatched the rest. The wind had shifted so he had to move the duckblind and now I could see his back as he squatted. He took off his coat to pump his fancy propane stove and light the other burner, and I could see he was well-formed, but not as strong-looking as a lot of the men. His shirttail pulled out so when he leaned a gust caught it and undressed him a little. I saw his longjohns, modern, not the stupid sourdough kind with the flap on the *nulluk*. The knobs of his spine showed too, and a patch of skin the color of dried grass. I stood up to see more while he rummaged in a crate, but no luck.

Although everyone freely borrowed things left at old camps, suddenly I didn't like that he was using Willy's duck blind. "Who said you could have that?" I asked.

He pivoted. "What?"

"That wood. It's Pataq's. He might not like you to use it."

The scientist looked guiltily at the bleached boards, maybe believing I would confiscate it. "What *is* it, exactly?" he asked, but I smiled to myself without explaining. He backhanded hair out of his face, poured something in a kettle and sprang up. "Gotta get more water." He grabbed the container and took off for the shore-ice, where he scrambled out to scoop fresh water from the melt. Water was good from there - only a little briny - and I was surprised he knew. Typical of outsiders, he couldn't keep his footing very well. I crossed my ankles and relaxed to watch the spectacle of a man tilted sideways with a bucket, slipping like a *kuangazuk*. No one else had ever worked so hard for my sake. I nearly softened.

When he returned out of breath I was wearing his sunglasses.

He thunked the water down and looked at me, panting. "These are a good brand," I said. And maybe he'd studied up on Native customs, because right away he offered them to me, ruining my plan to uncover a *naluagmiut* stinginess. I took them off to admire the wires. *Angukaa,* I'd never owned anything so nice. When I looked up the scientist was studying me, his arms folded in a protective whiteman stance. Quickly I stuck the shades back on my nose, turning him and everything into a weak tea hue. He seemed to be waiting for a formal thank you.

"Betchawanna know why I keep all those larvae in jars," he said at last.

"No." I was thinking he'd tell me anyway, but he didn't.

"Well, dinner's ready." He turned away. He served it, which made me uncomfortable again, a man serving. And it was a funny meal with no meat so I picked at it though I was ravenous: sour spaghetti with green specks, slimy canned fruit that looked like guts, and salty canned greens. The sand floating in the coffee turned out to be cinnamon. When I tasted the white thing like a fish eye on the edge of my plate, I spat it out, for it was a pill. Was he medicating me for an experiment?

He sat cross-legged on the gravel a little far away, and it did seem like he was analyzing me, though not with binoculars. He was starting on his third helping. "It's vitamin C," he said, "Just swallow it." I wrinkled my nose in a *no*. "Well, your *surra* is a better source anyway, and seal." He pronounced the Inupiaq fine. "You know," he went on through a mouthful of food, "I hear polar bear and musk oxen make their own C, which is incredible, because we have to get it externally every day. Passes right through." Food seemed to make him a little jolly. Maybe he'd been starving too, like a lean spring bear.

"What is it for?" I asked in spite of myself. "Vitamin C?"

"Prevents colds, infections. Maybe cancer too."

"People here get cancer but we eat *surra*."

The birdman looked unhappily surprised. His eyes were tracking ideas invisible to me. "That's a drag," he said, "Amchitka, maybe. Anyway, the medical guys don't believe it - not enough statistical evidence." He pulled a face. "They need to test it on five billion rats first. Expose a rat to enough radiation to kill a whale, then give it Vitamin C and see if it improves."

He was checking for my reaction. I heard the disapproval in his tone though I had little idea what he meant. Then I remembered the team of scientists that came through the winter before and had people lean over a machine that ticked, but never explained what for. They told Polly, as the health aide, that they'd be back next year.

I put my plate down, no longer hungry. He laid his empty plate on the sand. We looked at each other. I felt like I was in a dream - what was I doing here? "Are you gonna tell me your name?" he said, "You know mine."

Reluctantly I told him. My English name sounded funny but I would not reveal my Eskimo name. The birdman swallowed and reached out his hand from his crouch. I was supposed to shake it.

"How do you do," he said. I took his hand and let him wrestle with mine though I felt ridiculous and suspected he was making fun of me, or of the custom. His long fingers were cold. I wanted to tell him he shouldn't go around asking *Who are you, who are you*? like a moron. And now that he knew my name, I hoped he wouldn't start using it like a teacher: *Now Gretchen, could you tell the class...?*

He let go of my hand and re-settled. "So...you're from Itiak, I guess."

After a while I said, "Guess so."

He smiled in a pained way. "Right. I'm from Seattle."

I knew from teachers they wanted you to say, Oh, really? That's nice, or ask a question. If you were quiet or thinking carefully of what to say, they thought you didn't understand, and you'd just be opening your mouth when they'd interrupt or go off on a new topic or repeat everything louder. It was nearly hopeless sometimes. But the birdman had fallen silent. While sifting gravel through his fingers he kept glancing over, probably hoping I'd leave soon. Two loons were mating in a nearby pond - he watched them until it was over, so quickly. When we heard a *karonk! karonk!* he jumped to his feet looking upward with his binoculars pressed to his face. After a time a messy flock of black brant geese raced over us on the way to the mainland, very high up. Another flock of little songbirds ran like water in the sky. The birdman took his book from his coat and recorded things with his pencil. He studied the clouds as they turned into fishscales, lit up gold.

It grew colder. Suddenly he jumped up again. "Um...are you - ?" He cut himself off. "I'll be right back. Gotta answer nature's call." He hesitated like I was supposed to respond but I didn't; really, it was stupid to announce where you were going every second like you needed permission, especially for *that,* if I understood right. He set off for the beach and hid behind a pile of driftwood after checking to see if he was covered. Probably he just *qoq*ed behind the tent usually. I was ruining his privacy, his easy living. He re-emerged buttoning his fly to walk slowly back to camp, his face saying, *She's still here.*

"Kay-pee time." He dropped to his haunches to scrub the dishes with slush and sand, every once in a while shooting me a look. His hair blew wildly in his face; it reminded me of brown seaweed. Finally he got a string and tied it but it didn't help much. The wind was cutting now, and I huddled into my *kaspaq,* but the cloth was thin, so I balled my hands up inside the sleeves and

crammed them in my stomach pocket - it felt better not showing them anyway. If I was a smoker I'd have something to do, and I would have been a
smoker but had no money. The marsh behind camp was full of drowsy birds.
In the shore lead the flock of *aahaalik* had quieted except for one that kept
on like the kid who can't stop laughing at a joke after everyone has gone to
bed. The sun was north, the sky over all the sea and land turning a soft gold
and orange with an amber overlay from the shades. I took them off. I was in
no hurry to go home. I had to pee somewhere too but there was no way, with
the biologist around.

"Yep, pretty good place to camp I guess," I said. His head jerked up like
a startled fox. "Even if a lotta wind," I said, "because there won't be any
bugs."

"Good." He propped the dishes up on a crate to dry. "Thanks for letting
me stay here." He sniffled in the wind and warmed his wet hands on his neck
and fidgeted. "Want more coffee? Tea?"

"Tea."

Was he holding back a sigh? He lit the stove again and made a pot,
which I drank while he sat in the gravel, writing. "Field book, for birds," he
explained; it was a nice gesture, in case I thought he was scribbling about *me*.
That had happened when a scientist stayed at our place. For one week she
had observed me work on skins and diapers and she wrote about it without
even helping. I watched the birdman's inclined head and the movement of his
hair. Writing seemed to calm him down.

"Why do you always count goose poops?" I asked loudly.

Without looking up he kept writing and murmured, "Oh, not *always*,
but part of the time...it's useful to assess population...plant-herbivore interaction... nitrogen movement..."

I rolled my eyes to myself and poured a second cup. When it was finished
I said, "I can still let you move." *Let* was how Itiak said *make*.

"Let me?" Finally he stopped scribbling and looked at me from under his
brows.

"I might talk with the elders and they can let you."

He shut his notebook and studied me while gnawing his lip. It was hard to say whether he knew I was teasing. He glanced at the ducks in the lead as if for their help. When he jumped to his feet, it made me start. "Maybe you can help me out on something as long as you're here," he said, and he strode fast to fetch the bird picture book from the tent. "I got a problem with my research. I need to find a bird but it hasn't shown up, and it was supposed to be here by now. It might use Gyulnyev as a stopping off point and breeds somewhere north. Have you ever seen it?"

I thought he meant one individual bird; he was crazy to think he could find it. He was just a scientist, not *angutkoq* or one of those old hunters with special powers. As he knelt next to my log to show me I studied the goose he pointed out, and examined his fingers too, the little half-moons on his nails, the mud from digging in ponds. They were too long but the bones were nicely shaped, symmetrical, and the tendons stood out. I tried hard to find a sign of cruelty in them, some bad intention like they were just waiting to strangle you, hold you down. But they radiated a friendliness.

The birdman was so close his body heat and the smell of him reached me, the clean cold air with it, and it was not too bad. I liked it. With sun on his dark hair it showed red at the edges like it was on fire. It wasn't really like seaweed. His face was tilted down, presenting its sharp angles from the side. That was what they meant by a hawk nose. He gazed fixedly at the goose as if he'd never seen the picture before. His eyelashes were longer than mine and curlier, an effect some women aimed for with metal clamps. At eye-level, his lips under their *umik* looked soft. Slowly, I took the book. He withdrew to sit and watch me, as stock-still and alert as a hunter. If he was a dog, his ears would be pricked.

I saw he was in love with that goose. He was like the tiny boy an old couple found on the tundra. Tussock-Child grew up and went in search of the world's most beautiful bird, not eating or drinking until he found it. Everything was riding on that goose. It was large and like a Canada goose but browner, with black bars, more graceful than brant or emperor. "This one?" I asked.

"Umhm. That's the male. Tallin's goose." The birdman spoke quickly, poised for action, note-taking maybe.

"How come you want to find him?"

"Uh...they. They're endangered. I think it's their California wintering area that's the problem, turned into parking lots. This marsh is where a flock was last sighted. No positive identification...um...they aren't sure. Do you remember a group of old people with boots and binoculars a few years back?"

"*Naluagmiut*".

"*Naluagmiut*," he repeated perfectly, slurring the 'g'. "Does that mean... Caucasian?" His eyes met mine and shot away in an uneasy move. I smiled to myself, for *naluaq* meant seal skin you bleach in the sun, but I would let him keep guessing. "So...have you seen one?" he pressed.

"Old whiteman in boots?"

He snickered. "No, a goose like *that!*"

"Maybe..." I hedged. "I guess so."

"You have?" He scooted closer with eyes widened. Now he looked hungry, even crazed. His words tumbled as he explained how the geese were very sensitive to "ecological insult". They abandoned their nests if there was the slightest disturbance. Warier than cranes. They couldn't handle the modern world; they were "fundamentalist" birds. The scientist's hands were weaving. I had to lean back from the animated force of him. "And so if I do find them, I won't even be able to approach them, which puts me in a double bind!" Suddenly he stopped, aware that he had been too intense, maybe, but his expression was still like Maq's hoping for a scrap.

"Wait a minute," I said, "Now I think maybe I haven't seen them. Yeah...for sure I have not."

How quickly his face fell; even his shoulders collapsed. "You haven't."

"Not here. Maybe the mainland...near fishcamp." I pretended to search my memory. "But earlier. There was more ice. They just stopped and rested awhile...and ate a lot of grass."

He was writing so furiously that the thin lead of his funny pencil snapped. He stopped and from under his brows stared at me, a wolverine at a cache. It was nearly frightening. I said, "Their *anaq* was bigger. And greener than normal. They sound like -" I opened my throat and let loose a harsh cry - *ka-la-a-luk* - ending in a soft falling note. I did it twice.

"The *flight* note!" he exclaimed. "There's no recording of it! It got lost and the captive Tallin's won't do it, y'know? Can you please do that again in the mike?" He hustled to get the tape recorder and held the mike for me while I repeated the cry. I burst out laughing but he didn't seem to mind. I laughed at his serious expression and how he clicked off the machine with a satisfied look. He didn't know why - maybe he thought it was because I was shy at being taped. He had no clue it was a hobby in Itiak to throw interrogators off.

"Far out. I can edit out the human part," he said with a grin. "Thank you. Thanks a lot, man, it's a godsend. But the data was wrong. Now I have to think of a way to catch them next spring...shit...unless..." He was thinking hard, eyes moving back and forth, one hand tapping the pencil on the book, the other fondling his short beard. He was so elated and disappointed at once. I felt a little sorry and asked if he studied other birds too. He nodded, eyes still shifting as he plotted.

"If you don't find that goose, you won't get in trouble, ah?" I asked. He smiled ruefully, shrugging.

"More a question of funding. I have to show something for the money for all this stuff." He waved at the camp. "None of it's mine. And if I lose next year's funding I'll probably get -" He stopped, changing his mind about telling me. "Anyhow."

I stifled a burp rising from the dinner. It was considered bad manners by his people. I got up to leave though I hadn't even tried the *angutkoq* stare-down. It was probably midnight and too cold, the sun had dipped under and a deep scarlet seeped across the sky.

"Oh! Taking off?" The birdman clambered up and stood in front of me. It was a ritual I'd seen with the teachers and in movies; they didn't just leave or let *you* just leave. They made a production of it, pretending they wanted you to stay, walking you to the door, talking more there. "Well, it was nice having you over," said the birdman. Happily, he didn't say my name. After I had sent him down the false trail of that goose he had lost a lot of his reserve and I hoped he wouldn't try to shake my hand again or embrace me like they do. I kept a distance. And he made no move. "Well, take care..." he said.

"*You* take care, ah? People see things out here. Spirits." I hoped my warning would make him nervous, camping alone.

"Is that a fact."

I was unsure by his straight face if he believed me. "Yes. It *is* a fact."

"How far were they from your camp? The geese?"

"Maybe I didn't see them." I stared to get my message across, that he was being pushy. He got it, but a little frown gave away his hurt feelings, and he guessed I had toyed with him.

"Okay, well..." he said. "See you around." He kept looking at me in what seemed a more intimate farewell. Was he hoping for more goose lore, this time the truth? His eyes mirrored the low light, their color was like honey or varnish, pretty...so pretty it didn't seem right. An innocence dwelled there. I detected under the shyness a suspicion, and deepest down like at the bottom of a lake, a dark longing.

How could a scientist - a man - be so beautiful and complex?

I dropped my eyes. Quickly I turned to hike the long way back to town. From the safe distance of the cliffs where I could finally pee I saw the bird-man still standing there. He was a tiny figure on the great earth, like in the basket design of my mother. Hopefully he was not using binoculars.

Too late, I realized I had forgotten my pail at his camp.

AN ARTIST FROM EUROPE was lodging with us, taking my bed, so I was sleeping at Willy's. But I found that high-schoolers had invaded his cabin while he was hunting. They had just flown in from boarding schools all over Outside and were partying with the radio turned loud. Younger kids were running in and out, eyes full of adoration, wondering what to mimic first. I barely recognized the teenagers after a year. A few boys had long hair, for which they would get some grief, once the elders had decided what kind of grief. A girl wore jeans with floppy legs and a button that said *Eskimo Power*. They looked at me coolly, with smoke curling from their nostrils.

They were scary.

It seemed like each year the batch coming home for vacation was more awkward, self-centered, disrespectful and bored. What would they do when their parents asked them to go to fishcamp, give them the finger? For a time of recovery people spoiled them, like they had come back from a hospital or a war. I felt sorry for them too, remembering the shock of my return. Each May the village had looked more cramped and dull and backward, though dearly familiar, and Flo right away complained how lazy and *kuangazuk* I was at helping out. My fingers only knew pencils; they'd forgotten the *ulu* and needle, and the babies and seals and buckets were so heavy in my arms that had carried only books. I just wanted to sleep. Everywhere we went older people scolded us or gave us the silent treatment, though it wasn't our fault we went away for so long. The parents joined in with the whites, insisting on it for our own good. And it *all* seemed so useless, both worlds.

The highschoolers ignored me, though we were nearly sitting on each other's laps in the little cabin. The smoke was giving me a headache but no one would obey my hints to put the cigarettes out. When I couldn't stand it anymore I took my blanket and escaped, feeling like an old lady. I planned to sleep in the tall grass of the dunes near an abandoned *umiaq.* It lay upside down, its walrus hide disintegrating. It probably had never been used since the day its owner got an outboard, and that was fine with me, since if it was Flo's, I'd be at the oars rowing the huge thing. I closed my eyes, breathing in the sweet sea air.

The birdman immediately came to mind.

I went over and over things, not the words we said but how he moved, his narrow waist and hips when he leaned forward, his strange hair shifting in the wind, his hand holding the coffeepot, that last look in his eyes. My insides felt disturbed, maybe with remorse at my unkindness. How much trouble would he be in if he failed in his mission? Maybe I should tell him there was no goose like that. Finally I succeeded in forcing him out of my mind, and fell asleep to the calls of shorebirds fading.

But sometime in the dawn, the dawn which lasted for hours, I woke and looked up at the sky that was now as pale gray as seagull wings. While the grass whispered over me and one curlew whistled, I thought again of my birdman. *Mine,* that was how I had come to see him, like I had captured him in a net. And I didn't like him, I *didn't,* how could I? Yet I felt myself captured by *him* without his even trying. How could I be *angutkoq* if I lost my will so easily? Just by looking at me he had made me forget about my plan, and turned me into a goose molting all its feathers who cannot get away.

Compared to that, a stare-down and x-ray vision were silly tricks.

CHAPTER 5

I don't know myself, and God forbid that I should
GOETHE (NALUAGMIUT)

Sweet Analytics, 'Tis thou hast ravished me
TENNYSON (NALUAGMIUT)

HE HAD TWO BOOKS. One was for his grant money - his empirical, manly book. In that one he recorded like it wasn't true unless he wrote it. They had trained him that way; it didn't happen unless a scientist witnessed it and wrote it down: how many birds, what kind, their actions, their food, their poop. He was careful to not write anything but what he saw. But he had another book that was womanly, the one for his heart and no one else. With this book, it was more like *it* was writing *him*. He could write anything; it witnessed him, it created him and made him real and true. It was for his grant from the universe that let him really live.

ENTRY. ACCORDING to my book, Itiak was once a winter seal-hunting village with a network of trade clear to the southern Tlingit and across to China. Older sites follow archaic beachlines, strung out so they could watch the sea for prey or foes. These sites go back six to ten thousand years but if they are like Indians they might resent being told when they came or where they came from, and be suspicious of a land grab motive.

Families used to disperse in beautifully optimizing patterns until the missions coerced them into settling (though there's still seasonal camps). It was not so long ago. There will be people here who can remember. It's no small thing for nomads to shift overnight to towns, animist to Christian. I wonder how they feel about it. But I'm not about to ask; it'd be like asking my dad how he feels about Hitler's invasion of Norway and the torching of all the villages. Only here, the Nazis still occupy. The most fascist mission had a curfew and awarded an American flag to the best housekeeper. They planned a total assimilation to white values and lifestyle for the Eskimo, who seemed more willing than the rebellious Indians. It was a huge social experiment like the Occupation of Japan. But hold your tongue and stick to birds, not politics (though birds <u>are</u> politics). Patriots lurk in unlikely places, and maybe the tidiness kept away some of the epidemics that so brutalized this region. Records show only 51 Natives left on this vast coast in 1890. And famines: whites had wiped out bowhead, walrus, grizzly, musk-ox, beaver, eider. Caribou were gone. Society totally broken down, like Europe in the Black Death. They needed help and the missions gave it. They fed people, and they had medicine and people do anything to give the kids a chance. They might feel I am condemning their choice; they won't know I feel the same about the rest of the world, all the old cultures - even the damn Vikings - forced to give up their worship of the Earth or be put to the sword.

Entry. Ran into a strange girl asleep in the heather. I don't know what goes for normal here but she seems churlish and unhappy and like some kind of malnourished and disheveled stray. Who am I to talk, but other local womanhood seems to care more about their presentation. At the ramshackle P.O. I saw parka-dress thingies with pointy hoods, kangaroo pouches, some psychedelic, some made roomy to sling babies (no strollers here, thankfully) but all crispy and new. The younger women, of which there are few, have perfect Joan Baez hair and blue eye shadow laid on thick. All ages checked me out and found me lacking, but they were friendly and giggled a lot. They cling to each other. I doubt any of <u>them</u> would hike all the way out here to investigate.

But this lone girl, my somewhat unwanted guest. I don't know. Her severity seemed a tactic rather than lack of humor, because she laughed. I fear I was the brunt; she was on my case and using me as entertainment. They don't have sitcoms here and the evenings are very long. She may be destitute, a pariah? Self-conscious, disinclined to go home. Looks different from Itiak genotype, more Interior. She struck me as pretty sleeping in the buttercups and a bumblebee fertilizing a lupine by her cheek, but then I lost track. Those damn shades made her into a chaingang boss. She needs them more than I do for border patrol (People's militia?) so I'll dig up more communal spirit, though what did I get in return? Oh, right, use of her "sirra" land. Doubt she has influence but can't be sure. If I faux pas with one of the major cats in town, farewell research. Farewell Tallin's, Bering Strait and Chukchi coast, maybe life of the entire Outer Continental Shelf...maybe <u>my</u> life. And speaking of the Goose: General MacArthur knows very well where it is, and she was just leading me on with disinformation for political reasons. Or malice. Unreliable source. Still, her visit may be auspicious.

I am drawn to the ever-enlargening lead, the shining, moving waters "at their priest-like task". The oldsquaw are still out there chortling; such endurance. Kind of a derogatory folk name but they don't mind; "Clangula" is worse. Midnight sun has a powerful energizing effect, good for living things who need uninterrupted time to bloom, raise a brood, lay in stores of willow, run experiments. It's euphoric and you don't notice how spent you are until you keel over.

JAEGERS WOKE ME, wheeling overhead and jeering rudely. People despised the long-tailed birds - shithawks - because they stole right from the beaks of other birds, and from nests. It wasn't their fault, I didn't hate them, but I jumped up with a shout and waved my arms to chase them off.

Overnight something had changed - now I really felt afraid to go to the birdcamp alone. But my pail was bugging me. It was my only pail, and I had to go myself and rescue it, because if I sent a kid the news would get out all over town that I visited the scientist. A little boy hunting longspurs or even Paulette might see me out there, though. The idea of everyone knowing about my interest made my face heat up suddenly like the wind blowing over a flame.

On the other hand, the pail had done me a favor by giving me a reason to visit again. I went early. If the birdman was still sleeping I could just take the bucket and hurry off. Or maybe he'd be awake and brewing coffee...

As I got near the birdcamp I passed holes punctured in the wet tundra. Funny. Squares of marsh were marked out with string, a white feather fluttering on one corner stick. A container had black goo spilled down its nozzle and from the reeds drifted the fumes of something like gasoline. I didn't even try to figure it out.

When I saw that the birdman wasn't in camp - probably crawling in the reeds counting poops - with only a little hesitation I crawled into his tent. It was only to see if he had written more, yet I felt like a spy in a movie. The first book I opened was for science: *hypersalinity*, *grubbing density*...I'd be a useless spy, for even if he was gathering harmful information I could not tell.

His personal book was hiding under a wad of clothes he used for a pillow. *Izhigii* - horrors - it was about *me*! *Unhappy, unreliable*...what did that mean, *chaingang*? It seemed bad, brutal somehow. *That's* how I looked in his sunglasses? But the scientist thought that asleep I was - I read it again to make sure - *pretty*.

Slamming the journal shut, I fled the tent with my face on fire again. As soon as I found the pail I ran.

FOR A WHILE after that he didn't write about me directly, not in a way I could grasp. Think of a fox dancing around the morsel of fat in the trap, tantalized but sensing peril. Think of a goose stilled on its nest, pretending to be invisible as a fox lurks nearby. Maybe he'd discovered my snooping. He was a man of observation; I had put the journal back in a different place before I ran. But he wrote a question: *The visitations?* And then this: "*40, release of tension. You catch three foxes, good omen: like a fox, you can shapeshift.*"

ENTRY: I HAVE EVERY pair and nest site located in the radius, every plant keyed. It's the maniacal energy of no-night, like some kind of speed. Though many clutches are already laid, even hatched, some birds are still engrossed in courtship. The purpose of the lekking, this hysterical display of skill and beauty - and in owls and Corvidae, even wit - is for the females to weed out the less than perfect wannabes and find the one-and-only. But what is a desirable quality? Why does she stare before turning away? Does the male get to select at all? Don't know. Not my field. I strew crude over segments of their campsites to extrapolate their reproductive success if there's a little accident. It seems cold; it's their life and I can't warn them, anymore than I can warn Itiak of what's coming down.

The birds make me wonder about myself, why they go at it with so much more grace. Maybe it isn't easy for them either. I think of the poor canids stuck together helplessly while humans hurl pop cans at them in derision. And maybe it's easier for other humans who aren't me, not so nebulous. People misread me. "You're so scared of women, you'd rather fuck with birds!" said my girlfriend upon leaving. I said No, their cloaca are far too tiny. She left not even smiling, but who was she to talk? She was an astrophysicist; she probably came to quasars. Maybe she was frightening...

To the P.O. now; must gird my loins.

FIELD SCIENTISTS always entered the village for mail sooner or later. The prospect made me jumpy. If I ran into him in public someone might guess my feelings, though I wasn't sure what those feelings were. Within an hour the whole village would know, then how they would mock! The women, I mean -

men didn't seem to notice me. It wasn't only because he was a scientist and *naluagmiu* that they would tease; they'd always find something. But they were hard on each other too, the women of Itiak. Without raising a fist, with a soft remark, an imperceptible action, a woman could slam you to the floor. And the keenest-eyed hunter who could scan a blank terrain and find animals could miss the action in his own home. Women saw, and kept tally.

In spite of my fears I wanted to run into my birdman. I hauled in rainwater and washed. I oiled with reindeer tallow, combed and scissored my hair, took in my hand-me-down pants and replaced my *kaspaq* with a flannel shirt of Willy's. She didn't make me, but I gave all my monthly checks to Flo for supplies and hunting gear, and never bought new mailorder clothes. In the small, cracked mirror I studied my results. Still unhappy-looking and unreliable. A "somewhat unwanted guest". I tried smiling like a sweet village girl. Of all the words I had looked up that he used to describe me, *malice* was the worst. He thought I might be *auspicious,* which meant seeing good "omens" in the flight and feeding of birds. I had to look up *omen* next - it was right next to *ominous.*

Willy tramped into the cabin, worn out. He'd left a good catch of seal with Flo, who was on the beach now peeling off hides, flensing fat, slicing meat from bone. I'd have to go help. Willy looked at me hard. "You look different!"

The bridge of his nose was gashed and scabbed up where his rifle had kicked. "I don't," I said. "You sure the hell do though."

"*Ayii,* you *are* different." He was grinning. He said we were probably an old married couple in another life. He narrowed his eyes and walked around me to examine each profile. Then he murmured, "*Angukaa...*"

"What?"

"I don't know..."

"Shut up or tell me."

"Okay. You're prettier. Beautifuler."

I changed the subject by complaining, "Those high-schoolers - that Joel and them - they took over this place. And they were so mean to me."

Willy laughed. "It's because you're so mean to *them.*"

"Ayii!" It's not so.

He shook his head and turned away to wash his hands in the basin, splattering blood. He left his white canvas parka in a gory heap. I didn't mind cleaning it; he had been hunting for days with no sleep and little food, always chilled, in danger of freezing, drowning, or being trapped on a floe until he starved. All to get food, which I would also eat. And Willy didn't gripe about being a provider. But he could groan like a seal as he struggled out of his wet mukluks and rubbed his feet. They looked awful, wrinkled and ivory like they'd been in water a long time. Whiskers had sprouted on his chin and his eyes were bloodshot. Except for a pale band where his sunglasses protected his face, he was a rich, dark brown. He fell back on his cot, stretching.

At least he could say he was a hunter and it was enough. Under the pressure of the old men Willy had dropped out of high school in order to study with Abe and Fred Senior. The other young men who had kept on with school still had no work, but nor could they hunt like Willy. They lost face. Some stopped trying. They played cards and put it behind them, like letting an *umiaq* rot on the shore, or storing a *kaspaq* and a drum out of sight.

"Anything to eat around here?" Willy mumbled. He rolled on his stomach and leafed through an old *Rolling Stone* with droopy eyes. "Get some meat from Mom, I'll eat later," he ordered me, in the manly way. "You do look different, you know. Whatcha been doing..." He was asleep before I even got out the door with my bucket.

In the blood soaked dunes Flo was up to her knees in four giant *ugzruk*. One of the seals had a light-colored pup in her womb. I felt strange inside my own when Flo's *ulu* revealed it and we looked at it with a wonder, though we'd seen it many times. Seen the miracle, I mean, but also seen the baby itself. When a hunter took proper care the soul would always return to him, so he kept killing the same creature. Only disrespect - of the man or of those in his family or even of his ancestors and descendants backward and forward into time - broke the cycle. Sometimes we younger people got tired of hearing about it; in fact, it was oppressive to always be thinking about respect, respect, respect. And didn't big game hunters still catch animals all the time?

Abe's sister Ethel and her daughter Rita came to help, armed with their sharpened *ulu*s. Rita's babies came too, the smallest *amaq*-ing on her back. Even Polly was there, although just to chat. From her ruling position on a sand dune, her legs straight out in the old way, Abe's mother watched and commented, trying to make sure the seals were praised and that no one bragged. She liked to decide how to distribute the meat; the trouble was, she mentioned people long dead. Flo was complaining to Abe while cutting strips of pale blubber. "Why did you have to teach that boy so well?" It was half-joking. Of course she was proud and happy. If she was angry at Abe she would belittle the game and pretend to feed it to the dogs. She believed the animals heard everything, even your private thoughts, but could tell when you were just flippant. Knowing her old mother-in-law disagreed, she used English to tease.

The artist from Europe had set up his easel so he could paint us at work. He seemed excited by our butchering and sketched rapidly, squinting, a cigarette hanging off his lip. His bushy gray beard hung down like a bib and his narrow face pushed into a large nose with a hook and cave-like nostrils. His blue eyes alarmed me as they zeroed in, and such hairy, wild eyebrows! Yet Flo insisted he was kind. He spoke no English and had to make requests with rapid gestures. I thought the biologist's nose looked far better than that, neater. I chased such thoughts away and tried to concentrate.

Soon my arms were covered in blood and oil and my legs ached from crouching. I was unable to stand the way Flo did, bent for hours at a steep angle over locked knees. While she flensed and flayed so swiftly, maybe she planned all those mukluk soles she would make. Abe watched from where he lay on a fur. He had twisted his bad knee again but he was in a high humor. He drank tea I fetched him from the camp stove and ate raw liver to make up for his hunger on the long hunt. The seal had not been willing to give themselves until the last day, said Abe, then suddenly "everybody wanted to jump in the boat!" Abe had even used his old-fashioned harpoon he was feeling so good and strong, but then he'd slipped in blood. He wondered what he had done wrong, or if Flo had said something bad at that moment about seal.

"*Ayii,* I never!" Flo cried, waving her *ulu* at him. "I'm not the one with the big mouth!" Abe told stories about his mighty youth, when he was lost at sea, how he had been trapped in a lead and stood in the ice water for two days, not like young men today who got kidney failure or hypothermia. He interrupted himself to instruct Flo how to cut, or - if Aka wasn't listening - to tell her what part of what seal I should take to what relative. It was always *his* relatives, since Flo came from another village. When she was born, their parents had agreed they would wed, and Abe got to take Flo home after he proved he could hunt. It put her at a disadvantage going far away. At last Flo straightened, panting, and pushed up her blood-smeared glasses.

"Who's cutting around here? Do I tell you how to shoot?"

"Yup, you do!"

Everyone laughed at their old game. Usually I enjoyed Abe in this mood - so much better than the other moods - but that day I found him annoying. I listened for the mail plane and kept checking the road to see if the biologist was on his way, so I slipped and cut my thumb like a little girl. Polly always carried bandages and she tended the cut, teasing me. I didn't care, I barely felt the sting. Everyone stopped for a rest and a meal then, but I wasn't hungry for my plate of boiled meat with sweet new seal oil. Flo smiled at me.

"Big game guide flying in today," she said. "That bad one with walrus whiskers." I put my plate down. "What's wrong with you today?" Flo asked in Inupiaq, peering at me. "Eat something, you're so skinny. And why are you wearing Pataq's shirt? That's for a man!" She patted my knee. "You look good though, bones and all. Me, I'm just *ugzruk*." She laughed but it was true: Flo was the fattest of anyone. Her weight made her awkward, like the big seal humping over land. She wore nylons under her mukluks and house dress, and her still-dark hair, from which she had her grandchildren pick all the white, was rolled in a bun. Her cheeks were rosy and radiant with crows-feet.

Flo was known for her generosity. It wasn't just because she was devout; it was in her *inua*. She was also famous for being headstrong. She was the closest thing to a mother I had. Still, I wasn't Polly. I had to give up my bed every time an outsider boarded at our house, and returned to find their unpleasant odors on my blanket. Polly always got to keep her bed. "Any *surra* out there?" Flo asked in a soft, petting voice.

"I picked some," my voice came out strange, "but it wilted."

"Got to pay better attention to what you do. To waste even the green plants might make them hide from you next time." Flo patted my leg again and smiled, eyes narrow and kind, and Polly sent me a look, because I had cut myself and wouldn't eat and Flo was *unga*-ing. Flo didn't usually coddle me, though she *unga*-ed everyone else. I must really be in bad shape, I thought, or Abe told her about my activities and she was just being extra nice before she went in for the kill. Yet she said nothing more.

At last the older ones took pity on us younger women and let us go. The post office was closed and I felt a needle of disappointment right in the stomach. I was going to sneak off and nurse thoughts of the birdman alone, but Polly hooked my arm with her elbow. She liked to use me as support if her heels were high, or in winter to keep from slipping in her hard pointy boots. There was no denying Polly. "Let's go to the store," she said, "*Ki,* come on. I'll buy you a Mister Freeze."

I loved those cold things. Why was everyone being so nice - did I look so funny? I was giddy and my heart beat in a hectic rhythm. Maybe it was the virus Polly said was attacking Seward Peninsula. I waited at the house while she cleaned up and changed, taking too long as always. She bought stylish clothes on her medical trips Outside and had a personal supply of expensive shampoo, while the rest of us just used soap suds and ordered clothes from Sears or made our own. When she was in her finery we set off for the store arm-in-arm. *Leif,* I thought - *that's his name* - and my cheeks heated. He thought I was pretty...and malnourished...why did I care what he thought? Maybe he could cast a spell even if a scientist didn't believe in spells, and people could tell I was under his influence just by looking at me.

Suddenly I didn't want to be in public and I dragged my feet, but Polly pulled me along, oblivious. People smiled in our direction, as they always did if I was with Polly. She cast a bubble of bright goodwill around her. Maybe that was why she was a good nurse, a healer. Though I studied *angutkoq* things, I could not make others like me; instead I erected a shield of darkness. Polly never had to do that, she always had it so good. She was Ugungoraseok.

The new store was built up on tall pilings. Just as we began climbing the stairs the birdman came out with cheap new sunglasses pushed up on his head. He started down two steps at a time with a thundering noise, shaking the building. As he passed us he nodded and flashed his teeth at Polly. Her grip on my arm tightened. She cast me a wide-eyed look and turned us on the stairs so we were looking down at the biologist, who had stopped short. Too late, he realized who was with Polly, because he had been all eyes for her. His smile collapsed. He was thinking of how "churlish" I was.

"Holy cow, who *is* that?" Polly whispered, and hung off my arm as if her legs had given out.

"Who knows?" I said loudly. "Maybe a senator."

She threw back her head to laugh in peals, though it wasn't so amusing. She said thoughtfully, "I bet I know..."

The birdman was staring at me and seemed to be deciding something. *Don't say hi, don't, don't,* I prayed, and warned him with my look. He couldn't see through my shades - that is their disadvantage. But he switched his eyes to Polly fast. With her free hand Polly flipped back her glossy black hair.

"Hi, you must be the biologist, is it?"

"Ya." It was a funny "yes", sing-song. He looked even taller in the village.

"So we meet at last. I'm the health aide here." Polly knew how to do formal introductions well from her work with doctors. And she had her profession to throw out first thing, like the whites.

"Oh! Far out." He looked impressed. "Hopefully I never have to come see you." When he smiled again I dimly recognized it, although no man ever did it to *me*. He was flirting, in a shy way that alarmed me. I could feel the effect of his charm through Polly's hand.

She beamed, showing her dimples. "I'm Polly, Niviak. This is Gretchen, but her other name is Kayuqtuq. That means fox, the red kind."

He gave me a strange little nod like a bow from another country or century, and his face grew serious and watchful. "Hello..." His eyes traveled to my hands; I hadn't washed up well and my fingers were bloody. My bandage was already dirty.

"Let's go," I muttered to Polly, who ignored me.

"What species are you studying?" she asked the scientist brightly, her head cocked raven-like. His eyes shot back to her.

"Right now anything that lands here. But I specialize in...uh...the goose-duck-swan family. *An-a-tea-day*."

"Oh! There's lots of *them*!"

"Ya." They smiled. "So what do you do when no one's sick?" the birdman asked. Polly giggled, her hand weaving to her mouth, her eyes twinkling. Unlike me, Polly of course was sanitary. I noticed her clothes then, the snug flared pants and her jean jacket open to show her gauzy blouse that puffed around the breasts. Her bra-less nipples stood right up in the wind. Flo would be shocked. And her nails - pink! She started to tell him about health aides and how something always came up. He watched her with a curious and it seemed admiring way.

Suddenly a group of *naluagmiut* burst noisily around the building. It was the principal Bill, Dolores and a stranger with a walrus moustache - the big game guide. The schoolhouse was used as a hotel by outsiders, and *eskuulkti* always took their more difficult boarders for a long walk to tire them.

"Hey, look at that!" the stranger cried, "Got 'em even around here too?" He strode right past me and Polly, interrupting her. "Checking out the local fauna, son? Or is it daughter?" He guffawed and punched the birdman in the shoulder, who stepped back from the blow but the guide lunged forward to grab his hand and pump it. "Waldo Barnes! Missouri! I was beginning to miss you hippies! Right on! Ha Ha! No really, you must be a wild and woolly biologist!"

"True..." The birdman smiled a little.

The guide turned to the principal, who was trying to light his pipe in the wind. "You didn't tell me there was a goddamn BIO-logist here! We're going to have to invite him to our feast! Roast duck!" he told the scientist, whom now the teachers gave a look of pity. "So what have you seen game-wise?"

"Oh...well, I uh...I'm not really..."

"Oh, he's a bird man!" cried Dolores. "On a wild goose chase. And I bet he wouldn't tell you if he spotted anything!" She grinned broadly at the birdman as her green eyes flickered down his body, taking his measure. He seemed at a loss. He glanced at me and Polly and widened his eyes a split second in play-horror. We burst out laughing, but I didn't know if it was Waldo or the teacher who frightened him. He wasn't doing too good with his own kind.

"Well, come on," Dolores coaxed. "Aren't you here on some kind of covert operation against the oil companies?" Now he looked completely surprised. I felt a suspicion coming from the men. Funny, I thought, Bill ought to find the scientist okay: they both had beards, they both read books. "So, are you?" pressed Dolores. They waited, arms angled in whiteman poses.

"Um...wow, word gets around. But it's not espionage; they're sponsoring me and all the other oh-sea-ess projects. Outer Continental Shelf." The birdman said the last part like it was a joke, but dead-pan. "Prior to drilling."

"Oho," said Bill. "Gives you a lot of incentive to find something disastrous, doesn't it?" He smiled tight-lipped around the pipe as the biologist's brown eyes turned wary. The principal then dove for his hand too. The action seemed like an apology, or as if to say *I jokes*. "Bill Stern. Dolores, my loyal companion. We run the school here, and I hope you do come for dinner."

"Um...well..." The birdman looked up the road, down the beach, and then straight at me so my heart jumped like a dog hit with a pebble, for what his face said was, as clear as the sky: *I would rather eat with you.*

The teacher tugged his arm. "Come on with us right now!" she cried with glee. "Save us from Waldo's bear stories! Hi Polly! Hi Gretchen! How's life?" She waved at us, and Polly waved back, though we were standing only a few feet away. But we were in different worlds. The birdman cast us a look of regret as they dragged him down the road to the schoolhouse.

"They stole him," said Polly, laughing a little. She spun toward me. "*Angukaa*, he's gorgeous! And he's so -"

"Let's go in! Store's closing!" I interrupted.

POLLY AND I wandered back to the house, hoping all the work was done. Before we got to the door she said slyly. "You met him before." Of course I knew who she meant, for who else was in our thoughts?

67

"*Ayii!* I never!"

"*Saglu.* You did. Where did you get those sunglasses? What's he like?"

"I don't know. Ugly. *Naluagmiusak*" - that meant "whiteman-like". "Funny." By funny we usually did not mean amusing.

Polly snorted in disbelief. "I'm going to go out there and visit later. You want to come along?"

"Why?"

"Visit!"

"No way."

"*Ki.* Come on." She jerked my arm. "I can't go alone, ah. Don't let me go alone. He might do something funny. Attack me. I jokes."

"You mean you might attack *him*. What do you need me for? Hold him down?"

Polly studied me, her black eyes sharper now. "Okay, come later and fetch me" - she looked at her watch - "around ten." Like I watched the clock like her with her radio schedules and prescriptions. She needed time to curl her bangs and put on mascara, I recognized it: she was on the warpath. She'd sampled all the eligible men in town - though to be fair, there weren't so many for a woman related to nearly everyone - and maybe some not so eligible, and now she had to go after the scientist.

Back at the cabin Willy was still snoring. I studied his sleeping form, comparing him to the biologist. Of course he was more handsome. He was the perfect Itiak man even if he never had a girlfriend. We weren't blood, not even related on paper, and here we were living together with our beds end to end like siblings. He had rescued me from the torment of the other boys when we were little. When they pelted me with ice balls loaded with rocks he refused to join in; once at the risk of great mocking he had gone on my side so it was twelve against two. He pulled me from the cold surf when they threw me in and I was panicking. There was an evil spotted dog that one family turned loose on me now and then - the "*itkiliq* hunter". It hated me and would track me down in the village like a black-and-white spirit. People would tell me, "I hear she is out looking for you," then chuckle at my terror. In secret Willy shot that dog.

When we grew older he fell into the role of my "teasing cousin", someone who pestered and bugged and pointed out a person's follies when no one else could. The whole village was my open critic, so I didn't really need Willy for that. He was also the other kind of "cousin" though, the one who always stuck up for you and let you confide. It was love but not man-woman love. At times I felt like touching his back, his arm, to feel the sinewy muscle. It was a remote desire. Only *I* knew he wanted to be a musician, and he never played his guitar in front of anyone else.

I tickled his lower lip until it twitched. "Hey you," I said. He could keep me company, maybe give me an excuse to avoid Polly. We could play cards all night, double spit. But Willy kept snoring, though he grunted and flailed when I stuck my fingertip up his nose. I left the cabin, intending to pick *surra* again.

As I was passing the schoolhouse I saw the whites near the swingset in the low sun, still shouting, still keeping the birdman hostage. From behind the fuel-oil tank I had a clear scope on them. Waldo was going on about Eskimo this and Natives that while he and Bill smoked. The principal looked mad and the birdman gazed out to sea where terns played in the wind. Dolores laughed loudly in his direction at every opportunity, *Ahawhawhaw*. I edged closer around the school and craned to hear better.

"No, no! You take a bottle of...of...I don't know...Lysol or vanilla extract or *antifreeze* and dangle it on a string, half these guys will follow you anywhere!" It was Waldo. Flo suspected he ran booze into the village.

"Ah, what prejudiced bullshit." The principal's bald forehead had turned dark red. By the unsteady feet of the *naluagmiut* I guessed they were drunk on the teachers' illegal moonshine, though it was hard to tell with people already so uninhibited. But the birdman was sober.

"It ain't big-a-tree!" cried Waldo happily, "It's God's truth. Dry laws don't do squat. I seen guys blinded by fucking wood alcohol for chrissakes." I had seen it also: old Isaiah. Someone had sold it to him back in the thirties and he didn't know. When I looked at the birdman to see his reaction, he was just staring at the guide without blinking.

"Now guys, cool it," said Dolores. "There's a time and place -"

"And the time is now!" cut in her husband. "We won't make peace just for your lousy duck dinner," he hissed at her, making her shrink down in her parka. He turned on the biologist. "Well, don't hold back on us. I'm sure you *too* have ass-toot observations. We saw how you...er...study the local endangered chicks." Waldo guffawed. "Be careful out there, it's a bog," the principal said. With one hand on his heart, flourishing his burning pipe with the other, he sang off-key, "More geese than swans now live, more fools than wise..."

The guide found it hilarious, and even the teacher was smiling again. "Yeah, what are your *findings?*" she asked. But the birdman had grown as stony-neutral as a mad Eskimo. Now he was leaving, saying something about his experiment to the teacher's high exclamations of protest. I was relieved, for they were surely teasing and I hated Waldo the guide on sight. *Eskuulkti* didn't act that way around normal people; I wondered if this was their natural state, never meant to be witnessed. As the birdman took off for the shore they looked crestfallen like children who had broken a toy.

Once they went inside I ran past the school. He was using the beach for a road in that fast lope of his. Up on the cliffs I followed him nearly to his camp, ducking low in the grass when he looked back, then I turned inland and wandered restlessly until the sun rolled south again.

Polly would be mad at getting ditched, but I was not sorry.

BOOK TWO

"Unspeakably Far Away"

Whose are those three heads with evil looks
I see before me to the North?
Daughters of Calatin, wise in enchantment;
the three witches killed by me
their weapons in their hands

(ANCIENT IRISH. *NALUAGMIUT*)

The wild hunting wastes make mad the mind,
and objects rare and strange, sought for,
men's conduct will to evil change

(ANCIENT TAOIST. CHINESE)

The sea, and fire and women: all three evils

(ANCIENT GREEK. *NALUAGMIUT*)

The great sea has set me adrift...
Earth and the great weather move me
have carried me away
and move my inward parts with joy

UVARNUK (WOMAN ANGAKOK. IGLULIK)

CHAPTER 6

There is joy in feeling the summer
come to the great world
and watching the sun follow its ancient way...
TATILGAK (UMINGMAQTORTIUT)

HERE, STUCK INTO his journal around the entries of this time is an old sheet
of lined yellow paper. In the hand of a woman:

"My dear Leif, Have you found your geese yet? You don't write
but I know you're so busy. I hope you're not too absent-minded on
the tundra, and that you have found some friends. Don't forget
to eat, I sent a care package..."

His mother, working nightshift in a convalescent home. When I hold the
paper I can still feel the yearning, as if I reach out to hold something but my
arms meet only air. A flown bird, my son. *"Now here's your father. He's been*
having some angina and shouldn't he out fishing but he insists on it..."
And in a different hand, in coarse black lines with foreign shapes, only this:

"Hope things are fine. Fahr."

As fleeting as a line of geese high up in the cold wind. I don't care to
touch that bleak writing; it seems so deliberately short, but that is how fathers were to children who disobeyed, who followed their own ideas. An arrow, tiny but full of meaning, points to it in the son's blue field pen.

A bent photo is taped to the letter, trapping the ghosts of a middle-aged
couple. She, her hair in one curled braid and dark like the son, a familiarity
about her black eyes, the spirit of Leif. She smiles tiredly but the man beside
her does not smile. He is Nordic, tall and stooped and with a greater version
of his boy's hawk nose. There is mowed grass, a tree in pink bloom and a
white house, very exotic. "Ballard" it says on the back in the blue pen, the
word full of irony and affection. There is a pain.

A water mark near the bottom of the paper blurs that black, cruel writing and makes it flow at one edge. A stray snowflake of thirty-five springs ago? A fleck of sea foam stirred by a gale? I close my eyes and feel its history. It is a tear...for the father's last imprint on the son's soul. These people did not use telephones, not long distance anyway. Talk about primitive culture.

I DID NOT RECOGNIZE my condition or know it was growing and growing until it was full-blown. That settled pond was getting stirred - hundreds of reindeer were running through it with sharp hooves and my insides felt trampled. While foraging I kept away from the birdcamp, or far enough away that binoculars couldn't find me. The seal harvest kept me busy and Polly was preoccupied with an outbreak of flu - Itiak had little resistance to outside bugs, and even colds could turn serious. She gave shots in the classroom clinic and arranged medivacs to Nome or Kotzebue.

Soon most families would leave for the summer to far-flung camps on the mainland until the snow. At these camps women netted, fileted and dried salmon as they entered the rivers from the sea: chum, pink, silver, red and Dolly Varden, then chum again. We picked berries: blue, crow, the precious cloud - we called them salmon for their color - and cranberries last. The men put out the nets and hauled heavy tubs of water to wash the fish if we were too busy. They lazed around. If they tired of women endlessly cutting fish, they could hunt birds or boat back to the village to get supplies and check on the elders or visit other camps.

And they liked to protect us from possible bear attacks - *aklak* were drawn to the easy fish. I saw one once, shambling blonde and hump-backed on a high ridge. They were coming back since their extermination and they seemed mad. Other families told of *aklak* tearing down tents, ripping scalps off, grabbing helicopters from the air. Abe was sure there was always a bear lurking near us. He smelled their rank odor in bushes and talked so much about it Flo made me sleep out of the tent and a little away from camp when I was on my period. "It makes them so angry." Polly didn't have to though.

Flo was antsy to get out in the country, though the fish weren't running yet. She used the campsite of Abe's mother, whose ancestors had used it since *taimmani* - "back then". I went along; there was so much to be done, and

Polly did no work. She'd visit awhile being pampered and bored then let Willy boat her back to town. When the kids were all in diapers and Aka too old to babysit, Flo used to make me stay in Itiak with them. I pined away. People diagnosed me correctly as "campsick", for even those who had flown to a city tried to make it home every year for camp, just like the birds. It was hard work and not too comfortable, but it was so good to be outdoors in the country in summer. These days Flo didn't have any trouble finding a girl relative to take care of Aka and Willy's dogs, a pale girl who hated mosquitoes and animals and sleeping on the ground, and just wanted to put on make-up and play records.

But now I didn't want to go, for if I left the peninsula I would never see the birdman again. Not that I planned on visiting, but I might spot him from a distance. He hadn't come into the village since the whites teased him. I kept waiting, all my radar turned south to the marsh, prepared to race to the post office where I could bump into him. I knew it was strange, this willingness to trade my dear summer for a glimpse of a *naluagmiut* scientist. I had told no one my plan, but at the inlet camp as I was helping Flo bundle up the tent and remember all the things we needed to pack, she said, "There's cornmeal from Uncle Jay in the back. The dogs can have that every three days, and when that Alder has pups, feed her every day." So I *was* staying in town!

"That bird fellow," Flo continued offhand, "he's coming out that way with us." When I grew still she looked at me funny. "*Eeee.* Niviak met him, Pataq too. He wants to camp near us. Maybe he'll count some poops out there." Flo chuckled to herself, then she got started and couldn't stop laughing until she had to wipe her eyes with the hem of her dress and catch her breath.

I wasn't laughing with her. My heart had closed like sea ice, abruptly, my mind filled with the groaning roars of pressure. Polly never told me they had met again. I was going to be left here with the dogs! An old story came to mind. Abandoned on an island, an *aka* was forced to keep the company of a little green worm. At first she fed it scraps from the beach, then it grew and started hunting for her - hares and birds - until it was huge. In the fall when the worm saw the villagers returning, rowing the *umiaq*, it writhed down to the beach and killed everybody as they landed. The *aka* ran, so the monster chased her and killed her too. I had to go, I had to see the birdman again, I could not be left behind, I could not!

Flo was peering at me. My eyes grew hot and I hung my head. "Can I go to camp?" I whispered. I had to ask directly like that. If she refused, we'd both be uncomfortable forever after that, for she had let me down. That is why I never asked for anything important. I had thought long and hard about why Flo had taken me in eight years before. There were many churchgoers in Itiak but none of them had stepped in, so I wasn't sure if was belief in Jesus I could thank, though that was Flo's explanation. It might have been pity. Yet the unpleasant truth was, for years Flo did not interfere when I had been just a slave, right up to the events that made her so outraged, and she didn't mind putting me to work too, to let Polly have a life of leisure. Still, she was mostly kind. And she worked herself hard as well.

"I don't want to stay here," I whined like a baby.

Flo raised her eyebrows in surprise, and made a soft sound in her throat. "Seemed like you wanted to stay here."

"I *did*." Tears spilled beneath my sunglasses. "I changed my mind."

"Oh, poor *aninang*" - baby, Flo was calling me - "Let me see you, Kayuqtuq. Take off those things!" I pushed my sunglasses back and looked down, wiping my silly tears of relief and - I didn't know why - grief too. She patted my hand and shook her head in dismay and amusement. "Now you hear me, we are always happy to have you. And you cut fish good, even if your berries are not clean. You always have too many leaves, but you're fast. And you find them for me." I sniffled, fighting my urge to crawl to her bosom and snuggle.

"Buy jam, Crisco, canned milk, and onions. There's enough cash, that painter paid for his mukluks. And don't forget to pack seal oil and my candy this time." Flo turned back to tightening the rope. As if to herself she said, "*Eeee*, I met that birdman. He seems real nice. We'll invite him to eat when Niviak is there. She likes him too."

Her words were softly spoken but hard like stones, dropping into the pit of my stomach. And she was glancing up under her eyebrows again to see if I understood. I did, very well. *Don't you fight with my true girl* , she was saying, *because she will win*.

ENTRY. RAN INTO POLLY again and met her mom. Everyone has two identities here. Polly was eager to inform me that Niveeack means "cute and lovable", and remind me that Kayooktuck means red fox. Vulpes vulpes. Not sure how to spell words. Can't figure out the kin position of my wild maid-of-the-tundra; possibly a retainer of the Oogoongorawseeock clan. She seemed skittish and subdued in town, shadow to bright Polly. Oddly, while she seemed devious before, now she seems guileless, just a little waif who fends for herself. An ingenue. She's disconcerting and somehow...fey? "I am ANGOOTCOCK in these parts," she said in that braggart's tone. Could it mean angakok, which is shaman in Greenlandic? If so, that's an interesting fantasy. Like those guys who re-create medieval sword fights. Half-hoping I'd see her again but no luck.

Strange how things turn out. The hunter returned to my camp and disclosed that he is Polly's brother. They look alike. Willy (or Putuck: bone marrow) is the one who built the unnamed board-thingie I usurped for a windbreak. Which turns out to be a duckblind. At first he didn't want to reveal its true function, and joked that it was a "one-dimension outhouse". I think he poaches, because his rather whimsical face closed off during this topic. Maybe I am suspect of law-enforcement connections, ulterior motives (why does everyone think I'm a spy?) I was nonjudgmental. And I am without bias, as long as they're not shooting the last pair of Tallin's geese on Earth. My camp might interfere with his subsistence (more than willow disruption!) but he is cool about it. So we have a detente.

Willy is also an astounding mimic of bird calls. I played the recording of Gretchen's call minus the chortles, and he laughed wildly. "That's the Kayooktuck bird! You talked to her?" he asked, as incredulous as if she's a deaf-mute. When I said she was my key ethnographic resource, he wanted to see the Field Guide too. "Maybe" he had sighted Tallin's on the mainland, though he didn't specify where on the long coast. The custom must be to know more than you let on. I asked to record his imitations of brant, Canada, emperor, snow, whitefront, swan, etc, which seemed to delight him; they're good enough to entice a bird into a challenge or other behavior. He invited to take me to the mainland. Why not? Two sites are better for the experiment and I can search for Tallin's, so my reasons are valid.

Later: My second pair of binocs were missing, and I realized he had borrowed them. It's not stealing, I'm not using them, and I could take something of his no problem, but white explorers always misunderstood. It means we're buddies. Or like family.

Entry. This mainland camp is a pristine site, and the salt marsh perfect for a control. Beautiful, with a serenity underlying the frantic birds. "To one who has been long in city pent, Tis very sweet to look into the fair and open face of heaven." It all falls away here; there is no humanity, or inhumanity. No atrocity. I don't listen to the news. The battery is low anyway. The sea changes from cobalt to lapis in the perpetual sunlight, depending on currents. Arctic lunar tide is minimal and the ice keeps the swell low, even dead calm some days. Air temp reached 50 degrees (if it gets any warmer, I'll swim). Past the marsh the landscape undulates like frozen waves up into crags, at midnight lit up by a primeval glow.

Sighted gyrfalcons and golden eagles. A pair of snowy owls on a pingo; their nest is lined with dried lemmings. A swan nest fully seven feet wide and very tall, fortress-like. Red-throated loons in a nearby pond take turns letting one gray chick ride on their backs while the mate hunts at sea. The chick seems spoiled. Too cute, but there's close competition in the cuteness scale with some arctic fox kits tumbling outside their den. Little balls of brown fuzz with mischievous eyes. A gray whale drifted past doing the backstroke in a lazy way. A dead beluga juvenile washed up with hematomas on its white skin (maybe it got caught in a current and smashed on the rock island). In the riparian: otter, muskrat and a lazy porcupine. Estuarine: tiny sand flounders, the ever present kittiwakes and terns, many ducks, brant. A rank boulder den filled with scat and cracked femurs: wolf or wolverine. Willy says people can go a lifetime and never see either, they focus their extreme intelligence on avoiding humans (he and Abe find them though). Reindeer roam all over the Seward Peninsula until rounded up, Laplander style; they were imported in the '30s to replace the caribou and ward off famine. Willy is one of the herders. He says they'll come to the beach when the flies get bad. Probably won't get to see musk oxen, since they are only now being re-introduced from the breeding farms. Mastodons wouldn't surprise me here.

The only sighting I hope against is Ursus horribilis...yikes.

Willy has visited a few times and seems curious. The Ugungoraseoks (now I can spell it) are camped upriver a few miles as the raven flies - four if you follow the winding of the Iron, and he comes down in his boat. He warned me about a rabies epidemic and to watch out if a red fox came too close to camp acting "funny". I don't why he was amused but many things amuse Willy.

Here is one of our discussions. I was trying to tell him why I didn't like the term "wilderness". Anglocentric. The land just appears unpopulated to outsiders. As Willy pointed out, every inlet and hill has a history, all rivers and mountains were named thousands of years ago. I never understood the thrill of assholes imagining they are the 'first whiteman' to step foot somewhere, what does that really mean? That other people don't matter. (I can pick on the word 'remote' too: it is New York and Seattle that are remote. Alaska is on the edge of the barbarian zone). Anyway, he just laughed like I'm a little touched.

"How come some scientists who don't live here and don't even eat geese worry so much about the marsh?"

"Are there other scientists studying the marsh here?" I was ready to get jealous of those others. I feel possessive already.

"No..." And he dropped his eyes shyly. So he meant me. I tried to explain without sounding like a frothing-at-the-mouth zealot how the Arctic needs more protection, because the birds reproduce here and plants take so long to grow back, like the dwarf birch at our feet, centuries old and only one inch tall. In Seattle's ecosystem hemlocks that old would be three hundred feet high. Willy's eyes got bigger. "Is it? I would like to see it."

"But they cut them all down."

"Vaa." He contemplated the little tree. "So...last frontier, ah?"

"Well, I don't like that word either."

That made him laugh. He said he didn't worry about the Arctic like city people did. "We Eskimos know how to survive."

"Even Eskimos can't survive if the ecosystem collapses!"

I must have sounded too angry, because it made him withdraw. We sat in silence for awhile while he smoked a whole cigarette and I was determined to keep quiet too, then he gave me a conciliatory grin, like it had been his fault. "Hey, wanna see an island?" So off we went in his boat. I guess it was partly to show me, to let me see with my own eyes so I could stop "worrying." He took me to the rock cliff island to check out the pelagics: murres, devilishly-horned puffins, chubby auklets (and those cormorants I saw fly over!). There do seem to be billions of them. The ammonia smell nearly knocks you out. Proudly, Willy said they used to climb down the walls with ropes to gather eggs and make parkas from seabird feathers. I withheld my private thoughts that this, too, is imperiled.

Entry. On the other side of the river are the grassy humps of a sod village ruins. Willy says it's haunted. Northerners massacred everyone by smoking them out and spearing them like "sicksick" (note: ground squirrels of which it takes one hundred for Florence to sew an old style "parkee" only outsiders wear). The butchery was due to a blood feud, always originating with "woman trouble". In a vendetta male relatives had to take revenge, tit for tat, but they'd bide their time. A boy could grow up under the roof of the man he had to kill someday. Maybe his enemy would never return from a hunt. The relatives might be offed too, so no witnesses or future avengers. In fact, the people of this ghost village had once given a feast and invited their foes in order to slaughter them unawares. Trojan Horse deception. Willy told me about the Chukchi tribe from across the Strait, here long before the whalers to war, trade and mix gene pools. They took female slaves, who were not allowed footwear to prevent their escape. Both sides slew with arrows and devised shields, samurai-like armor and fortresses to use in epic battles. Willy says Itiak-miut above all relished killing Athabaskans from the Interior (gulp) and men got a tattoo for each "Itkeelick" they slew.

(But murder in the community was never tolerated. Criminals were banished naked into the tundra to be tortured to death by mosquitoes. And just sixty years ago when two youths in another village killed a miserly schoolteacher, their own uncles and dads hunted them down and made them choose between shooting and strangling. The boys chose bullets and were fed to dogs. My god. Over a mean-ass missionary. Perhaps they thought they'd better execute the boys before the whites killed <u>everyone</u> in their frontier "justice"?).

Maybe without oogrooks and vast flyways the people here would have been too busy scrabbling for survival to fight or keep slaves. I like the theory that warfare occurs only within a certain range of resource-availability. Look at songbirds. The most aggressive "land claims" posturing occurs among species co-occupying a zone of rich resources. In scanty zones, there's collaboration. With primal humans, if the resources fell below a limit, the tribes dispersed into far-wandering families that shared with strangers. Like Hudson Bay. Even the "Skraelings" and Vikings were willing to share at first (like when my mom and dad first dated). It turned to battle axe when the Norse got paranoid and fell into plunder ethos (my parents, again). For peace and harmony there has to be low population, both sides: you can't feel outnumbered? This mechanism wouldn't have operated on the bountiful coast here.

Of note: just like the Vikings, enmity could only be shown to relatives and others in the tribe by sanctified insulting, a public blowing off of steam through taunting poems. Otherwise, keep it bottled up. Only shamans could be in-your-face. Now I know the local standards are nice and accommodating, so what's Gretchen's story? I will meet her again, it seems, for Willy says I've been invited over to eat. Some trepidation. I managed to find out just how old she is by asking how old everyone in his family is. He thought it was funny. He thinks she's twenty (same as him).

I-Ching says the wild goose arrives at the river and the soul is born.

I pour the crude tomorrow.

WE SET UP THE TENTS on the bank of the Iron. The water gurgled by, snow only a few hours earlier, and the air was pure. The grandkids scampered up the hill back of camp with Maq, who was supposed to watch for bears but wasn't much more use guarding children than fishracks. They found a thrush's nest full of ugly little babies and the dog bolted them down in one gulp. Abe's ancestors had chosen this spot because it was so pretty nestled in mountains - that is what we called the high hills. Berries were good and the river narrowed without a fast current, making it easy for us women to set the net using a long pole if the men took the boat somewhere. Anyway, Flo didn't like the mouth where it was wetter and foggier and had all the scary terns.

Abe and Willy went on a crane hunt right off. With the men gone and the salmon not yet arrived, I could relax in the sun. I did *nak* greens and gather eggs and firewood. I shot curlews for dinner and built and tended the fire, fetched and boiled water, washed dishes, clothes and children in the river, but that was nothing. People were nicer out of the village and its two hundred pairs of eyes watching you for good behavior all the dark winter. At camp, the oppression and obligations fell away. You didn't have to worry about saving face. Best of all, back then the bugs wouldn't fly until mid-July, so we had a whole month of paradise.

Willy was amused when he returned from a visit to the biologist's camp. The marsh there was filled with goose *anaq*, and the naluagmiu got to work with his counting clicker while Willy was still drinking tea. "It's real interesting," said Willy. "He don't count every single *anaq*. He makes a square in a thick place, and counts just the poops in there. Then he does the same thing for a thin place and figures out the average."

I sighed. "Kind of like voting," said Abe. He was sitting by the fire with coffee and bannock and looking happy in a cloud of cigarette smoke.

"You fetch that boy here sometime soon," said Flo as she hooked a bannock from the skillet. "She'll be hungry after all that counting." She laughed hard at her own joke until she had to wipe her eyes with her hem. She wore a dress even out camping, with trousers under it and a *kaspaq* and sometimes even her apron, along with a number of scarves in the bold prints she liked. She would knit baby clothes on the riverbank.

"You count the shits," Abe told her very seriously, "then you know how many voters there are." That sent Flo off again. We all watched her, Polly and the men with enjoyment.

"It's so dumb" I muttered to Willy, not wanting to sound like I was lecturing to the old people. "Counting them won't save them."

Everyone looked at me now, with interest. I hardly spoke up with an opinion in a group, especially if men were there, though Polly certainly did. It was frowned on; it wasn't maidenly. "*Eee, tingmiaq*," said Abe thoughtfully. Birds.

"He find his special *ligliq* yet, that birdman?" Flo asked Willy.

"Nope. Somebody told him it stopped around here to rest. That's why he came to mainland."

"Hmm..." Abe narrowed his eyes through the cigarette smoke. "What kind is it?"

"He showed me a picture. It sure don't come around here."

"You tell her that?"

"I don't know." Willy grinned. "Pretty excited about that bird. He'll stay all summer so he can try see them fly in. You can't change their mind."

The old people laughed. "Maybe if you tell him, he will let you bring him back today to the peninsula," said Abe. "This very minute!"

"*Eee*, better wait until fall and tell him," said Flo, tittering softly. They are mean, I thought. But then, I was the one who had told the birdman that the goose came here. I didn't like how Polly pricked up her ears at news of him. The others seemed too intrigued, like they knew it was *I* who was really interested and they were teasing. I wanted the scientist as my own project, to withhold and tell riddles and send him off on false leads. Flo made a joke about serving goose when he came for the famous dinner. When her gaze landed on me I dropped my eyes fast.

She was laughing again, so happy to be out camping. Or if she was not happy, then she had a very good mask to face the world with. At times, away from all eyes but mine, I had seen Flo not so merry. Like when her first son died out hunting, bled to death. I knew that she longed to live in her own village, where she wasn't as judged, and that she often found her in-laws tiresome and bossy. All that cheerfulness was from pride. She'd learned it at fourteen when she was married to a stranger and had to live under the rule of Aka, and lost three babies to sickness.

People used to carve masks to reveal the *inua* inside every living thing, hidden but just about to take over. I saw them on faces. One of Flo's masks was a caricature of happiness: a wide curve of a mouth and crescent eyes, laughing so much it turned frightening: it was laughing at *you*. But it was better than my old foster mother's mask, so blank, with just lines for mouth and eyes and a maggot eating through the cheek.

It was better than mine. The old dancers used to alternate masks, turning away from the audience only to leap back with a transformation and make them gasp, or switch frantically, faster and faster to the drums until those watching were powerless with dread. I had two masks like that. On my first, the lower lip hung down in *ninaq*, a sullen, unforgiving anger at those who had wronged me. One eye was squinted shut in suspicion, the other was round and mean, and through the eye socket lunged the snout of a fox.

My second mask was the face of an indifferent slave. The ivory eyeballs were rolled back, the mouth slack and drooling, the teeth pointed and little. There was no demon taking it over; it *already* was taken over completely. The hair was real, human and black, but it was dead, dull hair. The whole face was dead. *Dead*!

Flo cackled on about the birdman, just having fun, but I thought I saw her mask and that she was mocking me. She knew I had misled him. I shut my eyes to squeeze out the image of her wide mouth. That can't be true, I thought - that was crazy. Suddenly I couldn't stand it in camp and I grabbed up my pail and left. I didn't say, and nobody asked where I was going, for if you didn't volunteer it people usually left it alone.

CHAPTER 7

Not for a moment could I now behold
A smiling sea and be what I have been
The feeling of my loss will ne'er be old
WORDSWORTH

Then all unexpected, I came upon
the heedless dweller of the plain
ORULO (AKA. IGLULIK)

NORTH OF CAMP a tall ridge humped along like a gigantic worm, or the backbone of the earth. It was dry and rocky up there, an easy road to the coast. That's where I was headed, under the influence of the birdman's spell. I pulled off my red *kaspaq* and wadded it in the pail so I would not be so visible on the tundra, especially to the keen-eyed hunters. A winter of shuffling over packed snow had changed my muscles and it was hard going as I jumped over sloughs, stumbled through mud and teetered on wobbly hummocks that collapsed underfoot. My leaky rubber boots didn't help.

Across such tricky lowlands the mountain always looked closer than it really was. At last the land rose steeply, slick with grass and flowing with mossy streams. Green sprang up, and flowers: the tall stalks of cow parsnip and Eskimo celery, poison blue monkshood and purple fireweed. Beneath the tender herbs, white quartz and black shale hid as keen as *ulu* blades. Raven fledglings bobbed their fuzzy heads from outcroppings, crying hoarsely. I had a soft spot for *tulgaq* ever since one made friends with me. It had just grown its black feathers and missed its family. For many summers it would wait for me in the hills and answer gladly if I called to it. They could live nearly as long as humans, but something had happened to my bird companion and I hadn't seen it for a few years.

As the slope got steeper and rockier I had to clamber on all fours or a misstep would send me rolling a long way down. Now only lichens grew. By the time I reached the spine I was gasping for breath and my legs were aching, but it was the top of the world and worth the suffering. There, the cold upper winds dried the sweat of my face and drove into my lungs, invigorating my spirit. Tall black boulders were piled along the crest like guards, moaning in the wind. The old people said long-ago giant men had carried them up so high to prove something, and angutkoq disappeared into them forever. Now people just used the stones as landmarks from the sea. Far below stood the white tents in the green, and Polly's dazzling pink spot of *kaspaq.* The river was a strand of silver yarn, a winding doodle, and terns and gulls drifted under me like snowflakes. *God must feel like this,* I thought.

I kept going.

After an hour's hike along the ridge the blue sea came into view with its belt of tan dunes. The rotten shore-ice was floating a ways out. As it did in late spring, a high tide had driven it against the land until it broke off, then dark seawater gushed through the crack, forcing a wide lead between beach and ice. The water was glassy there, with *aahaaliks* paddling around — their cackles reached my ears. Bleached logs littered the sand like the bones of mighty, unknown creatures. They had floated north from the Yukon in summers past and backed up into the Iron with the tides and storms. The river's mouth was crazy with terns catching fish.

And there was the tiny green pup tent, and a thread of smoke climbing lazily up. To the right, in the lush green and glinting water of marsh I saw the flash of metal: another oil experiment. A rust-red dusting lay over the marsh, the reeds in flower. Birds skimmed, swooped and swam all through it, catching the eye. Cranes were bowing and leaping on their tall legs in their ancient slow-motion dance; maybe one of them would end up in our soup kettle. My heart skipped when I saw the moving spot of brown that was the birdman's coat. I wondered if he knew how much he looked like a bear at a distance, and the danger that put him in from a near-sighted hunter.

My hogback ran straight down to the camp, easy until the dense willow and alder thickets that reached above my head. That was the kind of cover used by napping bears, which made me nervous, but I was more nervous about what I would say to the birdman. You had to give a reason to whites for a visit, didn't you? Or you'd be a somewhat unwanted guest. Several times I stopped to turn back, but I was pulled down the hill by the spell. The closer my legs took me, the harder my blood pounded and I was giddy enough to faint.

But I couldn't find him. He wasn't in the marsh or in camp, so I tried the beach. As I came over a dune, a high-pitched whoop arose from the lead. With a seal-like whiffling, a dark head broke through the green-black near the edge of the broken-off shore ice. I squinted against the sun. It was the birdman! Somehow he had fallen in from the ice! Or he had jumped in. Had he marooned himself out there, the *kuangazuk*? It was deep out past the dropoff, he would drown! Then I saw that he was afloat and he could swim. Well, he wouldn't for long. He'd be dead in a few minutes, unable to kick his legs. He'd sink. It was too far out, maybe fifty feet, and I was the only one to help. I whirled to look around the beach, pointlessly. There was no branch long enough to rescue him. I could try to tie some together.

But there were his clothes, hanging calmly on the roots of a big drift-wood. This was...planned? I turned back. On closer look, he did not appear in distress. The biologist was gliding parallel to the ice as smooth and happy as a duck. There were no frantic paws like Maq that time when she hadn't listened and we'd left her behind on the beach to try to catch up with the boat. *Alapaa*, how cold, he was crazy! I had never seen anyone swim except in a movie, I could count on both hands men who had drowned, and he had plunged in like a loon after a fish.

The birdman had turned and was heading straight for shore. His arms churned and splashed the water like oars, as fast as in a Tarzan movie. Suddenly his feet found bottom and he stood up, streaming lead water...*naked*.

I backed up, nearly tripping, and ducked behind the log. When I peeked out he had reached the shore. His winter-grass color looked golden against the light sand. He was close enough for the black trim of his crotch to jump out. Now he was sprinting on bare feet, not awkward like a water bird, and fast. Too fast. Toward *me*. He would find me skulking behind his clothes rack, squatting as if relieving myself...but if I ran, he would see! I stood, crouched, then stood again.

I ended up turned toward the dunes leaning against the stump as if to rest during a forage trip, nothing unusual. But my mind was reeling and my heart was sprinting too, so fast I wondered if people my age had heart attacks. I had not seen a man unclothed in bright daylight. My first sight of a *woman* really undressed was at boarding school when they made us shower together. Itiak was modest. The men once pranced around wearing only parkas in the summer and the women bare-breasted, but the missionaries had shamed them. Families of twelve in one-room houses managed to never expose themselves; it could be done. But longhairs - there were rumors of festivals where thousands of them ran nude. Picturing that made me cringe.

All too soon I heard sand crunch behind me, and frenzied teeth-chattering. "Where are you, towel?" The biologist circled the stump, hunting. In my haste I had knocked his towel off. When he saw my boots he started and his head jerked up. He froze. I stopped breathing. We were like two hares trapped in a sno-go beam, and the only movement was water dribbling off the ends of his hair into the little ponds made by his collarbones.

What else could I do? The universe gives us opportunities, in the way that an animal will offer itself for our dinner. You take it when it comes. It was like he was saying, *Do you want to look? Okay, look.* A normal woman might have bypassed his body to gaze at the sea, anywhere else, but I was more like a fish stunned on the head with a rock. I didn't know what normal scientists did. He made no move to hide his privates, but just stared back at me.

I couldn't meet his eyes. Helplessly, I dropped mine downward. I don't know what I expected: maybe fur, the idea you got from the principal's arms. But the birdman was smooth and sleek. His wet body skin was that golden shade and had goosebumps, tensed up and shivering in the sea wind. He was put together well, in the layers of bone and muscle. His nipples were dark. A few black hairs were sprinkled on his breastbone, an afterthought from his creator. From the little cave of his bellybutton a faint line of black raced down the slope, dragging my eyes with it like a tether with reluctant dogs straight to between his legs. It took over everything. Only that place existed in the world and all else fell away, the blue sky, beach, water, even the rest of the man.

And my fear was gone. They...it...did not threaten but were drawn back like on a little boy taking a cold bath. So undangerous. I thought of eggs in a nest of black lichen that you could reach out and touch. It was so surprising. More than anything else about him - race or college degree - these delicate things made the world think he was better than me. I wondered if the bird-man thought he was better, because he owned them.

How long did I look? I didn't know. I hope it was only a moment before I broke my trance. But when I peeked up at his face, color had risen onto his cheekbones. His pupils were slammed shut and he was looking at me strange-ly, as if mystified by my scrutiny. But he hadn't *stopped* me! The excuse - I needed the excuse.

"I'm looking for things on the beach," I said, and held up my pail. I meant sea cucumbers washed up after storms.

"Oh..." He gestured to the sand behind me. "Uh...I'll just get my towel..." I hopped aside. As he stooped I saw his *nulluk*, round as the moon and its ghost twin. What was the matter with me, gawking like a little kid? Blushing furiously at last, I turned away. At least it hadn't been *me* caught with my pants off. My whole life *I* had always been the one in trouble, misunderstood, the one mortified, trespassed against, forced to do things, stolen from.

He came out from behind the stump tucking in his shirt. "So besides the old subsistence what brings you here?" he asked as he fixed his belt, but I couldn't think of what to say. Now that he was all dressed his eyes were warmer. Dampness made his hair curlier. He shook it back, putting his hands in his pockets to hunch. "Brr. I call that my lim-fat-tick. Ever swim?"

"*Ayii!*" I tried to laugh and turned to go. Or at least forced my feet that way, because I wanted to keep standing there stupidly, my naked eyes to his. I tried to walk with dignity up the slope, certain that he was watching. Only when I was hidden by the boulders on the bluff did I run. Far away I stopped to catch my breath and collect my thoughts but could only think of his body, how he let me see all of him like that. He didn't do it to challenge me, did he? I didn't think it was to scare me.

It was...an invitation. My insides prickled like a foot just getting sensation back after frostbite, before it hurts. A wetness between my legs startled me.

I STAYED UP ON the mountain. I lay in a hollow and let thoughts of the bird-man pull me strongly like a tide. This time I could allow my eyes to wander slowly over him like with an intricate sewing, one you lay aside and then take out again and again. His male parts had the mute and mysterious power of an amulet. He had given me permission to look; he was like an ally you find in the Otherworld, who gives you a gift. We had a pact, a secret bond.

The wind was cutting through my shirt and the sun was flattened on the northeast mountains by the time I got home. Flo was still up, listening to the radio tuned to religion. She cradled Kamik, asleep with his bottle of Kool-aid. She was maybe worried a little. But she made no remark as she offered me last year's dry fish and leftover bannock, which I wolfed down. We sat watching the twilight and the few birds still awake, drifting. I didn't know what she was thinking: counting pokes in her constant inventory, plotting ways to give Niviak the upper hand. And I couldn't ask, a penny for your thoughts. How *naluagmiusak* to offer to pay to intrude on someone's privacy. But then, angutkoq could force their way into souls or penetrate like water, sneakily. If I wanted to, I could find out. But I would not do that to Flo.

I looked over just as she woke from where she was dozing. With a soft "sleep good" she carried the baby into the tent. Flo, I thought, how can I even think bad thoughts of you? But why oh why didn't you come sooner? She'd taken me away but a part of me was still enslaved in that cabin, with night falling. The years had gone by and the feelings settled, but the birdman had stirred them by coming out of the water as unknowing and innocent as a bird. Time had drifted over it but that night was still there waiting, and that part of me was always waiting like the little fox in the trap as the man closes in, who must chew off her own leg to get free.

I wondered if I told him I'd be set free, in the way the Christians con-fessed to a stranger, only instead of my wrongs it would be how *I* was wronged. The birdman would listen. It wasn't the kind of thing to tell a man or a scientist, though. Even if I'd seen him naked. It would be like undressing my soul.

HOW DO I BEGIN ? It is dark winter. A little girl's mother is dead - she's got no father. She struggles against the wind as she pushes a sled filled with ice, which she has chopped from a pond with her thin arms. Her mukluks are old, the fur shedding. Her gloves are not meant for the Arctic. Her parka is old, resewn rabbit skins so thin the gales blow through but just warm enough if she moves fast. The girl is fed last, when the poor parts of game are all that's left and no fat. They don't let her drink all the water she needs. At the school lunch she devours whole tins of government butter, she gulps water.

At school she reads about Cinderella and she wonders how she got into the story. If the work is done she too must sit in the dark corner. She must sleep in the coldest place near the door, on the oldest reindeer fur. When she is really small she does not know she is miserable or care about the lice in her uncombed hair, she does not know being hit is unfair.

But as she gets older she knows. She thinks about old stories where orphans turn into heroes and wonders when she will get the secret powers, when the animals and spirits will begin to help her. Or was it only boys who were helped? Did girls just give up?

Once, she tries to hide in the schoolhouse all night, but the teacher sends her home. Once, she doesn't stop at the pond but keeps going across the lagoon ice to the black mainland, until, when she looks back at the village, the lights have merged and narrowed into the nearly closed eye of a beast. Once, she sees a blue light bobbing like a star and wonders if it is a spaceship, and if they'll take her aboard, and leave with her. Once, she is caught in a whiteout and is lost. But she finds her own way back.

As she enters her foster home, the mask stares at her from the floor where it is sewing. The mask scolds her in hisses for letting in the wind and snow. It warns her if she does something wrong, the geese in spring will fly past without stopping and winter will become winter, with no summer. "Sweep the floor!" yells the mask, strident now. "How come you leave it so dirty? I work so hard all my life and nobody helps me. Why do I got to sit on a dirty floor?"

The girl does not hear the bitterness from the mask, that it feels it also is a slave. Slowly she sweeps, wearing her dead-eyed ninaq mask. Why are the others not scared of this? As she grows older she notices they do become unea-sy. Her look is that of a person harboring evil thoughts. A person who never smiles is dangerous. Someday soon I will truly become dangerous, she thinks...

No, no, I could not tell the birdman what came next.

CHAPTER 8

If witches fly across the night
I sing to make them lose their way
and steal their skins so they cannot go home
THE ELDER EDDA (ANCIENT NORSE)

I feel humbled and afraid
My grandmother sent me out
seeking the wandering fox
ORPINGALIK (HUNTER'S INVOCATION)

THE MOUNTAINS were not only good for reveries. Alone, I could practice the secret arts without fear of discovery. And it was clear why the old angut-koq always climbed the high hills where the giant rocks stood, for up there the power of the universe came from every direction, and a deep drumming throbbed up from inside the earth through my feet. The gale drove into me, filling my lungs until the world spun, and one day my spirit broke loose and I was soaring above the ridge and over the plain with my arms spread and feet trailing out like a crane.

Little Betsy called out from far below and pointed up at me, but nobody heard her or looked up. If Flo saw, maybe she'd just yell for me to come down and get to my chores; she wouldn't know it was my spirit up there and that my body lay on the mountain, attached to my flying soul by an invisible line. Such vision I had now, of Itiak and another village down the coast, the looming black headlands of Siberia, a big ship at sea belching smoke. Many times I had come to the ridge, but never had I flown!

My *qilya* was getting stronger. And I knew it somehow was due to the birdman even if he had no idea, for body and spirit act together, and when one languishes or flourishes the other follows. Old Isaiah had told me.

Angutkoq used to fly to the moon and into the future. They saw what was coming to this land, the end of things as they were. They saw jet planes long before they were invented. No such understanding came when I flew over the Iron that day, except how wide the world was. But I heard *inua* voices chanting at me, their songs beating around my ears like great wings. Their language was foreign but they were telling me something important, maybe a warning, or maybe an encouragement. Of my return to the earth I remember just a nausea, a roaring and a thump as I came to, sprawled in the same high meadow with spittle on my chin.

Once, when Polly found me like that she wanted to take me to Nome to get treated for epilepsy. I refused to go, and Flo said it was fine, I was just sensitive and had learned to do that to avoid trouble when I was with the other family. I found the illness helped my lonely apprenticeship; it was like the magic bird skin they used to fly with. It was unpredictable and scary but it was *qilya*, and if it was a disease it was also a gift.

It always took time to recover. When I finally was able to sit up the action startled a red fox, who darted behind a boulder. It was a living flesh fox with shedding fur, not my *turnaq*. Thankfully no human had seen - a witness was the only thing I feared about communion with the Otherworld, back then. If the spirits were trying to warn me, I thought, wouldn't they speak in a language I knew? I stumbled along the ridge and down. Hardly realizing it, I had let my legs take me back to the birdcamp.

The biologist had sighted me, for as I approached he was standing expectantly, waving a wooden spoon. "Heey...Gretchen! Just in time for dinner!" My name from his lips nipped me like teeth of a dog. He was teasing - I didn't know he could tease. But his smile looked sincerely glad, too. I didn't dare answer for fear what might emerge - a spirit noise, a growl. So I just walked into camp and sank down on the log near the kitchen. The birdman perched at the other end, holding the spoon.

The wind had knit his hair into dark ropes. White triangles were boiling on the fire, another kettle held red sauce. It had been so long since I ate that saliva shot into my cheeks and some drooled. I wiped it off. When I glanced over at the birdman he was watching me curiously. Suddenly I felt dizzy and fell off the log as if bowled over. I pulled myself up and hung my head over my knees, nearly blacking out.

"What's wrong?" he cried. He sprang up and hurried to me. When he laid his hand on my back a shudder ran through me. He slid his arm around me, and was sturdy and warm and I could rest against him, sleep against him...In a swift violence I pushed his arm off me. His eyes got wide. "What..? Do you want to lie down?" he asked. I wrinkled my nose, but whites never knew what it meant. "Do you want to -"

"No!" I shouted. He scooted away from me, but he was still watching. My sunglasses had fallen off, and I felt exposed without the shades. I looked down. "I'm okay," I said, my human tongue finally working. I sent a so-what look straight into his eyes and saw the pity there under the amazement. "You look like I fell from Mars," I said.

He smiled uncertainly. "Huh. Sorry..." He fetched my glasses for me, brushed off the sand and handed them over. He was careful not to let our fingers touch - funny, since he'd already had his arm around me. It was embarrassing that I had struggled when he only meant to help me, but suddenly I had felt as confined and airless as blubber in a poke. I didn't take the sunglasses.

"I came here to give them back to you. I - I don't like them."

"No, they're yours forever!"

We looked at each other. He laid them on the driftwood by my leg. Fine, I'd take them back then; who cared if they made me look like a general. He started to say something, then killed the words before they got to his lips and just walked to the kettle and dished me out some food. I wondered if he still thought I was like a stray puppy always coming to his camp, *destitute.* "It's ravioli," he said, when I didn't start eating but just stared at it. There was never any meat.

"I know," I muttered. " I used to eat every day in a cafeteria."

"Really." The birdman considered me. "Bummer." I didn't know that word. I didn't know a lot of his words and he didn't even know I didn't know. It was like talking with elders when we had to guess a lot, and could not explain, while they talked circles around us in Inupiaq. Words like terns diving at your face. It was a weak position, making you want to lash out.

"You don't always have to offer food," I said. "Did you read in a book that's what we always do?"

94

He seemed half-expecting some malice. "No-o...my parents taught me to be nice to my guest. Aren't you my guest?"

"Do you think we just eat blubber?"

"What? No!" The food started to slide off his plate as it tilted.

"They want us to be backward...and *quaint*. Like those anthropologists. They're always so disappointed when they find out we know everything about the Outside." The birdman kept his eyes leveled on mine, but not exactly mad. I kept on; my fit had loosened my tongue like beer. "And they seem so sad we aren't walking around in furs. Waddling."

He grinned though I wasn't making a joke. "Just wait until you get tourists," he said. "And they'll feel even more ripped off. I mean, I know, I grew up in Ballard and had to wear huge hand-knit sweaters in tourist season." My lips twisted in a kind of smile. "Come on," he said, "I don't think anyone's backward and quaint here, all right? Unless it's me."

"*How?*"

He was still standing with his plate of food already cold. "Me? Well, the *anaq* counting for starters. Not only people *here* think it's odd."

I felt my lips relaxing into a better smile. It seemed to make him glad - his eyes warmed as quickly as embers in a gust and just as suddenly there were many things I wanted to ask him. "You are a scientist," I said, "so why don't your people respect you?" I was thinking of the principal mocking him.

"Ahah." The birdman's laugh was short. He looked at me and seemed to agree that we would do this, I'd find out about him. He dropped crosslegged near me, not too near, and putting his plate in the sand, took a deep breath like he would launch a boat. "It's the wrong kind of science. I don't make bombs, I don't make them money, I lose them money. They don't understand protecting the Earth, because they don't realize they live off of it. They're so...removed, not like you. Ecologists are the antichrist. Someday they'll put us in jail like draft dodgers."

He had complimented me, I guessed. It struck me that he'd enjoy it in a strange way to be jailed by his enemy. "So, you think you are very important," I said, "but no one else does."

He snorted. "Right. Look," he said quietly, "I'm on your side, okay? Even if my methods look weird."

"You don't know my side." Flying from the mountain, talking stones, my *turnaq*...he would not understand.

"Well, give me a chance to know then. You don't really hike all the way out here just to rag on me...do you."

He shot me a careful look. I thought I knew what he meant by *rag*. I didn't really want to fight but he made me feel so disarmed when he showed pity and I couldn't stop thinking of him naked, or of what happened to me when those images came. And he'd put his arm around me. "You didn't eat anything. You probably should," he said.

I didn't argue. We ate our cold noodles. He watched me while I finished the kettle and looked like he was forming a question he didn't want to ask. Finally he did. "Have you ever seen a grizzly out here? Brown bear?"

It caught me off guard. In my dimmest memory, Indian memory, I heard the warning to never look at a bear, to never even look at a skin or touch one. I was a girl, and its spirit would destroy me, or the hunting. And even Abe said if you boasted that you weren't afraid of them, one would surely come to prove you wrong. I said in a hushed voice, careful not to name the beast, "Sometimes they come for fish and berries, but not so early."

"But they're hungry this time of year."

I looked at the biologist. He was scared of them. I wondered if I should warn him that they listen carefully to your words from very far, farther than walrus, even from their sleeping dens. "How come you don't got a gun?" I asked. "Even though they like a spear to kill them. They don't like bullets."

"Who does." The birdman thought, chewing on his upper lip, deciding whether to tell me something. "I *can't* carry a gun. Or a spear for that matter. I'm a conscientious objector so I pledged that I would never bear arms in my life, not even to save it. It's in the man's files."

"What man?" I asked. Bear arms, funny.

"The FBI, the Armed Forces. The war?"

"What war?" Somehow I thought there was more than one war going on. "You don't...? in Vietnam."

"Oh." An Itiak boy had died there. "How come they want to kill communist people?" I had heard communists were in Satan's grip, and so doubted that reason, since supposedly *I* was too. What was communism anyway? Nobody knew; we just heard it was bad.

The birdman heaved a sigh but it wasn't from impatience. "Well, there's a lot of oil and tin and rubber in Indochina and they want to keep it under their control. So they can be rich. Get *richer*. Same reason as World Wars One and Two." It sounded like Alaska, except for the killing. The birdman smiled in kind of a grimace. "Politics. Don't get me started."

So that's what "politics" meant: an explanation of how whitemen ran the whole world. I was fascinated and knew at once he spoke the truth, I felt it, and couldn't keep from asking more. "What is Vietnam like?"

"Well...they live in little villages too."

"Do they hunt?"

"Ya. Some still use spears and bow-and-arrow."

I tried to imagine that. "They must be losing then, ah?" He shook his head slowly. "Why did Indians lose, then?" It felt funny to utter the word; it was like a dirty word but I could say it to the birdman. He looked at the sea and seemed to be gathering his answers in the waves like they were fish.

"Indians were brave but nine out of ten died of disease. The ones left were sick and outnumbered, and their food sources were gone. And the young guys wanted to fight, but the old ones were afraid their families would get hunted down. And they were right. You can't compare it to Nam, they have weapons from Russia and farms to supply food. I mean it's bad, but the Indians were totally screwed. The whites even used germ warfare. The modern equivalent is nuking Vietnam back to the Stone Age; then they'd lose." He suddenly stopped and looked embarrassed. "I...sorry."

What was he was apologizing for? I hadn't been listening that well, since during his lecture I could watch his face watching the ocean. It was like he saw a battlefield in the water, a war that was over with everyone floating there, and he looked dreamy and sad. "Why *is* there war?" I asked.

"You want to know my opinion? My theory?" I raised my eyebrows, but he still didn't know what that meant. "Do you want my -" he started again.

"*Yes.*"

"Is this a test?" He smirked. It was the right kind of question if you wanted to get to know him, because he thought about war all the time, with his answer as ready as a dog in the traces just waiting for my command. "Okay, I have more than one theory but my latest is it's a kind of herd think, like a football game or theater or a mob - only bigger - and everyone is in an altered state. Like a spell, or hypnotized."

"Trance?"

"Like a trance, yeah, a long one, and a whole country can fall into it just like that." He snapped his fingers. "Overnight, from peace to war."

"But...*why*?"

His eyes drifted back to the waves. "Well, it evolved for *some* reason, maybe to reduce population or give a society the...I don't know... *gumption* to rob other people wholesale. I've seen even crows and seagulls go at it, warring at garbage dumps. There's a biologist studying apes who claims they have no war, but maybe she just hasn't seen it yet. She's only been watching for ten years. What do *you* think?"

I started, for his eyes had veered and were looking straight into mine, so his pupils were black bullets targeting me. "I don't know," I said automatically, as I always did to teachers, and looked down.

"Sure you do. You know your opinion anyway. Come on, I told you my crazy ideas; let me hear yours."

I thought war was an *inua* thing, a possession, maybe the same thing he thought. Instead I said, "Why did the whites kill all the Indian women?"

"Not *all.* There are still Indian women." He had a funny, defensive look

"You tried to."

"Not *me.* But yes, they tried to get rid of Indians, like they wiped out the big predators. They were clearing the land of competition so they could farm. And that's why people here weren't cleared off; the whites didn't want the land. *Yet.*"

I sneaked a look to see if he thought that was necessary, okay to clear the land this way, but his expression had darkened though he spoke calmly. I saw a revulsion pass through him. "Whites are always in an evil spell," I said. "They are always hypnotized."

"No quarrel there." The birdman felt his beard in an unconscious way. "They seem to operate out of fear, you know, circle the wagons! They seem all fat and secure now, but they came out of deprivation. Mistrust of the Earth. And after they got power they always had to be vigilant, make sure the slaves weren't revolting. But...this isn't to defend their culture, okay? But thousands of white people ran away to live with Indian tribes they liked it so much better. Even women and children that were taken as slaves refused to go back when they had a chance."

I was flabbergasted. "Did Eskimos ever fight the whites?"

"Don't you know?"

"Would I ask if I know?" I snapped. "The old people don't say much," I said more gently. "I read a book, but maybe they always lie."

"Good point."

I smiled and he smiled and we looked at each other in a startled way, for there we were, turned to each other knee to knee like the oldest of girl-friends. How long had we been talking? The tide had crept in. I never talked to anyone like this. In the silence the birdman's eyes changed; they were full of all the complexity again, and latched onto mine in a kind of appeal that had nothing to do with words and he probably didn't know he was doing it. His spell. I let him do it for way too long, and I took all his feelings in, thrilling myself - really, it was like seeing him naked. But it scared me as much as speeding on a sno-go near a cliff.

I stood up, nearly falling - my *nulluk* had gone to sleep. "I...I'm going."

"Back -" he cleared his throat - "back to camp?" As I left I heard him mutter behind me, "See you later." At a distance when I looked back he was studying the marsh with binoculars. His body looked perplexed, even let down. I felt fine and strange with a sharp joy, in a way like I was flying again, but high over an alien land.

And I had left my pail there, with my *kaspaq* inside.

LATER WHEN OTHERS were asleep in the tents I was still wide awake. I had flown, the *inua* spoke to me and the birdman let me into his world. He put his arm around me. I felt as if great things were coming and my body couldn't lie still. To sleep seemed like a waste of life. I went to the dead fire and awakened it to keep me company.

What was he doing now? Did he sneak into the marsh so late and try to spy on the settled geese? I thought of him stirring the kettle, the wind blowing his hair. The first naluagmiu I could remember was a traveling doctor, a frightening thing with his orange hair and paper-white face and the blood-red tip of his long snout dripping, sniffing, looming over me. The ruddy knobbed hand reaching toward my mouth was a crab, icy on my flesh. He may as well have been from a UFO and though he spoke kindly I didn't understand and wailed and screamed as he stuck needles in me.

My birdman was a different creature entirely. I thought of him swimming, at first just his dark head cutting the water, loon-like. He swam like the loon up from the deep, from the Land of the Dead, carrying messages...

Then something was happening, I was taken over by an unknown spirit that made me float toward the birdman instead of fleeing.

He rises from the lead streaming water, shivering before me, his eyes holding mine as if we are the only two people in the world. We are innocent, the first woman and man. He is unaware of his power to thrill me. He lets me see him as he comes from the sea, strong and frail at the same time, his body that will not hurt me. He smiles shyly and holds out his arms, he beckons, and with no hesitation I enter the embrace and we are floating. We are lying in a meadow in summer, the sun warms us, and of course there are no mosquitoes. He lets me caress him, the matching dark hair on his chin, under his arms, then between his thighs. He closes his eyes and sighs and it is a good sound, not the rasp of a violator but sweet. He breathes beneath me, he sighs, giving, I am giving way also...

When I opened up and fell apart in currents of black I had no idea what it was. Once I had experienced some versions of sex but the memories were only fear and rage, remnants of pain. Was *this* why Polly liked it so? She always insisted it was really something.

But this was not with a man, it was a phantom. When Calvin said angutkoq "did it" with spirits this is not what he meant! I wondered if the birdman ever thought about me, or if he thought of me while he did it to himself

- though I wasn't sure how a man "did it", or if scientists did it at all. Did he imagine *my* body, making me do whatever he desired? My face seared and grew cold, then heated again. Maybe it would be fair.

Then I had a worse thought: what if he fell asleep easily, to visions of flying geese? Then I would be truly alone in this craziness.

ENTRY. "DON'T CROSS river yet," scolds the Tao, "too soon, too fast. Fox soaks its tail, shame, regrets, you don't understand." Er...not really!

She had hypoglycemia, maybe. Don't they feed her, or is it a self-imposed fasting? When her glasses fell off I got a better look. My memory had been of fine and soft black eyes, often downcast even when playing her defiant game, like she can't decide between meek maiden or warrior. She is yin versus yang, polarized like the Arctic itself: look at this balmy summer and what antipathy lies in store for us. (Or maybe she's just manic depressive). Her hands are delicate, and her features, which she curtains off with hair. And she's not very substantial but when I foolishly hugged her I felt she <u>does</u> have breasts and hips, hidden under that odd 1920's coat-dress or the voluminous man's shirt. Then she reared in a panic and I got to look straight into her, with a shock. She's really beautiful, beauty leaping out in a lynx-like way. And I realized she is scared!

Maybe she should be, these solitary treks in country that daunts rugged explorers with big guns. It's doubtful other women traipse alone in these hills. Itiak males go armed, but her only weapons are her talisman pail and those eyes. But she seems at home in the wilds, as much as her namesake. She springs out of the hills like Artemis with no human parent (a changeling: no way is Flo her blood mother). I see more wildlife after she has been here; she draws them like a magnet, some kind of force field. She'd be a good research partner.

She must secretly like me or she wouldn't keep visiting. We seem to have some kind of contract that she finds my camps and we...do what? Try to figure each other out. It's a funny rapport. It's like my favorite scene from "The Little Prince", which I used to make Maman read over and over in French. Every day he scoots a tiny bit closer toward the Fox outside its den. The Fox understands it is being tamed but agrees to carry out this role. Good analogy, but am I the Fox or the alien?

Am I getting hung up on her? Ulp. Better not.

CHAPTER 9

*She lov'd me for the dangers I had passed
and I lov'd her that she did pity them;
this only is the witchcraft I have used.*
SHAKESPEARE

WILLY BOATED DOWN to fetch the biologist for dinner. I was anxious about my pail giving me away, and when the two men strode into camp without it relief made me giddy. I organized plates and wiped out bits of lichen from cups and tried hard not to stare. The birdman had fixed himself up, combing his hair and trimming his beard neat. It reminded me of the black calfskin we used to beautify mukluks. Other regions of his body swam into my thoughts and I had to push them under and hold them there.

Willy complained about how he had to wait while "this *tingmiaq*" preened himself, but no, it was because Willy wanted to watch him count poops, said the birdman. He and Willy shared grins; that they were already friends was clear. But his glances skimmed off mine like sandpipers down the shore.

The old people stood to meet him in the awkward way they'd been taught for a naluagmiu visitor. Whites were not popular in our home though we took in boarders; they made Abe and Flo ill at ease. Elders were used to deference, but whites - even young ones - were always there to tell them what to do, taking charge. The old people were more their true selves with the biologist, though, since he wasn't there to lord it over us. He was Willy's friend - and Polly's suitor even if he didn't know it. And he had the deference. When he returned their murmured formalities with a half bow like some kind of knight from a different age, their smiles were delighted and amused, not fake.

At once Flo began pestering him about his eating habits, how he couldn't possibly eat her Eskimo food. She showed him the macaroni she was boiling just for him and held up the box of dry cheese, something Abe hated and said was "stink". He looked alarmed, his eyes jumping from the macaroni to the real food: the new blackmeat swimming in fresh golden oil, and the simmering stew pot.

"That's a goose," said Flo, noticing his gaze. "But I always cook it the way whitemen don't like though." She meant whole, with the feet and head. When he saw the lone bowl with a fork set up on the card table, which Flo had brought to camp just for this event, he colored faintly. "So I made the noodles for you," Flo went on, squinting at the label, "Kraft."

The birdman thanked her though he looked unhappy. He flattered her with a *saglu* about rumors that she was the best cook in Itiak so she shrieked in denial. Then he did another endearing thing: he sat with us and gobbled up even the blubber (although he examined the webbed feet, probably identifying it). When Flo pressed him he took seconds and thirds, as was proper. He asked no stupid questions, let us eat in our normal silence, and paid no mind to the way the grandkids gawked at him. There was only one bad moment, when Flo said grace. I saw him looking sneaky. What did he worship, a goose? His sharp black eyebrows sometimes looked like the Devil's, and that beard. Fortunately Flo didn't see this, with her eyes shut.

By the end of the meal it was clear he'd won her over completely. But Abe was another matter. At first he was a gracious host, offering choice pieces to his guest on the end of his knife, "*Uvva*". Yet when the meal was over he told the story of the Man-Who-Unknowingly-Married-a-Fox, laughing mightily when the husband notices the musky smell in his house. "*Eee*, the red fox, she asked for darkness. In the dark she could trick the human beings and steal from them. But the Lord said, 'Let there be light.'"

I hunched down, hiding behind my drawn up knees, feeling that all eyes had turned on me. *Please don't tell the story of the dog-father*, I prayed. How whitemen were born from a girl who refused to get married, so her dad made her marry a dog. And the other puppies that loved to kill Eskimos became *itkiliq*, and they were set adrift in little boats.

In the silence Abe remarked as if to no one in particular, "Getting colder. We need more firewood, some of those big logs come upriver." The birdman jumped up, probably happy for an excuse to get away from more stories. Willy joined him with less eagerness. We watched the two shuck their coats to hoist and carry heavy logs up the bank, in the show Abe had arranged for us. The birdman seemed used to hard work. When they were finished he gulped water from the bucket, shook the hair out of his eyes and sat close by me on my log chair, so close I could smell the fresh sweat. I looked at the hills, the fire, Polly's deepening dimple as she sat across from him. The sign of God's blessing, Flo called it - His finger poked her cute cheek when she was born.

"You have an injury, ah?" Polly asked him.

"No." The birdman covered his hand with the other. "I just hit the permafrost with my core-sampler. I'm accident-prone..."

"How long ago?" asked Polly, her dimple departing. She had donned her stern doctor's mask. The birdman shrugged.

"I lose track of days...the sun...It's healing fine.

"You fix that, Niviak," said Flo. "Kayuqtuq, fetch her first aid kit."

"Don't get an infection just because you're too proud," said Polly.

"There's not much bacteria in the environment." There was an equally smug note in his voice, competing with the health aide's.

"People die of blood poisoning here all the time," said Polly, earning a warning look from her mom. To talk of death could bring it on.

"Nobody you treated, I hope." The birdman looked fake-worried, and Polly tittered. Everyone was silent while I fetched the medical kit and sat beside him again.

Polly bent over his hand like a fortune teller. "Hmm...inflammation." She flattened it on the log. From where I sat, the gash looked pretty deep. "Yep, it's septic!" She pushed up his sleeve to search for a red line. "No bandage and you're out there handling bird excrement."

"Actually I never touch the stuff." He grinned, impressed at Polly's professional manner. I usually loved the way she could handle the vocabulary, but not today.

"I'm going to use my scalpel to clean it out!" she said. He tried to snatch his hand back, but she hung on.

"Don't worry, Niviak's real good cutting," said Flo.

"Unless it's seal," added Willy.

The birdman cast me a nervous look but I couldn't help him. Though Polly had run out of novocaine she went ahead and washed his hand and laid it out on a log like she did with a slippery salmon she planned to filet. He tensed as she poised the scalpel. When she sliced in with the point, swift and sure, his entire body flinched as blood spurted. It was the same red as a seal's or an Eskimo's. Or Indian's. Flo had to turn away, for though she butchered animals this was different - the seals were dead. Calmly Polly sopped the blood. When she probed deeper her patient squirmed and tried to cover a noise of suffering by clearing his throat. He had turned pale.

"Hey, Naluagmiu, Leaf!" said Abe. He was relaxed against a log to watch and puff a cigarette. "*Sigaaqpak*? You want a smoke?" The birdman didn't answer, concentrating, I guessed, on not making a show for his audience. But when Polly went in for the final thrust he grunted and said *fuck*, and the children giggled. "No need to use bad language," said Abe, who was watching in the calculating way he used when carving, when he was first deciding what animal a piece of ivory would become.

Polly patted the birdman's shoulder and tied his hand up like a mummy's. She tilted her head to admire her craft. "I'll make a house call before I go back to town. Do you got a fever?" She had softened her voice, and stroked back his hair to feel his brow, then hastily removed her hand. "I should take your temperature." The two of them looked at each other in a meaningful way. His color had begun to return.

"Oral, I hope," he murmured, and Polly blushed. The rest of us did not get it.

It was then, in the pause that fell after a drama, that Abe started in on the naluagmiu. "*Eee,* Eskimo men, they never show pain." That was the lead-in. Now he was going to belittle him for that moment of weakness. Even if there had been no injury he would have found a way, I saw it now. "Yup, Eskimo *men*," he repeated. The birdman's expression was perfectly quiet, like he was used to being plagued by old men and knew he had to just listen and not defend. As Abe told about the hunter who crawled home with two broken legs he listened to the manly story with a calm interest. "In the whole world they are the strongest against pain," said Abe. "And Eskimo women too, by golly."

"That doesn't mean they don't feel it," said Polly. She and Flo smiled an apology at the birdman.

"Where are your people from?" asked Abe. His face was expressionless, which for him was mean. As an elder he had the right to questions. It was normal to find out the lineage of a Native person, since people wanted to see how they were related, and everyone knew whites required interrogation in social visits though we didn't like to do it, but Abe was being shockingly rude in a polite way to the birdman. *Why are you such a wimp?* he was asking.

But the birdman didn't understand, or pretended not to. "My dad was born in Norway," he said, "up in the Arctic too. He's a fisherman."

"Is it? What kinda fish?"

"Salmon. He's got a troller." At our blank looks he mimed two long poles sticking out, a boat rocking.

"Hmm..." muttered Abe.

"I bet she has a good mother," Flo said pointedly to Abe. "She raised a good boy."

Abe tilted back his head. "What people is your mother from?"

"She's French-Canadian. I have a picture of them." The birdman took a photo from his coat pocket like he'd planned on showing us all along. We passed it around. "Her father's Cree...and Slave," he said. And he glanced at me quickly. When we looked at him, startled, not understanding, he took a breath and explained. "Indian."

My jaw dropped. No wonder he liked Indians. And what was that look about? I felt like the impact of little bird pellets the looks everyone else shot at me then. Abe muttered the soft note of incredulity. He hawked and leaned to spit in the coals. The birdman took the photo back from Polly and looked down at his family lying flat and small before storing it in his pocket and composing his unhappy expression.

"That's a nice mom and dad," said Flo after a long silence, "They had only you?" It seemed prying, it wasn't a safe question.

"They had another kid," he said in a low voice, and Flo nodded slightly with the edges of her eyes getting sad. Abe began coughing and hacking in earnest then. His old TB was catching up to him.

"They say that people should quit smoking so much," chided Polly but Abe just tapped out another cigarette. Flo also condemned the habit - it wasn't Christian, and too expensive - but he didn't stop.

"They say that, ah?" He settled himself down. He wasn't done yet, though the Indian part had thrown him off. It struck me he was just being a father, checking out the interests of his daughter Polly. The wood-carrying was to test the naluagmiu's cooperation and strength. Now Abe was trying his background; next would come his humility. The birdman was lucky he wasn't being courted by a girl from one of those families where he'd serve the in-laws for a whole year, doing woman's work even. I imagined him sweeping the floor at our place. *Fetch water,* I would command, and he would have to go, if he wanted Polly. I would let him dump the honeybucket and it would serve him right.

Abe was talking again. "I forgot where all those whitemen come from. Before they go to Lower 48."

"Europe," said the birdman after a pause; he seemed to be trying to figure out whether it was okay to teach the old man, though he sure hadn't held back when it was *me* asking him questions.

"Hmm. Northway?"

"Uh...not too many from there. They're from a lot of different countries...like tribes."

"*Vaaa.* Heh heh," Abe laughed softly. "Lotta variety in people. Like them birds you go after." The birdman smiled and shook his hair off his face, relaxing. "You find your special bird? That's a *ligliq,*" said Abe. "Maybe we ate it for dinner." A second later the old man cracked a grin. "*Sagluraata.* I jokes. But I want to know something a scientist can tell me. How do they decide a bird is in trouble?"

Again the birdman hesitated in a tact rare in a whiteman. And now he looked uneasy. "Well, when the...gene pool...uh...when there's fewer than fifty left. A species can't reproduce healthily under that number. There's problems with the um...the babies. Chicks."

"Hmm...We see a lot of geese, way more than old days, but there are so many they eat up all the grass and there is just mud. I don't know what you people call them."

"Um, right, you might be talking about the Canada and snow geese? There *has* been a increase because they forage on farmland down south. The Arctic's carrying capacity...um...up here can't support that many and they're degrading...uh...there *are* too many. It's a problem."

"But I guess this is not your *ligliq*."

"No, Tallin's is truly endangered. It's not a farm feeder."

Abe laughed dryly. "Me too, I am not. I don't like that farm meat. Heh heh. Hmm...And if they decide a bird is less than fifty, what then?"

The birdman fingered the black tuft under his lower lip. "Well...they might try to get some of their eggs to make sure the babies survive, and try to breed adults in captivity. And they might make a refuge where the birds nest or stop over."

"*Vaa*, what will happen to us?" Abe wondered. "Eskimo people. Maybe there will be all kinds of Fish and Game, Fish and Wildlife out here bothering us more when we hunt. I take a shot in the fall, legal time, and there's an agent behind me making me nervous, spoiling my aim because of some research someone did. My wife's cooking dinner, agent's sniffing in the kettle. Turn around, whiteman's shaking his finger. Scientists make it real hard to raise a family."

Abe's victim kept listening, his eyes fixed on his own bandaged hand. It was the correct manner; maybe he had learned it from his Indian grandfather. The old man went on in the high-pitched monotonous tone he used for church testimonials, when he listed the bad behavior of youth. "An animal does not always give itself for our table. And when he says 'take me' you want to take him, because if you don't, maybe he never comes back. But we know when to stop. We have our special times for taking game that our fathers taught us. Why don't we Eskimos tell those whites what they can hunt, what they can eat? Because we leave others alone and live our own life. But we know it is whites who make the geese die off, like they made the caribou angry and leave. Before your people put tags on their ears, there were many caribou."

Abe paused, but the birdman knew better than to speak. "Maybe their science is to blame," Abe ranted on. "From the boat I see a biologist walking right up to their nests. They leave a scent trail, the fox can find her way there. And the scientists disturb the birds. It is a disrespect to always count. Nobody can raise a family easy with someone walking through the house and counting, bugging all the time. The fox is better. After the fox kills, she goes away; it is their agreement. She does not *count*."

Somberly the birdman met Abe's gaze for a long moment before looking away. "Will that happen?" the old man asked. He had reached his point, and it was a good one.

The birdman seemed to have lost the point though. He searched for it. "A new crackdown on geese hunting? More surveillance?" Abe raised his eyebrows, yes. "I don't know," said the birdman slowly. A good answer, but like he was thinking of the question for the first time. "I hope not. But I know it's not hunting up here that's depleted Tallin's goose. The problem is down south."

"That makes no difference in regulations for Eskimo people," said Willy.

"I guess not," said the birdman softly.

"Well, a man must do what she must do," said Flo.

"And biologists, they make mistakes too," continued Abe, ignoring his wife's hint of hospitality. "They say an animal's getting too few, or she will next year. But who is out here all the time? Eskimo hunters. We know the geese better but maybe scientists always think they're right. Do they think they are always right?" He directed this at the birdman.

"Well...no-o..." But I thought, yes, he does. I himself, anyway.

"You may think about that, young man, what I say tonight. And you may think about our dinner, what you shared with us, next time you write your report."

"Yessir. I will." The birdman was looking much better now, instead of faint, like he enjoyed being chastised in public. The rest of us were listening to the scolding a little stunned. Regardless of Abe's fame for long painful lectures, he never harangued *whites*. He badmouthed them in private. It had to be because this one was in a possible boyfriend position, or showed more promise. And he just let Abe have his say. Sir! Whoever had called the old man that? Abe nodded, leaned forward to spit in the fire, and settled back. It looked like the birdman had won him over too, before he had even gotten to the long hair part.

"Speaking of geese, you want to check around here?" Willy asked, careful not to look at his father. The birdman agreed quickly. Willy grabbed up his rifle, and they left, followed by the kids. I watched them grow small in the distance and stop, the biologist crouching to look in the grass.

"You were so hard on him!" said Flo to Abe. She wouldn't contradict or scold him before a guest or another man besides Willy. Abe just chuckled. "Pataq likes him," said Flo. "And he's a good Christian boy."

"Doubt it."

For some reason everyone glanced at me as one. I said, "What?" but no one answered. Were they thinking of that Indian thing? That had caught me utterly by surprise, like one of those war parties some people saw riding over the tundra, complete with eagle feathers. But now I understood why the birdman didn't look exactly white and why his mother's dark eyes were familiar.

The two old people began talking in Inupiaq in low voices, heads pulled close, so I couldn't follow much. They could speak fast down in their throats like water in a brook, and use sentence-long words to throw the younger generation off: useful for them, but in the end, bad, if they wanted to have a real discussion with us. Later Willy reported signs of large geese passing through that were not Canada. The findings had made the birdman cheerful. He explained about the need for "positive eye-dee" to get a grant so he could return next spring. He got the gleam in his eyes, which lured Polly in. I knew *she* wanted to be the one, not a goose, to spark it.

We played Scrabble then, while the kids played Eskimo and Indian around the tents, shooting each other dead and convulsing. Flo beat the pants off everyone, and the scientist, stifling a yawn, came in last. To celebrate her victory Flo told a UFO story - her sister had seen one near the Cape, hovering above the lava plateau. The birdman listened politely, but surely was no anthropologist or he would have interviewed her for more. I was embarrassed when she asked him about Martians invading; she had seen a movie and thought it was real. He didn't humiliate her though, he just said he didn't know about it.

Suddenly Flo gasped and clambered to her hands and knees. "A worm!" she cried, "green worm! Going in the tent! *Iii! Iqsii!*" We rushed over there, trying to find it. Abe beat around the entrance with his coat until Flo made him go inside. Frantically we searched, turning over the boxes and reindeer beds, then Flo saw the birdman outside with a caterpillar on his palm, rearing its head. "Kill it!" screamed Flo. "You kill it!" Abe seized the worm and hurled it to the ground, stamping it flat. I thought I saw the little caterpillar of a smile on the biologist, to himself. Flo held her chest, breathing in relief. She explained that it could grow and destroy a village.

"Ah," said the birdman, "Like envy." We looked at him. It was nothing to joke about, but his face was serious.

WHEN THE SUN was at its lowest the old people retired to their tent with the kids. The naluagmiu was talking with Willy, his face turned so I could look at him. At last I took off my sunglasses. Their low man voices fell away from my ears. I just kept watching that strange profile lit up by firelight. I wanted to see the photo again and try to find the parents in him, the half-breed mom. He was a mother's boy, maybe, getting along with women. But afraid of old men. The father...fisherman, foreigner, the origin of that *Ya?* He came into my mind as if standing real before me, and beside him is a little boy. He is as cold and removed as the moon, his eyes are pale blue. He shrugs the child off. I see him riding on a boat getting smaller and smaller. He does not look back at the child on the shore. And above him shoots a crooked black arrow of geese. Then the picture was gone.

I had seen straight into the soul of the birdman, to his spiritual bones.

The others were oblivious of my vision and chatted on - hunter, health aide, biologist. They seemed to sure of themselves and their paths. I doubted if they looked over at me they would see an angutkoq. Polly wouldn't. A scientist wouldn't. I'd seen that tiny smile when we struggled to find the worm, that studiously polite look when Flo described the flying saucer, how his eye-brow had humped in amusement as clear as a seal on ice when Abe told him the animals hated to be counted. I didn't blame the birdman for thinking he was right. At least that night I didn't, since he had been so kind to the old people and I'd found out about the Indian in him.

Suddenly he cast me a look. "Doesn't your sister ever say anything?" he asked Willy.

"I'm not a sister," I said. My voice sounded rusty; I hadn't spoken the whole visit.

"She's family," said Willy. "She was taken in, in the Eskimo way." Seeing my expression, he changed the topic fast. "Jeez, I sure wish we had whiskey so we can party." Willy never drank but he sometimes talked about it. "Does *your* father drink?" he asked the naluagmiu. It was a funny question, one you don't ask. Polly looked troubled but not by Willy's rudeness, and not because Abe drank - sooner would ravens turn white - it was something else...

"My dad *drink*? Like a fish!" The birdman sneered. I imagined a salmon tipping a bottle. We looked at him. "It's a Norwegian thing," he said shrug-ging, "They can't handle it. He's like...I found a log washed up here that a beaver chewed on? Only it chewed both ends so it's really short and useless for anything, and I was thinking that beaver was driven insane by its work ethic, you know? Well, my old man's like that, he can't stop working except to drink. The great war did him in too. He gets drunk and starts thinking of all the ways the militaryindustrial complex is screwing him." The birdman ad-ded darkly, "runs in the jeans," and dropped his eyes, glum.

We looked away, silent in our surprise that whites got in trouble with al-cohol - they seemed barely affected. "So uh...so I don't drink much, myself, but I got the alternative if anyone wants it," he said, and at our blank faces explained, "pot?" and shifted his eyes like a criminal in a movie. Willy agreed at once but I wrinkled my nose when the biologist cast me an inviting look. Yet I was curious, for marijuana was another link to Satan.

"No way, not here!" hissed Polly, "Go somewhere else if you do that -" She glared at her little brother - "and don't come back until it's out of your system. That's four hours."

"It scares the old people," said Willy.

"Right on. It scares my old man too, and he's a real live member of the party." The birdman sat back. It was clear to him Polly was the boss.

"What party?" Willy asked with interest.

"Communist." The birdman looked furtive again, whispering the word. It shocked me; he hadn't let on when we talked about Vietnam. "But outside of politics my dad's uptight. My hair is worse than a fucking fascist state." Ever since the old people had gone to bed he had dropped the "sir", the play knight. He was letting his hair down, or was trying his other selves out on us. I didn't know a whiteman could have so many. He said, "Excuse me, but where should I take a leak? I don't want to sully the wrong place."

When we women blushed and didn't answer - since when did a man have to ask *that*? - Willy pointed out the bushes with the trench I had dug. When it got too full we'd probably move upriver a ways.

POLLY ASKED about his hand when he returned. He held it up bent over like a paw. "Poor doggie," she laughed and patted the back of his neck, lingering on his hair. As if I didn't exist they smiled at each other, her dimple deepening. Willy didn't want to watch more of this either and said he was going to bed. The birdman could sleep by the fire, he hinted. I knew why: the old people wouldn't like a naluagmiu in the tent with two girls.

After Willy had thrown him a blanket and was gone, the birdman fell silent and reserved. Soon Polly raised her eyebrows at me in what I took as a "come-along" look, and stood. She and the birdman wished each other good night, and when she turned, as quick as a brown wing in the rushes came his glance. At me. It surely held some kind of message. I felt his eyes on my back as I left right behind Polly. It confused me, what did that look mean, what had *Polly's* look meant? Was I supposed to stay with him or go in with her? And I wondered why he hadn't brought my pail back. Was he in agreement that my visits must be kept secret, or did he want me to go back to get it, maybe so I could catch him swimming again?

Later I stole out of the tent but he hadn't waited; he was sprawled on his back, asleep. My muscles eased from a great tension, tired out from his long visit with everyone watching. The sky was a soft gray, windless and banded in fiery orange and scarlet on the edge where the sun had just dipped under. It would travel a short ways just out of sight and then pop up again, seal-like. Only a few birds twittered in the bushes near the river. Maq watched me from where she was tied to the fishrack as I knelt down by the birdman.

With the swaddled hand cradled on his stomach, his other was thrown back in the manner of a child. The army blanket half-covered him, his one leg sticking out with a red wool sock neatly darned, and his head bent to the side. He looked like a storm had tossed him there, the wrathful storm of Abe. I wondered if Abe was right, that he might cause trouble because of his research. The evening was hard on him too. He barely breathed, his long lashes sealing out the world. The tall cheekbones were the Indian part, maybe. His nostrils were larger than Willy's and shaped differently, like commas, and had tiny thickets of black hairs. No *kakik*.

Hardly breathing myself, like a starving person waiting over a hole in the ice for a tomcod, I gazed some more. *My* birdman, I thought. The little peninsula of black grew on his chin like lichen on a rock. No wonder Polly had wanted to pet him - his hair made gleaming ringlets when it wasn't beaten by strong winds. One was like the tendril of a plant creeping over his face. In the ruddy light of coals and sunset at least four shades of brown came out...more even than a *kapik* pelt. I marveled at that, how nature had made him like all the animals, and as unaware of his beauty.

Yet he was a man. Did he ever wonder why he was born a man and not a woman or a dog, a bird or a little bug? Did he feel lucky?

Under my hesitant touch to his moustache he did not stir. His breath trailed out, heating my finger. The skin of his neck was fragrant, the hollow of his cheek was warm, and the hair was soft. Stealthily I reached into the pocket of his coat; there was no paper or pencil to record our behavior at camp. I did find the whispery down of owl and the tiniest flight feather from a lark. The tooth of a fox, the perfect skull of a baby lemming the size of my thumbnail, a ringed beach pebble...he needed a little bag for these things to hang around his neck like people used to do.

I took out the photo and studied the captured spirits of his parents until he made a noise and his bandaged hand twitched. The scalpel cutting him in his sleep. I shoved the photo back, willing him to not wake and see me flinching and sniffing over him like a sneaky fox at someone else's kill. But he didn't stir again. Nothing moved in the world except clouds, the dark current of the river and the faint rise and fall of the birdman's chest.

Later the crunch of gravel made me start; it was Polly standing behind me. After a long moment she smiled. My face was hot; it was too late to hide my interest now. I lifted a water cup, pretending I had only come out for a drink.

"Fatigue," whispered Polly, eyes on the man. "I bet he never sleeps at his camp...like *aahaalik*." She stooped to draw the blanket over him before walking to the bushes to relieve herself. Niviak, always the kind healer.

I narrowed my eyes after her.

CHAPTER 10

Louhi, Hostess of the Northland
envy-laden, spake these measures
"Know I other means of trouble:
I will drive the Bear before me
from his caverns to the meadows"
THE KALEVALA

Then terror seized the heedless dweller of the plain
ORULO

POLLY WENT for her "house call". She was dropped off by Willy as he boated down the coast to visit a family, and he'd pick her up by evening. She never asked me to escort her though she'd be alone with the birdman for hours, and I couldn't invite myself with the prospect of my tattle-tale bucket sitting in his camp. And what if he had washed my *kaspaq* and hung it out to dry?

I saw Polly checking her medical kit beforehand. While she washed her hair at the river I peeked in and found a little box with a picture of a couple embracing beneath a sunset. The box was nearly empty of tiny squishy packages. I tore one open, puzzling at the wet balloon. Slowly it dawned on me what it was for. Polly found me holding it, frowning. She burst out laughing, clapping her hand over her mouth, then grabbed it from me, overexcited. "Kayuqtuq, you! You wasted it!"

"You can get more at the clinic," I said, "There's thousands and thousands there. Unless you used them all." Polly howled, clutching her stomach. I didn't mention that I saw her check her supply of birth control before going to the camp of the naluagmin. She started on her mascara and wouldn't be ready to leave for at least an hour.

Flo had mentioned her desire for eggs. With that excuse, I took binoculars and a string bag and hiked to the ridge. I hastened along it to get to the coast. From a rock outcropping that looked down over the birdcamp, I swept the scene with the high-power binoculars. The sea was calm and as blue as old trade beads, the waves sparkling. The birdman was puttering by a new rectangle. I watched him pour oil into its compartments with great concentration. Sensing that he was being watched, quick like an animal he looked up to scan the hills. And straight into the lenses. My heart jolted. For a long minute he stared before turning back to his project.

Now the boat was crawling around the bend of the river. I saw Polly wading ashore, the birdman's shy welcome, Willy leaving for the mouth, then a flash of white as Polly wrapped new gauze around the birdman's hand. They sat on the log and talked though I couldn't know what the topic was - science, maybe. My mind wandered and I moved the glasses over to watch cranes in the marsh. When I shifted back to camp Polly was leaning in close. I quickly worked the focus - she was kissing the birdman! He was motionless as if in shock, and she held his shoulders down in a restraint.

I could imagine well what she was saying now: *Leif, I really like you. You're so nice...*Polly had worked her knee between his thighs. *Angukaa,* she moved fast! What, would they do it out in the open like birds, right before my eyes? But slowly they rose like in a trance to creep into his tent and were lost from view. She had left her medical kit on the log: so much for her plans to use birth control. I pictured them in missionary position, Polly smiling proudly, not that stealing the object of her desire was ever any problem for her, the sexiest girl in Itiak. She was sighing, *Oh Leif* and he closed his eyes in great pleasure, not caring at all that he was just another victory...

He'll fall in love with Polly.

It hit me with a great paw, that idea, its talon puncturing my chest so the binoculars fell. All it would take would be sex, she'd have his *bibirak,* he'd move in with Abe and Flo and I'd do his laundry. But he was a birdman, it must not happen, he was *mine!* I had to do something fast, I had to prevent it. But I couldn't run down and pull them apart like dogs!

I was hyperventilating, desperate, my breath became the wind. I pitched forward as my mind was swept into a blackness through a hole impossibly small. From every direction the *inua* muttered and my inner vision brightened with a humming light as I came through the tunnel. I must have screamed. The instant I had entered the universe, the universe entered me, and I was a star that spiraled in a pulsating galaxy. I had finally done it, it was letting me! *Help me*, I begged, *help me stop them!* Again my mind darkened and filled with a roaring like surf in the fall, when chunks of land disappear overnight.

The spiritworld had taken over and it was no longer in my hands.

Once there was an old woman who desired a hunter who was courting her niece. They didn't realize she was a witch and they ridiculed her, until one night she killed the girl and skinned her. She laid the whole skin over her own worn-out body, all the while chanting a spell to dim the hunter's vision and trick him. When I came to on the sharp rocks of the bluff I thought of this old story, such was the dread in my throat; it was of the same caliber. My hair tried to stand on end like the mane of a wolf but it could not, the long heavy hair of a woman. I was drooling and half-paralyzed, trying to organize my mind. At first I didn't even remember why I was up there on the ridge.

I fumbled with the binoculars. My pulse was thudding so hard it made the lenses jerk violently and the land was a green fur being shaken out by a giant. I found the birdman outside, looking wildly around. He was shirtless and his jeans were undone like he'd pulled them on fast. There was a horror in the way he spun, his hands out to keep something from advancing. But there was nothing there. Polly came from the tent not scared at all, just tucking in her blouse with frustrated moves. The biologist raised and lowered his arms, unable to explain. Polly didn't want explaining - she snatched up her bag and marched to the riverbank, slid down it, and waited for her ride without looking at him again.

All is well, a voice whispered behind me, through a boulder, a thin spirit voice. *Do not fear*. With a gasp I let out my air. I had prevented a disaster, but had no idea what had uncoupled those two.

The birdman looked calmer now, and there was Willy turning into the mouth, marked by the glint of metal on water. He was right on time, almost as if collaborating with me and the spirits. Later he said he remembered that the family wasn't at that camp but a different one, so he headed back. The second he grounded Polly jumped aboard. He waved, hesitating at the birdman's feeble response, and he probably wanted to stop for tea but Polly wouldn't let him.

They left the birdman slouched on his driftwood. He leaned forward until his face was buried in his hands, a very sad picture. But no pity could stir my heart. The more I thought about what he'd done the worse it got.

IT SEEMED A MUCH longer journey down than before. When I arrived the birdman was in his coat and kneeling near his toy oil slick holding some kind of gauge. He didn't notice me. "Hey," I called from thirty feet away, not wanting to startle him. He saw me but looked as confused as a berrypicker on the tundra who forgot to memorize landmarks, when everything has become the same, only different. As I got near I saw how bloodless was the skin of his face.

I told him I just came to get my pail. He stared into the black crude, its swirling rainbows. Under its sharp odor drifted the smell of Polly's fancy shampoo, from the birdman. I stared at him. After a while he looked up. "Oh right, the pail. It's in camp somewhere." I felt a poke of guilt, then a greater satisfaction to see fear in his eyes.

"I'll get it," I offered, but he said nothing. I found my pail, and sure enough, my *kaspaq* was clean and folded neatly at the bottom. I picked up a science magazine lying on the gravel but it swam before my eyes. My brain felt heavy and dull. Only then did I notice blood drying on my elbows, cut by the shale when I fell. After a long time the birdman walked into camp. He looked almost glad to see me now.

"I saw a bear," he said, "before you got here. It came into camp."

Iii, izhigii! I thought, is that what they sent to help me? They knew exactly what he was most scared of. I shuddered and savored the idea. As if protecting his insides, he drew up his knees and tightly embraced them as he sat near me. "Sometimes don't they...eat people?" he asked in a hushed voice.

"I don't know. Yes." I smiled, conscious of my dog teeth, suddenly thinking they must look sharp, and he was looking at me strangely. "You could borrow a gun," I told him, "the government will never know."

He shook his head. "But *you* hike around without a gun all the time, don't you? Is it true if you shoot them in the heart they can still get you - the heart keeps beating? And if you carry a big stick they'll think it's a gun and run away?" He rattled on, but I understood: he'd been spooked at a pretty bad time. He looked around back of camp and up the hillside with the anxiety of an animal being hunted. I wanted to explain it was not a flesh bear, but how could I?

I said firmly, "There's nothing there, don't worry." And it seemed to help. His shoulders dropped, he slowly unfolded from his protective crouch and was sitting normally, cross-legged, trusting, and his color got better. He had no idea what I had done to him.

Though maybe he suspected because he said next, very softly, "You never explained to me what an angutkoq is. You uh...you said you were one."

"That's a shaman," I said, with a hard stare. In spite of his treachery, my stomach leaped at the innocence in the honey-brown of his eyes. "*Witch*doctor." I pronounced each syllable clearly, to be sure he understood. He swallowed.

"Wow, that's...that seems like a tough job...is it?"

"Yes." My eyes dropped away from the united gaze. I was answering *his* questions now, about me, and they tumbled out like he had too many stored up. I had been wrong to think he never thought of me.

"Can you explain what a shaman does exactly?"

I said carefully, "Exactly we have a line to the spirit world, like preachers say they do, but we really do. So preachers hate us."

We looked at each other. He didn't smile or try to keep from it - like at the worm - in fact he was very far from smiling. He cleared his throat like a fish bone had stuck in it. "What do you pull in...on your line?"

"Good things like the cure for sickness, and where the animals are. Hunting weather. And bad things, evil spirits. To help us when we need them, like for revenge. You look surprised."

"Well, you're pretty young for that calling, aren't you? I mean I always imagined ancient old men. Or old women."

"I'm training."

"Who's training you?"

"Spirits are," I said lowly, in case any were listening. He combed his short beard with his finger and thumb, studying me. I said, "Maybe it's hard for a scientist to believe me. I know how they think, I took biology in school. I got A's."

"I don't doubt it."

"But there is something important missing from science, and maybe you know what's missing. You always hunt for that goose..."

He searched my face awhile but I kept it as blank as new snow. "I don't know what you mean," he said. "What about the geese?"

"I don't know..."

"Oh come on." He smiled unhappily. I forced myself into another angut-koq stare, dead-on. When I didn't say anything he laughed at himself and scratched along his black lined jaw. "Um...I'm thinking I'm going a little crazy out here by myself, though I was fine up until today."

"Naluagmiut always crazy."

He attempted an insane smile, gave up. "No I'm serious, all this space and...time...it's...suddenly not very pleasant. But I always loved it before."

"Will you go back now to Itiak? Or Seattle?" My stomach hurt as I said it. If he fled it was my own fault. He shook his head, turning his gaze to track the long-legged flight of two cranes. Was that a glisten in his eyes?

"Sorry." He looked down, pinching the bridge of his nose. "I'm not nor-mally like this. He hastened to point out. You hardly know me and I'm laying my problems down. It's just that it was so...terrible." His voice roughened as he blinked and cleared his throat. "Sorry," he muttered again. All this effort to control himself amazed me; he hadn't tried very hard with Polly. It looked so difficult. Maybe he had stronger feelings than me, more kinds. Tears never came to me except for that terrible moment recently when I begged Flo to let me come along. I wondered if the birdman knew he was carrying out an ancient tradition, to lay one's problems down at the feet of the shaman. One's spiritual problems.

"But I *do* know you," I said carefully. "I know about your father."

He squinted at me, the glare from the waves beaming directly into his eyes. "*What?*"

"I told you. I am angutkoq so I know things."

He grew utterly still, expressionless. I waited, my angutkoq gaze not leaving him. "Look, I hate to be inhospitable but I have stuff to do while the birds are awake." He stood up abruptly as if no longer interested in my company. "And I was in the middle of pouring the oil. It all has to be poured at the same time -"

"Okay, I'm going, don't worry. You're a really busy whiteman. But I should tell you something." I stood up too, so that I was too close but he didn't step back. I was eye-level with his adam's apple and I found a pulse at the notch of his throat, fast like a bird's. He didn't want to hear me because now he knew what I was and knew I had a line to his soul, and he suspected about the bear. When I looked up his eyes were hooded around a wildness and he was fighting not to run from me, but at the same time he had to find out.

My vision altered, sharpening so I saw him as clearly and narrowly as through a rifle scope, but I saw the world around us and behind us too, the land and sky in its hugeness. Maybe it was the vision of *ukpik* - the owl. I felt the pulse of the world, its vast breathing. My own pulse had slowed to keep time with it.

"You hate your father," I said, "but you wanted to fly after him whenever he went out to sea, because you loved him and he turned away from you. He has the spirit of the goose. And you are afraid of him...he hurt you." Hurt you like a bear, I thought, when you were very small and he was big and roaring. The spirit of the bear, too.

From a great distance I saw the black of his pupils cringe, then pool, that I could know this. And with the fear I felt the indignation, that I had stepped over a line. This man who let me see his nakedness, the picture of his parents and of his beloved goose didn't want me to see that shadowed wound. It was not beautiful; it was raw and infected. And nothing a health aide could lance.

He tried to scoff. His voice came out uneven. "Come off it, it doesn't take a witch to know that. Sure, he hurt me. Sure I hate him. I told you guys he was a goddamn alcoholic, you were there, you saw the photo and you know he's a mean-ass redneck. You put two and two together fast, you're extremely intelligent. But it's not *supernatural*." He said the last word the way Abe said *Satan,* like it was the worst thing in the world, worse than war, worse than extinct.

"Someday science will believe in it too," I said in a faraway voice, "even in my lifetime."

He shook his head. "Don't delude yourself." But he just stood there, staring at me, unnerved. It was easy to go in through his eyes. He was the Blind Boy, I was the Loon, and his soul was the waters that would cure his eyes - while he didn't exactly agree to it - and as he clung to my back I dove, swimming down, further, deeper, hunting for a better fish, proof for him, evidence. At the lake's bottom I found the memory of the evil spirit I had called forth: Polly is lying on the ground with no clothes. A great brown bear is eating her, cracking her ribs to get at her guts. *Iiii, Niviak...dead!* The bear looks up, breathing fetid breath. Its eyes are small, its muzzle dark red with blood. It is female.

I might have screamed out loud. The birdman came into focus. He was staring at me with wide eyes. Polly had seen nothing. She had marched to the boat to ride off with her nose up without a backward glance and only her pride hurt. I imagined it from her side, the scientist scrambling off her - out of her - like she had suddenly turned into a horrible monster! If she knew I was responsible, she would never forgive me!

"Polly," I said, getting hold of myself. "You saw...the animal got her."

He inhaled sharply through his nose. "Jesus!"

"That was a spirit," I told him levelly. "She was warning you."

"About *what*?! I was just hallucinating! Wait a minute -" He held up a hand between us in a *stop* gesture, pressing his forehead with his other fingers. He dropped his hands. "Okay. Okay. You must have talked to Polly. You met her upriver somewhere. Goddamn! She told you!" His eyes skimmed mine, chasing understanding. "But I-I...I didn't tell her about...I didn't *tell* her! How did you - "

He closed his eyes, suddenly blanched. "You better leave now," he said, before clapping his hand to his mouth. He stumbled a few steps away and lost his tea. I could have told him the full truth, how the bear got there - and why - but he'd had enough. I guess I'd won. Not wanting to humiliate him further by watching, I rescued my bucket and left.

At my lookout point I found Flo's binoculars and hunted the marsh. At first he was nowhere - it was like he'd been abducted by the clouds. I found him on the beach in that crouch again; maybe he wanted the driftwood's protection, since he knew a tent was nothing to an *aklak*. He wasn't really the Blind Boy; he didn't want his new vision but stared out to sea desperate to get his old ideas back, to form them into a lecture. Everywhere looked deserted, the waves, tundra, even the sky was empty of birds. And the wind had stopped, the world held its breath.

You are angutkoq now, a whisper came from the boulders, or was it from the mountain across the river? I ran along the ridge for home. Several times I whirled to look behind me with trembling knees and there would be nothing but rock, wind, ravens. The fox wasn't there who had kept watch over me before, when I had flown. Tears were crawling down my neck though I had just convinced myself they never fell. *Birdman, Niviak, I'm sorry*. But why oh why did they have to go and do that?

The birdman liked Niviak, not me, and no bear could change that. The reality of it hit so hard I fell face down. I wept into the soft lichen and moss until I felt as wrung out as a dishcloth. It was strange to cry like that - when had I last done it? I could not remember. I coldly watched myself as if from above, my childish womanly tears, the kind of tears mocked by the owl when he stabbed the ptarmigan in her chest and said it was the fate of women, to cry like that. Then I was laughing in a gasping way, for I had finally done it, I was a true angutkoq, I had made it through the barrier on my own without even my *turnaq*. It wasn't as glorious as I had imagined.

In the middle of that strange laughing I felt with the certainty of an animal that something was indeed tracking me on big silent, padded feet.

Better me than the biologist alone in his camp.

POLLY WAS LOOKING mad and depressed, and I nearly hugged her, so glad I was to see her. We never hugged; people did not, except with little kids. But suddenly I felt like I had turned into the birdman, and I was embracing her with my man's arms, I was between her legs, thrusting into her, her grasping insides. My face grew as hot as a kettle and I ducked into the tent.

Willy was lazing in there with a *Rolling Stone* magazine. "You look like you seen a ghost," he said.

"Yeah. I did."

"A lot of them over in that old village. One time going by in fall I saw lights in there, like old oil lamps. Like the women were there."

I shuddered. "What's wrong with Niviak?"

Willy grinned. "Her and Mister Scientist. Lover's fight."

"Pataq, maybe you better go bring him here for another visit." I thought of the birdman covering his face with his bandaged hands and the long evening by himself, just him and what I had left in his mind for company. "He's too lonely."

Willy turned back to his magazine. "He's just got birds on the brain. You girls..."

Later Polly confided in me. "Maybe he's a war veteran. They're never the same - they can't get it up, or sleep, because they have nightmares even when they're awake, they had to do such terrible things there." I was hearing about the war all the time now. I wasn't going to argue with her.

"Well, I can't help him with that," said Polly, shaking her hair back. "I'm just a health aide. It's too bad, because he's nice. And for awhile..." She sighed again, making me remember with great discomfort my vision of her rapture in the tent. Was that picture worse, or the other, the bloody coupling of *aklak* and woman? I wasn't sure.

"I don't want to let him visit again," Polly said testily. "How come you do?"

"*Ayii*, I don't! Mom does, and Pataq."

"Oh shit, he can't come here!" she suddenly wailed. "You go *there*!"

"No way, not me. Just let Pataq."

SO THAT IS HOW it was, the whole summer, that Polly could not be in the birdman's vicinity. Flo missed her string bag - I had left it behind, of course, but I couldn't go get it. Willy reported that "naluagmiu looks pretty normal," and no mention of bears (I asked, when I got him alone a second).

With no comment he handed over the string bag full of gull eggs, making me flush as if I had hives. They had gone to the island to see storm petrels - the birdman paid for gas - and the birds puked over their heads because they felt invaded. The birdman was pleased to know what petrels ate without having to kill one. He and Willy had a good time and were planning to go hunting together. He wouldn't shoot though.

I thought, okay, at least he's safe. And he isn't with Polly.

CHAPTER II

Fear not the loose-haired maidens
Be not fearful of the women!
(ANCIENT FINNISH SHAMAN, TO A BEAR)

Dark-browed Sophist, come not near
All the place is holy ground
TENNYSON

I SAW HIM THOUGH, from the ridge. It was boring seeing him at a distance jumping around in the marsh like a little *izhigak*, the tundra leprechaun. Once I saw him fall down a hole; another time he was swimming in the waves, his head like a black duck. He always felt it if he was being spied on and would suddenly look up, just like a wary goose when it plucks grass. I would smile scornfully to myself, knowing he'd never admit he could sense things too, with the animal radar we all had. It grew stronger in him as he lived in the wild, in the way of a muscle you flex.

Abe joined one of the expeditions and formed a favorable opinion of the biologist. At sea in a small craft, that was the true test of a man's character. Tingmiaq, as they called him now - bird - was *puqik*, a quick study. He never complained, and took snappy orders from Abe. He brought good luck. His sharp eyes were a real point in his favor, for he spotted seals in open water. But he wouldn't even target-practice; what a waste. And he got seasick in pretty calm waves. Abe had teased him, wondering how he could help his fisherman father. With a shame-faced look mimed by Willy, the birdman confessed he was kicked off the boat. Abe appreciated that frankness. Itiak men got rejected from boat hunts, when the whole crew was in danger if someone turned unharmonious or lazy and was just dead weight. Still, it seemed harsh to kick a son off for getting queasy.

"I bet I know the real reason," said Willy. "He had his nose in a book when he was supposed to be steering!" Willy mimicked how the birdman had started guiltily when Willy caught him reading on the beach and saw the title before he could hide it. "About Eskimos, alright!" Reading was self-centered, a kind of trance outsiders went into when they tired of your company. The birdman had figured this out. And he knew we hated to be studied. Did he know *he* was being observed closely too?

ENTRY. WHAT'S WRONG with me? Besides a mild fever I had no other symptoms of blood-poisoning. Maybe it was punishment for eating goose like a cannibal: we descend from the goose totem, Maman says. Such bad timing too. Better to have stuck with the field biologist's specialty, onanism of the ornithologist. But the health aide is cute, persistent and very...er...adroit. Okay, I was giving signals, but the silent audience behind the impenetrable shades, the macaroni, the upbraiding from the wily patriarch and just human company made me lose my head. My awkwardness probably spurred Polly on. I could have warned her I'm not so heroic at one-night-stands and prefer the courtly style of the crane to the mallards' careless exchange of alleles. It's moot now.

And then my unsolicited psychiatrist: yikes. Methinks my favor begins to warp. I won't deny the possibility of the paranormal. Rodney wrote from Brazil about sorcerers and their psychotropic rituals and shared visions. He's a trained botanist. But he may have gone over the edge into this Castaneda stuff, had too many mushrooms and is dreaming up the whole tribe, a freak alone in the jungle. Animals have mysterious senses (of note, migratory birds), but these can be explained in the confines of the body. If you believe in psychic events the Newtonian premise is destroyed. I guess Einstein was doing that with his "spooky action at a distance" but that's particles, not a girl with a white bucket reading my mind. Worse, reading my unconscious, stuff I don't want to think about or didn't even know was there. And don't understand, like, why would my Id want to drag Polly out of the tent and eviscerate her? I feel transparent, like she's seeing into my skull. (Ah, but it's for the high seeress to unlock the secrets of a man's brutish soul). Hard to buy it.

It's more likely a Sherlockian brilliance, her dead-eye for minutiae. I had mentioned bears and implied perhaps stupidly that I feared how they preyed on humans. She tapped into my phobia, born from an old Norwegian fairy tale. It was supposed to be a rather helpful bear, a human living inside the fur, but in Fahr's drunken version the bear had a berserker quality and the human wife and child never knew when it would explode. Was it just a hell of an intuitive leap? The remaining and very unsettling question is, how did she know the bear ate Polly?

The rational explanation is just as scary, if not scarier than, telepathy. Such manipulation...for what end? In current anthropology the Freudians rule, claiming the witch was the sublimated aggression of a society. Like politicians or cult leaders, they gained by abusing the fears they implanted. Neurotic, schizophrenic, or so lacking in other talents that sorcery was their only means, the power of suggestion their muscle. An explorer advised, "look for the man who can't hunt well, with the nervous facial tic: that's your local wizard." And they were all fakes. But the Inuit claimed the powers were very real, and angakok were so feared that when they died (or were offed) their joints were severed and the body burned so they could not reincarnate. Even in the Enlightenment the forefathers of science burned all those women at stake, after finding irrefutable proof of danger. And Victorians seemed convinced; to whit," Witches feed upon the essence of things, leaving the tangible forms seemingly unaltered". I don't know, the satanic quality of arctic wizards could be missionary propaganda. If healers, they'd be a threat to Medicine; if leaders they'd compete with colonial rule, and thus must be maligned.

These shenanigans might be the Fox's only stab at power. Look at her niche in the hierarchy. They don't treat her like a big bad scary shaman, more like a surly field hand. I saw at camp how she's stuck with the step-and-fetch grunt work with no honor. Women's work: serve silently, labor on and on (hard labor too; I saw Flo heft a 200 pound seal), stockpile while the predators rest up and maintain order. Polly never lifted a finger, and she can rag on her old man to boot, but she's clearly the princess. Is this the egalitarian hunter-gatherer society? I always thought agriculture and private property brought down the female. If this is a pure example, not something corrupted by missionaries and Ladies' Home Journal, it doesn't bode well for the Liberation. Willy played dumb when I asked about roles as if a hunter can't even think about what the other division does, though he was sewing his pants very nicely in my camp. Don't know if I buy the Protein or Bringing-Home-the-Bacon theory of dominance, but what else explains it?

My own niche seems so ambiguous. Wish we could talk again of war and genocide; it seemed to smooth her hackles. Am I a hopeless romantic? Don't know. Mass confusion. I fear this is all moot now too.

THE BUGS put on their wings and lasted in their fury until mid-August, at their height during salmon-netting and berry-picking. We picked the net three times a day. I hated how they tangled their gills in the mesh. I cut fish but my scores were not up to Flo's standards: not deep enough, so the flesh wouldn't sag open as it hung and it stayed wet and rotted. Or *too* deep, so it sagged too far and stuck to itself to make places for maggots to thrive.

That summer much of what I cut would be dogfood, for my thoughts kept drifting. Flo let me do mindless tasks: lug water tubs, haul the bones and guts back to the river, sharpen knives, hang fillets, and pick berries even if we had to winnow them to blow out all my sticks and leaves. Gladly I left camp to pick alone. Though foraging was sparser there I kept to the high, windy ridges with no bugs and tried to practice my flights. But the spirit world had withdrawn from me. Even my *turnaq* kept away; he was mad.

By the time the bugs died, picking was over except for cranberries in rocky places, the last sockeye fileted and hanging red on the racks. We'd moved a ways upriver. The ponds grew a thin sheet of ice overnight and it was dark after dinner. It had drizzled a lot in late summer so the tents and dry meat were mildewed, berries were ruined, and Polly got fed up and returned to Itiak. Our clothes stayed damp and cold and we drank endless cups of warming tea. Sometimes the fog socked us in, blanking out the hills and carrying the ravens' "*gluk*" for miles. Birds were teaching their big babies last minute flight maneuvers. A flock of new Canada geese congregated nearby to practice "staging", a word Willy picked up from the birdman. Abe called it "going to school." It scared Betsy - soon she would go to school too.

And one morning while we were all relaxing in camp after a breakfast of *musuk* the birdman arrived to pay his respects. It surprised even Willy, who'd arranged to give him a ride back to the peninsula on no particular date; the biologist wanted to check on his oil squares there. When we spotted him ambling along the riverbank something surged in me. The blood left my head like surf pulling away, only to come rushing violently back in. He entered camp, it was too late to hide in the tent. I didn't want to hide, I wanted to see him! I didn't want anyone to see me seeing him, or for him or anyone else to see that I was glad to see him. Luckily, I got orders from Flo to prepare him food, so I could listen in and watch but not be part of anything.

The birdman said on Gyulnyev he'd watch flocking and departure, then he was leaving Alaska, and he hoped that his experiments hadn't caused any trouble. "Well, I stepped in one and had a heckuva time washing out my sock," Abe said. The others laughed hugely at his dumb joke; it was the season. The snap in the wind, the migrating birds, freeze-up and the reappearance of the moon in its larger yellow form stirred and excited us and we were tired of the discomforts of camp and longed to see the other families. But I didn't laugh. My birdman was leaving. Of course he was flying off; that is what bird biologists did - he wasn't studying polar bears or seals.

The birdman said he would try to return next spring to measure the damage to the marsh grass; it depended on the grant. It was doubtful they'd give him one. Oh, I thought, that was it then, that last time we spoke and he ran to throw up. That was how he would remember me.

He predicted some "meltdown" in the permafrost due to "escalating heat absorption", the kind that made tundra sink into a bog just from having vehicles run over it. He stopped explaining what he was going to do and fell silent. A funny look kept passing over his features like clouds racing over a hill, light-dark-light-dark. And he sought to make eye contact with me. I only let him do it once: people might notice, or worse, his effect on me. What was he trying to say?

He came close and I turned away but not before I saw that his hair had grown longer and as crazy as the curled branches of willow that hugged the ground in windswept places, and maybe he'd hacked at it with a knife, like it *was* firewood. His black watchcap beaded up with mist. He was nearly as dark as Willy now, and hollow-cheeked, with gnat bites. I thought he looked feral, but anyone would after a summer camping without even a dog to talk to. Geese were not very good company; they were standoffish, mean birds.

Flo gave him the half-dry chum I boiled into soup - we were using it up after rain softened it. He devoured it without pausing, so that Flo laughed with a kind of pity. "You run out of supplies?" He had, he admitted sheepishly. "Ahh, Pataq!" she cried. Not even asking me to do it, she hurried to find something more to stuff her guest with. "What will his mother think? How come you never bring him anything?" She complained to the naluagmiu while he gulped down blueberries how she hadn't trained her son well. But Willy hadn't known. "Someone" should have mentioned he needed food. Of course we were all thinking that a man should just hunt and not wait like an old *aka* to be fed, and even old *aka*s went out and found their own food if they needed to.

To change the subject Willy began discussing the biologist's tape recorder. He hinted how much he liked it. "But I'll never have one," he said mournfully, "unless someone gives me one they don't need." The birdman smiled, his teeth blue from *agutaq*. He seemed unsure if Willy was joking. When he didn't immediately offer up his machine, Willy got even by teasing him about a music tape in his camp - "whiteman traditional" - that sounded like a sick goose. "And that other one," Willy went on relentlessly, "that funny goose with girl's voice you always listen to." They chuckled as men do and cast me a look, the birdman's furtive and embarrassed.

Abe asked what would happen exactly if an oil-rig broke up off the coast. The oil would be washed in over the deltas in the first storm, the birdman said, and cover the breeding grounds of most birds. They would starve with all the grass and larvae killed, and then the foxes would go hungry. If the "toxins" didn't get them first. After that, who knew? How did foxes affect lemming populations? Science didn't "yet understand" the cyclical fluctuations in the Arctic. And oil spills would be worse for the sea birds and mammals, and the "seismic activities" that drilling caused might disrupt whale migration. He didn't know exactly. Nobody knew; it hadn't happened yet. But science knew the far north was the most delicate ecosystem on earth. I listened with a sick feeling. The birdman was giving us terrible knowledge and then he was leaving, without my explaining things. It was all tangled in a tight knot in my chest: disasters of oil, the flight of geese, and his own.

"Why didn't you tell us all that before?" It was me, with a withered, angry voice. Everyone else looked at me in surprise; I never spoke in the whiteman's presence and now I was being so rude. Under their stares I became aware of the *aka*-style scarf tied under my chin. It made me bold, turning me into a grandmother with the right to scold men in public. It was camp that had done it: the free life out in the hills made people forget themselves, or become more true to themselves. Whole selves could just be slipped on and off like in the old stories where angutkoq donned bird cloaks and flew, and birds and animals turned out to be humans, and vice versa.

The birdman stared at me. "Well...I just - " he faltered. "I just thought you'd jump to your own conclusions."

"We don't jump to conclusions with no *naluagmiusak*." I used the more insulting word. Abe guffawed and Flo made the raven-like noise of disapproval, but she was enjoying it. The birdman smiled wryly, fingering his beard. Now he wouldn't look at me. Quickly I took off my scarf. At least I wasn't tattooed on the chin or wearing nylons with boots. Too late I realized I hadn't washed or combed my hair for a long time. I never looked in Flo's camp mirror to see if my face was dirty, and no one remarked if it was. My hands were tanned dark, blue-stained, with old fish grime to the quick under my overgrown fingernails - we'd lost our clippers. I was wilder than the birdman. I hid my hands in my *kaspaq*.

"Maybe oil drilling will bring jobs for Native people," Abe was saying.

"Could be. But more jobs for Oklahomans, I'm afraid." The birdman looked down. We were silent. Was there something more he wasn't telling us, or was there more the oil people weren't telling *him*?

"Hey, how's your *ligliq*?" Abe asked cheerily. "Extinct yet?"

"Tallin's? I haven't sighted it. I'll try again next spring, if I can. If they let me." He'd never give up.

"Hmm..." Abe sipped his tea, exchanging a veiled look with Flo. The birdman surveyed our camp with seeming admiration, the racks of sockeye, kegs of berries and pokes swollen with food. He took special interest in the dried wing I used to sweep the tent and fan the fire. Flo had hooked the gull in its greedy throat when it was eating our fish. The birdman stroked the long feathers. "Glow-cuss," he murmured. Flo had hidden the goose wing, thinking it might be the kind he was obsessed about.

The old people didn't ask him about his further plans after Ituak. That was a person's private territory he might share only with family. And the birdman didn't want to reveal his future; he didn't seem sure about it, unlike other naluagmiut I had overheard who told everything to strangers, as if their plans were already reality and nothing could change, like they were God or living in *taimmani*, the far-off days when everyone had the power to create a thing just by speaking of it. The birdman was not like them; there was always a doubt, a hesitation, and he did move more lightly on the earth.

Even when he poured the oil it was tentative, like he was sorry about it. Was it the Indian in him?

Well, goodbye, he said to us. We didn't do that, not with those final words, and often people wouldn't even mention a leaving, but people would do it for a whiteman. His gear was all packed up, waiting downriver for Willy. Flo made him take a gunny sack of the best dried salmon - *her* cuts. When he carried it to the boat I was waiting there, kneeling by my shallow pool in the gravel bed and scrubbing dishes with sand. I'd washed my face and winnowed my hair with my fingers, dismayed to see a lot of berry leaves and stems and fishscales fall out.

No one in camp could see or hear us over the bank, under the bubble and chatter of the current. The birdman slung the sack into the beached skiff and stood only a few feet from where I rinsed plates. He leaned against the boat, stretching out his legs and looking down on me. Both our heads turned when a duck rounded the river's bends as fast as an arrow, with its feathers whirring. I shook water off my hands and dried them on my pants - clean now.

When I looked up the birdman was still staring and it made me jump. Because it was overcast, I didn't wear my sunglasses and he took advantage of that, his eyes traveling fast from one of my eyes to the other. Whenever I glanced away to escape he waited until I looked back to find him still staring. It would seem belligerent, if it wasn't the birdman. Over the summer with no company but birds something had changed in him. Or *grown*, wild like tangled hair. A hunger. Or had he just forgotten how to behave? Right now he looked as though he might lunge and bolt me down like a salmon.

"What are you *looking* at?" I finally said.

"You."

I pressed my icy hand to my hot cheek, willing my heart to calm. I should go back to the camp, I thought; this was a mistake, and I didn't like having to peer up at the birdman, him looking down on me like a raven. I stood, but my foot had gone to sleep from crouching and it buckled under me. His manner suddenly changed, or he remembered his manners. He dropped his intense gaze, allowing me to breathe.

"I've been thinking a lot," he said. Sure he had, all his long lonely summer. "I've been reading about angutkoq." My nerves settled at the words: we were going to talk about things familiar to me and give me the upper hand, instead of the silent staring. He was waiting; he wanted a go-head before continuing, in the naluagmiu way.

"Really?" I said.

"Ya, it's interesting. Very far out. They went to the dark side of the moon a long time before the astronauts." He shifted his butt on the gunwale. "I'm glad we can talk today. I lost it pretty bad last time we...and you ran off before I could...recover."

"I didn't 'run off'. I went egg-hunting."

"Oh. Anyway, I don't normally...uh..." He looked across the churning water to the opposite bank, where a gray seagull teenager was hunkered down neckless, begging its aloof parent to throw up fish for it. "I must have seemed...um...unstable."

"Polly thinks you're a vetcrinarian."

He slowly blushed, like sunset, like when I'd caught him swimming and stared at his groin. He laughed shortly, rubbing the back of his neck. "Veteran? But I'm *not*. And I'm not deranged, I'm not crazy. Well, not crazy *that* way, though I might be someday."

"I know," I said kindly. "It was an evil spirit, like I said."

"But why would a spirit appear out of the blue when I've never seen one before?"

"I don't know. Maybe because you're *here* now. Where spirits are."

"Spirits are only in the Arctic?" His tone had an insolence.

"Maybe."

"Hm." He thought about it, fiddling with his thumbs. "You said angutkoq called on them...uh...to serve. My mom used to tell stories like that, French stories of sorcerers and...not just Indian." In a quick move he met my eyes again; my heart skipped a beat and I couldn't look away. I hadn't noticed before but his eyes had tiny flecks of gold such as they pan for in rivers. He looked away first, his gaze ricocheting to the opposite shore. "Or do they sometimes just come out on their own?" he asked the willows over there. "The

135

inua? And angutkoq can send them away, kind of like dominate them? Dispel them?"

I struggled to untangle his meaning. "You want protection," I guessed softly.

"Yeah, well...you're the only angutkoq I know."

He spoke earnestly and a pride rushed through me, until a waver in his eyes alerted me. Did he only want to flatter? "You *saglu*..."

He tried to figure that out. "I'm joking?"

"You don't really think I can help."

He looked surprised I could read him so well, forgetting our last encounter, then he shrugged. "Okay, look, what happened can be explained by sensory deprivation: the featureless plain, isolation, add in your midnight sun and the lack of ah-ri-yem sleep, the repetitive roar of surf, and after a while, you start seeing things." His hand helped him list his excuses in the air.

"Scientists," I murmured. "They always understand everything and they invent and fix everything. Like nuclear bombs."

He didn't seem angered by that, but pleased, like I was his smart student. "Granted. A lot of us go to the dark side."

"But you aren't even a real scientist yet. They won't let you be one. They don't think you're good enough."

Now he actually laughed out loud. I was delighting him in the way of a teasing cousins. "True."

"What did you dream?" I asked.

"*Huh?*"

Calvin had told me this way to find out what *inua* were communicating. Normally people didn't want to relate a bad dream because it might come true, but they used to tell angutkoq. It was like confession. The birdman seemed really caught off guard. Whites didn't dream maybe; a teacher had told me it was just a way for the mind to rest. "*Do* you dream?" I tried again.

He folded his arms. "We have to, don't we? But I don't remember mine."

"You do," I guessed.

He snickered a little. "Okay...it's uh...a little revealing, but okay. I dreamed of *you*." My face blazed up instantly and I was sorry for pressing. What was I *doing* in his dream? "But it wasn't good," he said, "You were kidnapped. I was trying to rescue you." I still blushed - *rescuing* me? - but it wasn't what I had thought. "And then I was following tracks in the snow," he offered, watching my face closely. "It was getting dark. At first it was bear, then other animals, all kinds - I learned the tracks when I was little, from books - but then the tracks were of a man, and I was putting my feet inside his...like in that Christmas carol, 'in his master's steps he trod'."

The birdman waited for me to say something, which I didn't. He felt his chin as if comforting the whiskers, or making sure he really had them, that he really was a grown man and not a boy. "So what's it mean?"

"I don't know, you tell me."

He snorted. "Spoken like a true therapist. Is it more father issues, do you think? I have problems with authority?"

I hesitated, unsure if he was making fun of me. "It's *inua*. Spirits. Where were you going, in that dream?"

"I don't know...somewhere far."

"Were you scared?"

He shrugged. "Look -" he held up his hand like I was supposed to halt. I resented the princely whiteman gesture, and hadn't planned on saying more anyway. "Honestly, I don't think dreams are much use, even when they *seem* to tell the future, inexplicably. Like, once I dreamed of a cat in a sweater, then the next day I saw a cat on the street wearing one..." He chuckled. "Very important information. But back to your calling," - he brushed the topic of dreams aside with his hand - "You claim to have yes-*pee*." When I looked blank, he explained with an impatience, "Extrasensory perception?" He had words for what I *did* but which I had no words to describe. "Never mind. You said you can overpower a spirit, or make it do your bidding - right?"

I frowned. He was too excited, he was building up to something and acting really *naluagmiusak*. Was this why he had come upriver, to tell me this before he left? He'd been playing dog, showing his belly to throw me off then turning on me. His ideas had to be boss. He didn't wait for an answer.

"Well, you know, the old shamans didn't think they could control the spirits. They did a lot of coaxing and begging and then *maybe* they'd get help. And neo-fights like you, well, it's unlikely any would help you. It would take years of arduous training, and there has to be some kind of terrible initiation rite."

The birdman put his hands in his pockets and looked down his hawk nose at me, proud of himself for getting even. Lecturing *me* about angutkoq! He had laid a word-trap and I walked in. The only thing I could do was watch the gulls. Now the teenaged one was trying to peck the red spot on the mother's beak to force the food out of her. She got mad and attacked the fledgling with a huge, scary mouth.

I said, "So you're an expert now from a book."

"A book doesn't always lie," he retorted, "just because a scientist wrote it. But back to you. You know, if you want to impress people, dabbling in stuff that's outlawed seems kind of self-destructive. Aren't there easier ways?" He grinned like he'd won fifty points in Scrabble.

I felt something spill through my veins - rage, shame, I didn't know. *Impress* people? It was time to tell him the whole truth, and get my teeth on his throat, for I could play dog too. Slowly, to get all his attention, I said, "*I* sent that spirit."

Motionless, we locked eyes. Silence, several breaths worth - but we were not breathing. "*You* sent it," he repeated. His eyes went through an amazing journey in a few moments. Confusion and hurt passed through first. I could even see the little stripes in his irises shift like they felt pain. They ended up set deep and still, a glacier with something frozen in it, and fixed on me. That was how the Nordics did anger. It was worse than any form I had seen in any kind of person.

"Look, I don't believe in magical powers, I'm just trying to understand you. I thought we were...why would you want to scare the shit out of me? Assuming you could? You've been at me the whole time, man. What precisely did I do to you?"

"I don't know! I am sorry I spoiled your fun! Maybe I don't much like naluagmiut, or bi-biologists spilling oil on my land, trying to save birds like they own them! I bet you think we kill our old people and our babies. You always think that."

"*What*? I..infanticide and abandonment?" That threw him off, but for only a second. "Actually my mother's people were more likely to do it, and I happen to know every culture did it in desperate times and might have to again, but why are we talking about *that*? And I'm not the fucking representative of the white race, you know."

His words came at an intimidating clip but I wasn't going to give up. "But you *act* all whiteman! You think you can just jump in bed with Eskimo girls, ah?" I was gratified by the blood slowly flooding again under the high plane of his cheekbones. "Maybe you read it in a book, ah? Eskimo men lend their wives? You don't even know they did that so their children could be related."

The birdman had recoiled from me like I was a crazed fox on his trapline. My heart was thundering. "Did you try to rub noses too?" I asked softly. The pupils of his eyes had slammed shut. He sprang from the boat and stood tall, fingers curled, while little muscles worked on the edges of beard like he was chewing tough meat. I swallowed dryly. *You are not dangerous*, I thought, *I am*! I lifted my chin, my eyelid jumping at the lie, because I did not feel dangerous, I felt in danger, and we stared at each other. I tried to grin in the proper way of Eskimo battle, then gave up.

"Go to hell," he said quietly, and stalked to the bank and bounded up it with fury in his muscles, like a big wolf driven off by a weasel.

I kicked at the bag of fish we had worked so hard for. Why did Flo have to give it to him? He wouldn't give Pataq the tape recorder. He could not conceal his scorn, how he found me superstitious. *Savage*, the town kids used to call us villagers. Everywhere you turned naluagmiut were there, proving they were right, commanding, even on the television in Nome they were there too, still bossing! And I had brought this one with the science degree down with a few words; it didn't take a shaman to vanquish him! I had always imagined whites stomped around with hair-trigger tempers, blowing up but then instantly forgiving, a *kuangazuk*, like a toddler. Yet the biologist I found slow to arouse, a pot that would not boil. I had pestered until the *aklak* in him reared up. I had wrecked our strange alliance as surely as a foot kicking apart the wood laid just so to keep a fire going, as if we had never sat and talked about war and geese, our knees nearly meeting. I had touched his sleeping face, I had seen his body, his fears, he even told me his dream. But now he hated me, the whole world was arranged to get him to hate me.

Who cared - he was leaving for good anyway.

I could have thought of many more naluagmiut trespasses to feed my anger, but it had fled up the bank with him. Men used to cut off the heads of the witches and evil dwarves to destroy their *qilya* and make sure they could never return. They cut off the heads of walrus and wolves so they could not get revenge. I felt helpless like that. Everything I wanted and needed was cut off with just my arm and leg bones left for doing chores, and nothing inside the trap built of my ribs. I was new grass risen in springtime full of ignorant hope, only to find myself smothered in black oil. It was an old, familiar feeling.

I ran up the river, not wanting to be there when the boat left.

BOOK THREE

"I Feel As If My Soul, The One Within, Was Going Out"

*The rope will break
and the Wolf run free
Farther I can see
and more can say
of the fate of the world...
Seek you wisdom still?*

NORSE WITCH (ANCIENT NALUAGMIUT)

*Now o'er the one-half world
nature seems dead, and wicked dreams abuse
the curtain'd sleep; witchcraft celebrates....*

SHAKESPEARE

*All the wild witches, those most noble ladies,
For all their broom-sticks and their tears,
Their angry tears, are gone*

W.B.YEATS (NALUAGMIUT)

We do not believe; we only fear

IKINILIK (ITKUHIKHALINGMIUT)

CHAPTER 12

All spirits are enslaved which serve things evil
SHELLEY *(NALUAGMIUT)*

Great grief came over me
While I picked berries on the fell
(IGLULIK WOMAN)

ENTRY. GYULNYEV. September 9. Any inkling of my membership in the human species is now erased. I'm a racist scumbag interloper who ravished innocent Polly and must have bears sent to punish me. She thinks I'm a covert op working for the imperialists (the principal implied this too, the fuck.) I know nothing of loss or being under the boot. Her fully indigenous status makes her morally superior.

Yet "Polar Opposition" (yeah, right) changes to "First you draw the bow to shoot, then relax in friendship," and It tells me to seek marriages, that the hostilities are a misunderstanding. That a hunter should not close off all avenues of escape, so that the prey gives itself by its own desire. I don't think this is applicable. I'm not going to cast anymore about her.

Entry. Fair, nice after August's incessant rain. Birds depart every day. A few will remain, like the young ptarmigan turning white, very dumb and endearing Lagopus lagopus with their staccato call. They're flocking up for protection. Excellent startle reflexes but they flurry like snow against the russet of the willow to resettle a few feet away. They don't know Tennyson: "The ptarmigan who whitens ere his hour woos his own end". The cranes were awesome in their leaving, their rusty hinge voices so beautiful and strange. Gulls leave last, since they have a garbage subsidy, though I hear Ross's winter in mysterious open leads somewhere.

Ravens don't leave. They have a kind of anti-freeze in their legs. They ransacked my camp, neatly breaking into dry goods and taking off right before I got home. I saw them. They knew. Probably commissioned a fox to overturn the crates. I can see why farmers demonized the corvids and the Feds once branded them as Enemies of the State. Ravens form gangs and shit all over meat so no one else will want it. Willy thinks it's perverse, and yet I am to respect toolgock, "because he helps us hunt, and in the old story Toolgock-man saved all the people, in the flood. He found the land. And he brought the light." Willy showed me a wooden bowl artifact engraved with a peace sign, the footprint of this bird Creator (and hint-ed that I shouldn't mention these stories to his parents. He learned them from Gretchen, it seems. And they are verboten. Well, who did she learn them from?).

It's okay they took food except I'm low on supplies. Barely any cash left, nothing in the bank, I realized as if waking from a long dream. No sign of return fare from the Miser. Maman would deposit in my account but I know Fahr forbade her. Full of negative thoughts, no Zen, I-Ching just taunts me with "The roof of your house, the structure of your life, is sagging". Or worse: first telling me to keep my sense of purpose but then immediately warn-ing, "The bird tries to fly and falls. Don't do it!!" That helps a lot: don't do what? And then it tells me to hide my light to avoid injury. Not only must I enter the darkness but I must fly though my wings are drooping. Fuck oracles.

Had a bad dream and woke up in the black, a darkness kind of horrifying after months of light, a taste of things to come. The wind was screaming in crescendos like someone being repeatedly stabbed. The tent feels unsubstantial now, the land no longer forgiving as the days swiftly shorten, gobbled up. Found two mummified foxes still snarling in aspects of great suf-fering, like Pompeii. Then a common loon, shivering and immobile, something wrong with it, dead by morning. Blown off-course until it starved, I bet. Sad. The checkerboard patterns on its back were so intricate it seemed wrong it should die; to what end all that beauty?

Don't know why but I've been thinking a lot of birds from a different angle. Why were old cultures so spiritually bound up in them? The shamans' magic feather cloaks, Odin's raven spies, Leda and the Swan. What is that supposed to mean, being raped by a bird? (Better than a bull). I think here birds didn't violate humans; they married them, back when animals and people lived together and took each other's forms, though the unions didn't turn out so well.

And I'm reading Inuit mythology (maybe should not). There's Sila, the spirit who ran the storms and everything else, and softly crooned to mortals "Be not afraid..." because our tend-ency is to be scared shitless. Narrsuk, the male god of weather, despised humankind. The gods and animals were all so touchy, persnickety, vindictive, taking umbrage at the slightest offense. A wolf-like man-demon lived underground with his big-eared goblin henchman, who pressed that ear to the surface hearkening to the activities of man, the "heedless sinners". They too punished by withholding game. Oddly, the jealous, watchful moon also doled out the animals. The spiritworld was like a multi-headed police state with a constant, paranoid sur-veillance. It was confusing about who was in charge, who to appeal to, where to go when dead, a chaotic riddle that took a shaman to sort it out. Maybe it's a realistic paradigm of how the cosmos runs, how we humans run. Look at my master demons: Deans of committees, Secretary of Defense, CEOs of oil companies. I need a psychopomp.

Wildest of all was Nuliajuk under those seething waves, Greenland's Sedna. Willy doesn't know those names, though he pointed with his chin to the ocean without looking and murmured, "maybe the woman under there..." Could be she was obliterated by missionaries. She escaped from her husband, a stranger who was actually an evil storm petrel. Her family cast her off the boat to save themselves from him, little knowing what they were creating: a powerful scary goddess with her hands on the purse-strings (again, the animals). No sexy mermaid, the woman down there, and not sympathetic but mutilated, lonely, and very very angry. To placate her and bring food to a starving world a shaman had to sing and to make her lie down like Abi Yo Yo, so he could comb from her snarls the vermin, aborted fetuses, the sins. Her black dog-judge greets the souls of the dead as they enter her undersea hut, where all must wait for rebirth. Like Egypt's jackal Anubis, her hellhound counts all the taboos you broke. The Orphan has no patience for cruelty to animals, which were created out of her fingers her family had to chop off as she clung to the oomiak. And all because she ran off with a charming but alien bird-man. (Sometimes he was a dog).

Strong moral messages here. And far too many taboos to make life harder when it was hard enough. Such a nightmarish pantheon, though harsh existence seems to breed that kind of tale. Viking tales rival the Inupiat. I think of Fahr's Great Wolf devouring the sun and all life on Earth, and the Serpent coiled at the base of the world obsessively mulling on revenge. And those true stories from his boyhood! His village axed to death a witch who had hexed their cows. Her hair was "long, black and snarly", like a certain angootcock I know, hair I want to smooth, placate. Hmm...scratch that thought. Scratch all these morbid thoughts.

Later: This hair thing: the witch's comb in Snow White, Sampson, Norse sea-trolls who begged maidens to pick seaweed from their hideous locks in return for gold, the unkempt shamans of the Northwest whose power lay in their hair (forced to cut it by the whites), Puritan men executed for growing it long (it was a sign of turning Indian, the worst treachery against the State). What does it all mean?

Then, a freaky synchronicity. I was beachcombing when something lured me to the side of the cliff to dig. Immediately I hit a hard object, a wondrous relic: a comb. Like a louse comb, and so old the ivory is dark brown, with tiny hatch marks. I showed it to Lucy Meleyatowit at the P.O. and she looked sad, saying only that the marks were "for a woman's days" (for birth control? or to warn when the zillion menstrual taboos would hit?). I recalled an Indian legend of Maman's, the girl running from the predator Moon. When she hurled her comb behind her, it turned into a mountain range, thwarting moon. Wish I could throw this one southward.

Lucy did not seem covetous. After that first melancholy she didn't want to even look at the comb. Later, admiring it in the lamplight, running it through my own ratsnest - ow - I realized I'm an idiot. The artifacts are their heirlooms and I flaunted the comb. Hope I didn't mention money. But it's more than that: people seem nervous if I ask about the old culture. The old technology is a safe topic and is praised by the outside, but was anything else? Is it fear of ridicule? Fear of the satanic? Or overkill from all the experts studying them. Protective. Maybe it is like asking an Anglo about his bank account. I'll lay it back in its tomb and hope kind Lucy never tells anyone, especially you-know-who. And I'll try not to ask.

Entry. I should be happy to be migrating soon but I'm not. The directness of life makes other places seem like chicken under Saranwrap. Here on this desolate, surly coast I feel alive. It's not even winter yet, just the ragged tail end of summer. At dawn I stood naked and let the gales lash me with breaker spray. Cacklers hastened south following the coast but I didn't want to go with them. I admire the life forms here that choose not to escape. I admire the people that made Gyulnyev theirs, and the gnarly plants that hug the bedrock. I don't want to face the Master and his disappointment over results, or my old man and his predictable questions that replace a father's usual glad greetings. "Get your grant?" (nei) "Find a noble proletarian job?" (nei) "Then why don't you get killed in Vietnam, you useless piece of mongrel skraeling shit."

At any rate, the "play" slicks are looking oily and in character. The Pucinellia-Carex sward is dormant and won't know it's dead until spring. I can sit back and watch the staging and orderly departures. I beachcomb, though it is poor pickings for a biologist, with immense ice scouring and no tidepools so the intertidal zone's barren (though out on the O.C.S it abounds with life, a plankton-clam soup). And I have a shitload of data to compile.

Entry. I can't get her off my mind though it seems a finished chapter. I avoid town, knowing the Ugungoraseoks return any day for the start of school. Willy came back early and invited me to hunt cormorants. He wrung their necks while they floundered in the waves, shot. They taste horribly fishy, naturally. His boat gives him so much more freedom than landlubbing women and scientists. He wanted me to lend gas money but I didn't have it (well, I have a little but need it to buy kerosene, since the fathomless night comes so early; what would I read by? I've run out of t.p. and use moss). Gas, in its land of origin, is astronomically priced and these boats eat it up, so Willy ended up selling a stash of ivory tusks to an agent. But he didn't want to talk about it.

And I had another dream after interring the comb again. It was G, she lay down beside me, her hair strewn out with those bits of lichen, like that first vision of her napping, and I took the comb and gently raked it. She may have shapeshifted into a wolf, but a kind one, one who still liked me. If she visited again I could read her poetry: "From whence you owe your strange intelligence? What seest thou else in the dark backward and abysm of time?".

Sigh. This yearning after the unattainable. She will never visit again, Tallin's does not pass over. Now the wild goose draws nigh to the high plains but "the bird of the soul is cut off and has lost the way. Do not act with violence like the drunken idiot". Sure, thanks for the advice.

IN ITIAK we heard the birdman hadn't left the peninsula yet. Still waiting for that goose. While digging *mazu* roots I came near his camp but never saw him. I dwelled on his accusation that I dabbled in angutkoq things just to look great or something. But maybe he had a point. Maybe if people knew I had *qilya* things would change, or at least their fear of *qilya* would elevate me. I dwelled on the bear and the fear in the birdman's eyes and Polly crawling in his tent, but most of all how he had smiled at me before things got bad. Asleep in my camp, rising up from the waves, his arm around me...did he still think of me?

After going back and forth about it a hundred times, I visited Calvin, the bone doctor's son. Partly I wanted to show off. Calvin claimed he was involved in levels of *inua* manipulation far deeper than I could ever go. I needed to ask about the bear, though.

In their little cabin Isaiah sat on the floor with his legs out straight, smoking a long-stemmed ivory pipe. He was the oldest man, maybe ninety, with snowy hair and holes in his lip where once he had worn bone labrets. Not many men were older than Abe - their hearts gave out, or the elements took them - so even people who frowned on his ways treasured Isaiah. Once I had seen Abe sneaking around the cabin after a long dry spell of hunting: before he entered he glanced around nervously, like he was having an affair. But of course God saw him.

Calvin was divining with old seal knuckle-bones for a couple of middle-aged brothers who needed help with hunting. Isaiah had cast the same little bones three generations earlier, for hunters long dead. The brothers were making soft conversation and smoking as they watched Calvin analyze the strewn patterns. Their payment of a bag of dried salmon lay in the *kanichak*. They didn't even glance up at me when I peeked in the inner door. I felt it was a manly thing and retreated, knowing Calvin would be curious and come out. I hadn't visited for a long time, and he'd want to know what I was up to. Sure enough, soon he stuck his head out.

"Heeey, Kayuqtuq! Wait up!" He pulled on his boots. Calvin was what Abe called "soft man". That was the most dangerous kind of angutkoq, one who specialized. He was pudgy with a limp and never hunted, though the animals might have come to him with his old *ataata*'s help. He kept a tidy cabin and cooked, since no woman volunteered.

It was Calvin who had taught me words for the spiritworld. For younger people, Inupiaq was a language that had been beaten down, narrowed into a vocabulary for some animals, a few body parts and everyday items. Not just the spiritworld had vanished, but those long, long words strung together for emotions and relationships, and the old human and animal and weather ways that were so complicated and mysterious. The mission had tied Abe to a hot radiator for talking it, so he didn't want to pass it on to the grandkids even if Dolores encouraged it now. I remembered the feelings that went along with talking it: soapsuds up my nose, the sting of rulers.

But Calvin knew everything. It was because of his dad Isaiah, who was so old he had grown up wild and was already a man by the time the missions came. Calvin's narrow face was set with little eyes as bright and fixed as snogo headlights coming at you over the frozen inlet. His square, wire-rimmed glasses always slipped down his nose, and his stringy hair hung in his eyes in an old-fashioned bowl cut.

"*Kanoqikpin?*" Calvin greeted me once he was outside. Showing off. College was where he got the glasses and picked up annoying ideas. All the old shamans had been men, for example. Calvin was changing history: even the books talked about female "sorcerers". He had read that too, but he sniffed and said they were Canadians, caribou people, at a lower level of culture than here. From his own dad I had heard of the woman who drowned men in her house with magic, singing witches who led aroused hunters to their deaths and revived them, and *uiliaqtaq* virgins who lured whales with their combs. There were women-bear-angutkoq, and the *aka* who made Tulunigraq, the raven-man. And there was Lucy's great aunt, who knew healing songs. But "girls don't got what it takes", Calvin always proclaimed.

I was too shy to ask the old Isaiah to back me up. So why did girls become angutkoq then? I asked. Calvin didn't know, until he went to college and learned it was "penis envy." Now he was going to change his cabin into the old-style *kazhgi* so women could not enter. Since I was the only woman who visited, it seemed directed at me. But maybe he was just teasing. After all, he might have to change into a woman *himself*, and marry a male spirit if it was required. So he said.

"Just talk English," I said tiredly. Calvin grinned, showing his steel tooth. His father had pulled the original when he was young and no dentist. I hated his straight-across bangs; no wonder he had no girlfriend (though it was rumored he had a boyfriend. It was rumored he kept dogs as wives). "How's *ataata*?" I asked him.

"Pretty good. Pretty old. He says he will pass on before next summer. How was camp?" He and Isaiah didn't go to camp - it was too much work.

"Okay, I guess. Biologist tent near there."

"I know. Hear he's good-looking."

I made the raven noise. "Says who?"

"Old ladies."

Too shrilly, I laughed. Calvin's eyes pierced me just as a sun ray glinted on his spectacles. A passerby glanced over from the darkening trail and I could imagine her recording in her memory: *Calvin and Kayuqtuq met at his house*. Information for the gossip line. "Let's go for walk," I said. "Over to old house." I meant the *ini*, the abandoned sod house that was still standing on the cliffs, the oldest part of Itiak. People didn't live down there anymore, segregating the past.

"Right here and now," said Calvin. He didn't like walking.

"Yes. *Ki*."

Of course he would go with me; though he hid it, he was eager in the way a woman is greedy to see what others have sewn, or a hunter is alert to what his brother brings home, promising themselves they won't compare. Calvin trailed after with his crippled foot so I slowed down to be polite. At the *ini* I sat against the grassy roof; the whalebone and driftwood beams still held it up, but the other *ini* had collapsed or fallen into the sea as the cliff fell apart.

It seemed every change of season was my favorite time of year but autumn was really the best. As the sky turned crimson, seagulls flew across it, departing from mounds of trash. A hint of sharp wood smoke bit my nose. Further down the coast, the birdman would be cooking dinner behind the duckblind, no doubt. If I hiked there before the sun went under I could see the low rays land on his eyes, turning them that honey color...would he be happy to see me? I shut the thought like a door. Dusk was falling too fast and I was not going to see him again.

The clear voices of children carried to us from up the beach where they were playing a last game of baseball. I used to play ball like that, until it was too dark to see. They used to fight to have me, for they were sure to win if I was on their team. I knew what other players would do before they knew themselves, I could hurl the ball hard enough to break bones and run while dodging. It made me glad, my only chance to be popular. It was a way to keep warm. And it kept me out the house of my old foster parents for a time.

Calvin cupped his hand to light a Kool. With his hair blowing back he appeared nicer. That bowl-cut made him look like one of the poor mission boys in old photos. He would hate it if he could read my mind - often it seemed he could. "Like my new haircut?" he asked, turning his profile. "They always wore it like this before the whites. Old Nation. Sometimes they shaved it on top too. Should I do that?"

"No," I said. "Please." We giggled lightly. "Hey, didn't those men walk around without pants with their *ququluq* hanging down?" I joked. Calvin raised his eyebrows remarkably high, like a clown.

"Now I *know* I want to get a time machine!" he said. I had a fit of laughing while Calvin waited for me to get serious, for I was procrastinating. Just thinking about what I had done made me jumpy.

I said at last, "How did they know which spirits they were capturing?"

"Who?"

"Angutkoq."

"Angutkoq?"

"*Eee.*"

"What spirits?"

"I'm asking *you!*" I scolded, "How did they know what *kind?*"

Calvin was not surprised. He took a drag and shivered, huddled in his shirt - in a typical bachelor conceit he hadn't worn a coat. "They always knew which *inua*," he said, "or how could they capture it?"

"But...sometimes...did they catch powerful ones, bad ones...and not even know it?"

He thought, drawing in smoke every few breaths. "Maybe. That was a danger. *Izhigii!* Only the strongest angutkoq would mess around with that."

"How come?"

"They turn against you if you don't have good control over yourself. They do some damage you don't plan on, to innocent people." Calvin pushed up his glasses and squinted at the whitecaps beating the cliff below us, giving up, swirling back to try again. "Once a shamish and his wife sewed a spirit from the parts of all kinds of animals and he cast a curse on it. It was like *palrai luk,* you know, a sea monster. It was supposed to go after his enemies but the shamish didn't do it right, so it was like a robot, going after anything it saw. And it killed him and his wife instead."

I shuddered. Calvin had a story for everything, like Abe. "You don't want to call on bad spirits," he said His face was dead-serious now. "Those days are past, and there's too much man-made evil on the loose already. There's black and white magic. It's not a whiteman kind of white. But that's the only kind people should practice, that don't hurt others. Or they better change careers." He said it in a rehearsed way, like he had considered practicing the opposite kind. Isaiah would have a fit though.

"And they can be like me," he said firmly, "I follow the Higher Order, to help the community, not myself. If people would only come, I would tell the *unipkaaq* stories everyone could see in their mind while I spoke, more powerful than a movie. I would lead those seances, everyone traveling together in the spiritworld to heal this village...or heal all the Inupiat nation."

As Calvin stared into the distance he looked almost saintly. But then I pictured him in the throes of an old-time trance: nude, struggling against ropes that bound him into a human ball, swallowing then regurgitating objects, snarling, howling for hours while everyone watched, beating spirits with an *usik,* the walrus penis bone. Quickly I put that image out of my head. Calvin would no doubt enjoy it but *I* would never go so far as that. There were things from the old days better left behind.

Calvin was saying dreamily, "*Eee,* they will confess their sins, and I'll drive out the bad feelings that bring evil..."

"They do that in church now," I pointed out, but it made Calvin look sour. I didn't think about the village except how to protect myself from it, and I didn't want a congregation. I just wanted to be left alone. I didn't like the idea of the End of the World, when Tulunigraq the raven-man would bring all souls back to live in harmony, after everyone had died. Calvin looked forward to it. Maybe I was Lower Order.

"Anyway, you're a girl," he said. "*Taimmani* - in the old days - girls sometimes did get the *qilya,* but only after they were old and couldn't have babies anymore. Or those young ones who wouldn't have sex. But they were always bad witches, because women are naturally jealous. They turned the evil eye on men to make them fall sick."

"Penis envy," I guessed. Calvin tittered. Sometimes I suspected he was an "unreliable source", like the birdman had written about me. More often than not I suspected he was *saglu*-ing. But he was all I had in the living, human world.

I looked over the cliff. In the sand a man's footprints made a long pattern, walking north. It wasn't an old man, by the stride, and a hunter would take a boat. I knew whose feet they were...my eyes stalked them to the point where they disappeared. When I saw his penis I had felt many things, but envy was not among them...

"*Eee,* bad spirits will always turn against you," Calvin was saying, his soft words hardly penetrating my reverie, "but the trouble is they're like whiskey: you get drunk on the power they give you, so you use them more. I saw that scientist," he said offhand, making me start. "Post office. I think a very bad *inua* made trouble for him; he has that look. I wonder why someone wants to hurt him."

"I don't know," I mumbled, trying to keep my face still, "Maybe someone's just fooling around."

"If he met a bad spirit the others will try to come and get him. They'll wait until he's real weak and then attack, like a wolf pack. He might have to purify himself, but maybe a whiteman can't purify. They are too polluted."

Purify. I had never heard of that. "Other bad spirits?" I asked in a small voice. Calvin raised his eyebrows into his low bangs and dropped them, regarding me. The glasses made his eyes smaller, peevish.

"Even more dangerous ones."

I swallowed with a dry throat. "Can they travel far away to find someone they're after? Like to Seattle? Or Africa," I added quickly.

"The moon, Neptune, don't matter. Distance is nothing to them," Calvin said. "People who don't know what they're doing should stay out of it. They'll make it worse. And they shouldn't think the *qilya* comes from them, that they are better than other humans. It comes from *inua*. A hunter starts thinking he's smarter than the animals and he doesn't thank them, forgetting they allow it, and one day the animals are gone because they get mad at proud and selfish hunters. It is a sin. And one day they get even by taking *his* life."

I looked at Calvin sidelong. *He* looked proud of himself, like a preacher. "I could see that naluagmiu if it gets worse," he said. "I think I know what to do." He flicked his Kool to the ground. "Or *Ataata* will." I was silent, polite enough not to voice my doubts. As we walked back into town, I was thinking hard, while trying to shield my thoughts from the shrewd Calvin. I had to warn the birdman.

In my inner vision I saw him. He is trudging down the beach, head down. A loon passes over with frantic wings and her funny talking-to-herself, heading into the waves to catch a fish, one last fish to give her strength for her journey. But his mind has grown too heavy and dark to care anymore about birds. He won't take notes, and there is no smile to light up his face. Then he stops and lifts his gaze and with a jolt to my heart I see into his eyes. I see the trust shining out, the anger, and sorrow. He is skeptical, *kuangazuk*, beautiful...lost.

And he'll never find his goose.

I could not leave him dangling on a cord to hell with no escape, even at a university in Seattle.

CHAPTER 13

And wilt thou have me fashion into speech
the love I bear thee, finding words enough,
And hold the torch out while the winds are rough
Between our faces, to cast light on each?

BROWNING (NALUAGMIUT WOMAN)

ENTRY. SUNSET, early afternoon. The clock broke. The Wolf eats ever bigger chunks of sun each day (here it's a marauding wolverine who steals the light). Still no money: punishment from the Master for not reporting with unctuous letters, so I'm stranded. I saw a weasel-turning-into-ermine staggering off with the last of my dry salmon. I fantasize about juicy drumsticks.

Sleet and dreary leaden sky, some nights so cold that tall crystals grow in the soil and my bucket is solid ice. Camping's a drag. After an early dinner of nothing much I crawl in the tent, light the lamp and huddle "in darkness hatching vain empires", but the kerosene's nearly gone. It's so gusty and the wood and matches so sodden that fires won't light. I'm nearly out of matches. No laundromat, no dime anyway, and clothes won't air-dry so I don't wash them. My nose runs like one of the kids with their perpetual snot, and no tissue. My hair is stiff with sea salt. I stuffed my rubber boots with dried grass and it really works, but my fingers are insensate from the icy wind, knuckles locked up. No Hunter's Response, that trait that lets you work barehanded on metal in the winter; I missed that gene, damn. My eardrums ache. And it's only September.

But it is pretty in a melancholy way. Everything has turned, foliage and fur. The tundra is a patchwork of crimson and blazing yellow and even shades of purple, and each tiny leaf is rimmed with frost as if nature is a jewelry maker. Owls are all white now and I sighted a pied fox, half-white, pouncing on lemmings. A ridiculous sight. I almost expect to wake up a different color too, but I'm already "white" no matter what matter what color I really am, which is bleached (Willy clued me in to the meaning of my nickname "Hey Nalockmew").

The moon rules on clear nights, swollen and golden. In the overcast, the wind draws back the cloudbank and the moon looks down like a great shining eye...the Animal Master. Now I know the meaning of Dark, and of moon and stars. I found an archaic stone lamp in the cliff and am skeptical I could survive with it. They used to float little wicks in oil and that was their winter source of heat and light; it would take forever to melt snow or cook.

The ocean has turned a sullen hue and seems...I don't know...vaster, the breakers more alive and intentional. In the bird species still lingering I hear a note of desperation in their calls now, urging their clumsy juveniles to get with it. Some youths who hatched too late are left to flounder and lag in their own organizations. I wonder if they ever make it.

Am I slowly starving? This lightheadedness could be due to hormonal surges. Testosterone levels are highest in autumn, catalyzed by almost anything. Next time Willy goes seal-hunting I won't turn down a portion. I'll give him the tape recorder. Should look him up soon, but am not eager to run into either of his sisters. And I am grody.

Later: Oops, but I did kind of run into G, in the disastrous ball game. She didn't talk to me or anything, nor did anyone else afterward, for I was in disgrace. I hate sports. Enough said.

THE BIRDMAN could not play baseball. He could run fast and catch and even throw, but he had no understanding. He was on his way home from the post office when a group of young adults on the beach invited him to play outfield. I was watching from the path - I'd never played since I was twelve. He probably could tell his team was furious behind their smiles when he immediately let the other team get a home run, and he quickly left. When he was still within earshot I joined in the laughter as Stanley mimicked his *kuangazuk* way, holding the ball and looking dumbfounded while people ran around him like reindeer.

"Their rules are different," explained Polly, when she heard the news. "Jeez, didn't you ever see it in Nome?" I looked at her like she was crazy. "They don't all run together," she told me patiently, "only one runs; the one who hits. It's individualism."

It wasn't his fault then. No one had explained. He must have felt the way I did at high school that first horrible day when they gave me a locker and I couldn't open it but all my things were inside, and the town kids had jeered every time we villagers made a mistake or talked. I wanted to hurry and tell everyone why the birdman had played so stupidly, to redeem him, but thought better of it.

ENTRY. WENT INTO town, no mail. All families are back now from far-flung camps. People who had never seen me before stared. Don't know if it's the race thing, the hair, that I'm

156

a secret agent or that I'm just weird. I perceived no hostility except from the asshole store owner, and got some smiles when up close. The kids always love me. And those big puppies tore holes in my gloves and pants. At one point there were a dozen trying to pull me down; I was wading through them, covered in slobber. They don't do this to anyone else. The village watched, entertained. You are supposed to kick dogs and not worry about the Humane Society. These whelps sensed my reticence to hurt them.

Met a woman anthropologist swinging through on a study of child-rearing practices (I know why there's such an influx of them here: the war has shaken Americana like WWII did the Europeans; they want proof they aren't intrinsically bloodthirsty. Those Stone-age Tasaday recently "discovered" have them all excited. Hard to believe a society exists with no word for hate or murder). She's going next to Red China - Nixon has forged the way, and has been branded a communist.

The P.O. is a trip, a local hang-out. A vigilante operates the radio there. He's fervently National Guard, in uniform, hair bristling. He wants to intercept pinko propaganda from Siberia, or their plot to attack, so he studies Russian and monitors the airwaves. People ignore him, indulgent of, well, different behavior. Who knows what they say behind his back.

Visited the Ugungoraseoks. Abe was out hunting and Polly has gone to Nome for training so I breathed easier. I wanted to apologize to her before I left, and explain my psychotic break was a stored adolescent bout with acid working its way into the bloodstream as my fat cells shrink. But Polly's flown. G was gone too, whew - Flo said she was at a camp at the lagoon seining for "all different kinda fish" and had taken the children too, though it makes the teachers mad.

Their place is the typical one-room shanty of tarpaper, plywood and tin on pilings, a bit tilted from permafrost shift. The pilings are to prevent total meltdown. Outside: a driftwood cache with bloated bags made of seals, the funny "Muck" bouncing on a chain, dog unuck everywhere, a forest of reindeer antlers and one set of moose, a beautifully crafted wooden dogsled, and framed seal hides in various stages of processing. A ton of gear and fur and stuff jams the entryway-stormshed, which has inner and outer doors to trap cold and make it pitch black. I knocked on the outside, unsure if it was the right house (but it was Muck!) and no one answered but I heard a radio, so tripped through the dark cave and tried on the inner door. Flo's voice was in there, laughing, "Just come in!"

Inside, no plumbing or electricity; a foot-powered sewing machine and wind-up phonograph. They heat with an oil cook-stove, also a Coleman and woodburner made of a fifty-five gallon drum: looks dangerous. And boy do they heat; it was so toasty within a minute my tent-acclimated skin was sweating. I smelled seal oil, machine oil and oil paints with undertones of fish and blood, fur, fresh laundry, baking bread, Pinesol-human waste blend and turpentine. And my own underarms, yikes, I shall have to be more careful in this land where no one pits out. A sink drains waste water outside. A water barrel can catch any summer rain. A hole is cut in the wall for circulation with a coffee can inserted, the lid swinging as a flap.

The table's a low Japanese-like affair of plywood; there's also the card table, bread dough rising on it and a few chairs but mostly you sit on the floor. It's like you're between eras. Two-by-four and plywood beds line the walls, curtained off - for the adults I guess, since the kids were napping on a reindeer skin on the floor - and a cramped assortment of handmade dressers, chests and shelves. Like a boat's focs'le. A very ancient shriveled grandmother sat on the floor; at first I didn't notice her. A curtain makes a bathroom corner for the honeybucket. Another corner was full of ivory dust and a drill, a clamp, engine parts. A stiff seal hide ready to be scraped. A dried tail of a ptarmigan. Gretchen's little red riding hood thingie in a sewing pile. A calendar with an ethereal blonde Christ, and...an easel (!?) with a painting of the granny.

A behemoth oogrook lay on bloody cardboard, halfway flensed of its amazing fat supply and oozing oil. Flo brought it in because it was getting sloppy and dark outside. She butchers jackknifed at the waist. She didn't care to talk, seeming timid with only her and the granny there. I felt shy. Flo's "Eskimo name" means "shy", Ilira, so what a bind we were in. She was making soup from walrus blood (because they are so enormous the men butcher them out on the floes and save the blood-drenched snow). She didn't offer me that. She fed me some ribs, explained the dry tail was a napkin and told me how to get to Willy's. G lives there sometimes; right now they're housing an artist instead who spent all summer painting "Aka".

If I visited Willy I'd probably run into her. I wanted to. Seeing her coat-dress stirred me into forgiveness. Her "sending" the bear like it's a familiar is so anachronistic it's cute (never let her know). It's funny now, that part about rubbing noses: too slow for Polly. But touché. There is so much crap in the old tracts about "wife-trading", which really excited those self-important Victorian chauvinists. They took advantage. Their sick views of other cultures still predominate. I was too ticked off to let G know I <u>did</u> know: you could just as well call it "husband swapping", an agreement to enhance survival through more kinship bonds. Vikings did it as an alternative to pillage. Willy told me all about sharing: if you want to hunt or pick berries on someone's ancestral haunts, all you have to do is ask. They assume I don't have a clue, like only they are decent in the world, but maybe it's a view based on the specimens of whites they have met. If only I had a chance to let G know I get it.

No one was at Willy's hovel. The door has no lock but I didn't go in; people may roam each other's homes freely, go through things, that's cool, but I cannot. Though a red diaper baby I am not communistic and own a heart of bleached sealskin and a bourgeois sense of privacy and property.

When I passed the schoolhouse the teacher Dolores beckoned me from the window, so I went in. Their quarters are shockingly luxurious: lights from diesel generator, hot water, central heating, wringer and dryer, shag carpet, bedrooms. Still a honeybucket though. They keep a white cat abandoned by the prior teachers who broke contract and jumped ship. The village fears this cat; it's some kind of malevolent spirit. Maybe that's why the other teachers fled, in the spring, no explanation. But first they ran around the school stark naked with a gun.

Dolores had heard I've run out of supplies. Now I know why people stare: I'm a buffoon. Her schoolkids report everything as the town criers and spies. I didn't turn down her offer of food; even if I had cash, the store has only a few withered carrots. Well, tons of candy, cake mixes, Jello, Kool whip, pop and Sailor Boy crackers (plus bullets for getting real food). D fed me from government supplies and packed a box for me and hovered. I scarfed like a refugee or Hop o'my Thumb while keeping an eye out for the returning ogre.

She's quite open about the harm schools have wrought on Natives. Early schools were in charge of the trading posts, so had a stranglehold. Even now teachers hold some kind of exalted, paternalistic status. The Sterns hate it. She wonders what will come of the Land Claims Settlement, if Itiak will really benefit: at what price modernization? She says she is modern but something's missing; that's why she lives in remote places. Can you take the positive elements of the Outside - a road, a sewer - and leave the rest, or do you have to swallow the whole beast and sell your soul? Is she a hypocrite, to want to deny goodies to people? Do I know they are using the smallpox blanket method to kill Amazon Indians who resist roads, hamburger farms and mining, and isn't there a lot of oil under the jungle?

I just nodded, cramming in copious amounts of food, perhaps in an arctic frenzy like the bears before they hibernate. If she feeds me she can proselytize. Empty calorie whiteman food never tasted so fine. As I was wiping my mouth on my sleeve in came the Principal. He made a show of being glad to see me and I escaped, but not before he asked how I avoided military duty. Heh heh. I told him I wet the bed, and Dolores scolded him; it was a "John Birch question". It's taboo to pry into a fellow whites' past, why you came to Alaska. You could be a felon as soon as nature lover. Bill chuckled, avuncular, "Only a tribute to his youth, Door."

I can't figure out their vibes or the cryptic looks he sends his wife. There is an ineffable tension in that house. I escaped fast with my belly sticking out, like a gull or wolf, to regurgitate later for its young.

Later. Saw a poster at the P.O. for the movie at the "Center", which also has a generator. It sounds sublime: "The Good, the Bad and the Ugly" (missed last week's double feature of "Dr. Strangelove" and "The Grapes of Wrath" . Hmm, interesting selection of movies here). Willy can share my still untouched reefer and we can find the underlying messages. I'm curious about his philosophies. He's thoughtful under his fun demeanor, and tight-lipped about certain things such as his mysteriously linked sort-of sister. He'll go on at length about the behavior of animals (if he's not hunting them). But often, mum, like the mystics who will not pronounce the name of their god.

Maybe I had no luck at sighting my liglick because I kept blabbing about it. From now on if someone asks me a question I'll think about it a long time before saying, "I don't know," or even better, "Maybe."

Entry. How to describe events? I was beachcombing. A clod hit me on the head. She was up on the cliff with Muck...and the white bucket. I tried smiling but it felt weak, for I am a Conquistador. And a scientist is no better, for "Do not all charms fly at the mere touch of cold Philosophy"? She jumped down and seemed in a friendly, even contrite mood. Hard to tell under the omnipresent shades. The weather is a universal icebreaker, but I had to say something inane and eggheady, "cumulonimbus". See your goose yet? she asked, but like she meant it, not in that Itiak teasing. I said no, and there went my promise to obscure, the damnable truth-programming. "Maybe", I said too late, which made her smile.

Go up to the top, she said. "Kee!" (That means "come on, man"). She had me climb first, and at the overhang I pulled her the rest of the way but I over-pulled because she is light and she flew into the air and crashed. "Ungookaw. Strong," she muttered. "How do they get strong, those scientists?" I puffed up my biceps and told her it's from agricultural labor. My grandmere has a farm in Quebec where I mow the hay with a scythe. I mimed for her and she watched dubiously until I stopped, unsure if she was amused.

"You heal up okay?" she asked softly, then, Lo, she took my hand again and ran her thumb along the scar, feeling me like a blind person in shades. "Your hand's alapaw". That means cold. It was just an observation but I felt it was a slight, as in, "bleached sealskins are not made for this climate." My nose was running too, disgracefully. I wanted to tell her "cold hands, warm heart" but I wasn't sure how she'd take it. I heated up remarkably fast under this...er...ministration. She felt my sinews, maybe wondering if they could be used for sewing. "Slender," she said.

"Bony," I corrected. She smiled kindly and picked up her bucket and started off with her dog, both looking back like Lassie. I was supposed to follow. Bemused - that's the word - I hulked after her, a cyborg that had crash-landed from another planet and had been reassembled by an aboriginal High Priestess. Of what use would she make of me? Where were we going?

We came to an underground "eenee" like on the mainland. Its sod walls were overgrown with beach grass, saxifrages, heliotrope, dead poppies and fireweed, and were supported by old driftwood planks. Bleached whale ribs framed the long, low passageway. It's really a hobbity house, but it reminded me of a grave, a barrow. Or somehow uterine. She leaned against its roof, soaking up the autumnal sun. I wrestled with the urge to ask why we were there. They would beat me to death in a zen monastery with a cudgel. I could see Gretchen as the teacher. Whack. "Silence! It must not be explained! You will know when the time has come." At last she asked if I wanted to go inside, which I took as an imperative.

The idea of hibernating bears gave me pause but I crawled down the dank tunnel. Little caved-in plank nooks lined this passageway. After about eight feet of dark at a slight incline - cold trap - I went up and emerged into the inner chamber. Light filtered from a hole in the roof so I could make out a raised platform in the rear. It was surprisingly roomy. But the leviathan bones and darkness gave the impression of being in a whale's stomach, swallowed alive. It looked like there had once been a floor of planks, but these had been ripped out. For coffins, I read, during the epidemics.

The air had a clean dirt-grassy smell with a tinge of lemming pee. When I crawled out G had taken off the sunglasses. This seemed to be a signal that we weren't mad anymore. "How is it?" she asked. I thought it wise to be upbeat; the hut was important to her, maybe because it's a pre-contact dwelling. A heritage thing? A test maybe. I said it was cozy with good construction and she raised her eyebrows (it means "I agree"). "You can live here," she said. "It will get cold." She did not meet my eyes; hers were unshaded now but elusive, black and mysterious and fixed out to sea. A far horizon is useful here in the land of fleeting eye contact. She seemed different, as conflicted as ever but urgent, like she needed something but I was supposed to mind-read what it was.

"You can ask Village Council to let you stay here," she said, "and you won't have to pay room and board." So, the whole place knew of my penury. It's that shopkeeper William or whoever was listening in; I had stupidly tried to get credit at the store. He didn't let me and seemed pleased to see a whiteman down on his luck. I doubt poverty ennobles one anywhere, or endears you to the populace. But Gretchen's a fellow bum. I saw sympathy in her face, concern. She idly fondled Muck's ears with her small hand. She has a heart after all.

I looked at the sea, which in a few weeks will be frozen. I looked at the hamlet not too far away. And the angootcock, her eyes narrowed against the sun, noble profile, black mane thrashing in the wind like an Icelandic pony. Why should I leave, only to drag all the gear back at breakup? The feudal politics of the university, ass-licking, the rat-scrabble mazes to get the paltry cheese, the Dutch Harbor horror factory every break. The urbanity of it, the parking lots and lawns with plastic-geese of it: it quelled me. And no one like Gretchen. Anywhere in the world.

I suddenly entertained a ploy to get the Master to agree to my staying on; he seems to have forgotten my existence anyway. I could collect more ethnographic data and interview all the locals. Fuck the oil drones if they can't handle anecdotal evidence. What's existence like here for the majority of the year, in the grip of the ice and the Great Dark? What does Gretchen do? "I can't stay," I told her, regret clogging my voice.

"But...you don't need money. Putuck...Willy and them can let you eat, and give fuel. You like our food, you can hunt with them. You can put down reindeer skins and be warm. And you can look at birds in spring for free. What else do you need?" She met my eyes, hypnotizing me with a depth of meaning I didn't get. Was there ever a hipper question? Like Zorba's, and ingenuous, the words of a true hunter-gatherer. "And you don't got a girlfriend down there," she pointed out with her uncanny insight.

I think I laughed in disbelief; my head spun at the implications, at what she seemed to be hinting. I stammered, "But it's...er...duh...it's not really money." I won't try to record verbatim the gibberish that then spewed from my mouth: I think I went on about my indentured servitude, my balancing act with the geese on the open maw of the War Machine. It must have sounded so alien, so asinine. Case in point, if my radical mode is the face of the Enemy incarnate then why not shave and go in disguise, do I have a death wish? and when I saw her puzzling it out I said lamely, "Life down there is too complex and absurd to explain."

"So you will just wait for your plane ticket?" she asked with a little frown. I nodded. "But maybe I don't want you to leave," she said, so softly I thought I'd hallucinated it by sheer will. My mind stilled in a shock. Then she turned to face me in a ritualistic grace. She was very close. My senses had heightened after the dark hut. The low angle of sun lit up her face, her ebony eyes reflecting the rays so that they seemed to be burning oxygen in a subterranean fire. Her expression was as enigmatic as a Noh mask.

"So, have we made up?" That was me, instantly regretting the snottiness. But I meant it. I didn't know, had we made up? You're probably not supposed to mention any past ill-feelings. She gave no warning, no projection of her intentions. Her eyes had altered to a soft and velvety tenebrous night. She tilted up her face in that unambiguous species-specific signal, which triggered an instant and powerful reaction. My vision hazed over, my nether region flooded, almost painfully. I was thinking I should countermove but I felt paralyzed, and what about all that evil whiteman history she'd flung at me last time we met? When suddenly she had undone my belt. A glance down verified.

What can you say? The speech mechanism was locked up anyway and I couldn't breathe enough to operate it. She kept her eyes on mine, and hers were shot with an undescribable quality, something like...fear? combined with a detective's concentration sorting out the tangle of evidence. She never looked down, she kept those incapacitating eyes on mine. And she grasped me, warm beyond belief. In a remote sector of my mind I tried to figure out why. It seemed like a kind of contest; it was a mutual contract, I guess, yet I struggled to not be overcome. The dog watched the whole thing.

It happened bare seconds after contact and the noise that came from my throat was animalistic. I kind of collapsed backward, caught by the hut. She maintained the grip, assessing the changes in vascular tension, maybe. Her eyes held surprise. And she released and stepped back, seeming alarmed and confused by what had been accomplished so swiftly without effort. She looked in fascination at her hand that held my product. And then blushed (a bit late). My muscles were jellified with no strength to do the quick refastening of fly, etc. I could only watch as she wiped her hand on the beachgrass. Yeah, it was awkward.

So...the maid-of-the-tundra has a little gross and pragmatic knowledge, nothing subtle. She's picked up info from the sled dogs. But it's not her fault, no more than it was Mowgli's for acting like a wolf. Having had the honor of being introduced to the culture's sex through the fluent health aide, I'm not going to stereotype. And who am I to talk?

She slowly held out the pail with averted eyes and murmured, "Here." I just gaped at the strange, wilted sea creatures in the bucket. What more do you need, she'd asked. Food, shelter...orgasms...how copacetic! "You boil water and put them in. Don't put salt," she explained, as if their cooking method was what stupefied me, and then she pointed out some minty plant in the sand I could throw in the pot too (later in the bottom of the pail I found an assortment of smelt, trout, whitefish and herring, lagoon catch).

"Don't let anyone see," she added on an urgent note before heading back to the village with the dog. She could have given me her phone number at least, ha. I can't identify her motives any more than those geoduk-oids.

The oracle nods and says calmly, well, this is a connection between the primal powers. Yin is rising, and yang should give way and not try to control things. And I don't want to leave Itiak now.

THE TINGLING of my palm would not fade. That night after Willy slept I used that same hand to run over my skin until it ached and I shuddered, wanting to cast off my skin and fly. And as easy as water I slid through the air vent into the night and flew. Above me stars were like pinpricks on black paper held up to the lamp. *Tuttu*, the Caribou constellation, was digging in the snow with its antlers. Behind me the lights of the village winked in the blackness, below me whitecaps reflected the wan starlight. The ocean rose and fell, the chest of a sleeping giant, and under its deep sighing keened the thin howl of dogs.

Down the pale coast I flew. My goal was one small point of light, a beacon on the black, rushing leg of the channel. What kind of man lived so far from any village or friend? In legends it was never a man but a spirit dwelling in the Otherworld, or some kind of monster, and beware the lost hunter who moved toward that strange light.

I floated down until I hovered above the tent, which shone with a welcoming yellowy-green from its internal lamp. Through the fabric I could see the birdman stretched out, propped on his elbow. His breath smoked out white from his nostrils. He was wearing his hat and strange gloves with the fingertips gone, and he was writing and writing, confiding to his secret book. He blew on his fingers so he could write more. He frowned and smiled a little; once he laughed out loud. It was a dark laugh mixed with delight and many other unknown ingredients, which made me blush again in my spirit cheeks and regret I had flown to spy on him and hear it. Still, he looked happier, and that gladdened me.

It also made me fear. My plan was just to feed him and show him the *ini*, maybe lift his spirits a little. He would be safer underground, like a fish in a cellar. But with a will of its own my hand had taken his and felt the bones warm until both our hands burned. What I did next surprised me as much as him - even Polly would be amazed. He let me; if he didn't like it he could have stopped me, isn't it? But he seemed at a loss to do anything or say anything under my hand. And he had trembled. His eyes turned wide and then slowly lost focus as he surrendered, and he had to lean against the *ini* for support. I didn't know the act would exhaust a man; in my only experience they had slunk back into the dark like white-eyed ghouls, hiking up their pants.

And now he had the wrong idea! He had given himself to me, he offered himself just like an animal does to the hunter, and silently we agreed he was going to stay and he was mine after all, not Polly's. But what was I supposed to do with him *now*?

I watched him as with downcast eyes he read from a book near his elbow and took a note. Even my angutkoq vision could not penetrate his thoughts. When the birdman was in doubt he turned to his books and was self reliant in his little nest of a tent. But I had no one to call on. Calvin advised me on the spirit realm but he was useless in the earthly ways of men.

If my true mother was alive she could help me, she could tell me what to do besides flap around at night like a demon making trouble. She would understand and love me no matter how funny I was. But she probably would not understand. Surely she had feared and hated outsiders. She wouldn't know about biologists who didn't want anything from you, who won their way into your affection and talked with you until the birds slept and aroused your hopes and foolishness and remorse...and your body...everything, and then slept with someone else and made you cry alone on the mountain. And then tried to leave.

Do what is right, she would advise, *In your heart you will know.* But I do not know what is right, Mother, I cannot find my heart.

The birdman stopped the restless scratching of the pen to stare into the flame. His eyelids grew heavy. His face slackened from the trouble on it and grew serene as his head settled onto his arms. The pen rolled from his fingers - had I really held that hand? - and now his eyes were closed and flickering back and forth, already watching dreams. *Don't go to sleep with the kerosene burning!* My thoughts reached him and he stirred, reaching out to douse the wick.

In old times the angutkoq could see in the dark. But I could not.

CHAPTER 14

His soul shall taste the sadness of her might,
And be among her cloudy trophies hung
KEATS (NALUAGMIUT)

Using runes of love, I overpowered witches
(ANCIENT NORSE)

I WAS CARRYING MEAT home from the Apukinas, whom I often had to help because they were Abe's relatives. My hand bones ached. We had cut all day outside, the wet wind slicing through me like an *ulu* itself, with stray snowflakes. As I neared them, Willy's dogs sniffed meat and cried bitterly. Drifting from the *kanichak* was the pungent smell of burning grass. Puzzled and tired out, I did not realize we had a visitor. When I banged open the inner door the birdman was there, lounging on my cot in his bare feet with his laundry hanging everywhere to dry. He started and swung his legs over the side like he'd been caught. His muscles were coiled, ready to move fast. I thought he might either leap past me into the night or straight into my arms.

Inside a house and on my bed he was even more outlandish. At least he wasn't like some hairy whites whose odor hit you across a crowded room. No, I liked the birdman's scent, and didn't mind if it lingered on my blanket. But he couldn't be here! It was like a game of checkers - it was his turn to move in on *my* territory and be "a somewhat unwanted guest". But whose fault was that? I had gone down his pants and now he thought he was my boyfriend who could visit my house. It was fine for *me* to enter *his* camps far from society, on my terms, on foot or flying, but that was summer and in the country where only birds were watching.

Winter was different. There was no escaping he was *naluagmiusak*. The instant he stepped out the door the whole village would know he visited, if they didn't already, and speculation would fly from church to post office. And the birdman had seen my underwear I didn't put away yet - thankfully it was clean - and I noticed he had *papak*-ed my shelf and moved my toy troll, the one with blue hair. What did he think about *that*? I stood with my bucket, eyes on the floor in a confusion, and blushed as I remembered what I did the last time we met. In the thick silence, I grew aware of the gore in my hair and up my wrists.

Willy strolled in from the outhouse. "Hey Kayu! We're starving!" I didn't return his greeting. Was he happy to see me or just the meat I carried? All of a sudden the cabin seemed full of hungry men, the table littered with cigarette butts overflowing from a jar lid and crumbs everywhere like twenty children had raided the house.

"Pataq, for crying out loud!" I said, "You can't smoke inside." We had made an agreement.

Willy slid his eyes over to his buddy. "Long day, ah?"

The remark burned, and I was just about to drop the load of meat and walk out when the birdman sprang off the bed. "Let me take that!" He smiled close to my face as he stooped for the bucket's handle, and the grass smoke odor hung thick in his hair. I smelled soap too; he'd washed it. A lock hung like a corkscrew over his eye. I wasn't sorry for him anymore, just for myself, for having no place to hide. For a second I hung onto the pail, then let go fast so he lost his balance. "*Angukaa*," he said to Willy.

Willy laughed uproariously, sprawled on his cot. I was grimy and tired, and they were teasing me. "What shall I do with this?" asked the birdman. When I didn't answer he turned to Willy. "Should I cook this?"

"Gretchen," said Willy formally, "Did you know this whiteman used to be a vegetable before he came here?"

The birdman chuckled, "No, a vegetarian. But I want to eat some of this, I really do."

"He really does," said Willy. I looked from one man to the next. They exchanged a sly look like they'd pulled off a joke and weren't discovered yet. What, were they engaged to each other? I almost asked. The birdman carried the bucket to the table and found the cutting board.

"You don't know how to cook *ugzruk*," I told him.

He waved my *ulu,* which Abe had made for me. "What's so hard about it? Not to downplay the feminine." He lined up the curved blade with my eyes across the room, and sighted along it. "I cook, you rest." He dumped all the meat on the board and began slicing off chunks, but he was holding the *ulu* wrong; he was going to chop off his fingertips. He bent over to pick at a muscle layer. Suddenly he looked up and saw me still standing there. "*Ki!*" he urged me, cocking his head at a chair; I was supposed to sit.

"*Ki!*" echoed Willy, laughing himself silly. I didn't need a whiteman or any man cooking for me, and none ever had except this one. They cooked at camps only if a woman wasn't along. But if I argued Willy might get the idea the scientist and I knew each other better than I was pretending.

"Someone cuts funny even for a man," I muttered.

"Ya, it is yust nuts but dat is de vay vee do it in Ballard," the birdman replied in a singsong voice, and Willy had to wipe tears from his giggling face but I refused to smile. I went out to break the ice in the barrel, washing my arms and bangs in the yard before hauling the water in. Sitting on my cot, I pulled my knees to my chin, making myself small, feeling the smallness of the cabin close in, and tried to sort out the mess I'd made of things. The situation was as tangled up as the webbed underside of a beadwork.

The birdman said he couldn't explain the complexity of his life, but it seemed simple and free compared to mine. He was white, a man, an outsider and a longhair, so he could do whatever he wanted like he was the only person alive and it didn't matter that everyone was watching and judging. And he denied the spirits, not caring what they thought either. He had no idea what danger he was in, but his stubbornness kept me from warning him. He didn't believe I called the spirit and thought I just said that from spite, like I was evil. Maybe I *was* evil. And surely now he thought Itiak women were easy.

He found the kettle, filled it with too much water and plunked it on the stove. When he picked up my *ulu* again he looked at it like he'd never seen it before, fingering the antler handle and testing the blade. What was his problem? "Hey, that's for girls!" cried Willy, suddenly noticing the *ulu* in his hands. "It's the moon shape; you can't use it."

"Really? Far out."

The birdman seemed happy to be breaking a rule. He thought customs were stupid or old-fashioned. That was worrisome - what would he do next? Had he told Willy about us? He sliced the meat, and it was bugging to see he had figured out the right angle and could cut fine, though in tiny chunks only good for tomcod bait. A few minutes later for no reason I could see, a short laugh burst out of him, like at a private revelation. *He's nuts*, I thought. He threw the meat into the pot and shook in a lot of salt, keeping it on a high boil. I was on strike and didn't say a word. Let Willy suffer through the meal; it would serve him right for letting him stay. When the naluagmiu began to *papak* through the food crate I couldn't stand it.

"What's he looking for?" I asked Willy, who was softly picking his guitar.

"Spices," said the birdman. "Urbs?"

"Does he mean those green things?" I asked, but Willy shrugged, uninterested. The birdman was studying our dry goods with his head tilted to the side, the Man on the Moon visiting Earth for the first time. There wasn't a lot to choose from, since Willy always gave his money to Flo and didn't shop. If we needed something I got it from the main house, or we ate there. Finally he took a box of pilot bread and checked in the kettle.

"It's done. I guess. Come and get it!"

At the table Willy and I looked at the food then at each other. "Someone forgot seal oil," I muttered, and went to get it, the most important part. I had to admit the meat tasted like mine - only diced - but I had no appetite. When the birdman's knee touched mine under the little table I pulled away. We didn't look up from the food and the men were done as fast as dogs and Willy was burping.

"I'm paying Tingmiaq's way to the movie," Willy told me. "He don't even got a dime. You coming?"

I didn't have a dime either, I realized. I started to clear the table, but the birdman jumped up and took the plate from me, offering to help. I tried to grab it back and we had a little tug-o'-war until "*No!*" I snapped, and he let go. But he was in my way, and towering over me. I wanted to reach up and pull that funny coil of hair and see if it sprang back exactly in place on his forehead.

"Move off the *way*," I ordered, using Abe's tone if I got in his path. When the birdman didn't cooperate I put one hand on his chest and pushed a little. He slowly backed up with a curious expression, and sat again to watch me finish. Willy took no notice of our battle and had gone back to his cot to lounge there with magazines, belching. As I washed dishes at the counter under the window, my spine could feel the birdman's eyes still watching.

"So are you going?" he asked my back in a quiet voice. "To the movie?"

"I hate movies."

"Then I'm not going either."

I turned around. He looked serious and - I was unhappy to see - very handsome. The heat between his legs had amazed me, out there in the cold wind, and the silky-hardness of his sex inside his clothes and what surged out hot and startling, the life-force of the birdman. My throat was dried out so it couldn't swallow. "Willy, I'm not going," he said, eyes on me.

Willy sighed and put down the old *Life* magazine. He had been looking at the pictures of the dead villagers in Vietnam, again. The babies. "Okay, we can play cards then."

"Go ahead and play cards, just don't let them catch you," I said, turning back to the dishes. "Me, I'm going to movie."

"Kayuqtuq!" cried Willy, laughing. "She's like that, like the wind always play change direction." It grew quiet. When I glanced around again Willy was pulling on socks and the biologist was watching me, this time like a wolf trying to judge a trap, whether to grab the fat or run. *Ameguq.* When I caught him he looked down fast.

IN THE END I DIDN'T go out. It was *saglu* I didn't like movies - I loved them, and the Student Council wouldn't turn me away for having no dime. My problem was the Center we had outgrown, with everyone packed in and on display. Someone - Christine, probably - would come up to me the next day, smiling and batting her mascara eyes, "How's your naluagmiu?"

It was a moonless dark with big, wet snowflakes splatting down and not a good night for camping; still, I was hoping the birdman would go back to his tent right after the movie. But he returned with Willy - they were still laughing about some mysterious thing. I sat on my bed, paging through an old book a teacher had given me, *A Tale of Two Cities*. I was afraid he was going to test me about it or act surprised I read novels, but he didn't bother me. They pulled chairs to the stove and ate a whole box of pilot bread with Nabob jam and dryfish. It was amazing; where did they *put* all that food? The birdman was saying the *bad* cowboy was a symbol of everyone in authority, which made Willy laugh. Their topic meandered like a river, their low man-voices lulling me. Willy asked about the weather in Seattle.

"Mild," said the birdman, "it might bore you. Imagine a rainy summer day and that's winter. It snows once a year, everyone gets to crash their car on the hills, then it melts by morning." Holy cow, said Willy. And there were millions of cars, malls and condominiums "going up" everywhere, and multinational corporations growing in power. They sounded bad, like tall monsters, and when the birdman pronounced their names he had a superior expression, or like he had stepped in dog *anaq*. If I didn't *try* to understand the unknown words but just relaxed I could often see the images, what he was creating in his mind. I could do that with the old people and their Inupiaq. It was enough to get the idea. Plus I had seen movies of cities.

He talked of "cereal" killers and rapists of both women and nature, which put me on edge. He switched to weather again and it was worse. Disasters were on the way. In the future, the way cities were growing and burning coal and oil, the temperature would rise, the ice caps would melt and the coast would be underwater. Seattle too. There would be famines and wars all over the world. Nobody down south wanted to believe it. It sounded like the Eskimo legends, when people were punished for evil. It sounded like Noah's ark or Abe's Judgment Day. The biologist smiled as he predicted this. It seemed a villain's vengeful grin, especially with those eyebrows. Did he hate his own country so much? What would his parents do when it flooded?

Willy asked him that but he chuckled. "Oh, live on the boat. Or head for the hills with their falcon." I imagined them flying on the back of a big hawk. "Their car," he added softly, "their goddamn car." His swearing and this pessimistic, murderous mood shocked me. Maybe it was because of his work with the oil, but if he was so sure of disaster, why did he even try? I thought if the cities drowned, Itiak would too. Every fall storms bit off chunks of our peninsula. Willy was looking anxious. Once he had found ancient boats and whale bones stranded high on a mountain, when on a dare he hunted for dall sheep. It proved the stories were true. It could happen again. In the flood there were no birds left to fly away with souls, so the mountains were haunted with the undead.

"Gee, some people sure worry a lot about everything," I said behind my book. When I peeked over it, the birdman had the superior look.

"And some people should wake up and smell the coffee," he said to Willy. We glanced over at the coffeepot on the Coleman. "No, I meant -" The birdman smiled - his tone softened. "It's all right, man, didn't mean to be a downer. It's just a scientist's version of the Apocalypse, only we use population explosions or the pesticide menace. It's hard to prove anything."

"Like the birds going extinct," I muttered.

"Hmm..." The birdman cut me a fake-mad look, his eyes narrowed. He leaned back on the chair. "Anyway, nobody believes scientists unless it's how to build a better weapon, or a new product that can addict people so they keep buying it. I'm exaggerating, Willy, don't believe a word, man."

Willy grinned. "I don't. You're a scientist." When I snickered, the birdman grew livelier, encouraged.

"Ya, they won't believe ecologists until they wake up one day -" He raised his voice like a cartoon and pointed, his face screwed up in horror, "Hey, Pa!! What's that coming over the field?" He lowered his voice, "Why son, that's chlorinated hydrocarbons." Willy and I laughed, not because we knew what he meant but because he was being comical. And I forgot I had vowed he wouldn't make me laugh that night, leading him on. He watched us, pleased.

Willy lit a cigarette, but when I gave him the glare he went outside. Wait until he got married: he'd be happy I trained him instead of getting it from her. I was smug until I realized that now I was alone with my naluagmiu. The cabin was very still, so still I could hear snow melting off the roof. I turned the page, suddenly very absorbed. When I peeked over he was just sitting there, arms crossed, staring into the oil stove's flame. That foreign profile...I struggled to keep my eyes off it, and found it had grown familiar.

Finally I said loudly, "Why are you *here?*"

He started. "What? To visit Willy!"

"*Saglu,*" I hissed. "Go *home.*" I pretended to read. When I sneaked a glance he had a hurt-feelings look, and like he might obey any second. I regretted my harsh tone used for dogs. When Willy stomped back in a gust of wind and said cheerfully that it was really snowing and was going to stick, I thought, good old Pataq, he's a breath of fresh air himself. He could sidetrack the birdman.

Thankfully Willy didn't order me to fold the dry laundry. The birdman did it himself, so meticulously and slowly that I wanted to grab the clothes from him and just do it, get it over with. The men played cards, the birdman always losing even though he had a good poker face. If I was playing I would stare at it and forget my hand. They had lost all their earlier silliness and looked sleepy but still our guest would not go home.

The war came up again; Willy told about the Itiak boy who died down there. They had hunted together. Willy didn't know anything about it because he was Eskimo, and the birdman told him people saw it every night on the TV and probably understood it less than Willy. The war was supposed to be winding down but a hundred GIs died every week, and millions of Vietnamese were dead. The U.S. was dropping more bombs than World War Two and burning and poisoning the forests. The war topic always made the birdman even more talkative. He volunteered a lot of information in answer to Willy's shy questions.

I listened intently, trying to make sense of it. He was twenty four, two more years of draft age. He used to be safe in college but now they were changing the draft, and if he was called he could only finish that semester. But it was fair, because before only the poor got drafted (no, he wasn't rich, he was the son of a troller, not an evil purse seiner. His family had to go on welfare when his "Far" had an accident with a grappling hook. He went to school on scholarships and cannery work and researching for his master). He forgot to register for credits this fall until a friend reminded him in a letter.

Willy was impressed. "How can you forget?" The birdman shrugged like it wasn't a matter of life or death.

"I dunno...other things on my mind." He shot a secretive look in my direction.

"Absent-minded professor, ah?" The two snickered. But when Willy said offhand, "They drew my order of call number this summer," the birdman lost his smile. "I'm 1-9-5," said Willy. I knew he had been given some kind of number but we didn't talk about it or understand it - it was in the same category as death and bad luck. "Low is bad, right? That's really low, ah?"

"They're *all* low, man!"

Willy swallowed and asked timidly, "What's yours?"

"O-2-6". They burst out laughing. "Ya, I was in the first batch two years ago," the birdman said. "I watched it on national TV when that asshole pulled that little blue capsule out of the bowl. It was really bizarre, the whole world seeing my fate like a comedy show."

"So...you're A-one?"

"Reclassified to one-A-zero but I'm appealing it to one-zero. I don't want anything to do with them. I could get one-W for my work right now, y'know, alternate service if they agree counting bird poop contributes to the maintenance of national interest. Or even two-A if my doctorate committee can figure it out."

Willy nodded, pretending he understood. What were they talking about? Would they put ear tags on men next to keep track of them and hunt them down? It seemed naluagmiut knew many ways to try to escape. "I never do National Guard because I hate that commander. So I guess I just wait for them to call me, ah?" said Willy.

The birdman frowned, fiddling with his beard. "Raw deal," he said gently, and the two men slumped in their chairs, looking suddenly exhausted. Cutting seals and washing diapers was far better than war or waiting to go to war. I didn't envy men anymore that night. Maybe I had been wrong about the birdman living so carefree. When Willy lit up a smoke again I didn't bother to chase him out, imagining him lost in a jungle with a helmet and machine gun. He seemed so young then, like he knew nothing. He lit another Lucky from his own and offered it to the birdman, who took it, maybe in male sympathy - he was not a practiced smoker. He played with it, then pincered it like a crab, dragged in too deep and coughed so it went flying.

"Shit, those old congressmen," he murmured, "They can still make sure it isn't their own sons for the body bags." Willy gave him that anxious little-boy look. Did he hang on the birdman's every word?

"Why are you talking to Pataq like that?" I said. "He's not going to be no body anyway."

The birdman straightened, not exactly apologetic. "Hey!" said Willy in the silence, "Your pacifist thing - tell me about it!"

"It's hard, it can't look like a desperate act of cowardice. I wrote essays on the sanctity of life and joined strange clubs. It enraged my dad even though he knows it's a capitalist war. I sometimes think he wanted us to go over and die, while my mom plotted to move back to Canada and save us."

The birdman smiled to himself and stuck the dead Lucky in his mouth. It wasn't a fond or grateful smile but a twisty one, the cigarette hanging off his lip, a raised eyebrow. It was his Satan look but it seemed like he used it to hide an injury the way an animal tries to disguise a limp and I wasn't sure I liked it, but then I did. He glanced at me and stopped it, taking out the cigarette.

"You can string them along with appeals if it's not a unanimous vote," he told the fire, "and try to bog them down in the paperwork...it's a game you play...but it's relentless. I probably don't have a chance in hell because they know my dad kills fish and advocates the violent overthrow of the government and my mom's Indian, which doesn't help, and sometimes late at night I think what the fuck, I'll just give in and be a medic and watch everyone die. Or I could join the green *braids* and just go on a rampage and kill everyone. Or run *later*, in the jungle. But when morning comes I know I'd run *first*."

Willy had been sneakily staring at his profile too as he droned in a flat, tired voice. "Can Eskimo be C.O?" he blurted.

"Sure!..but, uh...without a religious reason you have to be against taking even animal life to make it believable."

"I don't kill any, except for food. It's not for fun; I'm a moral Eskimo hunter." Willy was serious! The birdman regarded him awhile. Something in his expression - masked but there - seemed doubtful and sad.

"Pataq, it's *saglu*. It's just to save their own life, not because they're *moral*." I quickly dropped my eyes back to my book after declaring this. Neither man said anything but I felt the disapproval radiating from Willy. The birdman was used to it. Maybe I sounded like that draft board. Maybe he would gladly die if he thought it was worth it. I knew it was brave to stand up to the government, which seemed so merciless. When he said nothing to stick up for himself it made me believe him more.

Willy asked him if he knew someone who went to Vietnam. The birdman nodded, keeping his eyes on the flame. *Us,* he had said. Go to Canada and save us. He had not been an only child; Flo had figured that out. Then Willy broke the taboo - on purpose maybe, trying to be like the birdman, or to face his own fears - and said heartily, "Know anyone who *died* down there?"

Like a freezing wind had just blown in, the birdman pulled in his legs and folded his arms across his chest. He sighed, fending off the answer. "Ya...Olly."

"*Who?*" I asked from the bed, though I knew very well.

"It's short for Olaf. He -" The birdman stopped because his voice had nearly broken. He tried again, "He uh...my little brother. Was. Last year."

Willy caught my eyes, his eyebrows up a careful fraction. We watched him, familiar with the grief of a dead relative. Who was not, in a village? But we had not thought it could touch a whiteman, not really, even if they had tragic movies. I wondered what the kid brother looked like, if he was good-looking. Willy said softly, "But he was a soldier so you don't have to go now, ah? "

"That's only for peacetime."

Willy scratched his head, trying to figure that out.

"How come he didn't object like you?" I asked. The feelings we glimpsed just under the surface in the birdman made me pry. I wanted to see more, all of it, just as I had desired to watch him lose control to the power of my hand. He didn't answer. He fingered the bridge of his nose and sniffed and the edges of his eyes grew shiny. If he blinked the sorrow would spill over, so he didn't, but stared into the stove. I think he was willing the water back into the lids. I was a master at that. I waited for him to shame himself, but he did not.

Finally he said in a normal voice, "Well, as they put it, he developed an objection. But it was too late."

"Naluagmiut cry more than Eskimos, ah?" I asked the question for Willy as if the birdman wasn't even there. With his eyes Willy flashed me a warning to back off. "Is it?" I asked the birdman directly.

His face had closed. "Pardon?" he said, with a thin blade in his voice.

"Whitemen cry easier, ah? Like girls."

"Jeez, don't listen to her," said Willy soothingly, and offered him a new cigarette but he shrugged it off.

"Try telling that to my old man," he said to me, frowning, "And it's no great quality, the inability to fucking feel. That's a whiteman for you."

"She didn't mean it," said Willy.

"*Ayii*, I mean it." I was being like Abe with his questions designed to arouse, so he could watch. But its effect on the birdman was so much greater when the needle came from me.

"When I was a kid he threw me across the room just for crying," he said. "Maybe like that old Norwegian custom of flinging your newborn in the ocean to see if it's tough enough to bother with. But times change, it's not a thousand years ago and I'm not a fucking Viking."

I let myself look back in his eyes. Men used to wear caribou rib coats against arrows and spears and the birdman needed something like that, he was too unprotected. He had armor made from "data" and all those ideas but it did not defend his heart very well. I wanted to see the scientist cry with all his masks off, cry very hard with a broken heart like when his little brother was killed. I didn't know how I would feel if someone I loved was shot in a war. My mother had died and I guess it was a kind of war, but I didn't remember.

The birdman was silently staring at me, his arms folded in a haughty whiteman pose. "I better get back," he said. He seized his bag of laundry.

In the *kanichak* I heard him jamming on his rubber boots and wrestling on his jacket. He must get cold wearing just that. The outer door banged as the wind grabbed it from him. I wanted to run after him and take back what I said, say the too-late "I jokes". I wondered if I was cruel like his father or like one of those boys who pulled legs off poor spiders, just because they could, even if grandmothers forbade it. No matter what I did he wouldn't hurt me; it was like his rule, his C.O. thing, but maybe he should try to hurt me back.

The cabin felt so empty with him gone. "How come you always do that?" Willy asked, looking stunned. "How come you don't like him?"

"I don't know, ask Niviak! And don't let him come here again if I'm here. I don't want to hang out all night with naluagmiut. And don't smoke inside. And I know you had marijuana with that hippie, so don't play pretend!"

"Old lady!" Willy jeered, grinning hugely. "Jealous we didn't invite you? Who wants to invite a mean old *aka*? Anyway, she's not a hippie, she...he told me, they don't like science. It's their enemy."

"It's my enemy too."

Willy looked at me then nodded slowly like he finally understood. "Whatever turns you on, man." He waited too long for the downbeat, "I fool."

"Jeez, you're talking like them now. I bet you take classes."

"You're mad. Should I go buy some Kotex?"

"*Ayii, you're* mad. Your nostril is getting big. Better have another cigarette."

It was one of the worst thing you could do, let it show, and the easiest way to raise someone's anger was to point it out. But this sparring helped me forget my dark ideas. Maybe that was the purpose of a "teasing cousin".

Willy said calmly, "I don't take classes from Tingmiaq. I teach her everything."

"Is it? Then teach him to cook."

And Willy laughed, high like a seagull, releasing us from the tension.

CHAPTER 15

Though I am free of passions there is sadness:
a marsh in a fall evening; a snipe passing over it
SAIGYO (ANCIENT JAPANESE)

The bird of Time has but a little way
to flutter...and the bird is on the wing
AL-KHAYYAM (ANCIENT PERSIAN)

I DID NOT FLY that night to the birdcamp, I did not watch over him. He was not mine. I was not his, and it was better to keep away so he wouldn't get more ideas. But I saw his father clutching his chest as his heart gave out, a heart as small and icy as a cod's. His pale blue eyes were like marbles and he flopped on the deck of a boat, his mouth gasping without a sound. You will never see your boy again, I thought, even if you want to. Never another chance to hurt him.

ENTRY. BLASTED COLD and only a postcard from Brazil with a lunatic's ravings. I petitioned the Council for permission to stay in the eenee. Willy warned me of internecine feuds; his old man is influential in the strongest clique. They ruminated for a few days and voted "aye", but it's not a democracy, it's consensus, people have to come around and that's why it takes so long. Meanwhile a long storm shocked the coast, maybe really it was a series of storms between blustery stretches when gulls came out (from where?) to fly sideways. All migratory fowl fled, "with wings as swift as meditation or thoughts of love." Plectrophenax everywhere, like snowflakes; one flew in the tent, cute. Far out to sea the pack-ice is waiting stealthily for a chance to lock us in, give the polar bear better access. My fingers are numb writing this, hence the mess: the holes from the pups' teeth let in the wind. This darkness sifts into my mind, drifting over. Who will be left of living men when three winters see no summer? the Norse ancestors wondered. For them sun and fire were the main succor. Ja, I do crave a longer photoperiod...and someone's rare smile breaking like the sun from behind that shadowy panther gaze.

I wonder why is it more shameful for a man to show tears than lurch around drunk beating up women and children, or machine-gunning them into piles and burning them alive with napalm? What's ironic is I always thought I'm repressed thanks to my lineage, and have been accused by women of being "undemonstrative", but it seems not enough for the Far North. It's twisted, but it is easier to ejaculate in front of someone, as if the crying function has been...I don't know...maimed. She finds my weak spots and strikes at them unerringly. Now I know how the birds feel when tricked into a display, keyed out (subspecies: sniveling whiteman). But if bleached sealskins are the target why snipe at <u>me</u> when a preacher, a principal, even a chest-thumping big game hunter are available? Or even that intrusive painter! It seems I'm the straggler of the herd, so she'll nip at my hamstrings little by little.

Entry. I dreamed of Olly. He'd grown his hair and hovered above the sea like a dark Christ in resurrection mode but then he pulled a shining bow and shot an arrow and was Ishi, last of his tribe. He transformed into a sorrowful-looking Willy, who cradled a dead baby seal. Then Willy became Fahr, the Old Man of the Sea himself. He seemed to be lecturing me mutely; he pointed to the old sod hut. Inside were many gaunt people. A shaman was breaking a dryfish into pieces so everyone could eat. Then two Tallin's sailed down, skimming beautifully into a marsh. They let me get close. But they opened up their beaks and inside were little human faces in agony, a man's and a woman's. Help us, they said. They were so afraid; not the geese, the tiny inner humans. I woke in a cold sweat.

There's something wrong with me, I'm in an altered state. Maybe I should go to Lucy's, anyone's, where they would automatically stuff me with whatever is available. But I don't want to leech off their generosity like that "funny whiteman" a few winters back, maybe a draft dodger. Hopping from village to village. People kindly put him up until he vanished. Willy thinks the freak tried to walk to Siberia over the ice but Nanook found him. As an aside Willy warned me to never eat the liver of a polar bear. Right, as if I'm going to go out and spear one for dinner.

I feel disembodied, unattached and floaty, and see auras; is it from starvation of the optic nerve? The body needs more lipids in this climate. Hunger and benighted cold were a constant for my boreal ancestors so I should be hardier, with an upbeat mood, a nose that didn't run, but no, and these sweeping vistas get to me. My book says the arctic shamans saw horrific visions in the wilderness, where steep mountains towered abruptly before them and bellowed "Puny mortal, how dare you!" before clapping together, crushing migrants. The land itself could be doing this to me, turning me into a mystic. Or maybe it's due to solitary confinement of the tent in the storms, like a sweat lodge minus the heat.

Later. I took the typewriter to the eenee to keep salt water off. During storms the breakers nearly reach my tent in long seething tongues; everything is salt-rimed. While I was trying to figure out how to move the rest of the gear, Willy magically appeared on a Ski-Doo bumping over the frozen, nearly bare turf with a sled in tow. He looked apologetic, as if responsible for G's backlash. He brought Stanley, who wears Clark Kent glasses and a 50's ducktail. They came to help me move in. When we brought the first load they seemed leery of the dark hole; maybe they'd never entered in their whole life. Willy murmured something mysterious: "This old house is an animal too, not just a house. They called it...animal. And when you come out of tunnel...I can't remember." He was deep in thought.

"I know," said Stanley, "It's awnee! Being born. When you come out of kunichuck, you get born." The two guys laughed, albeit nervously. Suddenly the whole idea seemed preposterous, and Willy offered his place instead. With the artist gone, G has moved back to his folk's. I declined, not wanting to intrude but also to avoid town. (I also avoid beachcombing, though another handjob would be okay, I jokes).

When it was clear I really intended on moving in Willy got excited and made Stanley hyper. We set our mighty thews to readjust the beams before they melded into the permafrost. They advised me to insert a skylight of Visqueen in lieu of gut, the kind polar bears used to smash through. A smaller rectangle above the tunnel was for ventilation and I'm to put the can contraption in there. We cleared lemming nests and made a stovepipe hole and Willy contrived an oil-drum stove for burning driftwood; there's enough down on the shore to last awhile. There's a frozen spring nearby so I'm set for water; I'll use the axe. Life will be very cushy now. Both guys seemed pleased to be fixing up the paleolithic home and I offered to reserve a spot for them on the platform. They could hunt and I could sew, I said. They were very amused and appalled. But the whole idea was really G's, and I told Willy that when Stanley had wandered off to take a leak.

That was when everything changed, in this massive gestalt: "Maybe she likes you," he said under his breath. "Watch out!"

"If that's the way she is to her friends, then I pity her enemies."

"She got no friends." When I looked snide he explained, "You don't know. She had a real hard life before we took her in." He dropped his voice further, and did that confusing gender switch, "He never had a boyfriend either. I was only joking to watch out, because he's too shy..."

I bit my tongue and waited. More was forthcoming, the lowdown. Incredible; I thought she was a drudge now, but her first foster family truly enslaved her; they were "very bad". She was born in an interior village, and when she was orphaned the state "sold her down the river" (Flo was the abolitionist). "And she's not even Eskimo, she's Indian. Half maybe, or maybe full. And lot of people here don't like 'Itkeelick'." Willy was sad when he told me this, and I realized he was pretty fond of this sort-of sister.

"But you're part Indian too," he said. Was that to imply that G and I should hit it off? "Isn't it?" he asked softly, without any rancor. I was in denial, but then came the real gestalt: he was actually saying, Go on man, what are you waiting for? And suddenly I didn't know what the obstacle was besides being pissed off. A slave deserves a crusty exterior and a deep suspicion, particularly of the ruling class. That's why she needs to command spirits, to feel safe. She can be a jerk and having a lousy childhood doesn't get you off the hook (see: Nixon) but I'll be her apologist. And really, what has she said that is so wrong? That I'm too sensitive? Insensitive? My father hurt me? Science is arrogant, and I don't know everything? I hate it, the truth, like we hate our therapists.

I was a jerk too, to go with Polly when there were all the signs that the Fox was wooing me. She'd been slowly courting me all summer. Now I understand about the bear. I admitted to myself then: she, not starvation, is the cause of my dementia. I couldn't eat even if I had food, and I can't sleep or compile data for thought of her. She's stolen the lauded niche of Tallin's goose. I want to sight her badly but am terrified of doing so. And I forgive her, mitigate her, suddenly like a blow to my entrails. And now I know why I haven't even called the Master for plane fare; this is passive aggression of the soul. I am thrall to it and her.

"Tis strange that from their coldest neglect, my love should kindle to inflamed respect."

I WAS AT THE BOTTOM of the stairs at the store with a bag of flour when Christine appeared. Behind the safety of her shoulder glinted the eyes of her sister and cousin. They were younger than me, fresh out of high school. "How's your naluagmiu?" asked Christine, leering, then all of them hooted and cawed. I ripped open the sack and flung a handful into their faces. They shrieked and wheeled, trampling in a panic to get away from me, their faces powdered white, but they were giggling uncontrollably. When I threw another handful the wind drove it back into my eyes and lungs. While I coughed my tormentors backed away, sliding in their high-heeled plastic boots. They tried to get the flour off before people saw. Someday I will make a doll of her, I thought blackly, an effigy, and do things to it.

My naluagmiu. No matter what the truth was, they would twist it. My reaction was as good as saying *Yes. He is mine!* There was nothing I could do about it, except to never be seen with him.

THE SEAL AND WALRUS were riding south in the floes and daylight was stingy. Late fall had taken over the land and I had switched to my long parka. It reached to my mukluks and was made of rabbit fur turned inward, with a red calico cover and a wolverine ruff for the hood. It was old-fashioned, but I had nothing else to wear in the cold unless I wore Polly's too-small cast-off ski jacket. Flo said she wasn't going to make me new mukluks that year; I would have to do it myself so I could finally learn, but I didn't, so my clipped reindeer liners were musty and shedding insulation hairs onto my socks and everything else, and the *ugzruk* soles were nearly worn through from climbing on snow as hard and sharp as rocks. It was stupid of me; we had all the materials on hand. But sewing was the last thing on my mind.

With the grandkids in school and the men still at sea hunting and Polly at the clinic, I was alone with Flo, working. The small house was filled with church singing from the radio. If Flo turned it off we just heard the wind whistling over the roof and the squishy popping and sucking sounds of peeling hides and chopped joints. Everything smelled of blood and fat and guts. After a few hours of steady cutting I would have to lay down my *ulu* and wipe my slick hands on a hare fur. I bent back my aching fingers and laced them behind my back to open up my chest bones and circled my hips to loosen things up.

Flo never seemed to stop. She worked like a cutting machine, but always with care for the newly dead seals, like she was changing a baby. She poured a drink of water into their whiskered jaws before we opened up their bodies. I watched her gather their bones - personally, like I'd do it *wrong* - for their burial at sea. "Those young women forget," she scolded me, though I hadn't contradicted her. She spoke to the seals, asking them questions and singing hymns like they were believers. She told me it was to soothe their spirits. It was different with the stiff hides we brought inside from their freeze-drying; we had to get tough with them, using our metal scrapers. I was glad we didn't tan hides - we never did - though Flo was thinking of trying a new method of making leather with battery acid. She had joined a skin-sewing co-op.

Flo gave me funny looks, I imagined sometimes knowing looks if I slept in and forgot to get the kids ready for school or to prepare Kamik's bottle. Early rising, keeping hands busy, this was what God wanted. Abe would return from a hunt and, once he was recovered, sit on the floor commanding me as he cleaned and oiled his land weapons and tried to figure out how to fix a snowmachine. Parts he ordered never came so he had to improvise with ivory and bone or leather. Dogs were better, he said, but still he used sno-gos.

He and the other old men were excited and nervous about the revival of the drum dancing, when they could show off at the winter feasts. It would be the first dance since Abe was a child and saw the burning of the drums. The preacher wasn't angered - he was the new type who thought drumming was harmless as long as there weren't masks or anything too angutkoq. Abe planned to go out on the floor and stomp around with the other men but he wanted to practice first; no one but Isaiah remembered exactly how to do it. And Flo didn't approve, even if God did. That was a source of strife.

I'm really going crazy, I thought. Not crazy like Abe thought, but strange even to myself. I had no further plan, I didn't know what I'd do next without warning. I didn't trust my own hands after what they did to the birdman, like something in a ghost story cut off from their owner. My body hummed like the northern lights, unable to hold still. Like a nervous dog I shivered but wasn't cold. When the sun was up I escaped the village to hunt for lemming trails and raid their supplies of *mazu* roots. I always left some behind, for Flo had taught me to never take someone's entire cache. I circled at a distance to see the *ini* no bigger than a *siksik* burrow, smoke curling from its roof. And I waited for something to happen.

Willy had gone to Council when the *ini* matter was decided, and reported to me though I hadn't asked. Most of the old men were entertained by the idea. Prompted by Flo - who often sat in at meetings against the rule - Abe had vouched for Mr. Trygvesen's good behavior and intentions. Abe said Flo might move into the *ini* as well, she liked the scientist so much. A lot of laughter. Flo said wait until Christmas when Abe won the old man's footrace and stood up to get his prizes and gifts. What would she hang around his neck? Flo got even more laughs at this coup. Once a woman had hung a chamberpot on William the storekeeper, and dangled a Mr. Freeze into it. All William could do was grin. But he got even by raising his prices the next day.

At the final meeting, which the naluagmiu attended so they could speak to him, the Council said he could live free of rent in the *ini* because it didn't have an owner. That was their face-saving: they knew he was broke. He promised to send copies of his research. Scientists never did that, back then, and it pleased the men. But William gave a long-winded speech in Inupiaq about freeloading longhairs. The Council tried to smooth things by advising the birdman to unload for William's store when the supply ship arrived. Able-bodied men were always short due to seal-hunting. William said fine, but he'd pay the rate for female workers - causing much manly laughter - to which Flo retorted that if the birdman worked as hard as a woman, then someone had a good bargain.

The old men moved into the delicate topic of who would offer up their boats for unloading. Due to storms and shifting pack-ice the North Star was late, due to hit right at the peak of seal-hunting. They could not agree. Finally, mad, William said that he wouldn't hire any naluagmiu after all. It was a blow to Abe, who had taken such a mysterious liking to this particular naluagmiu. So they decided the birdman was going to work only for the Native Co-op. They arranged all this in Inupiaq, so he didn't understand, but he listened carefully.

I pretended not to care as Willy reported, but I was thinking, *I'll see him then!* Watch him anyway. I longshored every year, so no one would suspect.

THAT EVENING THERE came a faint rap at the outer door, surprising us. Normal people came to the inside door and stamped around getting snow off feet and alerting those inside, then they walked right in. That custom shocked *eskuulkti,* and people did it to tease them. No one entered. I yelled out, "Come!" Someone was tripping over gear in the dark stormshed, *kuangazuk* for sure. Then I knew. Another timid rap sounded on the inside door.

"Now who can that be?" murmured Flo; she was on the freshly mopped floor kneading dough. Polly was out and we had no visitors. I was trying to do beadwork but my lines were crooked, the colors wrong. And Abe, he was squatting on his chamber pot, chatting with Flo while taking a leisurely *anaq.* You don't see that anymore. When we all three yelled "Come!" and the birdman stepped in, there was surprise all around: the old people's at his visit, his at seeing Abe on the pot.

But the naluagmiu handled his embarrassment better than me. With no more than a flicker of the eyes toward me, he smiled and said in a practiced way, "*Kanoqikpin?*". Flo and Abe chuckled, answering, "*Eee, naagarunga.*" When no one asked him to come in further he took off his boots, as was polite. Nobody wanted snow on their floor. He held his coat awkwardly before dropping it near the door. He carried a small tin box. I hadn't seen him for a few weeks and was alarmed by his good looks. I stood up so fast beads scattered everywhere with little *ping* noises, and went to hide behind the curtain of my bed.

"Kayuqtuq, come out!" called Abe. "This man sure didn't come all the way here to watch me do this!"

"Well...actually, I did come to see you and Mrs. Ugungoraseok. I brought this tea..."

"Come out here, make *sayu*," called Flo to me. She said to the birdman, "Did you eat yet? You get stew for him," her voice directed me. It was amazing how people could slide from the syrupy voice of hospitality to gruff orders. Silently I emerged and did as I was told, eyes down like a good daughter of the olden days. I wasn't trying to put on a show; I simply couldn't raise my eyes for long. What if something in them was revealed to my elders? Flo watched me curiously for a time as she picked beads from her dough and pounded it roughly. Then she studied the birdman's stocking feet to calculate their size. She never had to use a tape measure.

Abe and he were talking about the *ini* and how it was working out. At last Abe finished his business and got off the chamberpot, whooping as he hitched up his trousers. Swiftly I moved the pot to the back. The way I saw it, only the big man, the old hunter, would want to do it in the middle of the room; it was his house, he was the boss. The three of them sat at the low table and ate, while I stayed at the card table to pretend to do beads. The birdman's expression was of a modest visitor, self-possessed. He was on guard, but hiding it well; he hardly looked at my part of the room.

Flo brought him the family album. He studied each photo, flipping through as if searching for something in history. If he was hunting for my girlhood he wouldn't find it! He made dumb comments at each picture. It was a custom, I realized, maybe from Ballard. "Oh, look at that." "Really nice." "Is that Willy?" Could he just shut up? I caught a dark glance from him, unreadable. I had the feeling he was there in the disguise of a shy bachelor to research me in my weakest position: Flo and Abe's territory. If he came to fight back, how was he going to do that - measure the quantity of *anaq* in our bucket, or spread oil over me and see what happened? I pictured myself as a stretch of marsh staked out with white string, turned into squares so he could see all the different plants I was made of. But I had been doing the same to him, in my own ways. Over my sloppy curve of gold beads I analyzed *him*, trying to figure out his current spiritual state.

Soon I had the chance to find out, for Abe and Flo decided to go visiting before church. Flo told me to watch Kamik, who was sleeping, then they were gone in a big hurry. The birdman and I sat at the card table and drank more tea, formal. The old people had been his shield but they'd abandoned him to face me alone. He seemed to want to ask a question. He stared into his tea leaves like they held the answer.

I knew if I spoke he would have to meet my eyes, due to his naluagmiut training. He wore a sweater with holes in the elbows, crowberry-leaf green - good for his coloring. Red arrows of geese flew over the chest. "Nice sweater," I murmured.

"This?" He stretched the wool out from his belly to examine it. "Thanks. I made it. Home-ec."

Was he joking? "A boy in home-ec?" I asked mildly. He shrugged, studying the wolf trap hanging on the wall. I had been too mean and was tired of it; I was going to be kinder. "I saw Calvin," I said. When his eyes dropped from the trap to me they were as clear and deep as the tea we were drinking, without any sneakiness, and my stomach leaped and spasmed like I had gone over a dip on a Ski-Doo. A grievance still lurked in them, a caution I couldn't blame him for, but he wasn't mad. I did not understand why he tolerated me.

"Calvin? Do I know him?" he asked.

"He's angutkoq too."

"Ah."

"I told him about the spirit." When he made no comment, I went on. "Calvin said if a bad one like that comes then the others can get you too." But it was I who had given away the location, like a scientist accidentally leads a fox to a nest. I had drawn them to the door to the birdman's soul and there was no lock.

He smiled and put his cup down. "Really?"

"Calvin says you should worry."

"Regardless, I'm pretty sure it was just a flashback. You can get those from...a kind of drug that stays in your system."

"Angutkoq had drugs. In the red mushrooms. They always drank *qoq*... pee of the one who ate it."

"Hallucinogenic?" The birdman looked thoughtful. Maybe he wanted some.

"You don't believe Calvin."

"We have to agree to disagree, okay?" he said quietly. "It's like your parents going to church. Are you offended by that?"

"Yes."

He pursed his lips in an "oh" and laughed a little. "Fair enough."

"Bad spirits don't attack when you're feeling fine," I said. "They come when you're down."

"Well I never get down, so I'm safe. So no problem." He grinned; he'd lowered his guard. "Hey man, I got a new house and a job lined up, things are cool."

"I'm not a man."

"Pardon?"

"I'm not a man. You always play call me *man*."

"That doesn't mean anything; it's dialect!"

"Words always mean something," I said, and watched him grow solemn, like the sky, slowly, when the sun goes down. He glanced at the bed where Kamik lay, and turned his teacup like it was very fragile.

He said in a low voice, "I *know* you're a woman." My heart stilled under my ribs. The mood had changed - *he* had. I'd rather have him call me *man*. His words touched me on the back of the brain like a finger, and there came that memory again - his surprised eyes softening into a haze, his moan beneath my hand. I had not done it against his will, had I? And he had been so inviting..."But as long as we're talking about the power of words," he said, "why do you call me naluagmiu? I'm a man...not a bleached sealskin."

"But it's not bad!" I didn't know he took offense. "In old times *naluaq* was good. Your wife sewed it on your mukluks to show everyone you could hunt." I didn't point out that shamans also wore headbands of it.

"Really?" He looked doubtful.

"Yes, a real man." I changed the subject. "But you'll be a man in trouble if you don't listen. You'll feel bad pretty soon and they'll come."

The birdman set the cup down, his sharp eyebrows gathering in a vexed move, then he sat back with his hands on his knees like a picture of an old president. I thought he suppressed a sigh. "Okay, why do they want me? The *bad* ones. I mean, these ones to come, besides the one you already um...summoned?"

"Maybe you upset them. Maybe they don't like your research." I knew this wasn't true; he was an ally of the birds, anyway. He was in trouble because of me. When he still looked unconvinced I added, "There are bad *inua* who always try hurt people even if they do nothing wrong."

"No offense, but this sounds too much like the church. Why do people blame things on malevolent forces instead of the real enemies?" I heard a contempt there, an anger, but not at me. I didn't want to argue even if he wanted to.

"Just be careful," I said. "They'll go all the way to Seattle and find you."

"I'm not going to Seattle."

"How come?" I faltered. Yet I knew, I heard my own voice at the cliff rising out of me, taking me by surprise, *Maybe I don't want you to go...*

"What's the use dragging all that equipment down south when I just have to haul it back next spring? I can type up my stuff in the *ini*. It's amazingly warm you know. And I can help Willy hunt, like you said."

"You don't shoot guns."

"True, but I'm okay with a knife. I've cleaned a lot of salmon. And dissected."

I smiled indulgently. "You can't cut. That's for women."

"Then I'll get a sex change operation. I jokes."

I was shocked, hardly understanding, but we laughed together. His eyes crinkled at the corners. I was relieved the serious mood was past and was watching his face with enjoyment when he stopped the merriment and leaned forward on his elbows to fix his sights on me. "I came here to see *you*," he said.

My hands tightened on my cup. "Too bad."

"Why?"

"Because I'm going to church now." I got up and looked for my mukluks.

"You are? But I thought -" His expression turned crafty. "I was on my way to church too, actually."

"*Ayii,* try fool; you're not Christian."

He grinned evilly in his black beard, standing too, which made me nervous, and then he was following me around the house. "Ya, but I was curious about an institution that singlehandedly destroyed a culture. Thousands of cultures."

But it wasn't destroyed, I thought. Maybe when Itiak first took Jesus they just adapted him, like fastening an iron head onto an antique harpoon shaft. Maybe they kept the parts they liked about the old ways and got rid of the rest and it wasn't all just whitemen forcing them. Abe wasn't a destroyed man - he was proud and happy. And Flo too, she wasn't a poor victim. "What do you mean? We're still...we're here." I stammered, feeling inadequate in language.

We were standing near the door. The birdman looked down at me; I don't know what kind of expression my face had. I was hoping desperately no one would walk in. "I know," he said, and leaned against the doorjamb. "Everyone's managed to survive in some form. At least until television." What did that mean? He was thinking, eyes distant, then he moved his hand in a funny kind of pointing, maybe at his sudden idea. "For example the raven was very important in Europe too. That Odin stuff in Norway was shaman-ism, and Raven was there, flying souls back to reincarnate. And then in Ire-land as the goddess of death and war. But then the Church turned Raven into the Devil…"

He shifted his body, looking deep into my eyes. "What was I getting at? He's incoherent," he muttered. "Oh, now I remember! Um, but at least until industrialization they still believed in ravens as omens of important changes. So…well, isn't that creation? So it survived." I didn't really know what he was saying; I was not thinking of *tulgaq* but of this man's mouth, its tender-ness as he rambled, his white teeth.

"You know nursery rhymes?" he asked. Did his mind always go like this, a coal lying in wait, never resting? I had just thrown a heap of kindling on him and blown. "Not for kids. They were secret codes to pass on pagan ideas with-out being burned alive, and the slave songs were code to help them escape. Everyone's been playing the man's game for centuries but all along they were passing the torch underground…in the sodhouses of the soul."

He stopped, I guess at my strange expression. "Am I talking too much?"

"I don't know. Yes. But…how do you know all that?"

"Bookworm. Burden of proof falls on the whiteman, y'know." I guessed he was joking. He seemed a little combative, like his ideas wanted to wrestle with me. But playful.

"Why do you read so much?" I asked. "It doesn't help you."

"It's knowledge! That helps a lot."

"How." What I had picked up from books - the half-baked angutkoq ideas, the details of how the old ones had died - seemed to have made my life harder. "Reading too much can make you sick," I said. "Shamans had to pull papers out of an Indian's head after he went to school and he was dying from thinking too much."

"Really? I believe it." The birdman grinned. "But how do you know about that? You read it in a book, didn't you?"

I blushed. It was true. "And why do you *write* all the time?" I plunged on, excited at the novelty of pointing out a man's flaws to his face; you wer-en't supposed to but the birdman let me, if I steered clear of certain dangers.

Like fathers, brothers, his race...the *real* spiritworld, not the book one.

"Why do I write?" He shrugged. "I don't know...because I'm a weirdo?"

"I know why you *read*. It's because you don't want to think about your own life. But I don't know why you write, if it's just boring stories of what you did that day."

"But that's not what I write about!"

"Then what?"

"Hmm." He bit his lip and searched up at the ceiling as if unsure. "I think I write about what I think about, and read about." When he looked at me straight-faced we burst out laughing. He was so willing, trusting I wouldn't go for the vein. Like the gentle thaw of the boot-snow in the *kanichak,* I felt a warmth in my body. When our laughing had simmered down he took a breath and said, "And I write about *you*."

We both must have looked startled in the same way, knowing he'd gone too far. He cleared his throat. "Anyway. Back to mythology. So what do *you* think of raven, I mean the Inupiaq god?"

"I think he was a rapist," I said. The taboo words flew out on black wings from an unknown place, my own self-revelation, I guess. And they had the power to straighten him from his slouch in the doorway and turn him speechless. I watched his eyes puzzle and darken like I had switched off the light in him. He looked away.

After a long silence he said, "Um...I - " but I stepped into the *kanichak* before he could say more. "Are you leaving me with the kid?" he asked. I had almost left Kamik alone.

"A-Aka," I stammered, "Aka said she would watch him, so I have to go get her now." Abe's mother was staying for a while with her other son. I was making it up of course; Aka was far too old to watch babies, and except for funerals I hadn't stepped foot in the church since my Confirmation.

"I can stay with him; he knows me," the birdman offered. I widened my eyes ominously without answering. "I'll tell you what," he said, "I get Aka, you stay here, then we *both* go to church. Lutheran, right? Just like in Ballard! I'm sure it's exciting."

He pulled his mouth down at the corners and I didn't know what he was doing until he pressed his palms together: poking fun at his father's people again. Was he also making fun of my village or just trying to lighten things? Had he seen how my hands were shaking? "All right?" he asked. I raised my eyebrows to a noncommittal level. He hesitated, trying to figure that out, then began to struggle into his wet rubber boots. "Kay, catch you later."

"*Ayii*, wait!" I'd had a horrible thought of the birdman wandering into the wrong house, door to door, "Um, excuse me, Gretchen needs her grandmother". Darkness engulfed me a second while I hurriedly shrugged my parka over my head. I didn't bother to tie my mukluks.

"*You* stay," I ordered, and brushed past him, pulling the door closed as he stood with one boot on.

CHAPTER 16

Why wilt thou ever scare me with thy tears
And make me tremble lest a saying learnt
In days far off, on that dark earth, be true?
'The gods themselves cannot recall their gifts.'
TENNYSON

I PUSHED AKA on her little wooden sled over the drifts that now hugged the village. At the house I gripped her hands to lower her to the floor and brought her some of the new tea. Her gnarled bones could barely hold the cup, so I cooled it with snow and lit her pipe for her, the only person who was allowed to smoke inside.

She noticed the naluagmiu hovering near and started in on some distant recollection. I had little patience for the old woman as I tried to scheme out of my own trap, this church plan. With the birdman watching I was keenly aware of her snowy braids, her eyes vanishing into a web knit by so many cycles of storms and sun and cold. Her teeth were worn flat from softening everyone's footwear and clothing when she was young; she was already middle-aged before Itiak used steel to crimp hides. She was frozen in that bent seal-cutting position and her tattoos made her look like she needed a shave, or as if an animal had clawed her down the chin. The birdman would not know what they meant.

"How old is she?" he whispered. He didn't need to - she was not asleep or a sacred object that could break if he spoke aloud. She was a tough old lady.

"She don't know. She remembers the Gold Rush." And everyone dying, and starving, maybe eating the body of someone she loved. And people, those left, wandering inland to strange rivers or to distant coasts where they were not welcome and would always be strangers

Aka was often lacking in the cheerfulness the elders were famous for, a belief that all things were meant to be, that there was a set order. You can still see that idea, spread around the globe by an airline in the smiling old man painted on their airplane tails. Once she told me it was because her ancestors had been bad, so she had faced too many sorrows. Yet that night she seemed happy to *unga* a whiteman. She was getting blind and could not see he was good-looking. Maybe she thought he was a young man from another village come to court her. It was said she had been beautiful.

I moved away and from a distance watched the two of them. They were on the opposite ends of history and tradition and shared no language, yet they seemed to have a kind of instant bond. A kind of love. What would they talk about, even if they could? In the manner of *aka*s she petted his hand as her creaking voice wove a story. It didn't matter if it was just a rambling memory of some berry-picking trip. The birdman listened raptly, with wide eyes such as he turned on the beauty of birds, of the sea at dusk. He had fallen under her enchantment and she had him, just like that, without any bear spirit, without touching his sex, or any manipulation at all. And she would not abuse that power.

I wondered how a whiteman deserved a caress from her old hand. His kind had changed everything for her, whether she had asked for it or not. And they were still infecting us with a kind of soul sickness, Calvin said, turning us into angry people like themselves, full of wants and needs that could never be fulfilled. Maybe the birdman was being changed too, by us, but he had come to the village of his own free will. It was not fair. And if he wasn't an anthropologist or an artist or a politician who wanted her X on a ballot, then why was he so goddamned interested in an *aka?* Because she was a "real" Eskimo? And why did it matter? Aka was not mine, Itiak was not my home, *he* was not mine. These ideas he stirred up of vanished ancient worlds and vanishing animals didn't seem real, the loneliness and sadness too big, far bigger than life. What about *me*, and my own extinct life, my lost mother and the life I never had with her? No one talked about *that*.

When I was small there had been a really old *aka* who took pity on me. I didn't know her name - she lived alone. She used to give me drinks and thin soup, she combed the lice from my hair and braided it, and though she could no longer sew to make me new clothes, she took me into her cold bed and I would keep her warm and she would keep me warm. But she died - I was the one who found her in that bed, curled as if asleep.

A grief shook me so powerfully that the birdman looked over from where he communed with Aka. He came to where I stood and tried to see my face but my hair hung over it. "What's wrong?" he asked gently. His fingertips brushed my bangs aside but when I tossed my head he stopped. It was my fault he was like this now, with the right to stand so close, to touch me. "Do you know what she was saying?"

"How much do you know of *your* parent's languages?" I shot at him. "Norway talk? Indian talk?"

"Don't get mad."

"I'm not mad!" And it was true. It was something else.

"I'm sorry." His kind tone troubled me further. "Okay, I'll tell you what I know. *Ya, nay, tak for mowten, loota fisk*" - he made his voice go up and down - "*yai elsker doo*. That's all I know. She's still mad," he said to himself. "Norwegian just makes them madder." In spite of myself I was smiling at his goofballing. He was too at ease, like he planned on moving in. In the old days he would just have to try to sleep on my bed three times, I would kick him out only twice if I wanted him, and we'd be married. And I had another plan, to take advantage of his eagerness to please.

"I do know what Aka was saying," I told him, "She wants you to stay here while I go. She likes you."

"But I..." He glanced at Aka who was staring into space, nodding, mouthing her gums.

"No, you *have* to," I said, "He's elder." I caught myself. "I mean *she* is. Aka wants to tell you stories and you can't go against her wishes. If she gets mad he...she won't forgive you." Now that I was paying attention my grammar had worsened. "You better obey."

"She's the law, huh?"

"She's *aka*." I laid it on thick then, seeing how impressionable he was on the topic of old ladies. I told him of the law of never passing one on the road or sassing. Few obeyed anymore: people had schedules to meet and the *aka*s hobbled so slowly, and they didn't understand the new world so it was hard not to contradict them, but I didn't tell him that. I said they had powers like angutkoq just from being old, so you didn't want to get on their bad side.

"You mean they're like witches!" he said. "Why do poor old grannies always get scapegoated? Everywhere in the world."

"*Aka*s do have power," I said. Sometimes it seemed true, when they muttered in the language you only half-understood, that they still held an unearthly force the missions never got to. And that they had something against you, especially in the dark fall of storms when you met one on the path, bent so her chin nearly touched the snow. Surely they bore a grudge. The etchings on Aka's face were fierce lines of power. People said they meant only that *aka*s had reached womanhood, but I saw them as a warning from the past: watch out! *Aka*s had been "feelers" who turned babies, brewed herbs and understood dreams; they sang and cast love and hunting spells and people would go to a grandmother for help before an angutkoq.

Yet if they were really so mighty wouldn't *aka*s make themselves young again? It was frightening to realize they were once pretty girls flirting and laughing. "It's the power of their anger for being treated bad their whole life," I warned the birdman. "By the time they're old, they're very strong." I told him about the *aku* who put a spell on the boys in a *kazhgi* who had molested her granddaughter. She gashed her body until she ran with blood and then she led the bad boys on all fours into the hills, crawling and crawling in the snow until they froze into a line of stones.

The scientist regarded me silently, thinking. I made of show of checking the wind-up alarm clock on top of Polly's dresser. "Time for service. I'm leaving."

I WAS AFRAID he'd see my trick and chase after me but he didn't. Not wanting to give Flo a heart-attack from the shock and joy of it, I never went to service that night. As I traveled past the church Flo's nasal voice soared above the others in the choir. I pictured her, her reading glasses low on her nose. Later she'd give a speech from the pew, competing with other women to see who could find the most redemption. Naluagmiut hippies shouldn't make fun of that faith, nobody should. It took her from her troubles, and she was the one who had saved me. As she took my hand and led me from that cabin she uttered words I would never forget: "I *will fear no evil, for thou art with me.*" And it was true I had felt no fear at all through her plump hand.

Past the rows of white crosses in the cemetery, two bleached whale ribs marked the end of consecrated ground. The great bones curved toward each other, gleaming in moonlight like fangs or long *aklak* claws rising from the snow. One rib marked the feet of the last true angutkoq, one marked his head. When you stood close - not too close - you could hear throbbing under the earth. That was his drum. Decades later still no one dared walk between those bones for fear of his vengeance. How touchy the shamans had been, always imagining slights and ridicule. Or maybe they were just good mind-readers. Maybe the old people had accepted Christ for protection from them.

I thought for a while I had been followed by the birdman soft-footed in the snow, but when I turned there was no one.

THE SMELL OF TEA drifted from the vent. I peeked through the window to see the birdman still sitting at Aka's feet, in Willy's old spot. He did not look frightened. I fell into a drift of snow, my mind spiraling black and quiet as the sky above, protecting me from further thought in a dreamlike calm. A door opened and a snatch of radio leaked out. Reception was poor and someone was trying different bands; I heard Russian, maybe Japanese...I didn't know. Stars circled, sparks of far-off energy kicked up into a galaxy. People used to think they were lamps of the dead shining in spirit *ini*, and now it was Heaven. They used to believe that souls came back, but I didn't think that would be so great. Once I had read a poem in high school the year they tried to bring back our culture. It was an old Inuit song of a dead man asking himself, *Were you not happy on this earth?* The ghost decided, Yes, happy, when he had not been afraid of dying or afraid of people's teasing.

I would have to answer No. But I wished that wasn't so.

SO MUCH SELF-PITY...it is tiresome, but I was young. I would like to leave that girl for a time in her drift. I can read exactly what the birdman thought as he babysat, and if he grew predictable and sentimental, I can forgive him. Aka has been dead for a long time now. They're all dead, those who remembered life before; there never will be someone like them again. Maybe later young people came to see them as Leif did, instead of as a reminder that we were only two generations out of the Stone Age, damned if we didn't act like whites but damned if we did.

ENTRY. I FEEL LET DOWN. The Bird didn't marry the girl, he assaulted her. I shouldn't ask. Nor should I read books if I want to keep being an idealist. To whit: husbands would hamstring a run-away wife, rip her cheeks if she scolded, buy and sell her and make her sleep with assholes; she couldn't choose. And petty but awful, the men slept up on the warm platforms of the eenee and women were confined to the cold tunnels. (Oh, but a man's old mother could sleep under his bed). Other old women were killed and dismembered and burned in oil after bogus witch-hunts led by male shamans. There was never equality for Homo sapiens; can there ever be with such a dimorphic split? We're baboons, not geese. Goethe said power is neither male nor female but I wonder if his wife agreed.

Aka is uncanny in appearance but she patted my cheek so kindly. She has experienced the most radical change ever undergone by a human. All she needs now is the boob tube to complete her journey, join the nation in its weekly dose of the starship Captain (as he violates the code to never mess with other cultures) and his hapless alien lackey, the half-breed scientist-shaman yes-man. She can watch the carnage of war over dinner. The teachers brought in a video machine this week thinking Big Bird could teach the kids to read. And who am I to decry it: I've had the option to rot my mind or to scorn it. I should not have mentioned assimilation to G but I have the right, don't I, being an utterly assimilated partial Indian? But Aka is still hooked onto that line stretching into the remote past, the line time is reeling in. I wanted to lay my prodigal nuclear age head on her lap and hold tight...do not slip away...tell me the answers. I don't think you really have them.

And outside, the evening star, the harbinger. And G, hiding in a drift, or rather, flattened. She was distraught, but why? And why did she make a move if she didn't want it? She wanted to. Something happened to her.

THAT LAST PART gives him away - the researcher of the life science who would not record the most important things in life. More important in the end than culture or history.

I lay on the snow, my mind drifting like snowflakes. A skinned fox hung near our door with bared teeth, still trying to slip back into its skin and run away but unable to move. I did not move. I could lie like that a long time - it was warm and comforting, as I had learned as a kid. The huskies liked it, after all. Above me the black sky was cloudless, yet tiny ice crystals spun down into my half-open eyes. Black, black as a hole cut into bay ice before it slushes up. I was a char waiting at the bottom for spring, eyes rigid, and when the ice flakes landed on them I did not blink. Flo shuffled past me on the trail and into the house, not even noticing.

Suddenly the moon was up, a globule of golden fat in the black skillet. A howling rose from the farthest end of the village: Tuguk's hungry skeleton dogs. This was how I would die when I was old and useless, the little sled my only hold on life's slippery dark trail. I would push it across the lagoon and into the mountains heading east, toward Indian country.

It was the fall and the rising moon that made people think such thoughts...

He was bending over me. His face was black in silhouette with the moon behind him a lopsided, brilliant gold. I felt fear in his still posture, how he stopped breathing. "Are you alive?" he whispered. I didn't blink. I could not return quickly from these spells, with my spirit still loose. "Ohmygod." He was on his knees shaking my shoulders so my head flopped. He seized my forearms to pull me to a sit, then slung me over his shoulder as he stood so my arms flopped down his back. I felt muscles work under his thin coat, strong, but he staggered as he lifted. Was I that heavy? Like a seal, a haunch of moose, I thought distantly, smiling.

"Fuck oh fuck," he said, spinning around. My ribs hurt, crushed against his bones. This was not a good position to be seen in, *nulluk* in the air. He started toward the door, where he would call Flo for help or panic and do mouth-to-mouth. Picturing that, I revived and vaulted from his hold like a salmon. I slid down him until my feet touched snow. He grabbed my shoulders.

"Gee, stop it, let go!" I laughed. He snatched his hands away and stood there, panting ice fog. The whites of his eyes shone in moonlight, his skin reflected a blue light of the stars and moon on snow. What could I do? I laughed harder at his confusion though I didn't feel like it. Then I laughed more at his chagrin that I was laughing, and at my own embarrassment. "You're mad!"

"You *scared* me! Jesusfuckingchrist!" He wiped melted snow off his mouth.

"You are too mad!" I made the raven noise of derision.

He should have pulled himself together better, laughed a little too but he cried, "Lay off! Just stop it! What the hell is the matter with you?"

There was someone coming up the path below the bank with a quick step. "Shhh, be quiet," I begged. I clamped my hand over his mouth, which he shook off. But he was silent. I liked how he complied at once; you couldn't just shout in public like a naluagmiu, a drunk, no matter how upset. We stood there in the dark shadows. I listened to the rush of his breath as it calmed and felt my own speed up from its fish-like lethargy.

He whispered, "What *was* that, some kind of trance? You could freeze to death!"

"No, feel..." I stepped in and cupped my fingers onto his hot neck in the manner of a whiny little child with an older sibling. His blood was a furious current of blood beneath his skin and he shuddered under my touch. I thrilled at the power of life in his pulse: it sped for my sake, because he thought I was in danger. My hands crept into the chilly locks of his hair. I pulled his head down and rose on my tiptoes. It was just meant to be a light brush of lips, to surprise him again. His eyes did widen a second.

Then he surprised *me*, when swiftly with no forewarning from the muscles his arms hooked around my waist and he bent his head so I had to keep kissing. He closed his eyes and opened his lips so our teeth clicked together and his tongue touched mine, sweet and hot. His *umik* tickled my nose, the white mist of his breath went into my lungs, the good smell of him. He uttered a low sound like a man who was hurt, or a man throwing down a load after carrying it for too long. And he moved his hips into me. My own hips tilted toward his, amazing me, what was I doing? I felt like butter in a warm room, soft and willing enough to spread...

But his man's arms could squeeze the air out of me. He was so different from the time at the cliff, he was greedy, looming, I was being devoured!

I squirmed and leaped sideways, breaking the bear hug so he was kissing air. Slowly he dropped his hands, seeming dazed. He was breathing fast. One foot behind me, I waited for his next move. We were calf deep in a drift and my legs felt like dead grass in the wind they quaked so much, and when he took a step forward I sprang back, tripping. He halted at once.

"Gretchen, are you - were you - ?" He peered at me in the gloom, his face now lit in sudden moonlight, in a struggle. He glanced over to the skinned fox swinging near; it bumped his elbow like it wanted to say something, warn him or coax him, I didn't know. Thankfully, a racing cloud cast us in the blue-dark again and hid his eyes. He stood with his head bowed, then waded past me down to the path with a "See you around" and turned into a shadow.

I sank back into the white quilt of my drift. He was gone but the smell of him was still on me. My body still felt him, his lips, his pelvis, belly and thighs pressed against my entire front. He was still carrying me, the force of his heart shaking me as it pounded in ignorant fear. His bones worked under the flesh, laboring to make me safe.

Maybe he would help anyone in trouble and react the same to any woman: see how fast he had crawled into the tent after Niviak. Men were made like that: if a bird flew, their rifles were instantly at their shoulder, taking aim. They were hunters of whatever offered itself, indifferent - that's why girls used to be escorted everywhere and married off at twelve.

Of course I had never been kissed before to compare.

But it seemed pretty personal, the kiss of the birdman.

CHAPTER 17

And as the smart ship grew
In stature, grace and hue
In shadowy silent distance
Grew the Iceberg too
HARDY

Never lie with a witch in love;
She'll cast a spell so you forget the world
and you'll seek your bed in sorrow
(ANCIENT NORSE)

ENTRY. THE "NORTH STAR" gave up and went to more accessible villages. A viscous slush is forming in the sea, a milky young grease-ice that currents and wind keep breaking up. But it's cozy in my den and I could type fluently if I could just concentrate. No reaction yet from the Department on my wintering here. I may have to skew the data, paint a black chevron on a retrice feather.

Can't throw off a cold, vitamin C's out, the single phone of the village is now dead. Francis thinks the line was sabotaged by Soviet agents. I wasn't trying to call anyone. Saw those heathen teachers in the procession to the steeple, trying to ingratiate themselves to the populace. I'd go too if I thought I'd run into G, but fat chance. No sighting at the P.O. I think I am forbidden to visit. Other people remain friendly though I must seem to be the kind of lunatic-hermit they would, if medieval, send their progeny to stone. Although there's a natural racial prejudice here, maybe you're not so much judged by the pallor of your skin as your behavior. But feedback - the norming - can be subtle.

I have some allies; old ladies like me. Lucy invited me to dine at her house sometime, warning that she has eleven kids. They live in a Quonset hut. She had me follow her home to give me a "lingcod". It doesn't look like one, but that is what she called it. It's gone high into a lutefisk. She warned me not to cook it with reindeer (earth-land taboo?) but she gave me "toonook", which is reindeer tallow with the tastelessness of Crisco. It's good, I crave it. You chew it like gum, raw, and don't think of parasites. Lucy is so gracious; is it sheer altruism or a kinship deal since she's Abe's cousin and wife of Fred Sr, Abe's main hunting partner? Or is it a tithe, a hangover from colonialism? If I'm supposed to reciprocate, what could I give that's equal to a big fish? I could make her laugh; she finds me amusing.

It feels ageless here. These villages are the only society in the world. Except for weather people don't listen to news on the radio. Just Ptarmigan Telegraph with the real news: local births, birthdays, weddings. The climate is sure as hell direct, but social life is indirect. I err, shoot my mouth off, verbal diarrhea. You can run off at the mouth but only if you're over fifty and have proven your worth. You must not interrupt, same as with Indians (Maman tried to teach me but there's too much French blood). The underhanded insinuating style reminds me of Maman when teaching proper humility, Metis style. An exaggerated praise: "Oh, I bet you are the smartest scientist at your school, ah?" Meaning of course, "Silence, boy, you know nothing!" Wish I had a liaison to explain things more clearly than Willy. G would rather confound me. My books are outmoded. I may fuck up.

Entry. Dolores hailed me from the window so I went in and overheard Bill trying to contact the ship with the radio. Now she's jogging over the horizon in dark-heaving waves too rough to unload in. Teacher tried to engage me in political discussion. She's unhappy that her students don't know who the president is nor <u>what</u> he is, not that I'm fully cognizant of that either, Dory, other than a paranoid fascist.

Someone's dropped that I'm a quarter-breed, and Dory bent my ear about the American Indian Movement, the taking of Alcatraz. She wanted to talk about my ancestors: weren't the Cree and Ojibwe capitalists, unlike the Inuit, who prove that communism is the primal state of man? I was confused and told her by the 1600s those tribes had already broken up and depleted many species, debt-peons to the fur companies, if that is what she meant. Who could know their pre-contact state?

Anyhoo, more waiting at "curfew-tide." Desperate for staples, I tried credit again and William let me take a carton of eggs that turned out rotten, though I will use them. He has me humbled now (the others hate how he throws his weight around and tries to make a profit, and he does not avoid quarrels). Then by accident I found the other store, the unmarked "Native Co-op." Better luck there. The manager Jonas showed me a room filled with handicrafts and furs people had given in exchange for groceries, and asked what I planned on giving him. Then, "I jokes," a hearty laugh, and a sack of flour with only a few weevils, and canned milk. Later I found out he is the man I will work for - no one told me.

In back of that friendly store a lot of hunters stood at the stove drying their mukluks, smoking, and rapping softly in that uvular Inupiak. Because William wouldn't tell, I asked Abe when the ship unloaded. He grinned like the Cheshire Cat while everyone discreetly watched. A pregnant silence, then Abe said, "Vaaa, I don't know." A warning hint. But I imprudently said I'd overheard the captain on the radio and he sounded close. And when Abe kept silent, I asked if he was going out hunting when the weather let up. I was hoping he'd invite me so I could get a share with honor instead of a handout (though they won't let me go without cold-weather gear; I'd have to borrow). Maybe I miscalculated our depth of intimacy. He said "maybe" after a lengthy wait. And then, with great impudence, I dared ask, When? disrupting the delicate and mystical balance with nature and its crypto-encoded schedules. In reply, with his little finger he exposed the red underside of his eyelid as if the answer lay there - very droll - and the other old cats laughed. I recognized a scolding you give a child. The disingenuous Abe.

Don't tell me people don't make plans or give information; they'd die otherwise. True, they have to be ready to change course fast, for the best-laid plans go awry. The weather systems are so fluid; it's not like you can use a seed-calendar. Abe told me of this fugitive family of yore on an island they thought would have good hunting in winter, but they starved because in that particular mini-ecosystem the ice never froze, so they couldn't get seal. Abe's moral was "Don't think you know it". He is hardly haphazard; I bet he's plotting a hunt right now, ear to the wind. I can dig not inquiring about animals who might be listening, but why can't I ask about the ship? I feel at sea.

Later. I found out from Willy it's a bad topic now, rife in clan politics, the unloading scene a heavy power struggle with Abe at the fore. So it's not a Taoist thing, it's more tangled. And also I was too forward barging in on the elders like that. Probably interrupted someone's soliloquy - they pause so long, and everyone waits. Maybe I made Abe lose face; he's my sort-of mentor, or at least my guarantor. Maybe he just wanted to tease, but I'm a frustrated whiteman blowing any veneer of dignity. Withhold everything except the smile. Above all batten down a temper. From now on I'm just going to let things unfold and they can tell me when the time is right, to ask or even to return a kiss.

Lucy saw me on the path and took me home to give me some fresh seal and said to return the first night of longshoring for dinner. "First Night" - sounds significant. I'll be there.

Entry. Storms. Willy says the ship's holed up in a cove. The sea's thickening like Jello, and in the few hours of murky light under a sky leached of all color I watch its wildly coiling breakers. Froth sets into gritty shore sculptures. A beast of blowing sleet, slush and darkness darkness. I'll never see sunlight again: is this what post-nuclear war is like, once the Wolf has been set free? I can't see moon or stars from the cloud cover. Snow fell, melted and fell again (like people's hair and foxes, it takes a long time to turn truly white). Most of the snow cover is blown here in fall blizzards across hundreds of miles. It's actually "desert".

The seal harvest is suffering. No planes, and radio contact often failing or you pick up something bizarre like the Deep South: atmospheric skip. You can't travel by land without destroying your snowmachine track. We're truly out of touch. Maybe all these dogs are an insurance policy and not a nostalgic reminder (of a not-so-far past! Sno-gos only hit two years ago). You can run dogs or even eat them if the Outside broke down, all supplies cut off. No one uses them now except Willy, who runs a team for fun. He says huskies are like a radar for incoming nanook, once the ice is sealed. Polar bears eat the chained dogs first before they get to any stray children. Windago bears. Grendels. Some have ten legs. Lock into a kill frenzy and wipe out fifty dogs per minute. Nice survival trait for when the bears find a herd of sleeping seal. I should get a dog alarm, then I'd have a few seconds to know I'm a goner. They remove your skin and then every shred of meat from your skeleton.

The frail little bush-planes, shit. The radio reported a disaster north of us with an entire family gone down and the pilot Bob, the one who flew me. These acts of nature become so personal. It seems malevolent. No one blames the pilot. I feel bad, everyone feels bad, I sense it. Death is so plain and frank here, the skinned naked animal body, the grisly head. On the beach kids were using a putrefied walrus for a trampoline (minus its valuable parts). Is that what a battlefield smells like, or when they exhume mass graves after a nasty re-gime falls? It's my damn northern genes, this morbidity. Sometimes I feel like the whole family died in this dark hole of an eenee, perhaps of a virus. Some outsider like me brought them. Lucy said during one epidemic Itiak posted guard and shot travelers who wouldn't heed their warning to keep away. A mean-ass village with a protectionist ethos. They survived that one plague, but other plagues made it through.

I stumbled on a trench with skulls and bones, just lying out in the open. Kids told me it was from "old time war". Millennia of death in clandestine layers in the permafrost. Take a hike and you tread on past lives, their dreams, all gone. There is no creepiness about it, just a melancholy heightened by the wind's moan. Well, maybe it is a little creepy. The land is haunted, Willy claims, and I see why, and grasp the traditional uncertainty of existence. Then you near the hamlet of today, bubbling with animation. Buttery lights, smoke, yipping puppies and kids sledding on drifts. And your heart lifts, somewhat.

Maybe I'll never get out of this place. I could live here gladly if one boon would be granted. To tell the truth, I'm on a downer. Shows, huh.

Entry. Looked out this dawn and saw my version of the Cargo Cult: a mighty ship at sea. It's a dark, troll-like presence, looming in and out of reality as it bucks the deep troughs. It's ominous on those black waves, crossbones could unfurl on its mast, but they have to try to unload. Gotta head down to the beach. I can pay off Flo for the parka she's sewing me, and if I don't earn enough I'll indenture myself to her or until she pays me to leave Itiak.

Later. Hands totally locked up, hence this garble. It's arduous but there's a harvest exhilaration with every able-bodied person turned out. The landing craft stops before the surf, men heave fuel drums into the breakers and we longshorers (women, eighth graders and I) run to nab them and roll them to safety. I can appreciate now these eyesores marring the coast. Think of the millions of them in the future, slowly rusting. But they are a form of beauty: security. And they keep coming. A thick slush cleaves to the grim metal, cruel on the wet hands, the drums roll and slip, crushing knees amid the stench of hydrocarbons. It is a strange harvest of kerosene, diesel, gasoline, propane, fuel oil. Petroleum literally keeps this community alive. (Willy says some years there is no driftwood available due to current changes. Imagine the eenee with only the seal-oil lamp, or the coffin-dark if the seal failed, followed by certain death. Would I have the guts to paddle to sea in a skin boat to light my lamp? I should be chastened in my dogma, but...petroleum is still evil).

Meanwhile skiffs steadily brave the surf for cargo. They have to be thrown over the crest in a frantic launching. Beside oil comes supplies, snowmachines, even sections of prefab house. No TVs though. Another storm is due, so we keep up a mad pace. My legs were cramping and I couldn't bend them or my fingers because the women expected me, the he-man, to salvage barrels from the waves. They made me warm up at a bonfire then sent me back in. Willy is manning his boat; he knows why I didn't go out with the other men, the seasick problem. He might roll barrels later because "that's where all the girls are."

Many Gretchen sightings in distant work parties, her red parka in the gray light. No shades anymore. I saw her bent over, "umuck-ing" a huge crate. She's not going to come near today. I sense her tracking my movement. If I get a little closer every round of barrels, she may not notice until I'm right there.

WE WORKED clear into the dark. Using carton stacks as windbreaks, we built bonfires and made tea. All the women were of a single mind: to finish the miserable job and keep the village going that long winter. Too busy to make trouble, we laughed and called out jokes, and even enemies were nice to each other. That is why I loved the *North Star.*

The birdman saw the goodness in it too. In the masculine way he exerted himself, not rationing his strength. He rescued oil from the surf, and saved a few women from getting hit by barrels caught in a surge. He was agile; how could I have called him *kuangazuk*? He was happy in his vitality and radiated a joy, smiling as he worked, and it made women of all ages watch him and smile back. They stared as boldly as they wished, for we were working together and that changed things. Every time he came toward a flock of teenaged girls they giggled and screamed, throwing their arms around each other as if in great danger. Even Christine tried to talk to him, protected by her band of followers. I saw the birdman flash a smile at her as they took a barrel from him.

During a lull from the boats the sun set with no more than a deepening of the gray sky and sea, but then a band cleared on the edge of the water into a gold. In the belt of flame rested the black silhouette of the ship, and white seagulls rode the wind there. The birdman stood and watched, his hair blowing wild. He surveyed the little fires up and down the beach as if in love with the world. He was just taking it in; it seemed I was not part of his adoration. The older women waved for him to join them at a fire. They were sharing a pipe, which amused him for some reason, and they were laughing merrily with him, entertained as well. And I was hit by an unbearable confusion so that I slipped and let a carton of cans crash on my foot. I had to sit and clutch it, rocking back and forth in pain that brought tears. Now I was jealous of *aka*s, jealous of the ocean and sky and even goddamned seagulls! If we were in some kind of contest, he was surely winning.

They used to catch fox by coating a knife blade with fat. The fox would lick it while the cold numbed its tongue so it didn't know it was cut, and it kept licking as it bled, licking until it fainted from blood loss. I was that silly, craving fox. My heart was one of those oil barrels tossed back and forth in the waves. Would it go on forever like this, these feelings surging and withdrawing like surf, slowly eroding me? I was exhausted from my vigilance, worn out by what the birdman did to me just by living, just by smiling at someone else. He was free, while I couldn't be free at all. All my longing and the fear of my longing, the fear of being discovered, the fear of him finding things out and the fear in my remembering them, the fear of losing him...or losing myself: it was too much work.

Something had to change. And when I saw Willy sauntering down from the village, a plan suddenly formed that would change things.

Willy was smoking with a tired but satisfied air. His hair was down to his shoulders, held in place with his red bandanna - he looked good that way, confident, like an old-time warrior. He was a man you could be proud of, who would keep getting better if life served him right. I didn't think long about that though, for we had to carry out my plan - the plan with Willy as my spearhead - before I lost my will or night fell. The golden band of sky began to close fast, and the time was now.

Some men were standing on the beach chatting about a past seal trip and gas prices. When I walked past them they fell silent, abruptly alert. Hunters can always recognize another. Willy raised his eyebrows at me in a question and I sent him a follow-me look as I moved up the beach. The angutkoq eye in the back of my head was open. It saw the birdman watching us from the warm-up fire; he had stopped joking with the old ladies. Willy was trying to figure me out too as he walked after me, for he sensed a difference, a faint whiff of danger. If the line plays out too fast you lose your game and the harpoon too. But I didn't know.

We reached the final tower of cartons. Most people had already gone home; the plan was working out. Out of sight behind the stack, Willy pushed his headband back on the broad plane of his forehead and waited for me to say what I had to say. He tried to light a cigarette but his fingers were stiff from grasping a wet rudder all day, so I struck the lighter. He dragged in once then stubbed his smoke out in the sand and looked at me and it was time for the next step. I hung my head.

"Pataq, I'm feeling so bad today..."

He studied me silently, surprised, maybe with a suspicion. I tried to look more depressed and less sneaky. I had to give off the right signals. Good hunters practiced this with animals; it was not just an angutkoq skill. They imagined themselves to be invisible, while their thoughts lured the beasts toward them. "It's that ship maybe...I don't know...the fall time, with all the birds gone. Don't you ever get like that?"

Willy smiled, relaxing. "No, I like it. But I go hunting. You girls stay in the house too much. You want to come along next time?" He touched my shoulder gently. When I looked up his black eyes were sympathetic. "It's okay," he said softly. "I'll take you to reindeer camp when the snow gets thicker."

I leaned against his warm chest where his jacket was open. Didn't he feel the cold? "Put your arms around me," I whispered tearfully. And it seemed real then, it was real, my sadness. Right away Willy did that, and I was in the caring circle of a man's arms for the second time in my life and I felt his heart thud and how his muscles had filled out from all that hunting. But it was an awkward hug; he wasn't used to it either, not with anyone. "Pataq, I'm not your sister," I said into his collarbone. It was not so hard to do this, I just had to free the small desire I had for him. He'd feel it and do the rest. "We're not even cousins."

"I know." His voice was husky like he needed to cough. I looked up and his eyes were even more surprised. Excitement had dawned there, then a need, smoking them over. He tightened his arms around me, I kissed his lips. They tasted of Lucky. His crotch stirred and he shifted closer then pulled back, laughing a little, unsure what we were up to.

"Don't you want to?" I asked.

"Yeah," he said at once, like a gasp. "Sure I do. But you never wanted to before..."

I kissed him again harder so my teeth cut his soft lip, and it was nothing like the birdman. I didn't like it. It was only a practical move, like biting off thread. As I felt the urge rise in Willy, for a moment I was afraid. I was going to let him enter me, I who never let men do that, not since my right to agree or refuse was stolen from me. But I was even more fearful of my reason; that was unclear, as dark and roiling as the sea. I wondered if Willy truly desired me, or if he was just taking the opportunity.

Then I closed down doubts and everything else so even my body was numb and we lay down on the beach. I took him inside fast like I was gulping dinner, no chewing, and he was plunging in all the way to the hilt so our bones ground. We did it there on cold, wet sand where people might see, a storm coming, the rising wind blowing between our legs. He knew it was crazy and wanted to finish it. As he thrust he grasped me as if I'd slip away, but I lay still. I was a fish. We didn't look at each other. He bent his head down near mine, I heard his harsh breathing, and I felt little, nothing good.

OUR ACTIONS can grow through the future in unseen filaments like a mold. If only I'd given him more time and chosen a more friendly place. If only I hadn't done it at all. If I had only known his destiny, the man who was not my brother, whose carefully buried feelings I had chopped out so recklessly with a blunt pick. He filled me but my mind was gone, it had soared down the shore from us, removed. And I was on the wind.

The birdman is frozen in time near the warming fire, a metal cup in his stilled hand. I sing in his ear on the underside of the wind: *Go up the beach, hurry...*

He puts down his cup and stands, knees stiff, feet numb, the sweat clammy on his back. He shivers and turns up his collar, looking around for Willy, needing suddenly to ask him...he doesn't know what about, but it is urgent. He hesitates, staring up the darkening beach. It is beginning to sleet, his nose is running. He starts up the shore, following our tracks. I ride above him as he hunches against the northeasterly gale that slams into his face, whipping his hair into impossible knots. He rounds the last tall stack of boxes, where something moves near his feet. At first he cannot make it out, it is so rare, so unimaginable in this setting, in this grim weather. He recognizes Willy's back, though not the bare *nulluk*. He stares down amazed, interested, not understanding. He gets ready to flee before mutual embarrassment.

I swooped and reentered my body, which was being slammed by the full drive of Willy's bones. A thin line through my lashes allowed me a narrow vision of the birdman, how his unguarded eyes shot wide as he saw my face, how realization shoved him in the chest, making him stagger backward. He hung there like on a rope, unable to look away from my face. He could have caught a glimpse of my bare thighs, but he didn't.

Willy released at that moment with a shout and collapsed onto me laughing like he'd never done it before. I saw the birdman snap his line and back up behind the tower in great haste. Willy rolled off me while yanking up his pants in one move, I pulled my parka down. We heard the warning clearing of a throat, but it was more like a man was choking.

"Someone's there," Willy whispered. "Did they see us?" He jumped up and walked around the boxes. "Hey! Tingmiaq! What's happening?"

"The boats are back," came the other's voice, funny-sounding. Willy was making some joke to explain being so far up the beach; he said he was going *anaq*, which he went on to describe as he led the birdman away. I wasn't sure if the sharp-eyed hunter had noticed the naluagmiu's tracks circled back a little, from a perfect view.

I lay as if dead. Willy's heat seeping out of me was full of life but I knew I was not pregnant, for my womb was as barren that day as my heart and the cold sand beneath me. Maybe I was as shocked as the two men. It had happened so fast. It was bad, something out of control like the bear but much worse, because I planned it and carried it out myself. The spirits weren't in charge and I couldn't blame them, could I?

At least the stalemate was broken.

THE BAND OF SKY had bled from gold into a scarlet; over it crept veins of fire. Then it was the dark red of coagulating blood shrinking fast into black. They were beaching the skiffs and securing tarps over boxes. Willy was gone. The birdman was slouched at a fire staring into it but never in my direction. People were discussing him. He'd been so cheerful in the surf all day and now his joy was broken: was he a mad scientist or had he just worn himself out? Fred Jr. came to fetch him for dinner - Lucy wondered what was taking him. With head bent, he trudged after Fred up the beach.

A pain gripped my throat like a vicious hand, like boys were pelting me with ice balls there. My plan had unfolded in the right sequence but I was hardly free from thoughts of the birdman. In my mind's eye I had to see him recoil over and over in dismay and bewilderment from the sight of me. He couldn't believe he'd been so wrong. He would surely leave Itiak now - who wouldn't? If I was him I would run from me. Yet there was an image to turn over and over slowly and relish like one of the deep mysteries of nature, what I saw etched on the birdman's face later at the fire once he had time to stew. He was jealous, undeniably.

So things were more equal now. And if I'd been looking for proof that a kiss could not give, I had it now. It was gratifying. I was thrilled, scared, and scornful too.

As for Willy, I didn't think.

LATE THAT NIGHT as the storm built, I traveled to the *ini* in the way angutkoq once visited the bottom of the sea. The Orphan stored all souls there upside down, embryos in her dark *ini* for the day she would return them. A true angutkoq might persuade her to set one free. But I would never visit the Underworld; I did not know the way. No angutkoq would ever again visit the Woman to beg. If the animals left, no one could find them. If someone died, they were lost forever. What kind of angutkoq was I, using my *qilya* to fly down the coast to see what a birdman was feeling, too cowardly to go in person? What kind of woman was I?

I entered through the skylight and hung on the whalebone beam, looking down with my spirit eyes. He had made a tidy home in the old "semi-subterranean hut". I could barely hear the wind and he was right - it was cozy. But it was so dark the sod walls seemed to eat the light. The shadows cast by lamp and fire leaped around like the impish *izhigak*.

He lay motionless on his back with his eyes wide open and shifting. But he could not see me up there, and if he felt my presence, he would not believe it. I did not have to use *qilya* to know what he was seeing: the form of Willy writhing on a shore, a woman's face turning. He sighed heavily like he could not get enough air, and he closed his eyes. Beneath his eyelids moisture gathered and sparkled in lamplight like icicles under the roof in spring.

"Shit, oh shit," he whispered, as creeks glittered down his temples into his hair, and he wiped them away but more ran. He sat up, lunging for a box of tissue on the ledge to blow his nose. "God..." He flung himself backward with his arms out, breathing, and covered his eyes but was still held prisoner by his imagination.

Up on the bone rafter I wondered, impressed by his suffering. And no longer scornful. Hunters felt no victory or contempt when they found the bloody wolf stretched out after a long chase. The animals were to be thanked for their innocence, for agreeing to be tricked.

When the birdman snuffed the lantern and had curled up on his side and grown still again, I drifted away like smoke.

For a long time there was no entry in the journal.

CHAPTER 18

I tremble at the harsh northern wind
The waves cast me about...
and I tremble at the thought of the hour
when the gulls will hack at my dead body
(YUP'IK HYMN)

THE NEXT DAY the wind had settled enough to finish unloading. I was relieved that the birdman wasn't there, nor Willy. But Polly came to the
beach, wearing the new fall parka Flo had sewn her. It was short and zip-
pered with a deep blue velvet cover that matched her eye shadow and a
white fox ruff that made her hair as black and shiny as raven feathers. She
was surely not there to work. At first I thought it was to watch some young
men helping with the heavy cargo. She was giving me funny looks but they
were sly, so I knew Willy hadn't told; she would be furious, not amused.

Soon I found out what she was up to. Lucy came down to the shore with
Natmun, laughing in that special tone used for discussing a person's foibles. As
they passed our fire she said loudly, "*Eeee*, I never had such a sad guest, that
Tingmiaq!" Natmun asked if it was because Lucy had fixed *ushavak* - that
was walrus flipper buried until it ripened. No, Tingmiaq had eaten plenty,
Lucy just wondered what was eating him. Homesick, Natmun guessed. They
were talking in English for our sake, probably because we were seen as the
birdman's surrogate family. The women passed by, battening down their
scarves, and switched to Inupiaq. What did *qigluktuq* mean? I had
forgotten...

"Mom said he visited," Polly told me. "Is it?" She smiled sweetly. "He has
an interest in someone, maybe." I made the sound of disgust in the back of my
throat but she kept on. "Maybe *I'll* get interested again."

"Go ahead! *Ki*, take him! He's so bugging!"

Polly said play-thoughtfully, "I know why he's so sad: someone's being so
mean to him."

"I never."

"Pataq said you were."

"That Willy; what does *he* know?" His name flew out harsher than I intended. "I can be mean if I want. We don't need scientists here!" My ears took the heat of my words.

Polly looked down at a coy angle, picking lint from the purple braid of her cuff. After a minute she murmured, "How come people who are twenty act like twelve?" To my sullen pout she said, "Some people must have slept together the way they're acting. All jumpy." Her eyes twinkled up at me. "You like him." I didn't argue anymore; look where it had gotten me. Silence was usually the best sign of one's innocence, but Polly had made up her mind. She surveyed me, my face and body. "Did he get funny, in the middle?"

"Of *what*?"

"Sexual intercourse," she enunciated slowly like a disease.

"I never do that! Not with him! Or anyone!"

"*Never*?" she cried.

"You know I have," I muttered, flushing again - had she forgotten my history? When my meaning finally hit her, Polly gasped, both hands flying to her mouth.

"I forgot! But that doesn't count," she added quickly. I wondered if the thing with Willy *counted*. "Well, do you think you might?" she persisted, "With *him*?"

"Who."

"Naluagmiu."

"I don't like the principal. Or do you mean preacher?"

She snickered. When I finally shifted my nose in a no, she said sadly, softly, "Did they ruin it for you? It can be a lot of fun."

"You told me. So many times."

"Well, you should try the real thing, it turns you into a woman. Just don't get pregnant. Maybe you're not ready..." What did she mean by that? And the "real thing". What Willy and I had done, it wasn't real either; he was just my decoy. "Here, take one of these. *Uvva,* take three." She unzipped her medical kit, which she had brought to the beach for accidents, and crammed the foil squares into my limp hand like she didn't expect to see me later, like I was going to run off that second now that I had the proper precautions. Numbly I accepted them to be polite, and stored them in my parka.

"Okay, but I'll just blow them up like balloons and scare the old men."

Polly smiled but she wasn't in the mood now for jokes; she was being medical. "You have to put it on right away as soon as his *ququluq* gets hard, and don't let him stick it in bare, because even before they come there's a little drop. And be careful when he pulls out after - it could fall off."

"What falls off? The *ququluq?*"

She giggled dutifully. "Just don't make a baby. Unless you want one. But Mom's getting tired of raising kids."

"I'll give it to you."

She laughed. "Half *naluagmiusak*. Cute. I fool." She colored; the unspoken part coming late to her mind was, of course, "And half *itkiliq*."

I looked at her flatly. "I don't want him, or any man. I'm like *uiliaqtaq* from old times. Or maybe I'm one of those girl angutkoqs that has a wife. It makes you more powerful." Polly looked alarmed even after I added, "*saglu*." I was glad she finally shut up.

We saw the birdman trudging up the beach with his hands in his pockets and head down, pushed by the southwesterly. As he passed us he didn't look up, but he'd spotted us. Polly nodded to herself; that the polite birdman didn't even greet us proved her hunch was right. He silently waited near the other men and they ignored him. When people were obviously blue you left them alone until they felt better. It was rude to even notice; people needed their dignity.

He wanted to go out in the boats with the men that day and Nelson offered to take him. They had trouble getting over the high crest of the surf but eventually broke clear with oars and headed out to the ship. On returning low in the water they fought again with the surf, rolling and pitching. Nelson looked calm but the birdman's face had turned an off-white. He leaned over the bow and vomited, the stuff flying into the wind and attracting seagulls, who tried to grab it on the wing. When they made it near shore, the birdman jumped out with the line but he was knocked over by a wave and his boots filled to pull him under. Polly laughed nervously with me as a group of old women ran to help, grabbing the rope and beaching the skiff. It would embarrass a man terribly.

We watched him lurch to shore, where he dropped to all fours, drenched. The sea had stolen his hat. He looked like he was thinking very hard with one hand on the sand and pressing his forehead with the other. When Nelson bent over him to see if he was okay, he shook his head and retched again near Nelson's boots. A wave surged in, washing it away. "You kids better go on now," Nelson commanded the children who ran over to gawk.

The birdman stood up, making "it's fine" gestures. But he looked bad, dripping seawater and listing on his feet like a drunk, which the children believed he was. They had a custom of mimicking people reeling from a party. Now they were imitating him, play-stumbling after him as he made his way up to the dry sand. He sank down again, hanging his head. Polly grabbed my arm and wanted to go to him - she couldn't be kept away from anything medical - but I thought he just wanted to be left alone awhile and told her so.

People speculated that the naluagmiu wasn't seasick but ate something bad. That worried Lucy, for *ushavak* was the main culprit of food-poisoning; it could wipe out whole families. She hurried to examine the remaining upchuck and reported that there were *ushavak* pieces in there, alright. She was getting frantic, unable to be calmed by the other women. Polly settled it. "No one else in your family is sick, so it isn't botulism," she said in a that's-that tone. Nelson had convinced the birdman to come down to a warm-up fire, where he was shivering, wrapped in a blanket and wearing Nelson's Arctic Cat hat. Polly and I went over. He managed to laugh at himself as Polly talked to him. He didn't have enough "Norse" blood. His "Granfar" had rowed a tiny dinghy into the high sea every day until he drowned.

"Like I s-s-said, accident-prone," he said to Polly in a cold-tensed voice. Ignoring me. "And this ecosystem's the most accident-p-prone in the world, like one unt-t-timely freeze and the chicks are g-g-goners and no time for a second c-clutch."

Polly and I looked at each other behind his shoulder. "You go home and get dry," she ordered him. She warned him about hypothermia, which killed many young men who thought they were tough. Flo wouldn't mind if he couldn't pay her. I shot Polly a stern look, for Flo was using the best quality materials for a parka *and* mukluks, and she already had to give away many gifts at the festivities to people who counted. He kept insisting he was fine until Polly snapped, "Don't be stupid!" She told of the whiteman who went hunting with Eskimos and they got marooned in the ice floes. The other men ate raw seagull meat but the naluagmiu refused and he died, he didn't listen.

The birdman obeyed her and started for the *ini*. I kept from watching his back, and returned to work. Soon, though, Polly told me to go check up on him. The wind had risen again and the temperature was falling fast. I didn't argue but hurried away without even sneaking, with the health aide's orders as my public alibi. As I headed south a worry grew in me until it was a dread. I broke into a run.

He was sitting at the bottom of the cliff almost to the *ini* - his legs refused to carry him further. When people got too cold they gave up, it was the body shutting down. The elders said it was a gift to protect you from the pain of death. You slipped into a dream of summer, dozing on a field of flowers. The birdman was halfway to that meadow, holding himself up by one arm. But he looked scared, and I felt by the humming in the air that the *inua* had visited again just as Calvin had predicted, right at his lowest point. I had undermined him. Willy and I had shocked the resistance out of his soul.

He shuddered when I reached him. His eyes were glassy as he stared at the surf. I saw nothing, just churned up dirty foam and tangled sticks in the waves rolling in monotonous and gray. But I knew the *inua* was still there, keeping its distance like a wolf. I tried to think of what kind of spirit might come from the sea to molest a scientist and frighten him out of his wits. Then I had an idea and my heart stalled in me.

With my body I blocked his view of the water. My spine crawled at what was behind me. I held his stunned eyes with my own and talked to him softly, like when you calm a child terrorized by a dog. "It's okay, Leif." Carefully I said his name - I had never used it before. "It's okay. I can help you." I waited for some reason to return to him, and after a minute it did, I saw it come back to his eyes. He pulled himself up from the sand, pulled himself together.

"Tell me what it looks like," I said.

"N-n-no, there's n-nothing there..." His teeth were hitting together so hard I could hear it. Shivering and shivering - *uulik.*

"Is it an animal or a man? An Eskimo man...part seal?"

At my words he shook in spasms, hugging himself. He had to get dry. If cold didn't kill him then pneumonia could later. He stared at me, his molars clicking like bone castanets. "How d-d-do you kn-now that?"

"I already told you. You never believe me." He shook his head. "There are more than five senses," I said gently.

He looked around my legs to the ocean and it seemed the spirit was gone because he closed his eyes in relief. His mouth worked. "Drowned..." he said, with a great effort keeping the rattle from his words. "He...c-crabs in the eyes. That must have been some acid, m-m-man." He tried to laugh. A drowned *inuk*, I thought in a wave of horror. That it was dead was very bad. They could help you hunt seal, they could be good, but only if they hadn't drowned. People used to find them dead in seal nets and then the relatives came to get revenge, even if you didn't mean to kill their kin. They tried to drag you into the water. They had long hair floating like black weeds, and white headbands made of bleached sealskin. *Naluaq.*

"Let's go away from here," I said. But the birdman was rooted to the sand, shaking. "*Ki,*" I urged him, tugging his hand. I led him down the beach like he was a toddler who'd given up on a long hike. He didn't whine or say anything though, just stumbled after me. I knew his joints were locked up in his wet clothes, but he managed to climb the bank and crawl into the *ini.* I built up the fire and told him to undress and get under the reindeer covers. But he just propped himself stiff-legged against the platform and worked his shoulders. I looked around the *ini*; it was exactly as I had envisioned it, when I flew there.

"I'll go get Calvin," I said.

"No, I'm fine. D-d-don't get Calvin." He added under his breath, "Just the men in white coats."

"Then I'll get his drum."

"What are you t-t-talking about, exorcism?" He began to cough with a deep-chest phlegmy sound. "I said *no!*"

"But...why not?" I faltered. "We need to find out what you did to make them send a warning! Maybe it was something your father did...at sea. Sometimes the spir -"

"Just k-keep my old man out of this, all right?" It was like an animal had growled. In the silence he glowered at me, eyebrows fierce. But the scowl altered slowly into a doubt. "What do you mean?"

I didn't explain; it was useless. The wood popped in the oil-drum stove, a hollow sound. The birdman looked in the fire and seemed to be trying to force his features into a blander expression, the science one that knew everything, though it was too late. I had already seen. "I'll stay with you," I said.

"I don't need babysitting. "

I handed him a cup of tea at arm's length. "*Ki*, drink it to get warm! And you need water because you...you threw up." He took it but immediately set it down, like what I gave him was tainted. "You'll be safe here," I said, feeling my stomach wringing like I might throw up myself, and my voice came out too high and thin. "It's a good place; whoever lived here was good."

"That's reassuring."

He had stopped shivering, and that could be a bad sign. "Let me feel," I said, reaching for his hand, but he pulled it back. "Blood all goes to your insides," I explained, "Maybe you even feel hot, but you're in danger." Silently he drew his sleeping bag around himself. "Change to *dry* clothes," I ordered.

"I will, as soon as you *leave*." He cut me a look full of darkness.

I added more fuel to the stove; he had split his logs perfectly, like it was artwork, but it was running too low. Funny priorities. He looked so wretched huddled in the bag, having accidents that could kill him. I was treating him like a kid, but he didn't seem strong anymore. He had slipped so helplessly under the waves; what had happened to his loon-swimming? "You better get more wood soon; it's hard to find under snow."

"Doesn't matter," he shrugged. "As soon as the phone's working I'm calling a friend to send plane fare."

We looked at each other across the room, and though his expression was aloof and he had found some kind of armor, alright, I saw through it like it was just water. Of course he was dwelling again on what he'd seen up the beach last night. Was that worse than a drowned merman? He dropped his eyes first, with a faint frown, as if my look would harm him. He'd cut himself off from those too-long exchanges of ours, he'd cut off his trust that had nourished and delighted me, and - I suddenly realized - had become the greatest pleasure in my life. But *I* had cut it off when I lay in the sand and became a line that marked the end to our friendship, and he had stepped over it.

I wanted to say something to make it better. I could tell him that, like the infant in his story, a long-ago part of me had been thrown into the cold waves and left there to try to swim. It had crawled out and somehow found its way back, but there was something wrong. I could tell him of the misshapen *palrailuk:* patched together with so many animal pieces, mindless, only able to follow simple orders that could backfire. Everyone could make such a mistake. If hearts were suffering they drum up all kinds of bad things. I wanted to explain we were good actors up north, who hid our feelings because others were so good at hearing the unspoken. We were mimics who could lie with our gestures, laying false trails to survive.

Look at the lemming that everyone wanted to eat, pretending to be big and ferocious when jaws were closing in. Or look at the birds, pretending to be grass so no one could see their nests. Like these small creatures, women were in a weak position, so we had to be false and test things; we had to make sure. We couldn't be as simple as men. An ecologist could understand that. It wasn't really the survival of the fittest but of the sneakiest. He'd said it himself, how we had to go undercover to adapt. But it didn't seem like he would understand anything now. I wanted to remind him the *inua* could follow him all the way to Seattle, but he looked too miserable.

"Flo is making you a real nice parka," I said, to no response. "She's the *best* sewer! And...and the mukluks - "

"I'll give her whatever I earned." The birdman interrupted me again, though he knew it was rude, and looked pointedly at the door flap.

"Okay, I'm going. But chop wood tomorrow, not today. Your heart can play stop."

The birdman grew a small, twisty smile as he looked down, one meant for himself. "My heart?" he murmured.

"Yes! Please let it rest, promise."

And he nodded but it seemed like he didn't care if his heart stopped. It was one of those chances in life that you must grab before they close off, like the fiery long eye in the dark sky opening and letting birds through then shutting again, leaving you in the night for who knows how long. All of us humans were given tongues. Why, then, is it so hard to ask directly the vital questions? Maybe it is because we know that although words can mend us and work magic, they cannot convey the full meaning. And they can lie. I could have said something. He could have asked the most important question in our two lives. He let it pass, afraid of the answer. I tried to pass the knowledge to him through my eyes in that more ancient language, but he wasn't looking in them anymore.

I VISITED CALVIN anyway. As I entered from the *kanichak* I saw Calvin yank a cord, like he'd been just waiting all those weeks for my arrival. A wooden duck puppet hanging from the ceiling moved its wings, and sticks beat once upon four tiny drums. "What's *that* for?" I asked, unable to help myself; it was better to not ask. Calvin peered at me with his bright weasel eyes and he had changed his hair again - now it was in a greasy, combed back way I still hated. He grew more unsettling with the years.

"A woman is entering *kazhgi*," he said, "Duck announces."

"So *now* what?"

"So now...nothing. But we are aware of the dangers now." Nervously I looked around but the only *we* in the cabin were Isaiah and Calvin, who already knew I was there. I stood in the doorway, unsure. Maybe I should just leave. "I jokes," said Calvin, "Sit down."

I tiptoed inside and sat before him on the floor, the client's spot. He said in the old days the angutkoq always went to the client's house, but no one wanted him to visit so they came here. He looked at me. "Well? What do you want?" he said. I took a deep breath, knowing no one else could help me.

"Calvin, what does *qigluktuq* mean?"

"Huh? It means very sad." He lifted an eyebrow. "You're here about that naluagmiu again, ah? I hear he's sad because they made him work with girls."

"*Ayii,* that's not it," I muttered. "He likes girls, not like *you.*" Calvin just sniffed. As I told him about the *inuk,* he listened with an odd light behind his glasses that made me wonder if he was envious again; maybe he'd never had a client who saw evil spirits. I wanted to tell him he was lucky. He questioned me about the naluagmiu's "attitude". I said the birdman thought it was just brain chemistry - a "new-row-transmitter," which sounded like a radio.

"Scientist," sniffed Calvin. "Kayuqtuq, did the preacher ever tell you, can you get into heaven without believing in Christ? I would tell him to give something to the sea because it wants something from *him.* But he is an unbeliever." The angutkoq lit a cigarette and tilted back his head, regarding me without any expression until I got his point.

"Come back when it's not science," he said, looking tough like a hoodlum. "Maybe when he is *really* in trouble. You know what an old whiteman said, everyone believes in God in a foxhole." I thought he meant a real fox. "A *war,*" he explained, and sighed. "I only got so much energy, I can't waste it. And I warn you it is different when you're involved with a client. It confuses you; you lose direction. If you want to help someone, then look at yourself first. People who think they are angutkoq, who think they can mess with spirits to get things for themself, *inua* teach them a lesson. What is most dear to you?"

I swallowed, looking down. Calvin said, "That is what they might take from someone stupid. The thing most dear." He held his hand to his mouth and closed his eyes for a time as if listening hard. "Think about nets, that drown the seal-men. Think what kind of net your heart is, trapping things it should not. What did you dream recently?" He waited, but I wouldn't tell him. "Don't just think about what's hunting your scientist friend," he said in a strangely liquid voice - almost like he was drooling. "Is something hunting *you?*" His eyes shot open then and sent me an angutkoq look that scared me so much I jumped.

Yes, something was pursuing me, since summer camp, since I called down the bear; I had felt it coming behind me several times. My heart was pounding hard and fast.

Calvin stretched his lips in a wide smile. He had fangs, white and sharp! I let out a little scream. Calmly he removed his beastly teeth and I saw they were just a carving, which he put in his pocket with a satisfied smirk, swallowing his spit. "You have to go alone into the spiritworld far from man," he said, "and maybe one of them will have pity on you and teach you. I can't help you now."

NOR WOULD CALVIN let me borrow his drum. *Sauvaq* was part of an angutkoq's own body, he said; would I want to take his arm or his leg? He was a moody man, who seemed to be getting worse. Last time I'd seen him he was helpful but this time he seemed peeved with me, like everybody else in town. As I left his cabin I was thankful night had fallen, because I could not keep my feelings off my face. I had no one to blame for this situation but myself.

Abe had brought in a walrus and I asked Flo if I could have the stomach. She raised her eyebrows, not asking what it was for, though a drum was the only thing you made any longer from one, since pane glass took over. Maybe she was afraid to bring up the subject. She did, however, take the opportunity to lecture me about not learning to skin-sew. By twelve she could sew mukluks by herself. A woman might have to rely on others if she didn't sew, and she had to buy everything from a store. Sewing made you a better wife, too.

Polly never learned either, but I made no retort and simply looked down at my feet as if listening and agreeing. The stomach was so big and heavy I had to drag it on a hide to Willy's, in the dark so no one would see. When I inflated it to dry it so the membrane wouldn't wrinkle it was gigantic, as big as me and pretty hard not to notice in that small cabin.

At the Center I had seen how men steamed wood to bend it into the runners and rounded backs of sleds. I would make my own *sauvaq* in the shape of the sun with the power of the woman in the sun. I'd try to help the birdman and fix things, though he wouldn't believe it. If only I had the power to keep the phone broken so he couldn't call; I needed time.

CHAPTER 19

A crane calls from the reeds
Its child answers.
"I have a full cup
Come and drink with me..."
THE I-CHING (ANCIENT CHINESE)

I KNOW NOW what Calvin meant about getting involved with a client. Angutkoq could have sex - that could even help them spiritually - but if they fell for someone their powers could get ingrown. Imagine an insecure witch, one lovelorn. The old tales were warning us. That's probably what Leif was thinking as he tried to type up that summer's findings of goose droppings in a dark, abandoned sodhouse. Trying to chase out the images in his head of a bear, a drowned merman, and Willy's nude, pumping hips.

The dream I did not want to tell Calvin was this: a whiteman, an old time trapper, comes to a trading post with his dogsled full of furs. It is Indian country, with the thick stands of spruce trees from my infancy. The trapper starts unloading the stiff, raw furs to show me, and he comes to one that wears a red *kaspaq*. It is the hide of a girl about twelve, with empty eyeholes just like a skinned animal. This is the best one, he says, and he want to give it to me for free in a special deal. He smiles in an evil way. *That is me*, I think, when I was young; he is trading me myself. But I refuse to take it, I feel too sad and horrified, so he takes it back to sell to someone else who will not care.

I tried to understand how this dream had a connection, what kind of waters I wanted to cast my net into. And I realized Calvin had helped me after all.

WHEN THE MAIL PLANE finally made it in, a premonition told me to hurry to the post office. The government checks were late and the shack was crowded with people who'd wrung all their credit out of the Native store. Flo had me exchange skin slippers for sugar and tea but that was it. William didn't want to even barter. There wasn't any cash left anywhere in town even if the checks did come. It was right before a big snow; I could smell it coming.

The birdman stood near the counter, his eyes on the pile of letters as it grew shorter. He muffled a painful-sounding cough in the crook of his elbow. After one dismissive glance he paid no attention to me. I knew his mail carried bad news. Sensing it too, Jacob handed everyone else their letters before he took up the birdman's, which he'd shuffled to the bottom. At last Jacob held out the final letter to the naluagmiu who had been visiting his office so fruitlessly. "Mister Try-give-sen," he read off, "Finally got his mail, ah? From Seattle..."

The birdman opened the envelope slowly, like his fingers also knew he didn't want to read it, but his eyes skimmed down the paper. His body reacted before his face. Blindly he exited the building, bumping into Ellie and the doorjamb. His mumbled apology came too late for Ellie, who he knocked off balance. I pushed my way after him. People were watching, attuned to disaster in the post office, where bad news often came. I didn't care.

But he was too fast for me to catch up until he reached the *ini,* where he leaned against the snowy roof, coughing and out of breath. He studied the paper with bowed head, so engrossed he didn't notice me. He didn't see me fall when the humming started in my head and grew into a roar, and my vision darkened and opened up into the other plane where the truth is known in images. Under a black sky I saw the boat of his father, but it wasn't moving. It tilted, run up against a reef, and the bow was ruptured. Then my mind went as black as that sky and I was on the ground with snow in my face. I tried to lift my head. Snow cascaded heavily, the soft wet flakes dizzying me as they spiraled from a topless gray into my eyes.

The birdman was staring down at me. He could have been a boulder on a far-off hill - cold, dull and misted. "What's wrong," he said. I sat up, my limbs awkward and loose. "Why are you always following me?" he asked. "Are you trying to fuck with my mind?" I shook my head. "Is the phone working?"

"I don't know." My voice was slurred. He looked down at the imprint of my body, my snow angel. His face was pale, like a true whiteman's. It was scary with the stark black of *umik;* I thought of a volcano's sides cut with jagged patterns of snow.

"Just tell me if the goddamn phone's working, it's important!" He was shouting, his eyes black on mine.

"I said I don't know," I muttered. And I didn't know, though I knew that his father was dead and that the sea had indeed wanted something from the birdman. He marched past me swift as a caribou again, galloping toward Soola's house. That's where the phone was. I found my voice again. "You don't have to make no phone call!" I yelled as I climbed to my feet. "Because I can tell you. But it doesn't matter," I said to his halted back, "He never loved you and you won't hear that he cared about you on no telephone!"

He turned and plowed back to me in the fresh-fallen snow. "What?" he said softly. His bare fingers curled at his sides. It was like facing off with a gunslinger in a movie. Who would shoot first? I guess I'd already shot. I was no cowboy, I was angutkoq, much deadlier than a conscientious objector about to fall over. I didn't want to hurt him again, I didn't, but he was looming on me, his eyes cold, and I was that lemming. "What did you say?" he repeated.

"You want to know how it happened," I said slowly and clearly, "of how he passed away. She couldn't write it. He had a heart attack and he fell off. He drowned. The boat ran onto a rock and they can't find...the remains." I had known those grim details of his father only as I spoke them.

His body leaned towards me as if impaled on a spear. His eyes ran over my face as he imagined these details. Suddenly he inhaled sharply and coughed hard into his hand. A lot of water was in there, he was drowning too. How sick was he? I wondered in a calm nest in my thoughts. He got control of his lungs and fell back a step, shaking his head. "Drowned? No...he has a crew. They'd pull him out."

"He couldn't afford them because the fishing was bad, and they made the season too short," I said. "Limited entry. He went out alone." I had never imagined whitemen having such troubles: loss of a fishing season, government rules, death at sea. Maybe it was worse for them; in a village people would have helped his father for free if he wasn't too mean. He wouldn't have to pay a crew.

"No. He-he wouldn't go out -" The birdman was stammering, and so pale. I thought I must be pale too. "Why are you -" he began, and stopped. "How -" he tried again, swallowed. And his body and face collapsed in a little dip before he caught himself. I was the hunter who wounded an animal and now sights the gun for a more lethal spot to fell it completely. Scientists needed "empirical evidence" and I had it. More snow silently speckled his hair. His face was carven again in that same far-off boulder.

"Why do you feel so bad?" I asked him. "When he was dying he didn't think of you. He was no father for you, worse than mine, and I don't even got one. What's the date on the letter?" I asked when he didn't respond. "When did they say it happened? You knew when. You had a dream."

Something stirred in his eyes, an awareness. At last you understand what I am, I thought. "I have to go," he said, and was half-loping, half-stumbling north, a dark form in white as soft flakes spun slowly down.

I was sorry I rubbed the death in. But he needed me to release the pressure, in the way feelers used to drill in people's skulls to let out demons. In the *ini* his journal lay open, but there were only a few scrawled lines: "*Beggar to beggar cried, being frenzy-struck, 'The wind-blown clamour of the barnacle geese' "*...and one page back, "*The desire of the moth for the star*". Was he going crazy? The paper had not been touched for days.

When the birdman didn't come back I went to Soola's and found out the phone was up. There were onlookers so I pretended to want to call about an order, but I had never phoned before and Soola watched me curiously. Visitors could listen in on conversations, the reason there were always so many visitors, I guess. Pretending to read the numbers on the wall, I listened to talk in the main room. Sure enough, the topic was the birdman - he'd been there. Someone *had* died because he asked how it happened and he told someone to stop crying, he couldn't understand them. There was talk about a funeral and he hung up fast - he had called collect. He seemed angry and was curt to Soola, and he was then seen walking south using an inland route, not along the cliff. That was to avoid me, of course.

He wasn't at the *ini*. A large animal could not hide on the windswept

Gyulnyev; the little willow and alder grew sideways and made no thickets. In the dim light of the fast approaching evening his boot tracks made dents in the slush. He was heading to the channel. I pulled up my hood and bent into the wind at a half-run, in the way people used to travel in winter. The wet snow worked through the cracked skin of my mukluks but I hardly noticed. I thought someone - or something - was behind me, tracking *me*. "I don't *need* you! Go away!" I shouted, turning, but only the wind answered. The landscape was empty.

He was hunched on his old camp log near Willy's duckblind, which had fallen over. The snow had stopped. A fine spray blew in, bitter. I tasted the salt. "I followed you!" I called out, thinking I may as well agree that's what I did before he accused me of it. He stood up in the manner of the prey with no fight left who just hangs its head, agreeing in that time-honored pact.

"You believe me now," I said.

"I don't know what I believe," he said slowly, not meeting my eyes.

"Are you afraid?" Afraid of *me*.

He shrugged bleakly. "A person has to be a little afraid. More than a little..." His hair was blowing in his eyes but he just let it. He was tired.

I let his words sink in: it was the first real acknowledgement of what I was, nothing play about it. And it was from a scientist. This was what I had wanted, but I didn't want it anymore. No one likes an angutkoq, not when they saw to the core of things, no one could stand living with that. And now the birdman didn't even seem to be the birdman anymore, or the man who joked and made me laugh. He was lost, adrift on an ice pack, wondering if he was heading to the steep, dark coast of Siberia. And I missed him.

"Angutkoqs don't have friends," I said.

He narrowed his eyes at the white line of surf. "Why did you come here? Do you want to see me cry to prove your theory? Well, I'm not going to. And you're right, I should be happy he's gone."

"No, I didn't mean it! There's a story the old people tell -" I searched for a good one - "about the Boy Who Hated His Father. They lived far out of the village, because people knew there was black magic in their house. The dad had a line going down into the floor all the way to Hell. He was fishing for demons. And the boy was afraid...but -" I paused, thinking it should end differently for my purposes - "but he still had to love his *ataata.*"

The birdman frowned. His knees looked wobbly; he was on the verge of blacking out. "Look, I don't want to listen to a story right now..."

"Well, it's over!"

"Then leave! Please, I just want to be alone." He allowed his knees to give, and slumped back on the log. He shivered and started coughing again, trying to keep from it. He was hatless, gloveless, and only wearing the green slicker with no insulation. The wind on the channel chilled the marrow. I hoped my body protected him from some of it. "I need to think about how he died," he said, "It just seems...pathetic." He gave a short laugh. "He'll never get to Valhalla now, where he can endlessly drink with his comrades. You have to die in battle, you know, not like some poor old man. A *heart* attack. God."

He hit his fist on his chest. I tried to find something else for him to think about. "What about the funeral?" I asked. Maybe he'd have to fly out on the next plane, or charter one. He shook his head, staring at my sodden mukluks.

"None. They don't believe in funerals. He's from halfway around the world and my mom doesn't have the money anyway. They're all so distant and nobody speaks the same language. And my mom decided to drive to Manitoba to her sister on the Reserve..." He rested his forehead on his hand. "But I'm not going," he mumbled faintly.

What an impossibly strange family. "Let's go to my house," I said. "Everyone will feed you now in town." He shook his bent head - there was a disbelief in the motion I didn't understand. His hair was covered in fine drop-lets from the sea. In the silence that followed, my throat ached like the wind was buffeting through a hole chopped in it, a tomcod hole. Was this how he felt? I barely heard his question.

"Can you tell me something? What are you and Willy...to each other?"

That was on his mind at a time like this? I changed the subject. "I was wrong today what I said. I get so mad when you don't listen, but I'm sorry..." Then the words rushed out in their simple sincerity; they were the truth also. There were many truths, and you chose which one. Now I chose a kinder one.

"Because your dad did care. He went out fishing alone because he...he was saving money to give you...and he felt bad he hurt you. It's just when you started growing into a man he was afraid. Sometimes fathers are, when they think maybe sons are better than them."

The birdman gazed up at me, appearing hypnotized. At that point I saw I was free to influence his mind and there would be no resistance. I tried to make my voice soft. "But when you were little he would come when you slept and just...*unga*..." I slowly reached and touched his hair, "like this..." and I petted a strand of it back from his forehead, which had a line of pain. The brown stuff was cold and wet, and fine like the fur of *umingmaq*. I tried to comb out some of the unspeakable trapped sorrow that a lost orphan feels, that I felt.

"And he would say, 'that is my boy' and he called you Lucky after a man who left his country in a boat -" the whole name came to me - "Leif the Lucky." My fingertips trailed down his temple, over the bluff of his cheekbone. I hoped the spirit of his father wasn't trying to drag him into the Land of the Dead, to keep him company. "And you know that, because you sometimes just pretended to sleep."

"You're right," he whispered. I looked in his eyes, willing him to break. He could not bury this, or the *inua* would find him more easily. They would sicken him. His heart had a glacier, it had to melt and break up and free the living things that had frozen there long ago.

"Yes, he loved you. You were his boy," I said like to a child, "*aninang*..."

With no preparation of the face, his tears welled up and spilled out. They reached my hand, scalding it, and kept on falling as swift as a brook off a sheer cliff, as fast as a cut vein. He closed his eyes but they sprang from beneath his lids and flowed. His nose ran clear. It was a completely silent form of crying. He didn't move anymore than a carved figurine, nor was he breathing. He *was* melting, and like a glacier he suddenly broke up and fell in pieces into the sea. He grabbed blindly at my hand, and squeezed so hard the small bones ground together. I let the pressure hurt me, it was good pain, like prodding an infection. Through it I felt the strength of his anguish.

He let go. Hiding his expression in his hands, he finally released sobs, wrenched from deep in his stomach. I had never witnessed a man's crying before either; drunks do not count. I know Abe did it when his son died, he had gone hunting alone in order to let it loose. I had never even heard the sounds from a man in the dark, only from Flo or Polly when they thought everyone slept. Would anyone ever mourn like that for me someday? Would the birdman, if I died? Maybe I had cried like this when my mother left me...

Because he leaned against me, I petted his hair and his shoulders. I could not imagine that I was doing this at the channel, in the wind, holding the weeping birdman. But it felt very right. "Oh god, what are you doing to me?" he asked, his voice drowned out by the wind. I thought he meant the universe. We were like that until it grew darker and so cold I was shivering too, and he had stopped. I gave him a wadded tissue from my pocket that I saved for children.

"If you won't come to town I'll bring you home now." He nodded but didn't get up, so I took both his hands and pulled him to his feet. We lost our balance, he sort of laughed. It was good, he was going to be all right. But on the way to the *ini* he dragged his feet, coughing. We were walking side by side in the snow, and I was lightheaded.

I made him collect some driftwood with me on the moonlit beach, where branches stuck out like white bones from the white. We tossed it up the bank. I beat the snow off and dragged smaller pieces into the pitch-black of the *ini*, telling him to light the kerosene. He knew where the matches were by feel. By lamplight I chopped up damp wood with the hatchet and started a fire with one of his science magazines but it took some time for the small, reluctant flame to catch.

He was sitting on the platform watching sadly. By the light I saw his eyes were bloodshot. His life had fallen all to pieces. "Jeez, winter's coming. You really need to get more fuel," I said. He just smiled ruefully. "I'm going to get some food for you now. You get in bed."

"Yes Master."

"Give me your foot." When he didn't move I took his leg and tugged the rubber boot off; his foot was ice. I rubbed it and pried off the other boot and looked for dry socks, but his extras were still wet. I would bring him some of

Willy's. I looked around the *ini*, at the typewriter with paper in it, only a few lines typed, no food but pilot crackers and peanut butter. And *tunuq*.

When I turned back he was lying sideways with his eyes closed. I found his jerry-can with water and brought a cup and tapped his foot. He mumbled without stirring. "Drink this," I said. "*Ki*, sit up." He obeyed. "You're getting sick," I said kindly.

"No, I'm fine, I'll be fine. I just...I just got to get hold of myself." When his eyes flooded again I was alarmed.

"I'll go get Niviak..."

"Polly? No!" He wiped his face again. "Don't embarrass me."

"She's health aide."

He cleared his throat. "I have a cold, true, but what's wrong with me is not exactly a health problem. It's...do you understand?"

I did. "But you didn't want help from Calvin either."

"It's not in the bone doctor realm either, far as I know." He seemed ready to cry again, but stopped it. "Unless *you're* a bone doctor." We looked at each other a long moment, my heart skipping around. I held my hand on my neck as if warming it, or as if strangling myself.

He said lowly, "Oh, you're so beautiful," and I stood there, blushing. He thought I was beautiful, but didn't know he was too. I wished he had some bird *anaq* around to study or something. What I saw in his eyes did not seem like desire - not lust, anyway, which I had seen at an early age. No, I was a distant bird, a swan on a far lake across a stretch of tundra he had no way of crossing.

"What *is* your sickness?" I asked in a small voice.

"I don't know if I can tell you. And I wouldn't tell you except -" he shut his eyes - "except you're here. And today, I mean..." He lay back on the bed with his arm over his face. "I'm not very clear on things."

I tried to make sense of his groping half-sentences. Did he mean about Willy and me? He had tried to ask but I hadn't answered. Could not. "You think I'm...good-looking?" I asked. His answer came late.

"Ya, I do..."

"I'm Indian."

"I know." He said it like it was a good thing, precious.

"Willy told you."

"I knew already. But he did tell me."

"Pataq doesn't care about that."

He breathed in and out several times, his face shadowed by his arm. "Then he's no fool," he murmured. I hesitated, certain he would say more, another shadowy half-hidden phrase. But he was silent for a long time.

Strange thoughts came to me, that if the birdman was dead he would forgive me from heaven, or the moon, wherever his soul was kept. And that if he was dead I could tell him *everything*, in the way women used to confess to reeds growing in marshes, knowing they'd never tell. I could tell him that *he* was the one who was beautiful and the one I wanted to lie down with. I wanted him to be like the goose, who would never leave his mate behind if she got injured. Even if it was time to go south, even when the snow fell and geese were supposed to be long gone, he would stay by her side. He *had* to; he was a goose.

I covered him up and hurried to get reindeer stew and reindeer socks, but when I got back he was asleep. His feet were warm under the fur, but I put the socks on them. He had kind of long toes. I didn't wake him to eat; what he needed, far more than food, I was afraid to think about. It was easier with him asleep anyway, and I could study his face without worry that he'd catch me. It had transformed somehow so that it was not exotic or alien anymore; it wasn't birdman or longhair or part Indian or naluagmiut or the handsome outsider who turned heads. It was just *him*. When had he changed - while I was getting food?

"Leif," I whispered to him, and he stirred, like my saying it gave me more power over his soul. But he didn't mind. And I just sat there while the moon flooded through the skyhole onto his face, now free of care.

BOOK FOUR

"Be Not Afraid of the Universe"

For the sin of killing the birds who cannot cry
I myself have no voice
For the sin of killing
the molting birds who cannot fly
Now I myself cannot flee
MOTOKIYO (ANCIENT JAPANESE)

Whither is my soul gone away?
Whither is my soul gone away?
It is gone to the northward
Of those who live northward of us
HEQ (ANGAKOK, UMINGMAQTORTIUT)

What medicine shall I use?
What medicine shall I use?
Your dear face is what I long for...
(HAIDA SONG)

Do not give him medicine;
His ancestors wish for him to dream
(K'UNG! HEALER, KALAHARI)

CHAPTER 20

The last time I saw him
he was flying over the ocean
with a long string of goslings, lord, lord lord
(TAQSIVAK FOLK SONG)

THE RADIO sent out an all craft warning. Willy returned safely from a hunt, arriving just as naluagmiut caribou hunters blew in from the north with Waldo the guide. The married couple boarded with us - Abe didn't like sport hunters but we were short of money. So I moved back to the cabin.

Willy had shot seals but they sank before the boat could reach them. His hunting partner Stanley was luckier, and his mother sent over a share of *ug-zruk*. As soon as he lay down Willy was asleep, though not before letting me see his meaningful grin. *Izhigii*, oh no. I cooked the meat and waited for him to wake up. There was no way I could keep living like this, but where else could I go? Maybe Polly would move in with a man; then I could have her bed...but maybe the man would move in with her, and they'd have babies and I'd be stuck at Willy's forever.

He snored on. At last I blew in his nose until he slapped at me. "Pataq!" I cried. He bolted up, his grogginess vanished. "We can't do that again, ever!"

"Do what?"

"Don't *saglu* - you know what!" Willy swung his feet to the floor, his crushed bangs sticking out like black wings. Had I truly lain beneath him? I couldn't touch him again, not even his shoulder, not even stand close! It would be like that old rule where a young husband didn't dare brush the hand of his mother-in-law or meet her eyes, or a terrible thing might happen: would he try to jump her, out of control? Would *she*?

Willy was studying me. "How did it happen, anyway?" he asked. "Out there on the water I thought maybe it was my imagination. All those years, and then boom." He studied the seal grime under his nails. "Didn't you like it?"

"No! We can't again. Pataq."

"But you play-start it."

"No way. You did. You let me."

"Is it?" He looked eager to believe me. Maybe it was more manly that way. "Anyway we sure did it. And...you know that naluagmiu saw us? Shit, he sure was surprised." Willy's chuckle sounded forced. "But even it was someone else, why is it so bad? They know we're not related."

"Pataq -"

"Don't worry." He heaved a sigh, stretching. "Those *ugzruk* - they sure keep away from me. What'd you do, cast a curse on me? I jokes," he said immediately, but his eyes were different; trouble had hidden in the grin of his return, a lurking quality like a *nanuq* behind ice, and not just unhappiness at failing the hunt. Out there a man had a lot of time to ponder. "Girls get so worked up," he muttered.

"What do you know about women?"

"More than you know about men. Anyway, we're not so different." Willy picked at his fingernail where it had torn. "Who do you think is more different," he added slowly, "me and you...or me and Leif?"

That name struck me in the gut. I swallowed and looked out the window. He went to wash up in the basin. "It's okay," he said quietly with his back turned. "I just don't think you need to do that. He likes you good enough without playing a game. Men don't like to play those games. Whitemen either, I guess."

He was much smarter than I had known. He turned around, face dripping, hands out; I threw him the towel. "You be careful," he said into the cloth.

"Careful of what? *You?*"

"Don't be mad. Maybe I should be the one mad. I mean be careful going for a naluagmiu, even a good one. They don't stay." He dropped the towel on the table, looked at it, then picked it up and threw it on the drying rack. That was a first. "Dinner done? I'm starving." I went to get the bowls, aware of his eyes on my back. "Someone passed on in his family," he said.

"Father," I blurted carelessly. No one else knew. While I brought the kettle Willy looked on with his elbows on the table, with his chin propped in his hands.

"I remember when *Ataata* killed himself," he said. I thought he had died in an accident, the mother too, and Willy saw my surprise but changed the subject. "How's he taking it, Tingmiaq," he asked evenly.

I shrugged, eyes downcast. "Maybe you should visit him." I was hoping Willy would go see the shape Leif was in and help him, chop a lot of kindling, and make him go to the old folks for a meal. After a silence, Willy laughed.

"Goddamn, have you seen those caribou people yet?" He mimicked Waldo's whiny voice: "Hey, you cute little Eskimo you, look at me! A real *big game hunter!*" He dove into the meat, chewing so vigorously his jaw muscles bunched.

I laughed too and was relieved he was going to drop the whole subject, yet I didn't know how I could keep living there.

FLO NEEDED ME FAST: she was in a panic and sent little Betsy to tell me the naluagmiut hunters wanted dinner. "What am I?" I asked Willy, "the expert on whitemen now?" I was not happy to be around sport hunters either but I hurried to the house to rescue Flo.

The middle-aged couple were at the card table playing blackjack, which Flo forbade, it was the Devil, but she never spoke up with naluagmiut. The woman had yellow-white hair like a *nanuq* and gray, worried eyes. She was smoking too, stubbing butts in a seal-oil dish. Her husband dealt out the cards with long hairy arms and he frightened me; I wouldn't look at his eyes to see what color they were. The couple looked glum, probably wishing Waldo had never brought them to a village. They were not fascinated by our culture and were griping about the lack of a bar and TV and the oncoming blizzard that kept them stranded. Flo was nervously boiling macaroni, while Polly stood near the door looking outraged.

"*Alapaa!*" I said loudly, remarking how cold it was. I saw Abe smile to himself at my double meaning. The whiteman stared boldly at me and I wondered why he was so interested, until I saw him watching Polly in the same way. Right in front of his wife, and worse, in front of the old people, their hosts! Polly was getting ready to escape, now that I had arrived for Flo's moral support. She took me aside by the door, her eyes showering dangerous little sparks. If she was a dog her ears would be laid back.

"Don't let that asshole give Mom and Dad anymore trouble. He thinks he's so amusing." She told me the whiteman had been joking around, asking how much they'd sell Polly for.

"How much they say?" I asked. "I fool," I added hastily. "You think I can stop him?"

"You got the evil eye," Polly assured me. "Me, I'm getting out of here." She tied off her mukluks at the ankles with furious movements. "That Tingmiaq was here a while ago," she said offhand. "He paid for the parka but Mom just gave him the mukluks."

I made no reply. If Polly wanted a conversation about Leif, let her make it herself. I was thinking, *he bought a parka instead of plane fare!* and my insides were rejoicing. I was thinking, *angukaa*, Flo must really like him. She had sewn the boots from glossy reindeer leg-skin, the white patches on the dewlaps matching his own ankle bones. The *ugzruk* soles were crimped in perfect tiny ridges, dyed red-brown from alder bark. Diamond patterns in black and white calfskin trimmed the tops, and floral designs in her best jewel beads, red muskox yarn, pinked red felt and Laplander pompons. It was stunning footwear such as lucky men receive only at Christmas and worth a lot of tourist money. They were for church and feasts and for the seamstress to show off, not for hunting.

"His father passed away," said Polly. "He still didn't seem recovered," she went on into my silence. "Kind of feverish, maybe that virus, so I want him at the clinic but he won't come. He bought food at the store too."

"That's really interesting," I said. She smiled at my sarcasm. Just then the woman hunter won at blackjack and let out a whoop that made everyone jump. Her husband swept up the cards in big, grumpy motions, his red nose seeming to throb. When he winked at us, Polly and I looked away.

"You should have seen him," went on Polly after a pause, "Tingmiaq. When he saw those naluagmiut." Miming, she shifted her eyes over to the hunters and did a double-take then glanced sidelong in disbelief. I snickered in spite of myself, trying not to blush; his feelings were so exposed.

Polly whispered behind her hand, "And they were asking him all kinds of questions" - she made her voice deep, continuing her spoof - "You live in this godforsaken place, boy?' - and he said 'right'." Polly copied Leif's curt tone perfectly, and we giggled but stopped short when the hunter turned his head to watch. "Jeez, I'm leaving," Polly said.

Flo called me over to murmur in Inupiaq about the guests. She was anxious about asking for payment. I wished she would do it right if she wanted to board outsiders. She was embarrassed to take money for food (though not for sewing, for which she drove a hard bargain). And Abe wouldn't even talk to naluagmiut like these, pretending he didn't speak English, which was ridiculous, a sixty year old. Only the really old ones didn't speak it. But what did whites know? Flo wanted me to tell them the rate. I couldn't deal with them any better - there were whites and then there were whites - but she was desperate.

Slowly I approached the card table. "Hi, honey," the woman said in a smoky voice. She reeked of perfume. Her fingernails were pointed and red like bloody claws, yet a sluggish kindness swam in her silver eyes. The man's eyes bored into me like an ice auger and I evaded them. Close-up, his arms were mottled with spots and moles and his giant hands had seamed knuckles like he was part old walrus. How would it be for the woman? Would his *usik* be like a walrus's long ivory shaft? It was a disturbing picture.

"Room and board is thirty dollars a day," I told the woman in a loud voice because outsiders never seemed to hear right. "Maybe you better pay *now*."

"Oh, listen to her," she said to her husband.

"Cute little thing." Their accent was so different I had to strain to understand. "Why sure, we can settle now," the man said, winking at me. He rolled back and patted himself with what I imagined was self-adoration until I realized he was hunting for money. Usually they carried it in wallets on their *nulluk*. At last he grunted and whipped out a billfold and removed a thick wad. He wet his fingertip to shuck off a bill with a flourish, holding it out to me scissored between gold-ringed fingers. A fifty. I'd never seen one. Every action of his was strange, even more than the European painter's. He said, "Though I don't know, seems a mite pricey for a shack..."

"Sam. He's joking, doll," the woman said to me, "Your folks have been right hospitable. It's a mighty nice little home." But her face contradicted her words: her thin nostrils were pinched, maybe to close off the smell of seal-oil and dryfish. Their own brew of odors made my head spin, and I detected alcohol.

Sam kept holding out the money. Abe and Flo watched without expression, none that these whites could read, anyway. "Come on, come and get it," he wheedled. He pursed his lips and made a kissing noise such as they do when they trick wild horse; I had seen it in movies.

"Oh honestly," said the woman, and rose in her skin-tight jeans to grab the bill. She laughed nervously and maybe with apology, but not to me: it was for daring to correct him. She pressed the fifty into my hand. "Don't you mind him." As she leaned close to my ear as if to whisper something confidential, I pulled back. "That there is a fifty-dollar-bill, you understand, but you all can keep the change for your perseverance. Why don't you buy yourself something, a pretty girl like you." Her eyes traveled down my body with a compassion. I looked at her boots - pointy cowboy - and felt some kindness toward her as well. It was interesting these days, how I was getting compliments for being cute. Or beautiful.

I brought the money silently to Flo.

The hunters would sleep in my bed, and I'd air the blankets outside, after. I wondered if in their own land they snored in a large canopied pink bed like in catalogues, and if that night they would hump noisily like walruses so everyone had to hear. I was about to leave when Flo beckoned me again, this time for advice on what to serve besides macaroni. I said, "They're from Texas ah? They always like blubber. And *ushak* and *quaq*. They especially love it." I meant the fermented flipper and the frozen, raw tomcod slivers.

"*Vaaa...*" Flo looked skeptical. I shrugged. "Okay," she said, "I will give them that then."

I was secretly howling at their dismay when the food was finally served.

Flo looked vexed with me, because with strained expressions the naluagmiut pushed the food around with forks and the woman timidly asked what animal each meat came from. Then they ate only the macaroni. The man kept beginning comments but his wife kept her sharp boot firmly on his instep. She asked bright questions for a while before she fell silent, watching the children eat as though they were cannibals or animals devouring human beings.

When they were done she turned to me - I was using a crate to sit at their table so Flo didn't have to. "Tell us, honey, where do you go here for fun?" She batted her eyes, which were fringed with black spiders. I didn't answer; I was looking at those lashes, so finally Flo told her there was a movie the next night at the Center. *Guess Who's Coming to Dinner*. "Why, who ordered that?" the woman asked, and turned to Sam. "Sidney Po-tea-aye."

"Student Council ordered it," said Abe sternly. "Grade Eight." They blinked in more surprise, hearing English come from him at last.

"The children order the movies," said Sam, shaking his head. "Under the influence of that beat nick teacher, bet you a grand." I thought I would surely go to see this film he hated so much.

They retired behind the blanket, where they laughed until they started arguing about their caribou racks, what to do with them in Texas. There was a zipping of sleeping bags, an unscrewing noise, a gurgle. Abe stiffened; he never allowed bootleg in his house, but he was in a tight spot because he had to be a tolerant host, always in a good mood. There was also the fifty dollars. At least they were being discreet. Sam's voice crept out in a soft little school song:

Oomiak, kayak, igloo, mukluk, that's how Eskimos talk...

VERY LATE, when I was asleep in the cabin, Willy stumbled in. He barked his shin and fell heavily on the bed without undressing. Funny - he was usually so graceful with his body, as sure as the fin of a killer whale slicing the water.

ENTRY. I HAVE TO THINK of when my quest for the Wild Goose began. Was it Mother Goose, that old dame flying in the night sky? Some kind of goddess the Victorians cut down to size. Her downy breast huddles over us, poor chicks. But I don't think it was Mother

Goose. Because I was not deprived of mother-love, though Fahr tried to keep Maman from me, as if the feminine would ruin me. Or the Indian. She grew scared of him. A part of me wants his soul damned to hell - not the entire soul, just the vampire animal layer. Why did so many cultures believe in triple coexisting souls, so at death one flies to heaven, one reincarnates, and one lingers near the bones forever, gnashing its teeth? "One flew east, one flew west..." Acknowledgement of the cortex and the reptilian brain, our sedimentary intelligence.

He never hit her. Didn't have to. I want to ask why the fuck he married her. He was like that man in the Greenland myth who fell in love with a woman who was secretly a goose, and when he found out he killed her, and the children ran away and he was sorry but he broke his own heart, the unrepentant jerk. But it was never a secret Maman was Indian. I can't focus, feel so cold, then hot and cold at once, maybe the flu. Polly wants to give me a shot. That is all she does these days, but I won't bare my butt to the zealous health aide. It won't help anyway.

Entry. Back to the Goose, got to find the answer. I keep thinking of the Canada goose he blasted when I was five. Some kind of catalyst. So graphic my recall: the beady eye, the perfect ebony bill bubbling red, the drop of green guano, the black webbed feet, and feathers dense with shades and meanings I couldn't fathom. Fahr carried it by the serpent-like neck and tossed it on the counter as if he hated it. Why, I wondered, and still do, because it was so lovely, and it had given itself to him like my mother. He knew she was of the Goose clan; she wouldn't touch it and was so upset even when he apologized after he sobered up. And the bird haunted me...

In my bout with anthropology I found geese in every culture. Other birds are the creators but the goose is always the soul, isn't it, in its flight between realms? "Bird thou never wert"... Suddenly a memory comes up of Fahr reading to me "Though it's a Swedish tale": a callous teenager gets transformed into a tiny boy - a soul, see? And he rides a barnyard goose to join a wild flock flying to Lapland, where the geese teach him to respect nature and other peoples.

Vivid dreams. I was being borne on an Itiak-style sled through the sky at night like Santa, only it was drawn by a goose...it might have been Tallin's. I don't know where it was taking me. Then, a nightmare of men in lab coats as servants of darkness. It was a montage of science gone bad: naturalists filling vast halls with stuffed animals in a crazed taxonomy; pseudo skull measurements granting European men the right to enslave and murder, Nazi medical experiments. Oppenheimer and Einstein appeared white-haired and frail, hugging and weeping like Hansel and Gretel lost in the the woods before they find the witch's cabin.

There was a panel of judges, all of them Indian women, and I was pleading, "I only count goose poops to help them!" but they pounded the gavel and wouldn't hear it. I was the enemy too. A woman's voice softly chanted Hardy's message, "What we gain by science is, after all, sadness."

I dream too much here. When I woke I opened a book to this, I swear: "Our meddling intellect, Misshapes the beauteous forms of things, We murder to dissect." Doubt I was born to be a scientist. But what was I born to be, and why do I have to <u>be</u> something? My bug lingers. Maybe I am run-down, low white cell count, but Maman would say it's because I want something or I'm on the wrong path; it's a Cree idea that so inflames her doctor. Didn't G say something like that too, in her diagnosis of my soul: "there is something missing, and you know it." There is something missing besides Tallin's. I <u>want</u>, but what can I do about it? A shot would be easier.

Entry. Waldo materialized with clients, here to vacation from civilized behavior. I've forgotten what whites can look like: the familiar teachers and my own mongrel face in the hand mirror don't count. That couple seems like a goblin-primate hybrid. How fast the brain reverts to the archaic xenophobic mode. They may have thought I was the village idiot (my role here, I fear). Nouveau riche, oil, macabre. Pity G to have to live with them, pity the geese who must use Texas as their flyway. This is their new colony too, I guess; more will come once the pipeline flows. The tendency here to smile when humiliated is misunderstood by whites: "A happy-go-lucky people."

CHAPTER 21

Woe to the world then
battle-axe and sword rule
storm-cleft age of wolves
ere the world goes down
(ANCIENT NORSE SEERESS)

THE WORLD was speeding up since the caribou hunters hit town, and events and spirits were converging like the winds that kept their plane grounded. I felt it.

Once, when I was very little I ran to tell my foster mother about a voice I heard on the beach. I thought I had better tell her, since it seemed like a warning for everyone. The men of the family were out seal-hunting. The voice that came in the wind had been soft and soothing, an *aka's*. *What did it say*, asked my foster mother sharply, and she looked frightened. *It is all right*, I told her, *She said it's okay; don't be scared*. Yet that seemed to make my foster mother even more upset. She hurried to the beach to look out at the horizon where storms came from and she saw nothing; there was not even a whisper of clouds. Very soon, though, a gale hit while the men were still at sea and they nearly didn't make it back.

Whatever was coming, I knew Leif would be involved. And there was little time to get ready.

ON MOVIE NIGHT I waited until the lights were off before sneaking into the Center and standing against the wall. The place was packed. When the children saw that the actor was a *taqsivak* they pointed and laughed shrilly, ready to laugh more because of the old movies where *taqsivak*s were just clowns. But they soon fell silent and then restless, for it wasn't humorous and the *taqsivak* spoke like a book. I watched the girl character closely to see how they behaved Outside. The mean old whiteman reminded me of Abe somehow. Halfway through, the big game couple and Waldo came into the Center and lurched before the screen with cowboy hats in silhouette. Once they found seats in front with all the children they joked and commented loudly for the whole movie, their laughs raucous. When the lights came on they were swigging from a bottle in a paper bag in defiance of village law.

The younger people lingered in the Center to dance to records, or, like me, to see what would happen. Abe had stayed too, the only elder present. He did not approve of rock and roll dancing anymore than card-playing. He didn't even like movies, probably due to an incident Flo told me about, in the 40s. Abe was a soldier then. They went to the theater in Nome but were told to sit in the balcony, the Eskimo section. Flo needed glasses and couldn't see from there, so they came back down and a whitewoman called the police. Abe had never gone back; in fact, he tried to stay out of Nome entirely. I understood: in Itiak he was a big shot, but in the town he'd been scolded like a stray dog and read signs on stores that said "no natives or dogs." Now he was watching the hunters narrowly, maybe hoping to catch Sam outside of his home to make a citizen's arrest.

Leif was on a bench next to Willy, watching the naluagmiut. He didn't seem to recognize me. Soon Abe made as if to leave but instead he halted at the door, thinking, then shuffled toward the sport hunters. They were camped out on the bench now, down parkas shucked and passing the bottle around. Sam hid the bag under their bench like a guilty teenager. "Hi, Abraham!" cried the woman, as if glad to see him, and Waldo smiled too, but his lips made a thin line. With his parka off, the guide was clearly powerful. We adults had fallen silent, while the children, always alert to social changes, stopped their game of tag along the benches.

Abe, who had faced scores of treacherous bull walrus in his life, knew how to keep going through fear. He pulled himself erect before Waldo and spoke softly. "You cannot have liquor here. We are a dry town."

"What liquor, Abraham?"

"That there." Abe gestured with disdain to the floor. "Someone could try to hide bottle in there."

Waldo picked up the bag to peer in, playing surprise. "I'll be damned."

"Hey, I thought Prohibition was over," cried Sam happily. "They in some kind of time warp out here?" He said to Abe, "We have to drink like a bunch of old winos on a bench! You all need a decent bar!" In the audience, I saw signs of agreement and smiles stifled behind hands.

"Seems like you are drunk," said Abe, still quiet as snow. I felt the room's admiration of his old man's dignity, standing up to them alone. "This is a bad influence on the young people," Abe told Waldo, who was scratching his chin, "and we want to know why you are here, bringing outsiders with you."

"Hey, where's the sheriff?" yelled Sam. His hat flew off. He was clearly the drunkest. "Are we under arrest? Where's the poh-lees?"

"No police, but they got a village council," said Waldo.

"And a radio for the State Troopers," said Abe gruffly. "But we don't want to have to make no call."

The woman turned serious. "Give him that now," she said to Waldo, who shrugged and eased his body up, strolled to the wastebasket and held the bag high over it, letting it fall with a clang. Wide-eyed, he checked out Abe's reaction. Abe nodded once, then shuffled out of the Center with his pants riding so baggy on his bowed legs I felt a painful twinge of embarrassment and pity. The whites put their heads together to confer, disagreeing over what to do, where to go next. There was nowhere else to go.

The wise little twelve-year-olds of the Student Council lowered the needle to Credence Clearwater Revival, full volume, and the tension eased off as people stacked chairs and benches to clear the floor for dancing and dimmed the lights. I saw Polly tugging at Leif's arm but he pulled away. He just wanted to sit staring at the hunters with a strange, unblinking look. He was very pale. But that was better than watching him dance with Polly out in front of everyone. Somehow I doubted he even danced.

Sam was out on the floor. He'd retrieved the bottle to drink more and was dancing in a funny way, with his chin thrust forward and his arms hanging with bent knuckles. He stuck his lips out and beat his chest. We had seen King Kong, the resemblance was close, and people laughed. But when he came up behind Stanley and seemed to be aping *him*, they made the connection. Stanley looked behind himself. Seeing the horrible sight, he faltered in his steps. In case we still didn't get it, Sam flapped his hand against his mouth, gabbling and whooping. All around the Center faces grew stony, as if being compared to *itkiliq* was a worse insult than the first, and Stanley left the dance floor in disgust.

The song had ended - it was deathly quiet while the Student Council found another. From the middle of the room Sam squinted at his audience. I imagined how he saw us: an unknown race, savages, he was thinking, *real* hunters. There was only a fine line between a seal and a man, and he was in our territory, surrounded! But we were a peaceful people. Sam waved at us. He didn't know the great-grandfathers were warriors who took heads, smashed enemy skulls with spiked clubs, drew bows to pierce armor, and eagerly trained all winter for battle. He had no clue how he hurt us. I envisioned his broken body on the floor in a pool of blood.

With the next song he grabbed his wife and they pranced over the floor in their pointed boots. They believed they were great dancers, showing us, making everyone move out of their way. Waldo tried asking women to dance but they shook their heads and hid their faces. The last member of the caribou party charged into the Center. He was blonde. He also wore a cowboy hat and was lanky and tough-looking, like he wrestled cows. In one hand he raised a fresh bottle in a toast to the room, while his other arm held a short, giggling woman. Together they stumbled and careened, hanging onto each other for balance.

The woman was Anette, who always giggled at everything and had only one talent I knew of, which was having babies fathered by naluagmiut polar bear hunters who came every winter. And now Waldo had set her up with a caribou hunter. He didn't seem to mind that she was homely and dressed like an *aka*, with her hair straggling from an old-fashioned bun. The cowboy held the bottle to her mouth and she drank deeply, then he chuggalugged. He shouted *yee-haw!* and swung Anette so her feet left the floor while she cackled in aimless peals like a ptarmigan.

The song now playing was *Put a Candle in the Window*, my favorite, and the whites were spoiling it. But with Anette's arrival everyone else had relaxed and was enjoying the show. She could take all the ridicule and protect them from it. She could be the clown. No wonder Anette got drunk, even if she was too stupid to know the joke was on her. I was about to leave, though Leif was there and I wanted to keep an eye on him.

Just then the needle screeched, killing the song. All the harsh lights flickered on; the naluagmiut and Anette stopped dancing. In the brilliant silence we looked around and it was Leif - he had done it. He leaped over some benches and moved fast toward the hunters, who dropped their jaws and backed up.

He did look dangerous, maybe insane. His face was bleached out, his eyes were too shiny and his hair was matted. He was breathing fast though he hadn't danced. And the overly fancy mukluks - they were too much! For his sake I blushed.

"Is there something we can do for you, son?" asked Sam. He cast the others a bug-eyed look with a little grin. Yet he was polite enough, to another white.

"Hey! You still here?" Waldo said. "You gone native or what?" He looked down at Leif's feet. "Nice mukluks! Groovy!" Someone tittered in the audience. Leif backhanded sweat from his forehead.

"Can't you see, it's not just drunk? She's mentally retarded!" he appealed to the whitewoman, who gaped at Anette like she hadn't realized. Leif had caught the men off guard but now they focused their slow, red stares on him and took in his height and build. Most animals you could reason with and they'd decide to leave without attacking, nobody really wanted to get hurt. But certain bull walrus had no choice but to try to drown you.

Let them take Anette! I begged Leif silently. She could keep them occupied, and she was so drunk and shameless and the damage was already done, what did it matter, it was a tradition. But then I thought, yes, tradition...

"You better go," Leif told Anette, who just giggled behind her hand at all the attention. Waldo stared at Leif, who stared back, and they reminded me of a couple of wide-eyed lynxes meeting in the bushes.

"Who the fuck is this coming out of the woodwork?" asked the cowboy.

"A scientist," Waldo explained.

"A draft dodger," drawled Sam, "holed up here bumming off these people." I saw who he really hated then. It wasn't Eskimos.

"He's been out in the field too long, thinks he's Jesus Christ our Savior," said Waldo.

"And you think this village is a free fire zone," retorted Leif. "You bought a hunting license to act like animals!" He shook his hair back and looked down his nose at Waldo. He didn't seem scary anymore but insolent - he'd decided to attack with just words. I didn't think it was a good idea. The cowboy lurched toward him but Waldo trapped his arm as if wanting to hear more of Leif's opinion.

"You got something against hunting, boy? Karmadarma vegetarian?" The guide's voice was mild and he appeared relaxed with the little smile under his moustache, but a force was gathering in him. I saw it wasn't just the whiskey but his *inua;* he craved fighting, and he had killed many people too, from an airplane. At his leisure, and he had taken trophies from these humans, as he did from the bears. Parts of their bodies.

"Only *your* kind of hunting!" said Leif. "Wall in the caribou with a pipeline and fucking search-and-destroy from the air!" He was right. Sometimes they brought their little children and would land the plane on the ice so that each kid with an expensive rifle could take down a polar bear too tired to run. For their Christmas present. Leif gestured at Sam with a contemptuous hand. "He's in oil, am I right? Buying up Congress? You know, it's not just a species you're wiping out; you're total Earth-destroyers!"

"Fuck you! Fuck you!" exploded the cowboy. "Let me go, let me at this motherfucker!" But Waldo still held his arm. Sam roused himself, the bulk of a bull sliding into the water, tusks ready. Willy and Stanley had edged closer along the wall with their arms hung out from their sides, ready for something, they didn't know what. Everyone else in the Center watched with open mouths. It was way more interesting than the movie. I was suddenly angry at Leif. Did he think he was that old hero who singlehandedly saved a village from monsters? This was a kind of bragging; the men of Itiak might not like it. And he was white - bad enough! But fever had demented him.

"Look around you, everyone hates your guts. Only someone drunk and retarded can stand you, so why don't you just leave," he said.

Waldo snorted. "Shit, guess who's coming to dinner at the top of the fucking world." He was keeping track of Willy and Stanley from the corner of his eye.

"I take it back about animals, they're better than you and I only know two species that rape: humans and mallard *ducks*!" Leif spat out the last word as the whites jerked their heads back. I pressed my hand to my mouth to keep from laughing out loud.

"Why you -" fury choked the cowboy's next words. "I'll rape *you*, you sonuvabitch!" He tore loose from Waldo and swung a wild fist but Leif just stepped aside. Waldo laughed as the cowboy lost his balance and sat down on the floor.

"They don't really care," he said to Leif, "so just mind your own business and we'll let it go." I didn't know who he meant by *they*: Eskimo women? No...he meant Eskimo men.

"You know you're wrong, man. That's why you're so pissed."

I had crept down to Willy, who was watching Leif with puzzlement, maybe some envy. It wasn't unknown for Native men to get killed by naluag-miut and the charges dropped. "They won't hurt another whiteman," Willy assured me, as if Leif had the charmed loonskin through which no arrow could pass, but just as he said it, Waldo drove his fist up into Leif's stomach and Leif doubled over. Waldo grabbed his hair and forced him to his knees in a praying position. I could almost hear the little roots tearing as hair ripped out, and Leif and I grimaced as one. My own scalp remembered what that felt like.

The woman was yelling for him to stop, and Waldo did pause like a dog with a lemming, waiting for Leif to get his wind. But he kept his fingers twisted in the long hair, loosening his grip only to get a better hold, like he had a lot of practice doing that. Probably on women. When Leif tried to get up Waldo shoved him while letting go so Leif pitched toward the floor, and he seemed off-kilter like he had no strength, and he didn't catch himself. He just fell. Sam had quickly drained the bottle and rolled up his sleeves in an old-fashioned whiteman's ritual. Now with a dance-like move he stepped in to kick Leif in the ribs. I felt people around me flinch. The pointed boots were hard but it was more the act that shocked us, the lack of respect. Then the cowboy took a turn. He lost his balance and tried again. The boot driving into belly had a hollow sound that made me yelp. Leif writhed on the floor, airless, trying to get up while the men circled, and everyone was standing, craning to see the violence better. Suddenly Leif lashed his foot into Sam's crotch. Luckily for Sam he was wearing those derided mukluks. With a roar Sam staggered back, and Leif scrambled up.

"Oho, the peacenik's gonna fight back?" cried Waldo victoriously.

"No -" Leif gasped. *Oq* was dripping red from both nostrils and he looked astonished. Maybe he had never been beaten up before - though it seemed like whites were always fist fighting in movies - or maybe scientists didn't fight. Having never seen such a fight before, I was amazed too. Leif held up his hands. "I surrender."

Waldo smiled, shrugging. Leif slowly turned to limp outside without his coat. But he only got a few steps before the cowboy picked up his bottle. "No, fuck you!" he howled, and from behind he smashed it in an arc. As it hit Leif's temple and glanced off a soft groan rose from the audience. Leif held his skull, blood streaming between his fingers. A line of it shot down his cheek. The sport hunters watched as he bent forward and swift points of red dribbled onto the boards and his mukluks. It was so quiet I thought I heard the faint raindrop sounds. On the bench Sam rocked over his groin, and Anette had flown the Center.

"Shit, I'm getting someone," said Willy in a shaky voice. "Oh, maybe they'll stop now." This time he was right. Leif swayed, his knees buckled and in slow motion he collapsed and was stretched out on the dance floor. Something in me had shattered like glass and was stretched there with him.

"Okay," said Waldo after a moment, as if Leif had learned a lesson well, "Okay." He and the cowboy looked down at their prey, murmuring to each other, pensive. Was this how they got after they killed their game? All the anger had fled out of them. I half expected Waldo to take a knife and start skinning. The whitewoman tiptoed over to Leif and bent over him, wringing her hands. A puddle of scarlet grew beneath his head, it was flooding my insides. Uselessly, she pressed a hankie to his temple and asked whoever was listening if Itiak had a doctor. Like in a seance everyone was standing back watching the big game hunters and the fallen biologist. Even Willy. If that's what the hunters did to their own kind, then what would they do to an Eskimo who interfered?

Waldo shouted at us, "You come and help your friend now!" His pale blue husky eyes darted across us. I was not afraid of *them* now but I was afraid of a village, and I could not be the one to go out to Leif. Then Polly was banging into the Center with her medical kit - she'd run for it when she saw the fight starting - and she pushed aside the whitewoman. She staunched Leif's head with gauze in one hand while taking his pulse with the other. I felt some relief.

"I don't reckon I hit him that hard," said the cowboy. Polly ignored him. She told Willy to get the sled, she'd take Leif to the clinic. In the next second Abe arrived with several of his brothers. Nelson was large, the heaviest man in town, and carried a pistol stuck in his pants so the handle showed. The caribou hunters stepped far back, collecting in a tight knot. "He attacked us!" said the cowboy, "He must be on some kind of drug!"

"That's right, self defense," Waldo said calmly, and lit a cigarette. "He needs a shrink." Abe was studying the guide with his eyes pulled nearly into seams, like old style snow-goggles.

"You people just stay out of the health aide's way," said Nelson. "And there's no smoking in here; that's a city ordinance."

With a shrug Waldo flicked away his Winston, motioning to his hunters to follow him. They wouldn't be staying at Abe's that night. As soon as they were out I hurried with everyone for a closer look. Polly let the children crowd in, just as they watched every event in the village. Leif was sprawled on his back. The blood was a shocking red against his drained face. Polly examined his rolled-back eye, which made the children shriek "*izhigii!*" He had a shallow scalp wound and a mild concussion, she said - his internal organs weren't hurt, maybe, but after listening to his chest she thought he had walking pneumonia. She had been warning him but he wouldn't listen.

Abe fetched the bottle from where it had rolled and blew out an unhappy sigh as he read the label. "Never seen naluagmiut carry on this way, not since *eskuulkti* tried to shoot the preacher, what, ten years ago." Nobody ever tried to stop them before, I thought to myself. We cast our eyes down on Leif's still face. I had been imagining the naluagmiut in a bloody heap on the floor, and this is what happened.

Polly murmured, "It's the Lower 48. It's like a war between the generations, and the sexes and the races; everyone hates everyone." Softly Abe uttered the sound of disbelief. Was he thinking it was becoming so in Itiak too, a widening lead of misunderstanding and mistrust? I wondered if whole cultures could have the evil eye, an ill will that could harm you across the distance. Maybe the whites hadn't even needed germs and guns and traps and poison to kill off the Indians and the wolves and bears of the Lower 48. They could have turned their dark thoughts against us in their millions and we would have perished. Maybe that is what had weakened the people most, all that hatred beamed against them from afar, from those who wanted our land.

Leif came to just as Willy returned. He didn't know what had hit him. When he saw me standing over him I was worried he would say something like, "I did it for *you,*" but he just fainted again into Abe's arms when he tried to stand.

Abe and Willy carefully hefted him - it looked easy for them, so strong from hauling *ugzruk* - and carried him to the sled.

CHAPTER 22

With love's strongest thoughts
lift the dead man's frozen body
lift his spirit to earth's warmest life
(WITCH'S SPELL, INUPIAQ)

A pard-like spirit, beautiful and swift,
A Love, in desolation masked...
SHELLEY

NO ONE EVER found out. If Polly knew, she would blame herself for nearly killing Leif out of pride at being the best health aide in the world, when she decided not to medivac him. Most people would accuse the caribou hunters. Willy would blame himself for not stopping Leif or for not helping him. But I knew who it really was.

HE REVIVED on a classroom table, and seemed amused to be sharing it with hamsters and a *Curious George* book. Then he grew shy with Abe and everyone, even *eskuulkti* and mice watching Polly stitch his scalp. He wanted to know what hit him. "Bottle of Jack Daniel's," said Abe. I wondered if Leif knew how hard Willy had to struggle to earn that proud father kind of smile that Abe wore.

Polly was thrilled to finally get his temperature and a chance to give him a shot in the "gluteus". She decided his ribs didn't need taping - they were bruised but not cracked. She washed the blood from his face and hands, all the while lecturing on the need to breathe deeply even if it hurt. But he wasn't listening.

I wanted to scold him. We weren't defenseless birds that needed saving. He shouldn't feel possessive like some white who stayed in a village for a few days and wrote a book titled *Life with the Eskimos.* But I knew Leif would never show off or make a profit from us, and though I hated to admit it I was proud of him too; I just wished he had beat up those naluagmiut.

We hadn't spoken since the day of his letter. When he looked behind Polly's shoulder and caught my eye a rush of feeling flooded in my chest, a pneumonia of emotion so powerful it scared me. Someone was skillfully pulling sinews from inside me and joining them with his, lacing and forming a mysterious cat's cradle that moved and altered each second. I was hooked like a minnow by his eyes; I was swimming in him, though I didn't know how to swim. He thought I was beautiful. Surely he saw something wrong with me, something "marring" me like the rusted barrels he saw on our pure coastline. In the mirror of the window I looked odd and blurry; any moment I could just pass through and enter a different world, like the little white girl in the storybook. Maybe she had been a kind of shaman.

Willy showed up in the glass behind me with an even stranger expression as he watched his dad *unga*-ing Leif. The sky was like that when it turned grim over an open patch of sea. He didn't know anyone saw, or he would have put up a mask as perfect and artful as his carvings. At first I couldn't recognize the look, so rare on Willy's face. It was of shame. And anger, but not at Leif. At himself.

THE BIG GAME hunters flew out the next day, to everyone's relief. In the dark early morning the woman knocked to ask where "the longhaired boy" was staying. I led her to Willy's cabin, where everyone insisted Leif stay - I was back at the main house.

Willy was still asleep but Leif was sitting up trying to examine his ribs. He was peaked, with a bandage wrapped around his head. He stared at her, not in that hostile way, but mystified. She tracked snow in and stood awkwardly by the table. "What's your name, son?" she asked, and when he told her, "How nice. Is that a foreign name?" She lit a cigarette, but seeing my glare, stubbed it out. "We have boys your age, they're soldiers now." When Leif said nothing she sighed. "You know, you provoked them but you didn't deserve that. I want to apologize."

"It wasn't you," Leif said.

The woman smiled. "Well." She smoothed her *nanuq* hair. "So, what all is your specialty? In the sciences..."

He seemed to be weighing her question, all its possibilities of meaning. "I pour crude oil on salt marshes and measure the ill effects. And I census bird populations, analyze feeding habits, and extrapolate what a large spill will do. Once you degrade these vegetation systems they can't come back. And this area is a major breeding and molting ground for migratory species from all over the world, and they won't go anywhere else to do it." He shot her a dark look; the bandage made him look like a pirate.

"My, how interesting a line of work... and the birds are so pretty, aren't they? Sam has a small oil field. Listen, I have got to fly, so you take care, hear? Here's something...for the damages. Don't say no." She laid a stack of green on the table, smoothing it flat. "And God bless. I can find my own way back, honey," she told me. Leif was watching her with a stricken expression. The door ripped from her hand and banged as she went out, making him wince.

I counted the money. The bills were crisp and new and enough for plane fare. "Five hundred dollars," I told Leif, but it was Willy who started up in bed, eyes wide.

"*Blutgeld*," muttered Leif. "Hm..." I didn't understand. He wiped his eyes and carefully laid down on the bed, turning his head away. I heard him sniffing and swallowing. After a minute he said heavily, "Do me a favor, could you please give your parents what they lost in hotel charges."

Willy looked at me, his eyebrows high. Slowly I peeled off a fifty. Later, Willy told me "Tingmiaq" just wept soundlessly after I left, his face buried in his arms. Willy said maybe his head was cracked harder than Polly thought. I said without thinking, "But he's always been that way."

HE MOVED BACK to the *ini* the next day, too soon. The handwriting here has deteriorated badly from the neat bug print:

Darkness. The cold hurts my lungs but it's only ten below. Dogs yammer the live-long night, my head clamors with them, I feel decrepit and can't think. Willy dug me out from the last blizzard and chopped me some wood before traveling to reindeer camp. Everyone's treating me nice because I'm an addled idiot, I insulted the honor of Texas. Even G was kind. I should be felled more often.

Bereavement is my excuse but really it's the whole fucking world. I had a vision of that woman and her hunting party, Abe and Flo, G, even Maman all in a dinghy or an oomiak with a tattered skin sail. I was at the oars heading don't know where. The ocean was slick with black crude from a broken tanker askew in the distance and loons struggled in it. The land was flooded. Behind us on higher ground, a wasteland with bomb craters and snags sticking up from clear cut and empty parking lots stretching and on the highest hill a fortress where the last rich people fend off the rest of us with fighter jets and germ warfare and there were oil wells on fire in holocausts, dark satanic mills now in ruins, pipeline mazes over parched earth, nothing grows, no animals, ragged bony people with buckets tapping the line for a little fuel but the pipelines are dry and there's no water to drink, it's all in the sea. But there was one dark river, the Styx. It was the Cree Land of the Dead, Ragnarok after the Wolf breaks loose, no place you want to go, but I was the ferryman, rowing. Where was the black dog...

No malice to the Texans or even Waldo, because everyone looked so down wrapped in blankets and it wasn't anyone's fault, but all of ours, and suddenly on the dark horizon a rosy dawn Maman was smiling it was a dream but I was awake, functions slopping over no barriers have to stop now feel so thirsty so tired...

POLLY WAS BUSY with another flu outbreak and asked me to check on Leif. I pretended to resist, only giving in when she said she'd do it. She was relieved, for of course she was scared by the *ini* and the lonely route there. *Nanuq* came off the ice, night fell so early and no lamps from windows lit the way. I was supposed to remind Leif to drink plenty and breathe deeply once an hour and let her know if he was acting "funny". I said he always acted funny. Polly sighed. "Then tell me if he's acting normal and I'll know he's in trouble."

While it was still light - around noon - I set out, the dry snow squeaking under my mukluks. I waded through knee deep drifts until I found Willy's sno-go tracks and it was easier. The sea wore a dark young skin dotted with curly-edged pancake floes, its clogged surface breathing gently as if asleep. The boom of surf which had beat on our ears all fall was gone, stifled by crumpled shore-ice. It was beautiful but the call of ravens unsettled me. I leaned forward and half-shuffled half-ran as fast as I could on snow, until my lungs were on fire and I tasted blood, but I didn't stop until the *ini*. There were signs of Willy and his shovel - he had dug out the door, the skylight and the vents. It was too quiet, not in lack of sound but in the psychic way, like no one was home. Inside, the lamp burned low with a sputtering wick. A dim gray light filtered through the plastic in the roof. The stove had only one ember so my breath hung in a mist, near freezing. Still on all fours, I blinked a while, adjusting.

The sight of Leif face down on the floor was a bullet shot into my brain. It stopped my heart. My mind froze. It was my animal spirit that made me crawl to him, unthinking and without panic, ready to do anything. He was lying near the empty water container, dressed only in his longjohns with his bandaged head turned to the side. His skin was cold and still under his jaw. No pulse.

Maybe the *inua* had come to get him. But it was probably just the pneumonia, or the head wound. Why didn't I sense he was in trouble? What kind of *qilya* let me sleep and eat lunch while he suffered? A pressure was building behind my throat like someone held a knife there. A memory sifted into my thoughts: a deadly white sifted inside a cabin door, hunger, a child's sobbing, a long tortured coughing that finally stopped, blood reddening a quilt...

"Oh, why did you do that?" my voice came out in a thin, small wail. I closed my eyes to shut out the sight of his face as I rolled him over. His arms flopped loosely. When I smelled fresh urine, I thought there could be no more joyous an aroma. I felt his crotch. Still warm! I put my head near his nostrils, craning to see, and waited through a space of time agonizing in its emptiness. A faint line of mist trailed out, vanishing. With a shout I leaped up, my tears breaking loose. He was limp and heavy, but a strength burned in my muscles that let me drag him to the platform and lift him. I heaped his bag and reindeer skins on him and blew the fire back. With trembling fingers I poured kerosene and turned up the lamp, then climbed into bed with him.

He looked at peace, still freshly dead. His lips were chilly and tinged blue. If I had come any later, he would surely have died. If he'd passed out in an above-the-ground cabin he would have died - the *ini* had tried to save him, protecting him from the worst. He could still die. His soul was gone somewhere, leaving his body hanging on a slim thread of life.

Under the furs I undressed him and myself and wrapped my limbs around his, sealing him with my own warm skin, heating every surface. I thawed his lips with mine and tried to blow strength back into him with my breath. Carefully I unwound the bandage to find that his temple was healing under Polly's stitches - they were fine and neat as if she had sewn a handicraft. But blood was still dried in his hair, his mukluks were ruined with his blood, blood he had shed for me. He had neglected himself so, what sorry shape he was in, what sorry shape my heart was in.

Fiercely I hugged him to me, and unknown to him, my tears wet his cold cheek. I had done this to him. I had driven him to foolish acts, to his downfall, leading him on a snowmachine right over a precipice. He wasn't stupid; why did he let me? And I hadn't *meant* to! I hadn't tried to cast a spell over him like one of those old-time witches, but what was he still doing here in this *ini* as winter set in?

It dawned on me in a slow and vision-like awareness that this man, this scientist, had led *himself* to that edge and let his spirit go.

HE HEATED UP FAST but he would not wake up. I dressed, thinking Polly had better come, but a realization stopped me at the door. Polly would medivac him. He would not return. I had no doubt the grant was lost; he hadn't even written his report, for there it was: a blank paper in his rusted typewriter. It would all become a slippery dream. He would not believe he had once lived in this *ini* and in the camps. Itiak would grow distant, as unreal as his city was to me. My face, all our faces would fade; he'd never taken photos of us, just of birds. *Inua* would bide their time and come to torment him at their leisure. But first Polly would fly him to a hospital with its corridors and strangers in lonely beds and the bossy doctors who did not believe that a soul could be torn like cloth or get lost or stolen or invaded by spirits. They would not understand. And Leif would surely die there.

I built a roaring fire and hastened back to town to leave a message with Rita that the birdman was fine. Both houses were empty, easing my task. I smuggled out Flo's dried *sagrik* leaves that she kept for emergencies. At Willy's I swaddled my new drum in a baby blanket, but I could find nothing for the stick but a dried crane leg. The sky was lit with hundreds of stars, like sparks flying up when you kick a burning log. I hoped nobody would notice the regular trail my feet had plowed in the snow, before it drifted over. Women could recognize my mukluk tracks.

This time when I felt Leif's forehead I flinched in surprise. His skin was burning like a stovetop, in a dry heat. His breathing was shallow and fast with a labored sound and his pulse was still weak. Time was running out. He needed the *sagrik*, but there was no water left to brew it. I threw the covers off him and hurried out to get snow. While it melted I fanned him with a goose wing and made myself calm down. Maybe a high fever was good, a sign of battle. When little babies had fevers you bathed them to prevent convulsions, but I didn't know about adults. It seemed like Leif's body now had a plan, and interfering with it might be wrong.

How I regretted not paying attention when Isaiah tried to teach healing. Calvin wanted nothing to do with it either when his dad brought out the potent spirit plant. *Sagrik* grew everywhere, and every old woman picked it in summer and hung it upside-down to dry. They called it "stinkweed" due to its bitterness. Polly didn't like it in the house but Flo said it came from God, and when Polly wasn't there we breathed in its steam and wrapped Abe's joints in its leaves. It was the woman's plant and helped the womb, but it made you miscarry and killed you if you drank too much. "She strengthens the soul," Isaiah told us, "She wrestles with evil so that a man who appears dead can come back." He took a sliver of it and was going to stick it in Calvin's skin then light it afire - he said that would unblock a pathway for the good *inua*. But Calvin had scoffed - plants were for *aka*s; they weren't manly. Isaiah had put the *sagrik* away and now I did not know how much I should give Leif. A lot, I guessed. I hoped.

When it had steeped I cooled it with snow and held Leif's head up to give him a cupful. It was hard to make him swallow though his throat tried to obey. I drank some too for strength, and waited for the *sagrik* to begin its purifying effect. Now sweat streamed from Leif and the fur smelled of salt and the blood in his hair ran again with a fresh iron smell. He soaked through the towel I put under him. To make him more comfortable I laid a handkerchief filled with snow on his forehead. It melted very fast. His eyes began to shift under the lids, chasing dreams, and he started to moan. His fingers and legs twitched like Waldo was still pinning him down. I knew that feeling. To erase the memory I sang lullabies and the moaning stopped, but then he spoke garbled, foreign-sounding words.

At first I hoped his Indian side was emerging, climbing out from under the layers of whiteman they had piled on him so thickly the Indian couldn't breathe. I leaned close to his lips to hear. Maybe I listened for my name like in movies when the soldiers cried out to their sweethearts. "*Tack far*", he said. I made out some English, "statistical...significance..." - but I did not understand - "habitat...irreparable..."and at last, "Tallin's...please..." His unconscious tears seeped out like tributaries to join the sweat and melted snow. I understood those tears: they were from an orphan with no people, the lonesome wanderer.

Alright, so he called out to that goose, not me. He even dreamed geese, like that girl in the story, as if geese would not exist unless he constantly thought of them. Yet I was strangely happy as I waited for his fever to break. I was sweating too, and stripped down to just my underpants. Now it was really like in old times; all I needed was tattoos. I looked around at the bones of old whales and trees holding up the *ini*, the lamp burning oil made from long-ago plants, the tea leaves in the cup, my drum and the walrus and crane who helped me make it, skins from the reindeer, and the hut itself, made by the hands of ancestors: all given to make us safe, all containing their own spirits that held me and Leif in great affection. Everyone was waiting now. And Leif's soul waited somewhere while his body fought to live.

I fell in a trance as the water streamed off Leif's skin and glistened in the light. I thought how strange it was that all the blood and breath running through us lay under such a thin cover. How well I knew that from all the seals I cut and birds' necks I wrung. We could live a hundred years but die as easily as smeared mosquitoes; just a slip through a crack in the ice and we were "goners", like Leif said, so accident prone. We began in such small spurting movements: the planets and stars line up, the soul is released to the mortal plane, sperm leaps from a man into a woman, it bursts into the egg and in that instant we are created. A match is struck, the sun pops up from the sea, a baby slides from the mother - though that is not so easy - and from then on, either in sudden movements or slow, huge or tiny, we are taken on our slippery route to death.

The universe arranged so many ways to kill us it was a wonder we lived at all. What kept us alive but the spirits' protection? Fingers close around a blue capsule and turns a birth date into a death date, viruses creep into our lungs, a knife slices an artery and life jets into a dime-sized pit in the snow, we slip into hypothermia, fevers, comas, rages, laughter. A seal plunges into a hole and takes your hope with it, a man jabs into your body and in that instant, like the rip of cloth, you become someone else. Earth tumbles into surf, ice breaks ice, the sun glides under, summer spins into winter, light into shadow, the tide goes out, the birds are gone...and suddenly you are not a child anymore. You've fallen in love, tears shed from you as unstoppable as rain. And if one day you are old and no longer recognize the world, your heart slowly hardens until it stops. Your entire life is now just memory, vanishing like a dream. And the soul, a little fish, slips back into the Otherworld...

Is that how an angutkoq thought?

I allowed myself to caress his face and smooth his tangled hair. His skin was golden and even softer than I'd imagined. I laid my hand over his heart and belly, trying to send some of my life-force into the wheels Isaiah once told me about, wheels of energy that had run down. I bent his arm, marveling at the smooth, pliable action, and laid his hand over my heart. "I'm here," I told him, "I don't have to fly here at night to see you." I could look at him as much as I wanted now, without feeling ashamed or afraid. Why was it so wrong to see people as they really were, wearing only the skins they were born in? If he knew, would he be mad?

In spite of my encounters with them, the bodies of men were still unknown. It was vital that I knew. The lamp flickered and burned more brightly as if to say, *why not*? Why shouldn't I see the organ that - on other men - had wrecked my life? Leif's penis seemed such a poor, tender thing with no ability to enter me. But it had changed so quickly at the cliff. I wondered a little angrily if it mattered who touched it, if Flo or even Abe could get the same effect, easy, like running a dogteam. I imagined it inside me. It would be Leif inside me, but it made me fear. It was such a simple act, wasn't it - flesh moving into flesh, just pieces of meat. But it wasn't just flesh, for they had hated me and hated the body they broke into. They had taken part of my soul and removed it to a dark plane in the spiritworld, a haunted land that kept the stolen part of me hostage. But Leif would never do that to me, or to anyone. A man's sex was innocent, no different from the rest of a person; it was he who held it between his legs who made it ugly...or beautiful.

Leif did not seem mad at me for looking at him. His features were tranquil, his eyelashes curtaining out the world, and his hands lay palm up, open, just like Christ when he blessed people. I looked some more. Those nipples - what were they for? He would never nurse a baby and yet he had them, in miniature. Life is funny, I thought, and a sad pity-delight stabbed me like an awl to the heart. If I was a baby and he was a mother I would gladly suck at his breast, or even like we were now, man and woman and no milk, just to do it. Would it feel good to him? If he wanted to nurse *me* with those lips, he could, and if he wanted to go back into the womb to rest awhile I would let him into mine and build up his strength with my own blood, whatever he needed.

These were funny ideas. Surely a woman was not supposed to have such thoughts about a man. Abe would say they came from Satan but I let them flow and more came, from the wall of the *ini*, from the bones of whales...

The man lying there was actually *me*, and he was *myself* looking down, so I saw my own calloused, unbeautiful hands for the first time with kindness, and I loved my hands as much as I loved his. His tears and sweat were mine, it tasted like mine. I could have searched more, exploring other parts of Leif, but he seemed so exhausted and defenseless. A gratitude filled me. He had let me in on his secrets, maybe in the way a corpse's face in the coffin lets you realize the truth about life. Once a girl was taken by a hunter who only came to her at night, and though he had forbidden it, she was overcome with desire to see him. Fearing he was a monster, she drew the lamp close as he slept and saw he was breathtaking. I felt like that girl. And something wrong in me was laid to rest.

Years ago I had been wounded as much as Leif - more than him - and I was still lying cold on the ground in my own dried blood. Yet no one had come to help *me*. That part of me lost could not return just by my willing it, anymore than Leif could have heated himself as he lay near the door. There was no angutkoq to travel the Otherworld for me. Calvin was not the type. Somehow Leif was going to help me find it. I knew it. I gazed on him, thinking such ideas that Abe said came from the Devil.

I prayed then, prayed for him and prayed *to* him, as they once did to animals who were gods.

SOMETIME IN THE NIGHT Leif's fever broke. His breathing was clear but as slow as a little *siksik's* in its winter burrow, and his heart was steady but still faint. Under the lid his eye was looking up into his skull like he was dead, with no movement. What did he see up in there? In the white, tiny red vessels fanned out like a river delta. I swallowed my fear and gathered my strength again, knowing I would have to save him through spirit flight, for though the fever had released his body from the grip of the virus, he had still not returned.

I tried to remember what Isaiah taught me about a soul: if it was complete it acted as a shield, like the sack around the baby in the womb. It was not the same as the will to live. My mother had wanted to live. It wasn't belief. Surely the ancestors had belief - if they were anything like old people I knew - yet the angutkoq tried to save them from the viruses and failed. I didn't really understand, and wasn't sure Isaiah did either. I just knew part of Leif's spirit was cut loose and wandering. He needed his *turnaq* to guide him back, and somehow I had to find it.

My drum felt clumsy in my hands; it was made in secrecy and haste with no teacher, and before making it I had never even touched a drum. But it seemed to emanate a power. I moistened it and tapped the skin with the crane foot, watching Leif's still face by my outstretched feet. I was like a real angutkoq now, deep inside the *ini* with my drum. But what did they do next? *Come back,* I begged his soul. Then I thought I had better plead to the spirits too, and not just to any spirit but the highest one who bound the universe together, the unmentionable Sila. *Let him live, and I will sacrifice something,* I promised. Too late I realized there was nothing I could surrender worth the soul of Leif. I owned nothing much in the world. Even my womanhood had been taken.

My *qilya!* It was precious to me.

Without hesitation I vowed to give it up if I could just use it one more time. I began to beat the drum, letting the forbidden deep sound.

IN A FLASH OF RED my *kayuqtuq* came. The *turnaq* had been sulking since my wrongheaded experiment at the Iron but now it was willing to help. I ran after it across the plain of the Otherworld. We saw first a wolf in the distance, white like a specter and watching us with its head lowered in a way that scared me. My *turnaq* moved his ears back in a no, *It is not the one,* and we raced past, and the *ameguq* spirit did not follow.

We traveled far on a barren flatlands but I saw no portal and I was getting weary. We were surely lost, Leif was lost. The sound of the drum fell away. My spirit feet were bare and cut on the sharp rock, my breath tore my chest in painful sobs, but I ran and ran as the land darkened, guided by the white tip of my *turnaq's* tail. At last we saw the black stone of the portal on a hill.

And we saw the goose. It was far above us, shooting toward the portal like an arrow. It gave three urgent cries. My *turnaq* turned his head back, beckoning. *This is the one!*

We followed the goose through...followed it...

AT DAWN Leif stirred and woke. "Oh," he said hoarsely, looking up at me.

"You passed out," I said. "Your stove was cold. It's bad to pass out in winter."

He tried to swallow, but could not. "Jesus."

"No, it's only me." He tried to smile at my dumb joke. When I felt his forehead a shock coursed through me - his life-force was so fully back. His awareness made me shy again, and I was glad I was dressed and he was under the covers.

"Water," he whispered, like a man in a Western dying in a desert. I fetched him tea but he was unable to sit up and his hands wouldn't close, so I knelt behind him to hold up his head. Still, a lot ran down his neck, and he coughed, hurting his ribs. "Bitter..." He sank back against me, eyes closed. I wiped his lips and beard.

Carefully I slid out from under him, finding our position too intimate now, though I had liked feeling the weight of him. After a while he said, "Um...this is a real drag but I have to pee." He tried to crawl from the platform but collapsed with one arm hanging off. He was panting with the effort. "Pretty sad..."

"I'll bring something," I said, "I'll help you. But don't be embarrassed."

"Too late," he murmured. "Am I...naked?"

"I don't know..." Hot-faced, I fetched his coffee pot. "You can do it lying down maybe."

He shook his head.

"Then let me help you." He didn't have the energy to argue. I helped him sit on the edge of the platform. Things had been much easier with him unconscious. He grunted in pain when I bumped his ribs with my knee. Truly helpless, his head slumped down. At that, I lost my fear and delicately positioned the coffeepot.

"Cold..." he whispered with his eyes closed when the metal touched him. At least he wasn't a girl; what if he had to do this for *me*? I blushed again at the thought, but pulled his shoulders close to me because he was shivering. I told him it was okay to start but nothing happened.

"Do it! *Ki.*"

"I can't if you're watching."

"I'm not." If only he knew how much I had seen before! He tried to snicker, but sagged against me. I thought a while then pressed right above his pubic hair and the trick worked. I was *kuangazuk,* nearly dropping the can. He didn't have much in him. When I looked at his face against my shoulder, he had fainted again. But he looked relieved.

CHAPTER 23

To lose the self
to join the boundless one
is the creed of lovers
RUMI (ANCIENT PERSIAN)

Maidens, undress, be as you were
when you were born to the Mother
(ANCIENT MAYAN HYMN)

FLO WAS FUSSING over Polly, who had worn herself out and was sick in bed. With no comment about my absence, Flo had me go to the store for salt. While I was there Soola's girl ran in shouting, "Phone call for birdman!" She told no one in particular, for which I was grateful - not wanting to be seen as his ambassador - but I said I'd take the call. At Soola's I ignored people's looks as I gingerly picked up the receiver and tried to remember what to do with it. I breathed into it, listening to static.

"Ello?" The woman's voice sounded like a mix of the European painter and her son, for surely it was Leif's mother. It was a far-off voice - I imagined I could hear the Indian in it. "Oo is this?"

"His...acquaintance." Even to my ears my voice sounded low and furtive. "She can't come now because she hunt - he's - hunting."

More silence. It was hard enough talking to outsiders without a phone. "Well, please give him a message?" I raised my eyebrows then remembered to say okay. "They recovered the boat," she said, "and I have to sell it in that condition -" her voice broke - "And a notice came from the appeals board. He must fill out more paperwork. I'll send it. He must try, he must not neglect...the world..." She was hardly able to speak. "I am sorry, he never writes. Is he really fine?"

"He is," I whispered. "He likes it here."

"It is running in his blood," she said; it was scary until I realized what she meant. "I must hang up now," she said sadly.

She was a good person, the mother. She would not judge me. This crying was a trait she'd passed to her son - a kind of strength, maybe. And I loved her. The idea amazed me, coming out of nowhere like the voice from space. She hesitated and I sensed her yearning, how badly she wanted to talk to him - but he was gone, flown the nest, flown her world. "*Merci*," she said, and I thought she was asking me for mercy. I didn't know you were supposed to say goodbye. After a time I heard a click and a strange moan as soulless as wind, and I stared at the black thing in my hand before realizing it was time to hang it back on the wall.

LEIF WOKE TOWARD evening looking better, his color returning. I fed him and made him drink more *sagrik*. He let me wash his hair as it hung over the edge of the bed. I so enjoyed playing with his locks; someday I would braid it. I told him about his mother's call. He was silent for a long time before saying, "They should have burned it." He didn't explain and I didn't ask; if people are mysterious they have a reason.

He'd be up and walking the next day. I brought his toothbrush, warm water, soap and clean longjohns, then went out to fetch ice while he did his toilette. It was so cold my nostrils crackled and glued together. Puffy salmon-pink clouds sailed briskly from the north. Leif hadn't asked me to, but I had already cleaned the blood from his mukluks and done laundry and hauled ice. Soon I'd have no excuse to be at the *ini*.

Inside, I picked up my drum from its dark resting place - hiding place, maybe - and slid a look over. Sure enough, Leif was watching from the bed where he lay, dressed in longjohns. "I'm leaving," I said.

"Oh. Don't go yet. Please." He sat up painfully. He squinted like he couldn't see me well, dazzled by a strong sun. Was I sending out trails of light, connecting me to the *inua* world? "You played that drum, didn't you? I remember..."

He kept gazing at me so I couldn't make a move toward my parka. He watched me like he was seeing me change, not into a strange and frightening *palrailuk* or a fox he'd married accidentally, but he was Tussock Boy and he'd found the most wondrous bird in the world.

"Gretchen...Kayuqtuq..." The way he said both of my names made the hairs on my scalp and arms rise up to be petted by his voice. "What happened to me?" he asked. "Was I dead? I...think I was dead."

"No. Don't *say* that," I whispered.

"Could you come closer? I just want to talk to you."

"You *are* talking to me."

"Just a little closer..." His voice reached and gently pulled me to the platform.

"Okay, now what?"

"I want to hear."

"Hear - ?"

"Your drum again. And sing too. One of your angutkoq songs."

I wondered if he was teasing, yet his eyes were grave. I sat on the edge of the platform, tapping the drum and turning it a few times to fan a slight breeze. I moistened the skin with water from a cup, not wanting to spit in the way of the old men. He listened to the hollow thonk and watched so hard I couldn't make myself sing anymore than he could pee under my gaze, so I stopped and just sat there. When he asked to see it I handed him the drumstick. His fingertips touched mine, making me shudder.

"It's a crane tibia." He smiled, studying the bone. The damp ends of his hair were starting to curl again down his neck. He seemed not to breathe. You had better, I wanted to caution him - Polly said to take deep breaths.

"Before...when I gave you *sigrak* you talked in your sleep about things."

"I did?" He kept looking down, his smile gone. "A truth serum."

"Do you always think about birds the most?"

He was silent, still hardly breathing. I thought he might be mad about my eavesdropping, but when he looked up his eyes weren't mad. They were the prettiest alder color with lakes in their centers, shimmering with light and deep with inky shadows. How could eyes do that?

"I don't know about when I'm delirious," he said. "But I can tell you what I think about all the time when I'm awake. Do you want to hear it?"

But I couldn't answer, I forgot to breathe myself now, and he set the bone aside. I shuddered again. I laid the drum on the floor, not caring that it was too close to the stove and might crack.

"You like me," he said, and it was not a question.

"I like you," I whispered.

"I love you. I love you with all my heart." I stared at him. "You aren't...really with...someone else are you?" he asked. I shook my head. "Gretchen do you want me?" he asked in a rush. His face was open, waiting for my answer; he was such an easy target. How could I ever have tried to hurt him? His soul had returned, and this time we weren't going to let ourselves miss another chance, because now we knew how short life was.

"Want you for what?"

"Anything." He slid his body down so his head lay near my knees, his throat exposed. "I'm yours." I looked down at him, feeling my blood roar and pound. And slowly I stretched out beside him and laid my cheek along his to breathe him in, in the old way of kissing.

I lost track of time until I felt his lips on mine, and we both released a long sigh as something gave throughout our whole bodies and minds and we eased, moving in deeper through our lips with our arms circling, cleaving to each other. I felt a great thirst; he was water and I had been parched and spent with fevers, so I drank.

"Oh, god yes, I love you," he said ardently. His eyes were half-closed. I kicked off my pants and was on top of him, straddling and squeezing him in a bear hug. He gasped and laughed through my kiss. I knew I was *kuangazuk* but it did not matter. We were both breathing so fast, our hearts drumming together. He slid his hands under my shirt and slowly up my back, and I never wore bras - hand-me-downs with wires and rubber - so his palms sledded along my skin, and when I raised up on my arms they ran around my sides to my breasts and cupped me against his lifelines. He was careful - I could have been a speckled chick he was lifting back into the nest. In the slightest movement, no more than a feather's down, his thumbs brushed over my nipples. The sudden feel was astounding.

I pushed his longjohns down and molded my body on him, on the ridge of his bare sex. As I rocked against him and he caressed me under the worn elastic of my underpants, a current of wonder traveled through his eyes like he couldn't believe what we were doing, any more than I could. "Oh my god," he whispered, and in the next second he gasped, rolling under me as he clenched me with his arms so we were one, a human wave, and I was riding his hips in to the shore. My body shook and my mind swept out, spinning through stars in a kind of ecstatic spirit flight. When I returned I was lying on top of him. His eyes were closed and he was limp under me, everything, his heart thudding powerfully like he had sprinted. Too late it crossed my mind that he had almost died. And his ribs...

"I'm sorry! I hurt you!" I cried, clambering off him.

He smiled a little. "No, you cured me," he murmured. He made no mention of my strange form of love-making, and let me clean him and cover him in the furs. He could hardly move.

"Don't tell anyone I came here again," I warned. He nodded with no comment on that either, just reached up to my face before dropping his hand. "Don't tell anyone how you feel, either," I begged, but he was asleep. He didn't think secrecy was important. Now he would want to broadcast all over town and try to hold hands or take my arm to stroll with me down the village, or carve our names at the post office or on caches.

But I am happy! I thought as I ran through the drifts on light feet, under a full moon and the long dipping antler of *Tuttu*, the Caribou. This was happiness. I laughed and fell, still laughing, and leaped up to run again, covered in snow. He loved me with all his heart, more than the geese. His soul had returned and he had made love to me, I had made love to *him*! How strange and wonderful was the universe!

IF I COULD ONLY go back in time and become that moon riding above the girl whose hair flies behind her, whose lips still tingle from kissing. I would breathe to her through the medium of the wind, *Yes. Be happy! Be happy on that earth. It will not last.*

And maybe I am able to do that - my powers are still with me - so that I sing my warning across the field of time in a spirit voice. Because she stopped, the young woman who was I, right before she reached Tuguk's cabin on the outskirts of the village. Her smile faltered and she caught her breath, stopping the white, frozen mist from her lungs to gaze up at me, the moon.

A cloud moved over the face of it, throwing the snowy world into indigo shadow. As quick as lips pulling back from teeth in a grin, quick as the eyelid of a dog waking from sleep, it opened again to reveal the round, gleaming mask of moon. "What do you want?" I asked it, "Is it the bargain I made?"

I threw back my head and laughed again so the cold air hit the back of my throat. I was hugging myself because the birdman was alive and in love with me, I had made love to him. Take the *qilya*, who needs it now?

HOARSE SHOUTS spilled from the house as I came in from the night. Nobody ever yelled, so at first I thought a naluagmiu was in there. Willy's snow-machine was parked in front, the contents of the sled in a jumble. Though Willy was always so loving with his equipment, his expensive .30-06 and shotgun lay uncovered so snow blew into the chambers. He'd sure been in a hurry. I covered the gun with the tarp, noting the fresh blood on the canvas, and stepped into the *kanichak* to listen.

Her own voice strained, Flo was answering that shouting stranger. I entered the house. The intruder was Willy. He was flushed and bleary-eyed and sprawled at the card table in his tee-shirt. Flo sat across from him. Food had been set before him but he wasn't eating. A bowl was shattered on the floor, a hare dangled its long, bloody feet over the table's edge. Polly was hiding behind the curtain to her bed.

It took a long moment hanging like a whitefish at the bottom of a lake in winter, and then I understood. Willy was drunk. Abe verified my shock; he stood back from the table, wearing the slit-eyed goggle-mask. But he was not scolding, he just looked helpless. As I tiptoed inside Flo signaled me with her eyes. Get to the back of the room, they warned, don't attract his attention. She meant Willy!

She said to him, "We just want to know. You tell us now. Did Stanley bring the liquor?" Trying to put the fault on someone else's son, anywhere but on her perfect boy. Her plump fingers were still, in a play-calm. Willy began swearing. His head was weaving, his stink reached me across the room. Hare blood and vomit smeared his undershirt. I stole toward my bed behind his back, past the stony old man. All my joy of the night had flown, replaced by a sickening pang in my stomach. Polly's eyes glimmered from the crack of her curtain. I slipped behind it, still in my outdoor things, and sat on her bed. She was in her ruffled nightie and it made her look too young.

"He came home this way," she whispered. "Dad thinks they never went to reindeer camp and they just got drunk. But where *were* you? He went all over town looking for you, so now everyone knows."

"I just visit *eskuulkti*, it's not *my* fault! How come he's drunk?" I was confused - Willy looking everywhere for me? Since when?

"That's what Mom's trying to find out. But he's like this."

I peeked out. Willy was just mumbling now. Abe was overreacting. So his son got drunk once in his life; who didn't? Probably Abe had. When I came out from behind the curtain Willy saw me and flapped his hand. "Heeey, Kayuq! I been looking everywhere for you, man!" He was slurring and didn't look handsome at all - the liquor had changed his features. His eyes were crowberries shining in a swollen, red mask.

"Hi, Pataq," I muttered, rooted near Polly's bed.

"You were with that naluagmiu, I know you were...wharzizname! Out in the old *ini!* The *iiiniii*." He wagged his forefinger at me like a scolding schoolteacher. I blushed while Abe and Flo shifted their stares to me. "How come you with that birdman, that whiteman? You don't like em, so why you always play hang out with people you never like?"

It was not so much Willy as the sober spotlight of curiosity, the raised brow of Abe, that flustered me. "You leave her alone now, Pataq," said Flo.

"Leave her alone, leave her alone, leave her alone," chanted Willy in a kid's way. My insides cringed at the glitter of his eyes, which didn't seem to be Willy's. If it wasn't him, who *was* it? "How come you go there?" he exploded.

"She can visit anyone," said Flo. "It is her business." How long had she been trying to reason with him, keeping him under control and in the house where no one else could witness? Flo was the upright cornerstone of the church - her family was the model Itiak family. He was breaking her just like that cracked bowl on the floor, and the blasted, dead rabbit.

"How come you go there!" Willy shouted again. I made the mistake of trying to answer.

"He's been sick, Pataq. He's got no one else...to take care of him."

"*I* got no one else!"

"You got everyone you see here and all over town."

"No, no, no!" With his whole arm he swept the dishes off the table, like a one-year-old. "I got no mom and dad! I got no parents!"

"You got us, son," Flo's voice quavered. She sneaked her apron hem to her eyes.

"I got no parents! Fuck! I'm all alone!" At that, Willy laid his head on the table and seemed to disappear for a while. I hoped he had passed out. There was silence in the house then, a wail of north wind outside. His legs seeming to break at the knees, Abe sat slowly down on the corner of his bed. Polly watched from where she lay, sniffling and holding back the curtain and her tears.

"Why is he so mean to Mom and Dad?" she whimpered.

"It's not him saying that."

"How do you know? What comes out has to come from you; it's not really the liquor talking."

I wanted to believe it was due to a bad spirit in alcohol. Whoever invented it had thought so, those old-time naluagmiut. Why else would they name it "spirits"?

"I'm going home now!" shouted Willy. He lurched to his feet, holding onto the table so it rocked with him. "To *my* house! You take that hare I shot, Kayuq...where is it, oh here it is -" he pawed at the hare - "and you cook it, okay? You cook it! Cuz everyone's real hungry!"

"Okay," I said at once. Willy tried to focus on me, his eyebrows working into a parody of themselves.

"You think it's too small? I'm not such a good hunter?"

Was he still thinking about his one failed hunt? Was that what alcohol did, dig up fears you thought were gone but were still there, festering with pus?

"You're a good hunter, son," said Flo. Willy turned. He studied her, perplexed.

"Don't go, Pataq. Stay here." Abe finally spoke. He had stood again, and his fingers were clenching and relaxing in twitches. And his eye.

"Well, shit! I'm going! This ain't my goddamn home here. Nowhere's my fucking goddamn home." Willy jolted to the door and out, stumbling in the *kanichak*. We saw him trying to pull on his jacket, losing his balance and giving up. He left the door ajar so the cold burst in. My ribs over my heart felt bewildered; only minutes before Leif's hands had petted and smoothed them until they had opened and let everything in, and now they cringed and my heart felt shrunken.

Flo dropped her face into her hands. I went to close the doors firmly, wishing we had a lock. When I came back Abe was still standing in the middle of the room in his worn sealskin slippers. He looked long at me and heaved a sigh. I had never seen the parents so gray and old, and I realized in a quick, clear knowledge that they wouldn't be around that much longer. How would I eat; would Willy hunt for me? And what if he turned out - ? I cut the idea off. I couldn't live with Pataq anyway! And why did I have to depend on a man? I hated to sew, I always screwed up the butchering, I had to get a paying job or else I'd be like an old *aka* waiting for scraps from anyone who remembered, the village charity case. My thoughts were blowing around like that, in panicked flurries.

Then Abe said to me, "You go there, take care of him. Let him get in the bed, keep the place warm. And try to let him change that shirt."

"Let *him* do it," I said, "if he's dumb enough to drink." Flo raised her head from her hands.

Abe narrowed his eyes in the scary way but it seemed just a reflex. "He's not dumb; the Devil got hold of her. And you do what I tell you." He seemed too tired to think of words to punish my disobedience and that made me bolder. Or was it because I knew I was loved and had made love and laughed at the very moon?

"I'm not his wife. I'm not his mother, or even his sister, so why do I have to be the one?"

"You will *do* it!"

"I won't." I wondered how many times we could go back and forth, me saying no, Abe saying do it, until he gave up or lashed out and cuffed me and broke my eardrum like Nelson did to his daughter. Abe had never hit me but I had always backed down just in time, Maq the dog. Why was it so important that I obey? It must be more important than Willy's safety or he'd just go himself. I didn't want Willy to freeze but I was thinking of his red-rimmed, mindless eyes and being alone with him. An old anxiety rose into my chest. My knees began to shake out of control, as disobedient to my will as I was to the old man. Abe's squinted look had altered to a puzzlement. He had no idea.

"She don't have to go," said Flo then. That she understood troubled me more than anything. Willy had revealed a jealousy and nobody could be sure what he would do. "She better not go there," Flo told Abe with a meaningful look. As the old man became aware, the lines of his face deepened into cracks. His cheek spasmed but he didn't override her. "*Adiii*, I'm so tired," she sighed.

I began to clean up the mess to get it out of their sight, their troubled old eyes, hoping they wouldn't cry like Polly. I washed off puke splashed near the sink then took the mutilated hare and tried to salvage some meat for stew. The fur was wasted. Willy's shotgun had blown it into a colorful tangle so only the ears were white. I cut off the feet to use for tourist good luck charms. Abe sat on the floor with his drill and hacksaw and a piece of tusk in a clamp, blocking out the world. Flo left, gone to make sure Willy hadn't passed out in a drift; Polly quietly sniffled in back of her curtain. They would not speak of it in the future, just mull about it for days.

But I did not dwell long on Willy or how I had won the battle with Abe. I had already returned in my mind to the *ini. I love you with all my heart*, Leif had told me, so softly, and I had him repeat it over and over like an incantation, *I am yours, I am yours*, until I stopped thinking of the chaos at home and the ache in my stomach eased. It was a powerful medicine. I would see him again, I *had* to. We could do it again, what we had done. What had we done? Made love...make love...

I had to warn him. He shouldn't tell anyone he'd been so sick or they would think I had endangered his life. And with Willy like this it might be foolish to meet in town...

In that way my desire and fear quarreled.

LATE THAT NIGHT they were still warring. Abe and Flo were discussing in their bed, in Inupiaq. No name was mentioned but Pataq's but they were circling around another person, and that person was *me*. I was strange and crazy and a bad influence, Abe was saying. He wanted me to move here permanently and sleep on the floor if boarders came. Pataq must marry - he was old enough, a provider. And Flo agreed I was a little funny but I was doing fine. Becoming a woman, she repeated, like I was unformed. I had a good heart, but I had been hurt, I had a bad beginning that left me argumentative sometimes. Was that so crazy?

And when Abe wondered if they should keep me anymore, Flo protested that I had nowhere to go. They couldn't turn me out. Then I should get married, it would make me settle down. I should marry and start having babies with a man from another village, and move away from here. That would keep me busy, away from crazy ideas. If I wouldn't choose someone Abe would arrange a footrace like his grandfather did for Aka, and the winner could take me. That wouldn't work so well, said Flo, since I ran so fast I would beat all the men. That was a really bad idea. Besides, girls should choose their own husbands or life was no fun at all. There was a long silence - she'd hurt his feelings - and in an angry tone Abe brought up my drum. So, he knew about that! He ranted about the old ways, God and Jesus, Indians. Finally he uttered the dread word: naluagmiu. It seemed visiting Leif was further proof of my incorrigibility. Like my drum.

But the *ligliq* man was not a bad person, Flo said, and was he not part Indian too? Maybe there was a natural affinity. I hadn't been treated so well by some Inupiat, had I? But Abe said he still didn't want me living at Pataq's. Abe would find Pataq a good wife to take care of him. They stopped talking then, and fell asleep after tossing and sighing a long time.

So...I did have something besides *qilya* to give up. My home. It was not my real home anyway; I knew what Willy meant, though I was shocked he felt that way too. Take it, fine, I thought, but I'm not going to settle down with some stranger Abe finds me. Take my home and I'll keep my powers and choose my own man and live in the *ini*...

I smiled to myself in the dark.

IN THE OLD DAYS the *uiliaqtaqs'* power lay in their virginity. Refusing husbands, alone in their *inis*, they combed their long hair and drew animals from the sea. Jealous men took their *qilya* by forcing them over and over in gang rapes, foolishly undoing their own hunting success. The men asked for help from the male angutkoq, who used the blood of the witches, the blood from their torn wombs to lure the whales, and that was how power changed hands, I guess, from women to men.

Calvin liked this story and told it a lot. I don't know who first told it, man or woman, or if it was told to girls to keep them in line or force them to marry, or to remind them: *See, you once did have power*. Clearly I was not *uiliaqtaq* though, because I had never lost my *qilya* - it had strengthened. I was the other kind of witch, maybe, the kind whose powers are fed with suffering.

In a different story also told by Calvin, shamans gained *qilya* through sex, because copulation balanced the male and female elements that bound the universe together: moon and sun, dark and light. Physical union pleased the universe. Calvin said it was satisfied even more when a man angutkoq turned into woman and coupled with a man. I didn't know about that; it was confusing. But I felt my powers increase again that night, even if Leif and I didn't really quite *copulate*.

Maybe the spiritworld didn't even care about a promise. Sila might be like a storeowner who let you buy on credit, or a relative who never demanded repayment, because you were blood.

CHAPTER 24

It is the secret sympathy, the silver link...
SIR W. SCOTT (NALUAGMIUT)

MY POWERS INCREASED but next morning the flu had me, and though I wanted to run to the *ini* I didn't want Leif to catch it. Polly was up; she and Flo *unga*ed me, bringing me aspirin and tea. Suspecting they did it out of guilt, I let them pamper me all they wanted. They were going to tell me I couldn't live with Willy, the reason hard to explain without people losing face. Polly was going to visit several ill babies and said she would check on Leif too; I didn't try to stop her. She left in her best parka with frozen white-fish and her syringe needle.

I dozed in a half-dreaming state until I heard voices. Abe had gone to drag Willy out of bed; the elders couldn't stand lie-a-beds, especially hung-over ones. I peeked out to see Willy looking remorseful and sick, his wide shoulders drooping. He kept his eyes down as the parents scolded him in soft but relentless voices about how worried and ashamed they were, switching between English and Inupiaq, on and on, and he didn't dare interrupt or re-tort. He got the gentle approach. Abe had never beat him like some fathers. He was old-fashioned Inupiaq. When the grandkids acted up, Flo and Abe would implore and reason or tell stories in case the old souls - the *atka* - were in the children, listening. If you were too harsh the *atka* might be so offended it would leave and the child could die.

I wondered how old a man had to be before his parents stopped lecturing like that.

When they were done, Willy admitted he had bought the whiskey. He and Stanley had drunk in a tent but somehow they ended up back in Itiak, like they wanted to be caught. He had hurt everyone, Flo said, "even Kayuq-tuq", though it was the alcohol, not him, she assured him. They prayed. He would have to testify at the church, in public. After Willy tearfully vowed never to drink again, the old people went out; it was part of the plan that Willy was left in the house to make amends.

He sat on my bed, his eyes still fixed on the floor. "I didn't mean it, Kayuq. Whatever I said."

"It's all right..."

"I don't care if you want naluagmiu; he's okay. And besides, you're not my girlfriend." Willy was blinking rapidly. All this crying, it must be contagious. "I think..." he said slowly, "maybe you're mad because I don't treat you very good." He ignored my protest that I wasn't mad. "When you're not living at the place I do stuff. But when you're there I let you do all the shit work...so I can see why you're mad all the time."

He gave me a sweet smile. When I recovered from my surprise, I said, "Someday I'll go find out what my mother was like. Maybe I'll live where I was born." If I could find it, I thought.

Willy picked at a cuticle where the blood from many hunts had dried so deep he could never get it out. "At least she just died...not on purpose. Or killed."

I raised my eyebrows a little, in a what-do-you-mean look.

"I don't know," Willy said. His shoulders hunched forward. "What did I say last night? To Mom and them?"

I couldn't tell him the truth, not to his poor hung-over face. "Just *kuangazuk* things, like you aren't a good hunter."

Half-groaning, half-laughing, he covered his eyes and answered my unspoken question. "I just wanted to get stuff off my mind is why I drank. Like, what am I going to do all my life? What if there's no animals left when I'm thirty and have a family? I don't got no education like a scientist even if I know more. And what if they draft me? Maybe it's better if I go, I could hunt people, I could get a medal. Shit, I wish I live in the old days."

And I had imagined he was content. "Were people happier then?" I asked softly.

"Sure. Don't you think?"

"They had wars too, and they starved. I think they worried a lot about dying. And they died...a lot".

Willy shrugged, looking at me finally but with unreadable eyes. "Everyone dies. What you do alive, that matters."

I turned over in bed to face the wall and said, "I'm sorry for what I did too. Sometimes I act bad without even being drunk."

He knew what I meant. "We don't need to talk about it."

HE GOT BUSY hunting again, really hunting this time, and ran his huskies. He even started seeing a woman, Renee, who had a baby and didn't really want to be a hunter's wife. She wanted money. She wanted to be taken on a trip and to eat in a restaurant. I didn't stay at the cabin again. And I forgot about him, as much as you can forget someone you see all the time.

I felt different, like an *aka* who returns as a sled dog or her grandchild, only it was my same body with a different soul. My body was changed too, at times it seemed with a malady that sped everything up so the fat burned off my body though I felt no pain. I was a weed swaying in a fast current - I was the arctic cotton that swelled until I cracked open and apart, spreading over the world so I entered every icicle, star or snow-bunting. And I loved it all.

But I could only dwell on one entity, each word he had said to me, each glance. He was in all things: a drift was the curve of his flank as he lay; a wolverine ruff on a parka walking by was his hair; a raven, his beard; old varnished wood, his eyes; the sheen of light on the lagoon ice, his sweat; the sunset, his blood. I could see in the dark now with the eyes of an animal - but what they made out in the dark was not fearsome. No demons lurked there but my lover's form, waiting on a bed for my return.

Being angutkoq, it was hard to tell apart these symptoms from the ones I'd always had. Like everything else, I tried to conceal them.

I could not hide that well from Polly, though. When she came back from the *ini* that day, she sat on my bed. The birdman was feeling so well he was typing his report, she said, "Very cheerful..." She cast her eyes down pointedly.

Cheerful? I thought. Back to the goose? If he didn't need me, would he still want me? Now that he was strong, what would happen if I lay with him again? I shut my eyes and felt ill.

"Did you tell him?" asked Polly. We had to whisper - Flo was in the house.

"Tell what?"

"That you're in love!"

"*Ayii*! I-I'm not." I pressed the backs of my hands to my cheeks, feeling hot and cold at the same time, caught naked.

Polly studied me. "And he confessed his love," she guessed, "and then you did it. You consummated your love. Was it okay?" she whispered. "Did he come?" Her manner was that of a concerned mother asking a kid what grade she got in school. Blushing furiously, I let my eyebrows rise a tiny distance. "Did *you*?" she asked.

"Niviak! Don't tell anyone!"

"That you came?"

I punched her on the arm. "I won't tell," she said, giggling. "But it's modern times, and it doesn't matter if he's white, either. So why hide it?"

"I don't know..."

"You're like a man! They don't want to admit it, like it's weak, or a woman has control over them. And you never cry either! But secretly you're a romantic."

"It's the Indian," I muttered.

"Maybe *I* should go out with you...I jokes." Polly smiled at me affectionately. "I can't believe it. My little sister." My eyes stung. She looked so beautiful and like she really cared, so that I didn't mind being exposed - I could feel anything. With others I always imagined if they heard I had a lover, the first thing to jump in their mind would be me being held down and...

Polly's suddenly gasped, thinking of something. "Kayuq! Were you going after him at fishcamp?"

"No!"

"*Ayii*, you were!" She covered her mouth with her hands with her eyes wide above them. "If I knew, I would never -"

"It's okay!"

She pulled a sorry face. "You're too good an actor. You better tell him soon though. Because it's winter and there's no geese to keep him around. If you don't want to, I will." She made as if to leave.

"No!" I pleaded, grabbing her. She pretended to wrestle me off, laughing, but her dimple smoothed and her mouth grew wistful.

"Be happy, Kayuq, it doesn't happen much. It's a gift from God. I want to feel it, but I just lose interest. Too many cousins here, besides."

I was silent. Here I hadn't wanted to love anyone at all and it had sneaked up on me like the sun in early spring, brilliant out of the night, in the unlikely form of a birdman. While Polly hunted it with her great talents and it escaped her.

AFTER A LONG, fathomless sleep I was well and Abe and Flo were back to normal, joking with each other, sometimes cuttingly. I jumped out of bed and devoured a lot of food, anything I could find. The children ran in to announce the shivary was starting. I asked Polly who had married. "It's May and Barney! Where have you been?" she exclaimed.

"On the moon," I said, making my eyes dazed so she tittered.

I let her drag me to the shivary. Some men had already kidnapped Barney and were holding him for ransom out in the cold with no coat. They tossed him on their shoulders while the village gathered, smiling expectantly. The low, slanting sun cast a light that turned all the familiar faces beautiful, like angels in ruffed hoods. I was moved by a great kindness toward the people of Itiak, so any wrong ever done me was okay, at least for now. Dark memories had always been my whiskey, my solace, and a part of me fought to regain it. But a stronger force had taken over. Itiak had become dear, its people and all that had happened were part of a design that - step by step - had led me to this radiant instant. I wouldn't change anything.

While I was in that trance of goodwill, Leif climbed up the snowbank. He and the buildings behind him were glowing, the edges taken off so everything blended into the sky and red-lit snow of May's yard. He was not separate from the universe or from me, the cells of our bodies were vibrating and pulling apart so we were just energy and light, and I wanted to take his bodiless body fully into mine and turn ourselves inside out into emptiness. When he looked at me I saw that is what he wanted too. He remembered my warning and did not approach or even wave, but across the snow the two black points of his soul pierced my heart.

Someone play-screamed and everyone looked up. The mother and sister had clambered up on the house with May and a large box that contained the payment for her groom. They nearly slid off the icy roof. People howled like wolves, demanding the ransom. The women began tossing handfuls down; candy, cigarettes and gum rained as the crowd surged forward into a free-for-all. A shivary was the only time to be selfish and greedy *kapik*s like that, when grown men knocked aside *aka*s and little kids to get at candy like looters. I held back though, just watching. Although I had always enjoyed them, suddenly a shivary seemed a very peculiar thing.

I saw Leif stoop to pick up a chocolate that skittered to his feet. Baring his teeth in a doll's scary smile and with eyes fixed on me, he unwrapped it and popped it in his mouth, chewing while still grinning. I refused to laugh. He took one step toward me, cutting his eyes around like a thief. Nobody was watching. He sidled another step and I snickered uneasily. The spell had broken, replaced by anxiety. Maybe he thought it was silly, my avoidance, but he couldn't tease like this or he'd have to stay in the *ini*! When he took another exaggerated sneaky step, I stopped him in his tracks with a frown and his smile flickered out. It was just in time, for the shivary was ending and people would see. He turned away.

Little Paulette from the Tuguk family suddenly stood in my path. She had been elbowed in the nose and was bent over dribbling blood. It spread into a bright pool on the snow that just kept getting bigger. She was from a bad family and no one would help her. She seemed too small to hold that much blood. I gave her my tissue and told her to go home but she was stubborn and remained crouched, fountaining red, sobbing bitterly.

When I looked up Leif was gone.

ENTRY. SHE IS my Orpheus, she speaks to the animals and with her magic drum she descended into hell and took my hand. In our very cryptic debriefing session, before it became...well...carnal, she said it was not the land of the dead. I must have gone somewhere else, or my fugitive soul did. She would not elaborate on how she brought me back, and can I blame her? The placebo effect doesn't even explain it, since I wasn't conscious. Will she be coming back for her drum?

Entry. The mock abducting was interesting: must be Lutheran. G is so skittish. Are we illicit due to some hangover from an arctic Jim Crow or is the miscegenation in her own mind? There are kids who look mixed; the trouble is, where are the donors of the haploids: sport hunters? Military? That could explain her behavior: leery of the fly-by-night nalockmyoot in-seminators. Though it seems the paternity of children is irrelevant.

I won't be so maudlin, if that's the problem. She "likes" me. I wonder if Romantic Love operates in the Arctic. They say it was invented in the Renaissance, but it makes biological sense. It <u>must</u> operate; look at the dog-birdman who made Nuliajuk throw caution to the winds. Is it just the creative impulse to expand the gene pool? That always subverted the social order, the allure of the alien overriding the drive to murder it (anyway, her preferred style makes genetic drift unlikely).

Entry. The Committee okayed my wintering here to do the write-up and grant proposal, as long as I check in more frequently. They allow a grieving period. They are willing to vouch for this research as valid wartime service, and Master said he would attest at an appeal if I pay him back "somehow". What the fuck does that mean? The war seems unreal, the whole Out-side. Itiak is the center of the universe and the rest of the world could have been obliterated and we wouldn't know or care – except for the mail plane with the checks.

I'm plowing through the unuck data but make any excuse to go to town for a sighting, my true research. She's never at Willy's but I have to stay away from the main house, since it might blow my cover. I know, I'll contrive a duel with the principal and the preacher, let them beat me, then faint at her doorstep. I'd endure that scene with Waldo all over if I could reap her favor again. But she'd suspect a second time.

The I-Ching's hopeful note: "Molt, shed, strip away the old useless hide and expose the new. There is a fruit still not eaten." The wild goose draws nigh to the mighty stone, but I must penetrate things with great care.

BOOK FIVE

"Out in the Great Loneliness"

O cease! must men to hate and death return?
Cease! drain not to its dregs the urn
of bitter prophecy
The world is weary of the past
SHELLEY (NALUAGMIUT)

Forbidding is our task, you say
but think, ere we return to peace and calm
how boundless is the fate you flinch from
(HIGH PRIEST OF IFE, YORUBA)

A river bears westward through
a baneful valley; its name is Fear
Seek you wisdom still?
(ANCIENT NORSE)

By self alone is evil undone
By self alone is she purified
THE DHAMMAPADA (ANCIENT INDIA)

The way is opening before me...

AUA (ANGAKOK, IGLULIK)

CHAPTER 25

The valley spirit dies not
nor the female mystery
Long and unbroken does its power remain
used gently, without pain

(TAOIST, ANCIENT CHINESE)

I will visit unknown woman
search out hidden things behind the man
Seek thou under man
and under woman

NETSIT (NETSILIK)

ENTRY. THE SPIRITS answered me on Halloween night. They do it different here. This is the real thing, like Ireland a thousand years ago with an Inupiat twist. The kids don't go trick-or-treating; they stay indoors scared shitless. You don't need acid up here to blow your mind. If not the land itself, what is left of the old culture will turn your psyche on edge and drop you over.

I was at Willy's late. He was telling "true" ghost stories, which give me the heebie-jee-bies, maybe because we're so vulnerable on this polar coast. But the main reason is Willy believes them. That's influential, I'll admit; the mind is tugged by another's. As the wind beat at the door, Willy told of cannibal ogre babies who tunnel into eenees, the grinding teeth of children murdered long ago, dogs who cry like babies when someone's going to die, ravens who predict it, and evil dwarves who force you to run races you'd better lose. A boy comes home to find a giant has clubbed his parents to death. The beam of the Enlightenment dimmed. My, well, paranormal experiences here didn't help. I kept expecting kids to show up though I saw no bowl of candy. Then with a curious light in his eye Willy left the cabin and did not return. I didn't relish the journey home to the old sodhouse, so I lingered.

I was on the cot G seems to have vacated forever, reading her Dickens. There came a scratching at the door as if one of the dead seals outside had reanimated and was coming for a visit, like Banquo or quoth-the-raven. The door opened and eight demons filed in. They were painted black, dressed in black like commandos. I recognized Gretchen, Willy, some others, all young. They stared at me unsmiling, emanating a faint menace, and made me flash on Picts painted blue, the KKK, Sioux war parties, initiation rites. This was Itiak's aboriginal trick-or-treat, and I wanted to give them treats, for fear of the trick.

G was attractive in her shadowy get-up. I tried not to stare or approach in fawning adulation. Silently the ghoul who was Stanley pointed to the supply crate. Of course: you had to feed visiting shades, bribe them with fall harvest. They watched me start koopiak, but before it boiled they glided back outside, casting back looks of warning. G was last out the door. She was hesitating as if a demon only reluctantly, from peer pressure. I didn't know when we'd get another opportunity. We hadn't talked since the...(what do you call that? My rebirth), I hadn't gotten within thirty feet of her, and we can't pass messages like even the Montagues and Capulets managed. POWs must feel this way in the enemy camp. But she stepped back from my advance and whispered that she had to leave; people might see. I must have looked ready to make a "scene", maybe jump the next plane out, because she quickly promised to come out to the eenee. She didn't say when.

I tore home at the witching hour. A ghostly cloud stretched out across the newly risen gibbous moon like a phalanges, pointing to forgotten terrors from childhood. Willy had told of a man who goes to the home of his best friend and no one is there, but a bag is hanging from the rafters. He cuts it down and guess what? the head of his friend is in the bag, but they're not friends anymore! It grins, terribly. The man runs with the head in pursuit, in a ball of fire. I had the weirdest thought as I ran through the night that a head was chasing me...and it was Willy's.

The eenee had taken on the lair-like quality, and under the influence of all the fight-flight chemicals I had to force myself to crawl into the black tunnel. And the Fox sat on the shelf. I have to admit it sent a jolt to my heart, as in fright. She'd washed off the hell persona, but she was staring at the entrance as though lying in wait. The books say the old shamans had a special look, seeing the invisible; that is how you identified one. Her eyes had that look. I was out of breath, laughing at myself; I explained some stories had freaked me out. She also had a kind of new tension. I sat down but not too close, pretending we hadn't slept together; we were still strangers. I wasn't going to start. But we really needed to talk.

She looked at me with a kind of melting desperation and said, "I want to tell you a story too. Only it's about me..." The eenee grew very still. This was it. I was going to finally understand. And she told me, simply but graphically, starting with her sad birth in a spruce forest filled with ravens.

AND WHEN SHE IS TWELVE, *in autumn, she menstruates. She uses the arctic cotton she frantically gathers while the blood runs down. No one had told* her. Children run through the village reporting if they see a woman's stained underwear on a clothesline, but they don't know what it means, they just know it's bad. The mask sniffs out the underwear hiding in the slave's corner.

At first the mask pretends to be angry but then grows a different look, altering into a kind of fear. Is it afraid it will lose the slave-becoming-woman? Will the slave begin to fight back now? If the slave is lost, the mask will have to do all the work. So it grows a crafty look as it plans. The girl hears it telling everyone she has bled and is a woman now. This shames her completely. Such a thing is not mentioned to men; it is a secret domain, a process held in fear, a force men have no power against that destroys hunting prowess and virility. That is from the old belief. And from the missionaries, the double humiliation...

I looked up at his face to see if I could go on and saw that he already knew what came next. That made it easier.

On a dark night soon after comes the great betrayal of womanhood. First it is the father. Right after he is finished, it is the son. Never had the girl heard of such a thing, nobody had warned her. Is it the end of the world for her, or just another misery to endure?

The girl knows nothing, but I do later, as a grown woman, remembering for you. In some villages it was tradition to break in a girl like that, one with no relatives to watch over her. She would understand that she was not to get ideas. She was not to use her rising power. The custom served certain men, who could enjoy themselves without fear of revenge.

The girl obeys quietly, lying on her back and opening her legs like she's just a pair of scissors. And she does not cry. She tries to pretend it is just another chore, like going out for ice in weather you don't send a dog into. The men do it quickly and easily, like koq-ing and she's the pot. They hide their faces in her shoulder, their breathing is harsh. And the mother is in the next bed over, satisfied with her plan.

But the next evening when the girl is alone in the cabin the son brings his cousins, so drunk they have turned into not-men. Now she struggles, and wild-

ly. She is strong and nearly full-grown. She bloodies a nose with her fist, crashes a chair over a head. They wrench her arms, shoving her into the walls. They pull her hair, wrapping it around her neck to choke her, laughing that she's itkiliq, *throwing her down on her stomach, they'll do it that way. And that is when she has the fit.*

It frightens them through all the whiskey. They realize it is more than a sickness, it is a spirit thing and they flee. She lies on the floor with her pants down, with her eyes rolled back. She does not remember that part, only being found by girls - their screams rouse her. Soon the whole village knows.

And Flo makes her visit though she had never entered that house before, for Abe's family and this family are enemies. Flo scolds the mask. She prays aloud and takes the girl's hand and they leave, walking through the valley of the shadow of death. They carry nothing, for the girl owns nothing. The men are out hunting. When they return to find the girl taken, they are too scared of the Ugungoraseok clan and will not fight to get their property back. Flo never takes the money from the government that the family receives for the girl.

And right away she sews the girl a new parka and mukluks.

SHE LOOKED UP. I saw in her eyes a courage I have never known. She wanted me to look in her eyes and not flinch or turn away. But they glazed over when she said quietly, "And they grabbed my hair so I couldn't move, like I was a dog to put a harness on...or a reindeer when they cut its throat. And they took turns."

I didn't hide the effect of this story on me. I think she wanted to have me emote fully for her, to be her cathartic hired mourner. She couldn't do it for herself, because if she ever let her guard down and allowed herself to truly feel how she should, she couldn't have borne it. I let my tears flow; it was easy, it broke my heart. By now they're practically just parasympathetic reaction, I who used to never cry. And she touched them on my face.

I knew who she really was then: the poor Fox, finally allowing me to pet, and I did, I petted her. She huddled on my bed as fragile as the new ice out there on the sea, and I stepped out onto that thin ice, not knowing anything at all and envying that little white fox I saw leaping and mincing over it with such great skill, knowing exactly where to put each paw and with how much pressure. Who were they, I asked; I would report them, no matter how long ago. But she shook her head. How could it be someone in Itiak? Where were they hiding out? Surely they looked deformed somehow, with twisted humps and tiny red eyes. But no, they'd be the picture of normalcy: nice hunter, smiling seamstress, churchgoers. Now I know why she's on the path of the seer. In medieval times she would console herself in a nunnery. I told her she must have had a great mother, a really loving mother, because she survived with a sense of humor and grew beautiful inside and out. And stayed beautiful.

"Why did they die so easy of those sicknesses back then, so many people?" she asked. At first I thought she might be changing the subject. But actually, it is the same subject; it is all intertwined. Her hands were cold. I warmed them in mine, and told her how the plague killed half of Europe and Asia, more than once, and the flu with its millions. Not only Natives get swept away as if by a giant broom. There will no doubt be more, and they'll strike in an equality the world has never seen, because of airline travel. It will probably arise and mutate from ducks and geese, the enslaved kind, but be spread by wild migratory birds so people will want to kill them all, and drain the wetlands that are left.

This sad litany seemed to help her. What's so great about just surviving? she wanted to know. There was a woman who had survived a famine by eating her children - was she some kind of hero, to do anything to make her life longer? "I know they put animals in the zoo to protect them so they won't go extinct. But what is the point if your family or your land or your way of life is gone? Sometimes I wonder what's the point even if you have everything."

I'm going to lend her my existentialist books someday. I told her, "I don't know the point, but I'm happy you survived, because I love you."

Her eyes glistened like when a wave recedes from black pebbles at night and there's a moon, limpid. Then she stunned me by flinging her arms around my waist and crying into my lap, "I'm happy you're alive too! I want you, I want to be with you, ever since I saw you." She said I was like the sun when it comes in the spring. She didn't know what to do, she could only think of me, she couldn't even be angootcock.

I was in heaven and hell at the same time. Still am. I tried to pull her up, but she was rooted so I slid down and we lay together. I kissed her closed eyes, her lips. They did not part, I didn't try to go in, nor did she take me in. I understand things now, how what she suffered can make a body resist entry, any perceived invasion. She was trembling and it seemed partly in fear. Our last time together I had been non-threatening, I guess, my injuries leveling the field (some would say emasculated). So we just nuzzled, inhaling each other's pheromones, and I made no sudden moves.

"There is something wrong with me," she said, "But maybe you can help me." She didn't know how, but for now, she wanted just to lie down with me and let me hold her. And so she stayed the night, the best, purest night of my life, while I held her in my arms until they were numb. I kept vigil as she has done for me and watched her sleep, and knew that I will spend the rest of my life with her. "Tomorrow night," she whispered when she left.

Later. When she returned I knew a transformation was to occur, down in our cave. She had already changed. Our empathies seemed tied together but her eyes begged me to mind-read further, deeper. I made tea and told her an anecdote from my odd boyhood. She laughed but her body did not ease; it emitted a need and an apprehension. I wanted to give her anything and have her know that's what I wanted, to give, not abscond, and that she was cherished, the one being given to for once. But what could I say? There was the legacy of the forked tongue. We could only talk about ideas so long. And give what? Action, or inaction; it might be wrong. I didn't know. Nothing ever prepared me for this.

She was waiting and I had to show her I was the opposite of the drunk rapist. It had to be physical because that was the medium used to harm her. She liked me vulnerable, not perversely, but like with so many of the animals, symbolic infantilization that says "I won't hurt you - don't hurt me". That's why lovers use baby talk and feed each other grapes. I was out of my league, conditioned by the school of testosterone.

I asked her if I should undress. Maybe <u>she</u> should undress me. Her semaphore eyebrows, in their slight uplift, signaled "good idea", so she did that, and I stood there like a statue. Her eyes softened, then they kindled, the photons of their obsidian depths spinning out and touching my skin so it prickled and I felt less like a sculpture. But I tried to use biofeedback so my body made no demand, and she could be the forklift operator. I thought about geese, how if they sense your predatory intent they bolt, but if you aren't hungry they will calmly graze. Couldn't she sense I wouldn't hurt her, even if I wanted her badly? When we locked eyes I was nearly knocked over by the tangible force in hers. I was on the right wavelength. We stood like that a full minute, ten years, breathing in synchrony.

I said finally, "Tell me what to do." My voice sounded growly.

"Be...be a woman," she said, uncertainly. "I jokes. No...really." I still didn't know what to do; how could I be a woman? With angootcocks anything is possible; they are imaginal territory, shamanism and sex. But a woman, what is that? It's only what your society says is feminine behavior, or is it? "And be you," she said, "be the man."

And so...as Coleridge, that dope-fiend found, "All look and likeness caught from Earth, All accident of kin and birth, Had passed away".

HE STOPPED WRITING but I will finish for him. He was right - what did it matter how bodies were formed, his for going into mine, mine for accepting?

I saw his anxiety as he wondered what I was going to do to him, now that he was female. It aroused me to a tenderness.

"It's okay," I whispered; I took his hand and led him to the bed and pressed against him so he gave, bending back until he stretched out under me. And I kissed him again and again, *kunipiq*, the soft inner sides of his arms and legs, throat, hipbones, his nipples until they formed into beads. He shivered and looked surprised, like he hadn't known *either* that it could feel so good, and maybe he was surprised I didn't play-hold him down or force him, though he would have let me. But how would pretending to harm a woman help me? There was enough hurting in the world.

There would be no barrier this time. I undressed all the way and took him into me, gently until our bones met. And I looked into his eyes. It thrilled me, it took over my mind having him inside me. And he fit so well it was like God had tailored him just for me. I had taken him into me and the knowledge was sweet that he entered me, but I entered him too.

He didn't move, I didn't move, and the world outside of us slowed into a stillness. I knew we had reached that sacred plane of balance the angutkoq tried for. My heart sped, and his heart sped to keep up. If this was the Devil, I wanted more.

"Okay," I whispered in his ear. In that moment he became a man and reared up under me like the surf again but powerful now, and I was a little boat on it, unprepared. I fell forward. He cried out, clutching my hips to bring us closer, then in a sudden, opposite move tried to pull us apart. I was confused and clung, until "*baby*" he gasped. I understood then, but I held on - I wouldn't let him go - and I felt the fluttering drumbeat deep inside me, and his collapse.

We streamed, we were glued together with our moisture, I smelled ocean. Water is life, I thought. This is life. I had been a pottery vessel you find in the cliffs, made by a woman long ago but broken into shards by hard times; now I was mended with blood and sand and burned in the fire, and I could carry water again.

He lay beneath me, receding like tide. More water stole out, from under his lashes. "Are you sad *again*?" I asked.

"No...yes...a little. Sorry, I don't know why." He kept his eyes shut, thinking. "Maybe because I'm a woman," he said.

"You do it good." I said softly; I meant as woman-man.

"You too. But you aren't...uh... satisfied. A man has to be, you know, by tradition."

"Who said I was leaving?"

He laughed in sudden bliss, his eyes like stars in the Caribou. "I think I'm pregnant."

CHAPTER 26

I am a man so I hunt; let me go to the Moon
You are a woman; you go to the Sun
(INUPIAQ MYTH)

And sly Loki flew, his feathers roaring...
(ANCIENT NORSE)

TIME MEANS NOTHING to the spirits; they can wait so long you think they no longer exist, or never did exist. They watch humans play out their lives and make themselves known at critical points. But always they take part in our affairs, seen or unseen, and whether you believe in them or not makes no difference. Even if you've never seen the President far away in the White House, that doesn't mean he isn't making plans that can harm you. Or help you. That is what Calvin told me.

ENTRY. IT'S A LONG WAY here in the snow and cold and dark (for she can only come cloaked in darkness) and it's blowing hard so I can't expect her to come too often. I'd go to her if she'd let me but I am under orders. When she does come, she makes up for lost time: we get down at once, and she leaves before my tongue unties. Not to complain, but what's avoided is anymore talk about who we are, the future....What does she do all day? Work, of course, on animal hides. How many hides do they need? And what do I do all day? Wait for her, pretty myself up in vain. I feel like the Other Woman", kept in the rented apartment or the pumpkin shell.

The pack closed and anchored and the ice now stretches forever. With the seal harvest over and good snow cover for travel, men are roaming the mainland. Elegant creatures spring out of the white void, materializing for these relentless hunters (which we in the village see only dead): wolf, fox, wolverine, porcupine, weasel, mink, otter, lynx, muskrat, owl, pleistocene sturgeon and pike, dog-nosed hares as long as human five-year-olds, the rare moose. The game is dwindling as more hunters are born, with fancier technology. By the old law, once you have five foxes or wolves you have to stop or their guardian spirit gets mad, but I don't know how many follow it. Abe does; Willy says he even tells stories to his wolfskins, which he hangs up like an honored guest in the house. Willy claims he himself is a terrible hunter, but he has to say that because all the creatures have an ear cocked.

Entry. The sky and ice are the tender, non-threatening hues of baby blankets and Easter eggs. It's so frigid now my beard ices up. My new male parka has a white canvas cover, roomy for lethal action with rabbit liner for warmth and kupick ruff to repel frost. The periscope hood forces a tunnel vision, but it warms the air before it hits the teeth and lungs. Forget about the nose, hopeless. I feel like a real man in this "parkee", or an impostor.

Finally I tagged along with Abe and son on a hunt (for whatever moved, but we got nothing). Abe lent me big mitts and a sno-go suit but I covet his sealskin pantaloons. In spite of precautions I got mild frostbite but didn't shame myself that I'm aware of. Because I kept quiet, in fact, said nothing. We <u>saw</u> no mammals in two days except hares. And tracks. Bone-jarring sno-go ride for tedious hours over white. Curled up the endless, icy night in a little trail cabin, listening to a far-off wolf chorus. Abe was teaching me a few things like using stars or the ridges cut by wind in the hard-packed snow for direction, "though I should not be teaching a whiteman this, I guess, heh." Since I might steal it somehow.

I like it and can also dig how some young guys say screw it. Yet to give it up must be demoralizing to these fine-tuned predators. Their goal recedes like a point of light on the ice. The shroud of modernity and its restrictions, quotas and extinctions settles over the land. Fur prices are at an all-time low anyway; the styles have changed. You need a lot of cash to buy fuel and machines, which leaves plenty without the means to hunt even if they want to. They twiddle their thumbs. Women must still busily carry on in the home domain, but where does it leave the men with hearts still honed for the kill? Willy gave up fox-trapping and now carves pricey little figurines, very zen style. Doctors can line them up on their mantels and throw their chests out in the intelligentsia's version of the caribou rack. Whether it's real tradition may be moot; they were selling curios to whalers a century ago. If Willy can't hunt or carve I don't know what he'd do. He wants to run the Iditarod but can't compete with the rich whites with their fancy supplies and sleek dogs. Once the pipeline's been bribed through they may hire an Itiak guy. Maybe some of it will trickle down to G.

A more complex and darker side to Willy emerges. He talks of what he wants to possess and urges me to describe my "things" in Seattle, as if I have gleaming troves of riches. He's incredulous that I don't have a car and don't want one. I'm sorry to see this growing in him, but maybe he's just letting me in on more, and it's not new, the demon Mammon in his ear: "Buy buy acquire!". He let on that sometimes he and Stanley head-hunt walrus for easy cash, hoping Abe never finds out: they let the massive bodies sink, all that meat. One time they shot fifty, mothers too, orphaning the calves. He mimicked the sad bawling the calves make. And "they don't really tell or have powers like the old people think. They still let me shoot. They are just animals." He watched me carefully after this confession but I said nothing, kept my face neutral. Is it worse than feedlots or fucking dairy factories where they tear the calf from the poor mother, over and over? Except walrus are wild. I shouldn't be remorseful, condescending. Just accept people for what they are, not what I want to be. Willy can't be the Noble Savage, my vicarious natural man.

Lord Carver is waffling. Now he writes that the proposal looks okay only if I can verify presence of target species for the impact statement. He hinted about work in his fiefdom: doggie biscuit. I'll not be his lackey. I wait for my next initiation rite into the mysteries of the universe.

Later. But no visit, nor has she passed on any rendezvous coordinates. In limbo, holed up or roaming the snow. (Itiak thinks it's "funny", this aimless hiking: real men conserve their strength for the hunt). I can't imagine our lives together. Don't enumerate the ways it can't work. But "Let me not to the marriage of true minds, admit impediments".

Willy passes on the news. Some little boys were found passed out from sniffing gasoline. The other night an ancient aka walked out on the ice and the National Guard was searching. Her intention was clear, and she is not senile. Polly treated her for frostbite by immersing her in tepid water, and now her family will send her to a nursing home. Imagine her little sled replaced by a walker. Maman says they wither and perish within hours of admission. Makes me wish the aka had succeeded in her tradition. Well, I've been feeling almost as useless.

Entry. Overnight with ungodly groanings and a force that shook the conoo like an earthquake the pack crumpled the shore-ice against the land. Chunks of shattered pan shot up thirty feet and froze in a jumble of crooked tangs, a gnarly Stonehenge. Abe had told me offhand to beware if I go out there. Nanooks creep between the pressure ridges and Willy swears they slide on their bellies when sneaking up on you. It was thirty below but the wind lacked it usual harridan shriek. I sat, daydreaming, the renowned ecologist who saved Tallin's through the graces of the local sorceress who made him consort, and we present at packed conferences the world over. We make love in hotels, we send our parents money, Willy is guest speaker...

The ridges are ethereal, with a levity, and my spirits were rising from my eenee gloom. Then I heard movement from behind the wall of ice. My ursophobic imagination loomed with the great white predator. My only chance was to fake death but if I laid down it would hear me. How could I fool a nanook anyway, who smells a seal in a blow-hole fifty fucking miles away? Silence. Then squeaking snow, a muffled yip, and a mutter in Inupiak that I knew meant "shut up!"

Lo, the angootcock had appeared in the great white and was observing me, an otherworldly apparition in a frosted ski-mask and mane of fur with only her eyes showing. Maybe they were smiling, maybe not. Behind her was a sled and panting dogs fluffed against the cold. I must have appeared fairly psychotic to be sitting there as if at a picnic, but my observer has pretty odd habits herself. She looked cold. Her woman's red cotton parka is thin and she wears skimpy gloves. When she took off the mask and shook out her hair the inky blackness of it was breathtaking in the stark canvas of white.

We didn't even try to exchange a hi or some inane and pointless greeting. I just said, "When can we see each other again?"

"You see me now. And I see you."

She didn't seem in a talkative mood, gazing past me to Siberia. I felt clingy. I would fall on her (under her?), the dogs as witness. "I can't live like this, feast or famine!" My huge-mitted hands beseeched like a dancing bear's. She looked startled out of her inscrutability.

"I'm sorry, I don't know how to have a boyfriend! Especially a nalockmew one. A scientist one."

"I'm not your 'boyfriend'!" I cried, laughing at the same time in frustration, "Argh. I'm a...I'm your <u>man</u>, your soul-mate. We're kindred spirits!" Silence. With bare hands in perfect Itiak manner she grabbed her hair swiftly into a ponytail and crammed it into her hood and down her back, as insulation. She warmed her hands on her throat, her expression bemused, seeming ready to be humored. "I'm your husband if you want," I uttered, and was stilled at the words that had flown out. We stared at each other. The dogs were curling up as if for a long wait. I rattled on in the face of what I imagined was her stupefecation and extreme doubt, possible horror. "I'll cook and chop the ice and chew the skins. But it's okay to live in sloth, because cleanliness is just a bourgeois way to keep women down. And we don't have to do a shivary or anything, just common law."

Then I thought of Tennyson's very Inupiat "Man for the sword and for the needle she, Man with the head and woman with the heart, All else confusion." Hadn't I just finished brooding on how unlikely our union seemed? Men have so screwed up things by their supremacy trip; how can women want to live even with us, far less climb into the "blackened hearse" of matrimony. "We can..." I faltered.

"Shack up?" she finished thoughtfully.

"In Itiak if you want. Or we could -" I dashed the option of Seattle or anywhere south. Not an angootcock; they need the land, animals. "You want to live where you were born? You're Athabaskan, right?" I saw I'd gone past the Neutral Zone but I pushed on. "My Grandpere was part Dene, same language group. We could be eighth cousins." No response. "Well, if you don't like a village let's go to a forest or -"

"You're crazy, you know?" she said. I shut up at once, my teeth clicking together. I was glad she interrupted or I would have spun off into ever wilder graspings, and she was not amused. "I don't even know where I'm from," she said. "I never even saw a forest! Maybe I have," she admitted. "And snowshoes."

"You could have a trapline! You run dogs and hunt moose, I'll tan the leather with pee and make baby booties. And count owl unucks."

She laughed softly, her face abruptly merry. "Can't we just visit?"

"Like we 'visit' now?" Her eyebrows lifted in a yes; their pathos moved me. She didn't know what to make of my advances and neither did I. Be careful, I warned myself: beneath the pack-ice seethes a fecund world of plankton and gleaming mussels who time their egg release with the full moon; don't make her reveal it. But she wanted me to play the woman.

"I know traditional marriage is a kind of servitude...or the draft. Forget it, we can be exempt from it! I just want to be with you and -" I thought of what women probably hated most - "You won't have to wash any laundry. I'll do it. Or let's just wear skins. You don't wash those, do you?" That gave her pause. I plunged on. "You really need to get away from your family. How can you stand them ordering you around like that?" She frowned. Was she in denial? "Do you realize that you're like a slave now too? Not just in your past. NOW." I went into heady areas, how society can see it's slavery when it's men, they pass laws and go to war to free the men, but if it's female enslavement it is not enslavement, it's okay, it's natural. That raised her ire.

"I <u>know</u> that! You think I don't know? But how can I just play stop? You're a slave too, you said so. To your 'lord and master'. And to Abe and them when you hunt."

"That's kind of a joke, and it's short term and I'll get payback. With you it's real and it's forever." No grown man would put up with her situation for long. How long would she? She had so many excuses: they feed and clothe her. Well, they did that on the plantations too.

"But men work too. And Flo and them, they <u>all</u> work."

"It's the attitude, and you must know what I mean."

She turned her feet. "Okay, I'm going back right now to tell them." We started laughing. We heard a raven then, and a pair rushed over us, black on white, aligned as perfectly as fighter jets. They fell into an acrobatic tailspin-somersalt, then proceeded. Mates for sure, maybe the playful pair I saw sliding down a hill on their stomachs. My angootcock seemed to study them for spiritual nuance. The shamans used to learn all the many calls of ravens, and they communicated. But if she knew what they said, she wasn't saying.

She donned her mask and minced back to her dogs in the Itiak snow-shuffle. Well, Inupiak has no authentic expression for "goodbye." I watched her careen in a rooster-tail of snow from her claw-brake, dogs nipping, one of them pooping on the run, one with its leg caught in the line hopping and yelping while she struggled to right the sled. Soon she was a dot on the jumbled frozen wastes. I tried to find something philosophical in it.

Entry. But more. I was hiking out on the lagoon at sundown when Polly's Arctic Cat nearly ran me over as she practiced breakneck for the Christmas races. It was bitter and my lungs were feeling raw so I accepted her offer of a lift to her house for a warm-up. G was on her knees working some skins with Flo. As if on a cue, Polly and Flo departed, leaving us alone but for the company of a gorgeous wolfskin hanging alongside the laundry, eavesdropping. A picked-over bird lay on the dinner table, and snowy owl wings on the floor. After a dense silence broken only by a furious rubbing of the skin scraper, G sat back and wiped her face. Did she stop her chores whenever the old dame left the house? I think of those legends where to win a heart you have to undergo hideous cleaning tasks before dawn.

"How come you play come here with Niviak?"

"I was cold. I know how you feel about seeing my face in your house." My somewhat pale face.

"You never understand."

I lost it. "You're right! I don't! It's too hard to understand for a dumbfuck whiteman!"

"You are one! And I don't want to see your shouting face! Your eyes get all round like ookpik and you turn red and I don't like it! I don't know you!"

"You don't know me, you don't want to, you don't want to see my face, but you don't seem to mind using my body!"

I had vowed not to criticize her, especially her sexual methods. As she stalked to her curtain my anger swept out like a draft. I said to the implacable army-green wall, "I'm sorry, I adore the way you use my body. I mean, you don't use me, it's mutual consent but cut me some slack, I'm upset because I can't ever see you and that's all I want to do." No lie, and it was appalling. What had happened to free will? "You're all I think about."

"And Niviak," came her voice sweetly insinuating. "You were doing it at camp..." A sinister pause. "Only you couldn't go in." (Is every detail free game around here? And I distinctly recall penetrating). "And you <u>are</u> kwangazook; there's no Tallin's goose out there."

Kwangazook means utter retard. "Well I guess I was pretty stupid to believe you."

"I didn't know you then," came the muffled voice, an apology in it somewhere. I drew aside the curtain. She lay on her stomach, and spread on her overworked shoulders that raven current flowing into shadow. A shudder when I touched her. On her shelf were a few dog-eared paperbacks: "To Kill a Mockingbird", "Island of the Blue Dolphins"; given to a diamond-in-the-rough by some schoolteacher who didn't know books make you a weirdo? But she kept them. I lay down with her and took her in my arms and felt tears threaten, my incontinence of emotion. Fahr would be repulsed, though he too was at fault. But this never happened before I fell in love. There had been a plug, and life, she, had pulled it.

She turned over and grabbed me in her sudden warrior's embrace. "You're not stupid," she whispered, "but why do you always cry..."

"No, my eyeballs just water; I'm allergic to fighting."

"Eye-ee, you can't sugloo me." (I can't spell these words). We were murmuring in each other's ears. This is what I have come to live for. "I like it, though..."

"I can appreciate the contradiction." Mr. Controlled Experiment out of control. "Just don't make me do it too much."

"Promise you'll never die."

"I'm not going to ever leave you." And I meant it. She softened against me, and we were starting in the procreational direction. Too late I was thinking of buying some rubbers if the store had them. The door banged open and G clapped her hand over my mouth. We heard Abe clearing phlegm, puttering around. A silence, as if he was testing the air. A pensive fart.

"That old man!" G whispered, "always play be nillick!" She clamped down on my mouth so I couldn't laugh. "You have to go. He saw your parkee. Stay here!" she hissed confusingly. She left the bed cubby to engage him with a plea to break loose a poko from the cache. Abe joked about her sudden weakness and shuffled outside. When he returned, I was emerging from behind the bathroom curtain. He took it in stride. "Hey, Tingmack, looks like you need some dinner!" I smirked at G; see, I could too visit, and the walls wouldn't crash down. Her cheeks were a high rose and she was trying not to smile.

Yet now I think of polarized plugs, where you can't force it in the wrong way or there's fire: "Do not attempt to defeat this safety feature."

EVERY THANKSGIVING the young bachelors had to prove they could cook, not that this was a skill a husband used much. On camp stoves in the Center they fixed enough reindeer stew to feed two hundred, and chased away women who came to give advice. That year Willy was a boss cook and he had Leif assigned. When we crowded in ready for dinner and the games they were stripped to their tee-shirts, their glasses steamed up and blinding them. The stew was extra special with chunks of canned corn-on-the-cob and tomato.

The women - some visiting from other villages - were in their best parka finery and beaded earrings, with smiles and roving eyes. Like brilliant ravens in chattering groups they peered at the men, comparing. They could stare as boldly as they wished, it being Thanksgiving. And the bachelors enjoyed the attention, the comical ones goofing more and more as the audience warmed up. Leif wore a tall chef's hat from the school attic and spoke in a French accent. He bowed as he passed out pilot bread and looked pleased by the women's reaction, which was hysterical giggling. What was he doing? He wasn't eligible, he was a biologist, an outsider! And taken! Even if I wasn't going to let anyone know he was taken.

I sat with the parents, feeling drab without braids or jewelry or makeup, and picked at my food. Nearly choking when Christine and her sister called Leif over to their bench so they could take off his hat and feel his hair. They reminded me of first-graders who jumped on the principal, tugging at the long hair on his forearms and crying "monkey! monkey!" Next they'd make Leif put on the red suit from the school and play Santa.

"*Vaaa*," said Abe to Flo, "Someone sure got the evil eye. No one wants to share food with this part of the room!" They chuckled softly. I had been glaring across the sea of heads, and tried to make my expression nicer. But I'd lost control of it.

At the close of the feast the bachelors had to clean up so we could play the old games that helped pass the long winter's night. The contests were another excuse to stare at men, now to measure their strength and agility. We women didn't have to do anything but judge in our secret hearts. I think the men really delighted in hopping down the wood floor on bloodied knuckles or wrapping their legs around each other and straining their big muscles in the finger pulls. Leif looked happy enough. He lost at everything but the Indian leg-wrestling, since his legs were advantageously long and he was part Indian too.

He was the first man to find his mukluks in the giant pile in the mukluk game; everyone knew, of course, that it was really Flo who had won, for making them so extravagant that they stood out from two hundred other pairs. When we played *maq*, the game where you had to keep a straight face, people imagined a scientist would be perfect and old women fought over him for their side. But he cracked up right away when Lucy wormed and humped on her stomach toward him, turned into a seal wearing upside-down glasses. His team had to get rid of him before the old people got down to serious *maq*-ing.

The whole evening my eyes never left him, so I knew he never glanced at me, though he knew where I sat. It was my doing, I knew that; he was only obeying. But I was slipping backward into the broken vessel again, the empty skin, the old me, and I couldn't stop. Alone in a crowded hall filled with laughter, I struggled to remember, to hold on to the peace I'd felt in his arms in the warm, golden light of the *ini,* when it was only the two of us in the world.

But it was swift and inevitable, the re-taking of my soul. A giant paw had raked under the bed where I was hiding and dragged me out. And I had no one to assure me it was normal, that the journey of the angutkoq - or of a woman, for that matter - is one of slipping backward two steps into darkness for each three taken into the dawn.

ENTRY. I THINK I won't visit the teachers again. I don't know which was fiercer, the blizzard or the caterwauling emotions of the cabinbound educators at their holiday party. That stash of liquor and weed! No wonder they don't invite any locals. It's not elitism but fear of being expelled (the same impulse that forces them to church, the opiate of the hunter-gatherer). The storm rose so unexpectedly; it was just a westerly gale with visibility when I got to the schoolhouse, then it about faced and was a full-blown northerly blizzard. And I was trapped.

Dolores was coming on strong with all the allure of a hyena on a choke chain. Maybe she has a thing for field biologists - some do, because we're elusive and hung-up. She was saddened by the festival, a mere hint of the mighty "Messenger Feast" of yore, the social glue when warriors from all over came to compete and wealth was redistributed. She didn't like Thanksgiving and had thrown out the school's Pilgrim-Indian decorations; didn't I appreciate that? She wailed on about how she, an anti-Skinnerian, has to bribe the kids with candy to learn to read. She wants to preserve Native lore by bringing in skin-sewers, carvers, Calvin to tell stories, etc. (though from what I've heard he'd send the tykes scurrying under the desks). Dory is mystified why no Itiaker has volunteered but I know why: it would be showing off, saying you're the expert of the village. And then there's that legacy of beating people for speaking their language, and the fact that stories are from Satan.

Bill was all smoldering innuendo and an indirect hostility that grew more direct with each shot glass and not even followed with a "suglooraata - I jokes!". His beard white and black in a skunk's BACK OFF! warning, his eyes growing smaller as he drank more bootleg, shouldering into a male-hierarchy thing. He wanted to know what I read. I said Nothing, books do no good; look at that Shakespearean scholar who introduced to the U.S.A. every bird mentioned by the Bard: hence we got the starling. Dolores was fascinated by this alienness of intellect. "A real scientist," she breathed drunkenly, 'but part Indian!". But to Bill I'm a technoid, a sell-out analog-brained yes-man of the Military-Industrial Complex, a fake C.O. Of course, the Sterns are pure and came up here to find more purity. Bill asked me why I was in ecology. I said to make the world safe for wild things, if not for democracy, and to preserve the diversity of life, even evil life forms.

The Principal chuckled avuncularly, "Is that so." He stuffed his pipe with more home-grown and at midnight proclaimed he would kick a ball hanging near the ceiling, like the best of the Inupiat. "Of what possible need in hunting or battle is such a skill, but I'm going to do it!" He'd been impressed by the competitions at the feast, which he had not entered. To refuse was an insult, maybe, even if it was due to fear of failure. But the whole point was to say "so what" in good humor, and probably it's a public display of the older cats' flagging virility, for they must accept defeat with a grin to the ribald jests from the matriarchs, and step down. If you won't do it you can't be trusted, you're a narcissist. Which Bill is. But now he was liberated by wine and lack of aboriginal audience. He said Dolores wanted to re-enact the tradition of spouse-swapping that used to come after the games and did I want to join in? (I didn't point out that the eskooltee were the only spouses present).

The other unfortunate guests: a stormed in Black social worker, Jones. He laughed uncomfortably at the teachers' antics, weird charades where we were forced to act out scenarios from English lit. These beatnik parlor games are worse than that laughing game "muck". Jones kept his huge parka on, maybe against stray arrows from the ongoing civil war. And there was L'il Mick from Florida, who looks and acts twelve. Cannon fodder. I figure teaching here must be equivalent to defending one's country. He drank, occasionally lurching up to grope through cupboards in humongous bunny boots. Dory whispered that the lad had to ask her if the sun revolved around the Earth, for science class. The principal watched this human resource in gradually dawning horror: Mick is supposed to prepare Itiak's youth for the Outside, and in the Stern's subversive minds, also weave in the true but mortally wounded Inupiak culture. This dream seems more quixotic than the salvation of arctic salt marsh.

A fog fell over my brain. I could only think about G, surreal scenarios of us together. The Stare-of-the Angootkock had zeroed in on me all during the feast to make sure I wasn't looking. Okay, I was taking satisfaction in sticking to her command to never attempt contact while in Enemy Territory, and keep my front of Man-Who-is-Not-Remotely-Interested-in-Kayooktuck. When her back was turned I peeked and saw how waifish she looked in the collective, a misfit wallflower. She didn't dress up like the other show-off woman; she uses cryptic coloration, a little nondescript wren hiding out in the bushes. Her niche is so bad here. Her uptight rules are slave-mentality; I should have just swept her off her feet and carried her out the door to the eenee...but maybe she wouldn't see that as emancipation.

At the climax of the party Bill crashed onto his back, hurt, in paroxysms of laughter. While everyone tended him I fled. I planned on going home to Nordically brood and try to get sober; that one glass totally wasted me. In the school hallway I got disoriented in the institutional glare flickering as the storm whipped the line. In the window I looked gaunt, pallid from no sun. My eyes burned darkly like Rasputin, a feverish monk. Definitely a lot of white blood.

Dory caught up in the kanichack, that barrier against the howling ice-maelstrom. She was totally plastered. I wrenched open the outer door a fraction and the monster storm shrieked in, beating at the crack, smothering the cranked up sounds of The Band. With both shoulders I forced it closed, and tried to tie my mukluks. Dory sighed, leaning on me. "Blizzards make me feel so-o-o insignificant (hiccup). You know it doesn't matter if you're good or bad; God just wants to kill anyone in his path tonight."

The way she was draping herself on me seemed an invite to do bad, since it didn't matter. Inside Bill cursed and writhed on the floor, failed in his display of Alpha dominance. I sensed imminent peril. ""Winter is so-o long. What's it like in that lonely dark old sod hut?" the schoolteacher chanted. I said it was okay, and tried to extricate as kindly as possible. "You go out there and they'll find you in a melting drift in spring." She laughed boozily. "Sleep over. Don't be frightened..."

But the storm seemed a better choice and I plunged into the white and black fury, ice crystals stinging, howling at 80 mph across three thousand polar miles toward me, sole target in the whole dark universe. The mind screams with Narrsuk! In a few seconds I was disoriented, still inside the village. The canids' linear howls can be a straight edge home in whiteouts but tonight they were totally drowned out. In a trick of Abe's I found the vector of the dead grass and navigated south but after a few steps was lost again. Walking the cliff seemed a bad idea but I dared not visit anyone in my state. I tested the strength of the brutal gale, falling face forward only to be kept aloft, and tried yelling in the middle of town with utter candor, "I love you, why can't you love me to-o-o?" with the words safely engulfed in the howl of the Mother. Somehow I made it to the emptied-out Center, where I sat with the mangled Ski-Doos and sobered up.

At three a.m. the gale had died down to a whimper so you could hear the snow squeal underfoot. It was beautiful as I headed home, the new drifts unsullied and little tornadoes circled at my ankles, cute. The huskies liked it too and had dug themselves out and were singing on their chains. It was probably ten below but felt tropical, moon riding lagoon-side, a benign crescent in the tiny stars. I was in a mindless peace, my body small and furtive as a lemming's, "in the dead vast of the night." I saw the white shadow of an owl against snow. As I waded thigh-deep past the school a faint bellowing emerged like from a zoo's cement dungeon. A higher-pitched defense.

No, I'll not visit the eskooltee again, hip or ancestral affinities be damned.

CHAPTER 27

There is fear in feeling the winter
come to the great world,
and watching the moon
now half-moon, now full
follow its ancient way.
TATILGAK

So farewell, hope, and with hope, farewell fear
MILTON (*NALUAGMIUT*)

THE GRANDKIDS reported that Leif had partied with the teachers, and just *taqsivak* and naluagmiut were there. Though the envy hovered over the principal's head like pipe smoke, I had seen the way Dolores studied Leif with green eyes in the way of a fox at a hare den, trying to find his secret exits. *She* must have invited him. Maybe she sensed he was lonely.

I decided I'd better visit him at the *ini*. I'd tell him he could talk to me in public as long as he didn't bare his feelings so everyone wondered, what does the birdman see in the crazy Indian? Wasn't he ever afraid of what others thought, or did he only fear bears, and *inua,* or "ecological destruction"? We would make love. A baby frightened me as much as anything - with me as a mother what kind of life would it have? - but I didn't let him use a condom. And he always did what I wanted. When I felt the climax rise in his body and how he tried to pull back, to protect me and to keep a life from having to be born, it broke my last reserve, all memory, and all I could do was grab him closer and deeper.

Our baby would be a girl, with ringlets. I pictured Leif *amaq*-ing her as he waded through marshes and she waved her little arms from his back. He was like an Itiak man, holding *bibiraqs* easily when people passed them around to *unga* at the feast. He let them tweak his beard, and laughed when mothers made their toddlers mimic him. Anyone could see he would be a good father, like *ligliq* who tore down from his own breast to keep his baby warm and stood guard so fiercely...

I was careless; I did not use my angutkoq ears but burst through the inner skin door to surprise him and watch the joy leap onto his face as he threw down his papers. If he was asleep I'd wake him with a kiss. But the schoolteacher was crouched on the platform where I once sat to tell my story.

Leif sat on the opposite side, arms folded. Their heads jerked up with identical startled looks, dogs caught eating from the drying-rack. His expression changed to pure relief and the gladness I had come for. But I was too shocked to see it. Were they friends? How often had she sneaked here after the principal slept to confide in Leif with her snowplow mouth? Did he tell her things he told me, or things he *never* told me? How could he replace me so easily? I had an image of the schoolteacher straddling him with her head thrown back in pleasure.

The ribs of the *ini* closed in making it hard to breathe, and suddenly I hated the dark old place with its bones.

The *eskuulkti* settled back when she recognized me, but her white fingers twisted together. A bruise darkened her cheekbone, a silence as thick as congealed blood bruised the air. They were staring like *I* was the intruder and must explain my visit. Did I look so funny? Slowly I stood and looked away from both of them and felt the blood roar in my head. "Abe wants his mitts. For tomorrow," I said.

"Abe wants his mitts?" repeated Leif dumbly. "He sent you for -" He cut himself off, studying my face. "Okay, I'll get 'em," he said in a new voice, and vaulted from the platform. As he moved past me, deliberately near so I felt the vibration of his body, he shot me a look that said, *I don't want her here but what can I do?* He sorted through a pile of gear. "Here." He held out the mitts. "Tell him thanks." He hung on a second, his muscles insisting on something. I draped the cord around my neck. "Do you want some coffee...or...? Why don't you join us?"

He sounded like a movie actor, so *naluagmiusak*. I walked to my drum, which still rested with the crane leg against a crate of books, and I took it. At that, his face splintered. He opened his lips to speak but shut them again, his eyes cutting from the drum to me, back to the drum. I pulled up my hood with the fur unrolled so that I saw nothing but straight ahead. I did not know what to do. My heart was chilled, a fish in a deep freeze cut in the bank, but all my life it had prepared me for this day: I was to be alone. And so I left.

The north wind drove against me, trying to push me back to the *ini*. It scolded me in shrieks, "No-o-o, you made a mista-a-ake!!" but I leaned into it with my head down and hugged the drum to protect the delicate skin. When I reached Tuguk's dogs I barely heard Leif's voice downwind, tiny and far off. He was running. His mukluks were untied, he wore no gloves and his hair flew behind him. He seemed ghostly in the white parka floating out of the gray snow at night. Just before he reached me he slipped and fell like a kid. Snow was packed up his cuffs but he paid no attention.

The wind died down all of the sudden, the night fell into a glassy stillness. The yellow from Tuguk's window lit the snow, pale blue northern lights swam gently like salmon milt in water, and there was starlight. I could see Leif well enough, his outline, but not the inner him, the light of him. My eyes were numbed. I was just a puppet, Calvin's wooden duck pulled with a cord to beat its drum, I was a shadow cast by hands to make animal shapes, a string pulled into a cat's cradle, grass plaited into a design I hated. Nothing I did or said was what I wanted but I could not stop.

Leif was closing in. When he reached for me I pulled away. "It's not what you think!" he said, breathing hard. "He beat her up!"

"Well, why did he beat her up?" I asked dangerously.

"I don't know! Because he's an asshole! Because he's gone crazy, cabin fever; he's jealous."

"And I know why."

"No, no way, man. Come on -" He tried to laugh.

"She wants you and you let her. Because you're interested too! Don't try to *saglu*!"

"What should I do, kick her out in the snow? I feel sorry for her, that's all."

"Like you feel sorry for me."

"I don't feel sorry for you," he said quickly. "Her husband's in some kind of a psychotic break and there's no one to help."

"Is it? Just the whole village!"

"Like they helped *you*?"

"*Ayii*! Shut up! You always try change the subject! It's because he's...she's your kind. There's more to talk about!"

"What? She's not my *kind*."

"Neither am I!" The words hurt me, coming out of my wooden lips. I stabbed him and myself with a thin fish-knife into soft places. "Do you two talk about biology? Or do you just *do* biology?"

His eyes widened. They were gleaming from starlight and that light thrown back by the snow. With a rattle of chain a wolf-dog lunged at us from the silent drift where she'd curled half-buried. Her chain was long and she sank her fangs into Leif's pant leg. I kicked the dog so she cringed and backed away but Leif just stepped aside. He glanced at the tear in his pants, hardly aware of the attack or of the schoolteacher heading back to town skirting wide around us, her glance shadowed in her hood. The wind had picked up again and Leif shouted over its moan.

"What the hell are you saying? I can't talk to a white person or another woman? I'm not supposed to talk to anyone in the entire fucking *world* but just hole up in that old grave and wait for you? This does not bode well for our future and I see a fucking wall, like Berlin! What do *you* see for us? No, don't *tell* me what you see!"

I stared as his outrage spread to his arms. He was flinging them; he let it show in his whole body and didn't care. Once he had told me it was his "agitated Frenchman" when he gesticulated like that, when nothing else worked. His words built into a storm, a blizzard, and it was a good thing we were far from town. I saw that I should have visited sooner.

"You treat me like that starving dog tied up there, feeding me when you feel like it or just ignoring me! You take advantage of my feelings and I have a lot of them for you but sometimes I think you prefer me...I don't know... half *dead,* incapable of *anything,* so you have total dominion and I find that a little frightening, Gretchen! I don't know what you really want from me. Or *don't* want, more like!"

He dropped his arms. It was my turn to speak, I guessed. I was wondering too, what didn't I want from him? I didn't want him cozying up with that *eskuulkti*, but I didn't want to be a wife and told what to do, even though he never told me what to do. A man could change from a shy, eager-to-please suitor to the boss the minute the shivary ended. I'd seen it plenty.

"You never looked at me at the feast," I muttered.

"But you told me not to!"

"You looked at the others..."

I watched him struggling to figure me out. I knew it was hard for someone used to neatly measuring and recording things. He had not been unfaithful, I knew. I wanted to tackle him and hold him close to soothe him, let the wind veer around our bodies and meet on the other side of us. Let him talk me out of my fears, his voice low and melodic again, calm seeping through us. Let both our hearts slow.

But something powerful was operating in me, as strong as the channel pulling whole segments of bank with it. I needed his anger. I would see how firm his bank stood. When it crumbled I could go on existing as before, alone with my spirits, truly angutkoq. Calvin had been right about love.

"If she wants a man maybe she'll be sorry."

"What?" His eyebrows acted confused. "Look, if this is about sex, I thought you wanted it that way. But if you want *me* on top or any other way, great, let's start tonight!"

I felt myself blushing in the cold. "Who's talking about *that*?"

"Then what are we talking about?"

"I don't know..."

"What should I do, sign a Loyalty Oath? I told you I was yours! You have my word."

"Oh. Whiteman's word."

He shook back his hair. "That's bullshit, man; am I *still* the enemy? You know, hormonal reactions don't last forever."

"Don't talk science!"

"And when they dry up there'd better be friendship, and that's based on trust and equality. Because I don't want to be in a sick thing."

317

"You *are* a sick thing."

He put his hands in his front hunter's pocket out of the wind. "No, I don't believe I am."

"Counting bird *anaqs* all summer is really healthy." I mimicked his hippie words, "Whatever turns you on."

Suddenly he looked ready to laugh. I had mercy and handed him the mitts, which he put on, smiling flatly. "Okay, admittedly that seems a little ill, but only out of context. Even owls do it; they count lemmings to know how many eggs to lay."

"Context. Big word."

"The background! Where it's coming from."

"Well, your context is real sick whiteman culture, you told me yourself."

He was silent awhile, his breath frosting the air around his nostrils. Then he grinned ruefully and his eyes were warm. "Hey, at least we're talking! Maybe we need to fight more."

"We don't need it!" I yelled, angry at his ability to forgive me, like water running, changing shape, or deciding not to be mad. "And your culture is sick!"

"And Itiak isn't?"

"What do we have left? You took it all away and what's left is sick!"

"Oh, right. Like, Europeans six thousand years ago forced tribes to diabolize each other."

"What do *you* know? If you got some Indian, it's what? One arm worth? Or your big *ququluq*?"

"My penis? Thanks, but that's a helluva lousy argument," he said, grinning. His body had relaxed. He was taking pleasure in this combat now, faced off in Tuguk's dogyard in the bitter night, because it was just ideas; he didn't conscientiously object to that kind of war. I knew he was just glad to be with me.

"That's a helluva lousy argument," I imitated his voice but turned it into someone retarded, or drunk with my jaw slack. He laughed.

"Don't get childish. I think we should talk about this. Did whites force that family to enslave you?"

"Some social worker stuck his big nose in and had me sent here. And you invented slavery. Maybe your family had a *taqsivak* slave. And you invented alcohol," I interrupted as he started to protest. My list was wearing his patience and it was cold where we stood. He shifted his feet, sighing gustily.

"Oh, who cares who invented it."

"I care! Alcohol ruined everything!" I cried out, my voice a wail, "And you people have a fancy party drinking so much, and nothing happens but -" as I swallowed my throat made a gulping noise and the wind cut at my eyes. I clutched the drum before my heart - "but it *ruins* us."

"But it can ruin anyone," Leif said gently. "What's wrong? Hey, please... can't we stop now?" He took a step closer, mitted hands out. "Come here." But his face had smeared and taken on an inhuman look, the mouth in its pelt speaking gibberish, the eye sockets shadowed into empty black. His tall body reared up like a bear, shambling forward with clawed arms. I knew it was not Leif or the *inua* of him, but a vision. Yet I saw death. He had brought it. This vision had been biding a long time to make itself known, like that skeleton dog under the drift, while we played around like innocent children. I had forgotten things angutkoq. Who, who would die? Smothering a scream, I jumped away.

Leif stepped toward me with concern on his face. He was just a man again now. But his features dissolved back into a demon's and he was slipping in and out of humanity. "No, get back!" I cried, and I shoved him with one hand, grasping my drum with the other. I started toward the village with a frantic heart. My mukluks were sliding, unable to find any holds. Leif followed. He was unaware of the terrible change; for him it was still just a human quarrel, a girlish manipulation. I whirled to face him. "Go away! Go back!"

"No! I'm not going away. I'm going with you into Itiak to let everybody see. We'll tell your family we love each other! A proclamation!" He reached me in a few long strides and seized my wrist. I violently jerked away so my drum fell. The skin split, even on that powder snow, and from my feet a chill shot up my backbone at this omen.

"You made me break it!" I screamed. "I made it to protect you and to keep away evil!" I felt faint. Someone would die. He glanced at the drum but I saw he didn't really see, or care. It was only a silly toy I had better put away, to get on with more serious things: a man, him, life in the mortal world.

"I'm coming with you," he said. He was gripping me by the arm, dragging me toward Itiak. "You want to be a shaman? Then physician, heal thyself."

I kicked his shin and elbowed him in the ribs to break away, and maybe he was still mending there, because he gasped and stumbled back. "Don't touch me, don't ever touch me again!" I shrieked. I felt my face contort and the wind sweep down my throat so cold pierced all my teeth to the roots.

Leif was hunched over with his hand to his heart, the invisible shaft of my knife in to the hilt. He looked confused again, with no argument left. And he was no demon but a man, his fully human beauty swimming in my vision so I had to blink to clear my sight. I had hit him. My own heart was stabbed, bewildered, sensing danger still. What could I do to prevent it?

"I hate you!" I shouted. "I won't visit you again! You leave Itiak!"

I grabbed my drum from the snow and ran, slipping, righting myself. When I looked back he was still in Tuguk's yard, on his knees. Not the blow, nor even my words had felled him, but the terror in my eyes.

CHAPTER 28

Until you have loved, you cannot become yourself
DICKINSON (*NALUAGMIUT* WOMAN)

The wild goose cannot fly
You close your own self in a trap
(ANCIENT CHINESE WITCH)

TINGMIAQ IS LEAVING, Willy announced at the open door. The dark morning was so cold the younger dogs whimpered. Willy looked as unhappy. "She coming back?" Abe asked. Willy didn't know; Leif didn't want to talk about it but before the mail plane left he would come to say goodbye, like a whiteman. Willy was in the middle of hauling Leif's gear out to the landing strip. "Maybe she'll come back at breakup," said Abe. He looked puzzled, maybe even offended.

"*Eee,* you want birds, this is the best place," said Flo. A silence, then while they drank their coffee they slipped into fast Inupiaq, the subtle kind, and their eyes seemed carefully averted from me. Suddenly I jumped out of bed and pulled on my mukluks and parka. I could not be here when he came! People watched in surprise as I raced out.

I wandered around in the purple gloom, avoiding the main path. The sun rose and listlessly hugged the ice, soon to go down, and the fair blue of the sky was painted with salmon and gold. Dogs yipped in what seemed a joy at seeing the light. When I heard the plane from the east I ran up the stairs into the store and thawed a peephole in the frost of the window with my breath so I could look down on things. Ivan's sno-go and big mail sled growled past, humping over the packed drifts with a string of kids hanging on. Willy pulled up with his sled full of crates and equipment. Glum-faced, he cut the engine and knelt in the hunter position, one knee on the saddle seat, to scan the village.

And Leif came down the main path wearing his bird-searching face.

When Leif reached the store, Willy shook his head at him and scanned the road again. I could have ducked and hidden, but I didn't - Leif would have found me anyway, because we were still connected like magnets. His vision was drawn up the side of the building to my eyes in the peephole and we stared at each other.

His expression was not one you often see in a man, maybe never in a lifetime. He had fallen under the ice of a river and was looking through it at me and everything was still except the rushing of water and our inner blood. I could be God or a powerful old spirit in the clouds, and he was a mortal below with supplication in his upturned face, a man whose family was starving as he begs for game, or Jesus on the cross asking why his father had forsaken him. But it was the biologist who befriended me and then grew to love me. I hadn't asked him to, had I? I hadn't made him that way.

People outside were glancing at the birdman. No one could fail to understand the voiceless plea made with his whole body, or who he directed it to. But I didn't care; they could think what they wanted. The line attaching my soul to my throat, the spirit's umbilical cord, had been snipped with scissors and I hovered above all feeling. I pressed my forehead against the glass, meeting his eyes with my own, and felt as removed as snow when it forms above us before falling. It has no thought of what it covers.

Willy cast me a baffled look and asked him something, but he just shrugged. Breaking contact with me, Leif slowly turned away and leaned against the railing, staring down at his duffel bag now - it looked as cold and forlorn on the snow as a baby left for someone else to raise. And I took a snapshot in my mind of him like that, to look at forever: the last sight of him.

I didn't see Willy come into the store. "Maybe he wants to see you before he goes," he murmured behind me. He was watching Leif's hangdog form from the window. Leif was wearing that thin coat again, hugging himself against the wind. "Come with us to *tingun*," urged Willy, but I shook my head. "Then say something to him, or he'll just keep standing there. *Ki*." He squeezed my elbow, hard. I put on my sunglasses and let him steer me down the steps and plant me directly in front of Leif. Maybe he should have attached a string to my jaw to make it open, and recite for me too. I thought of a toddler trying to push his arguing parents together, his little face screwed up. After a moment he took the duffel and went to the sled to readjust the gear, pretending not to watch us. I looked straight through Leif's eyes to a point far beyond, somewhere in the sky.

"I'll do what you want," Leif said. He was staring into my sunglasses as if aghast by his reflections in their mirrors. "I'll be back in spring only if you -" he swallowed - "if...uh..." His voice shook and I saw his throat work; it was aching too much to speak. I knew that.

"Never come back," I whispered. He clenched his teeth, fighting to keep a composure in front of all the people. I listened to the slow, vague drum of my own heart as it tried to cut loose from him...

He spun and strode to the sled and stepped onto the ledge of the runners. Willy looked at him, at me, back at him. He yanked the throttle too forcefully, slipping, and had to pull three times before the engine started.

A CESSNA CLIMBS into the sky and banks. Beside the pilot a scientist is weeping, or trying not to. The low sun reflects off the ice, blinding him as it hits tears. Fumbling, he puts on his sunglasses, though it is already growing dark. He looks down at the gray ice rivers twisting across white. The pilot asks him something once, maybe as they round Troll Mountain. But he never answers.

WILLY RETURNED with the empty sled to find me still at the bottom of the stairs. I was gazing southeast and could hear only wind now - the plane was long gone. Willy eyed my face in the way he did the sky in inclement weather, or like he was trying to recognize someone he thought he once knew but wasn't sure. Sniffling, he shoved a folded paper in front of my nose. "Address." I stared past the paper and he removed it.

It was not until my part of the earth had turned its way into the shadow that I snapped out of it and began to worry. The spirits had seemed to demand that I cut Leif free. Cut *me* free. But maybe I was wrong. It seemed very wrong; what if it was Leif who was in danger and the peril that hummed around him by Tuguk's house was danger to *him*? Calvin had warned that the spirits could find him anywhere in the world if he was disheartened; they could vanquish his will again, as they had before.

I ran to Willy's. He was tuning his guitar again, trying to make it sound perfect before he really played it. But it would never be in tune. At his feet sat the tape recorder, once property of an oil company and a nature society, now an Eskimo hunter's. I tuned the transistor to KNOM. At first it was just the whistling you picked up from no human country. The news came on through static, the announcer's voice scratchy and thin.

Willy didn't comment on my rare interest in the radio; he just studied his fingers as they ran down the frets. There was no word of a Munz flight going down on Seward Peninsula. Leif was probably already on his way back to Seattle on the jet. How far away was that, a thousand miles? Ten thousand? It didn't matter; it was all as far away as the moon for me. Once angutkoq could reach from the moon, farther, they could reach from the Land of the Dead - but those were the old ones.

Now a group of King Islanders were singing; the harmony of the psalm was fine and poignant. My throat made a little noise as I swallowed hard. Willy glanced up and quickly down again. When Ptarmigan Telegraph came on the air I leaned forward to hear the whitewoman's nasal voice, mutilating the last names of people and villages. The messages were the usual: to a daughter in Noatak from a mom in Kivalina, doing fine, home next week. A kid's birthday in Teller. The announcer paused too long, then read the last one with a different, funny emphasis:

"To someone on the Bering Strait, not only a drum is broken..." The voice brightened. "Ahem. And that is all for Ptarmigan Telegraph, November 29, 1971." The trumpet made its call and sad music played that I didn't recognize, a song about a white bird. I sat on the bed that was once mine. Willy laid down his guitar and walked softly over. He sat down beside me and slid an arm around my back.

"Are you crying?" he asked in wonder. I hung my head so my hair covered my face and let myself lean against him. He tightened his arm and didn't let go. "Never thought I'd see the day."

IT WAS THE DARKEST part of the year near the solstice when the sun peeked over the rim at midday and sank at once, scared, weary and cold from blood loss, as if she really was the woman in the old story who was raped by her brother the moon before he killed her. I took Willy's dogs to the *ini*. The wood stove was still in the hut, some firewood, a jar of matches, and the oldest reindeer hide on the platform. By the light of the stove I could see loose reindeer hairs circling in the still cold. On the ledge above the bed perched a little ivory goose. It was Willy's art, the *ligliq* spirit so true it made my breath catch.

Something else caught my eye, a coppery glimmer in the firelight: a human hair, stuck in the reindeer's. Its colors sparkled when I turned it. Like a tiny fishing jigger I carefully wound it up on a match-stick and later sewed it into the hem of my sleeve. In the old times a witch could curse a person using parts of his body, but I would design a protective one instead.

After that I came every day to the *ini* and lay on the bed where we had lain. It was far from town, where no one could hear my sobbing.

CHRISTMAS FESTIVITIES had come and gone and the old men had danced without the sky falling. Flo gave me a new parka. In our close quarters it was hard to surprise someone, far less an angutkoq; I had already seen it in my mind's eye, the green velvet cover and fluffy red *kayuqtuq* ruff. And once I saw it on Flo's bed, but to be kind I played surprise. Though it was lovely I didn't care - there was nowhere to wear it but church anyway. But I didn't care about anything.

I went to help Lucy prepare a *nanuq* skin for the sport hunters. The gigantic white hide covered her entire floor. He was the last *nanuq* to be killed by naluagmiut, since there was a new law to protect marine mammals from them. Things were changing but it was too late for this bear, and his head seemed to snarl at me with a personal grievance at his bad luck.

As I was leaving I stumbled when I saw a postcard of Seattle tacked to Lucy's wall, from "Trygvesen". For a long time I studied the outline of the big city at night. The monstrous tower in the middle was shaped like a spinning top, and so tall if someone fell off they would definitely die. The longer I looked the more it frightened me. It was eerily beautiful, not something from this earth. How could he live there? He had told me he hated it.

Another time, my heart squeezed violently when I was in the store and overheard a voice saying "birdman", and much laughter. Stanley was showing around a poster of a whiteman they killed because he helped poor Indians fight in South America. A communist. I didn't even know Indians lived there. Stanley thought this man resembled the birdman. Did I want to see, he teased. Though Leif was more handsome, the wavy locks and *umik* and the shy but rebellious look did remind me of his, enough to make me stand there stupidly while the others fell silent: Stanley had gone too far and I couldn't hide it. Later I thought it was from sympathy, a respect like when someone died. It no longer mattered that the entire village knew.

I had cared too much about that. We had quarreled at the *ini* one of our rare nights together. He was sulking. I said I didn't understand him. He flashed anger from his eyes and said I would always misunderstand him, we would just go around in circles forever, like rolling murre eggs, and it scared me to tears and he apologized. But I was more sorry. I *did* understand - what *was* wrong with our feelings? Animals never hid their feelings. If people saw my true self maybe they'd treat me better - all they ever saw was my "slave mentality", that mask I held up. Leif quickly assured me most people had one. But still...

One day I was sweeping when a paper fluttered from Polly's shelf. In her round, careful hand, this:

> Dear Layf, I hope you are taking care of your health. I hope you come back in the spring. Everyone misses you, but someone especially. I shouldn't say, but she cried and cried and she won't talk to anyone. Maybe whatever she said, she didn't mean it. Can't you forgive her? Or if it was you who said something, maybe you didn't mean it. Could you write to her, please? Nobody ever wrote her a letter.
> Love Polly (Niviak)

I put the letter back on her shelf but couldn't see the floor to go on sweeping.

CALVIN WAS MY last resort. I didn't care if it made me lose face.

"What now?" he said while I stood in the *kanichak*. His blind old dad sensed it was me, or someone in trouble, for he spoke sharply to Calvin in Inupiaq. "Well, come in," said Calvin, sniffing. He had given up on his duck drum and his fake fangs. He never offered tea. As the old man listened from the corner, we sat on the floor facing each other. I was surprised to see Calvin had been reading a bible with his granny glasses, but he didn't hide the fact. Getting to know his enemy, I guessed. He waited, but it seemed like he was forcing himself to be patient.

"Calvin, I...I.." Suddenly I was crying, and in surprise Calvin lost his mask of scorn and looked kinder, and I wondered why I learned the power of tears so late in life. But when I was young they had not worked. He let me cry, looking away until I wiped my eyes on my sleeves. Maybe his other clients never wept, those hunters wanting to cast the knucklebones. *Tell me how to get Leif back*, I wanted to beg, unsure if you could ask an angutkoq such things.

But what I said was, "I want to believe in people; I mean...to trust...they believe in me."

Calvin's mouth fell open a little. "Maybe they *don't*. I jokes."

"No, I want to see better...clear. And believe what I see. When is it real spirits, or my own mind? I-I don't know." Fresh tears were running, hot, and my sleeves were getting wet.

He looked deep in thought. "You are a modern woman. In old times your own mind did not exist. Everything *was* the spirits. There was no division."

"I can't help being modern."

"Me too. We *all* are changed."

"But which way is right?"

His face lit up; maybe he lived for this kind of question, at the end of town just waiting out his life while others flocked to the minister. "You are having a crisis of faith. I have those. I don't know the answer. Think about it too much and it becomes a war inside. You know, I always drank when I was Outside, and now I know it was to shut down my modern mind."

"*You* drank?"

"Yep. Pretty hard to be shamish at the university with all those scholars. Drinking was a more acceptable way to leave the normal world." He snickered. "Well, not *that* acceptable, not a drunk Eskimo. But I don't drink now."

"Then what do you do?"

Calvin closed his eyes in a wise Isaiah-like expression. "Purify. Stop thinking with that part of your mind. Make a drum and go into the drum, with song. Ask the ancients for vision."

"Or can I just give *qilya* back to them and not be angutkoq and just be normal?"

"No!" Calvin was outraged. "You can't! They will be very angry. It's like spitting in someone's face if they give you a gift!" His small eyes brightened with curiosity and hope, like he wished I could give up *qilya*. "Why?"

"I don't know..." I couldn't tell him about the bargain I had made, he'd have a fit. His warning didn't worry me too much. The spirits always got angry, anyway, like Abe; you could never do anything right. How could they get any madder? It seemed I was stuck with my *qilya* and there was no going back. I remembered the word Leif had used, back when he teased me for being a "neo-fight" - I hadn't found it in the dictionary. "What is the initiation *right*?"

"*Izhigii!*" Calvin sneaked a look at his father, who still was listening carefully. Isaiah didn't know English, but maybe he didn't need language to understand. Calvin dropped his voice. "It's not for playing around! A spirit mortifies your flesh. It seems evil, but later you understand it helps you, after it rips you apart. It might put you back together, your bones." He reached for a carving on the floor, half-finished in a pile of ivory dust. "Like this..."

A little man's kicking legs emerged from the huge, grinning mouth of a spirit. He was either going in, or coming out like a breech birth. I stared at it, then at Calvin. "*Eee*, it eats you," he said, looking glad. He showed me another little man in soapstone stabbing himself in the gut with an arrow. Maybe Calvin was just trying to frighten me off from the secrets. But he seemed earnest. "You must be destroyed," he said.

"I *was*," I whispered. I was hoping maybe women didn't need to torture themselves or be taken apart to get vision, because...weren't they women? Wasn't that enough? Isaiah knew what I was thinking. From the shadows he muttered something in the old spirit language that made Calvin straighten.

"Oh. But humans don't count," he told me, and cast me a strangely apologetic look under his low bangs. "You will feel great fear, but after, you will be new. You will be master angutkoq."

"Born again?"

Calvin sniffed. "Christians do it, but our way is far older, and far more fearful. That is why the power given to us is greater. Without the fear and the death you stay blind, not blind like *Ataata*, but blind like you can't see the great design. Christ was angutkoq."

"*What?*"

"He was shamish of the highest order. Listen to his words: 'turn over any stone, and I am there.'" The idea was stunning. What would Abe and Flo think? On the other hand, maybe they knew. Calvin's smile was like he'd pulled a trick on me. "*Eee,* look at his death! He was being pursued and he turned to face it. Read the Bible with this in mind, not like it's in this world, but in the spiritworld."

I shuddered, thinking of myself skinned and hanging like a pelt from a pole and stuck with spears for days on end, as wind whistled through the holes. "Can someone make it happen?" I asked, "I mean, let the spirits get them...sooner? Because I don't want to wait forever."

"You can offer yourself but you can't force the *inua*. A lot of shamish don't get found until they are really old men. Or women..." Calvin conceded, a first.

"Have you...?" I asked in a small voice.

He tried to look mysterious, but he was slippery-eyed and quoted something familiar: "Wisdom lives far from man in the great loneliness."

It struck me that Calvin was still just talk, and no further along the path, even if he knew more. There was no way *he* was going far from man, to suffer alone. He never even went outside. Though a few months earlier I would have exulted, I didn't care - it was not a contest anymore. I thanked him and said I would pay him but he shook his head.

CHAPTER 29

When the Goose Moon rose and water ran beneath the ice,
he yearned for the sun for winter after winter the snow
had murmured of bones. He desired space, light;
he cried to himself about himself...
(KATHLAMET HERO TALE)

I STILL HAVE what Leif sent me in midwinter. People used to write letters back then - though not to me. I was amazed at how he wrote so I could hear him draw breath near my ear, and could see the movement of the ideas in his eyes, the feeling. The paper has grown soft from readings over the years.

"Gretchen, I'd rather be sitting in front of you so I don't get carried away. What happened that night? At first I thought it was cold feet, the sheer impossibility of us, especially since I was such an asshole and tried to force you. But now I think it was a shaman thing. I presented my research. On one side of the table, all my professors stroking their chins; on the other side the bored oil people, dollar signs in their eyes. At least I didn't burst into tears. In the end they extended my grant, which means I can come back. All I need is a word from you and I'll sprout my flight feathers. Distance makes no difference, a light year would not. I am not here, I am with you. My empty body is here, the sorriest dumb creature, and I can't explain what's wrong to it. If you would only reach out some night and fly to where I crouch in the dark rain with my head tucked under my wing, and wake me up and bring me back. We'll fly north together in each other's currents, taking turns like the geese. But I won't go unless you say it's okay, even if it means an end to my career. Because without you my life's ended. You keep the greater part of my soul. I imagined I heard your drum last night, out in the wind. I miss Itiak, your beautiful country, everything you ever touched or looked at. I miss the me who you touched. What can I write that you wouldn't believe in the flesh? Any lecture I ever gave, let me eat my words; let me eat crow.

I am yours, eternally. L."

p.s. I am supposed to be researching for Master but I go to the beach to feel the storm that will reach you in a few days. In the dungeon I read stuff forbidden to scientists even though it is written by them, but the authors are blacklisted, they have gone mad. People don't dare mention this far out research or they become a laughing stock, but someday, just like you told me, it will be accepted and we'll look back and call this the dark ages. I am talking about the psychic abilities of birds and other animals as well as humans, and thought transference and the unity of all consciousness.

It explains the raven and its uncanny tricks and how it became god and the bringer of light (light as awareness, light as the universe looking at itself). It explains bird divination and how wolves plan their hunt and communicate from afar, and how their prey know they are being stalked, and how a flock of thousands of starlings turns together in a split second as if one bird, and how geese find their flock when they get stranded, or fly in Vs when they can't even see the formation. It explains your abilities, my dear angootcock.

People who deal with the natural world always knew, didn't they? When hunters ask the guardian spirits of animals to help, maybe they are contacting the "field" of the species. I had plenty of opportunity to witness these things. But science is a cult and they burn heretics at stake; they cut off the grants and we go into denial. A scientist's mind closes and calls it coincidence or wishful thinking, and won't believe evidence found by other scientists. Even theories based on data tested for tens of thousands of years by Natives is ignored as superstition and "anecdote". So only the really brave investigate it, and the Russians. (Meanwhile the CIA and military have secretly been using psychics to locate enemy activity. The killers are more open-minded).

You'd agree with these far out physics guys I met, that the mind affects reality, creating it somehow. If we do an experiment, we can alter the results by looking at it, especially if we feel strongly. So how can we trust any results at all? Won't we find what we expect to find...or fear we will find? I met this doctor who secretly heals at a distance with his prayers, but not to a Christian god; he calls it the "big head" and says we can also fix machines with our minds, or break them (that explains my dad and his boat engine). Now that I have been cracked open I meet all kinds of crackpots like this. They use new terms like "subtle energies", "intentionality", "ganzfelt", "psi", and my favorite: "Direct Mental Interaction with Living Systems" for old ideas like "second sight", animal familiar, "the Evil Eye". The mind is not locked up inside a head. Space and time mean nothing, they are not factors in remote cognition. But love is; studies show that love dramatically increases the telepathic connection. And old poets knew: "more things are wrought by prayer than this world dreams of..."

Sorry, I'm lecturing to the one who cracked me open. I have been living under assumptions so powerful and rigid I didn't realize I was brainwashed. I hate now the doctrine that indoctrinated me and forces its way on the whole world like a missionary. And I hate myself for being its slave and don't blame you for hating me.

I stopped reading here and closed my eyes, dizzy. He did get carried away. I was going to have to bring the dictionary to the *ini*. But I was smiling.

p.p.s. But Kayooktook, I won't lie to you; on most days I don't believe in any god. Maybe there is a cosmic intelligence. Sometimes I think there has to be, but it does not care about any individual life form or species or ecosystem. It's not an old man or woman, or a bird; it has no personality or feelings. I don't believe in good or bad spirits punishing or rewarding us. Spirits may be real - as "real" as anything else we see - but we create them from our personal and cultural ideas, so we see different angels and demons (though it seems shamans can make people see their versions and, well, tap into other minds to find the scariest version). But we dream images coming from all of humanity and history that cross over boundaries.

And no heaven or hell exist except what we create while alive. Who can know what happens after that? I wonder about transmigration of soul, reincarnation. There are billions more humans than two hundred years ago, so where did all those souls come from? Mosquitoes? My logical brain has trouble accepting it, or the accuracy of premonitions and omens. My mother has them constantly, always negative, (she looks into a glass of water and sees bad news), and more often than not they don't come true. She's a worrywort, and it's probably just human nature to be pessimistic, to keep us on our feet for survival. They may be glimpses of just one possibility, and there are many, and you can change the future, the course of events. Destiny or fate may not be set in stone, which would mean there isn't really Fate. Or maybe it's like Shakespeare feared: "To win us to our harm, the instruments of darkness tell us truths to betray us in deeper consequence."

I don't really trust thought, and am suspicious of emotions since they are chemicals designed to make our brain remember something, a kind of trick. Although they are "real", feelings and the so-called "gut instincts" can arise from faulty thoughts which can be based on faulty perceptions, according to what we are trained to perceive. And the senses can be clouded by bad memories. You ask a racist how he or she "feels" when they see someone of the hated race. What is their "instinct"? To hate and fear. So how can we trust what we see or believe? Our own minds are the biggest liars and bigots and propagandists; we don't need politicians. And even love is really an addiction to a powerful drug (not to say it is bad. Sorry, this isn't so romantic, is it? Maybe I'm a cynic. We can agree to disagree on some points if you ever take me back.

But just to make me look like a hypocrite, I do consult an oracle. Don't be jealous, it's just a book written thousands of years ago. It's confusing and I read stuff into it depending on my mood, but it works, and it could not work unless the cosmos was interrelated, woven together like a spider web so that our thoughts are like vibrations of a fly across this vast web. We have an effect, even if it's not so big, and everything affects us at the same time. I don't know what the Spider is, and don't really want to think about that. But in many places the spider was considered the Almighty (while here and in my dad's country it was a spider-like woman, an aka who wove the universe on a loom). Maybe the Spider is all of us.

And I do believe in life and its phenomenal powers. I know I love. I am addicted to you, I feel awful withdrawal symptoms. I believe in you, and your powers. And sometimes I think a caring force really is looking out after me, because I met you. It let me meet you...

I DID NOT WRITE back, could not, not in the way he could. All those words just meant one thing anyway. My answer was in my heart, and he could hear it now that he was open-minded, couldn't he? He seemed so admiring of my abilities, while I had lost my faith in them. Maybe I was a cynic too.

I was afraid of flying to him, so far I could not find the way back. I was afraid I hadn't really ever flown and had just dreamed it, like in a fever. I was afraid that if I flew to him he would change again into a fearsome thing. Was he right, that our memories and beliefs could manipulate us like we were puppets, making us see only what we wanted or didn't want? I didn't really see death that night. Omens, what were they? Everyone dies, everyone fears it; you live your whole life being afraid to die or seeing a loved one die, then it happens anyway.

I had seen Leif turn into something out to destroy, but maybe it was my own fear taking form, or an omen to warn me about *me*. It was *I* who could destroy others, and my chance at happiness. Maybe Calvin tried to tell me that. Angutkoq had to study deep into old age because they could fool themselves too - and look at me, untrained, scavenging ideas and making the rest up. At least Calvin had his dad to keep him in line.

No wonder in the old days they sent disturbed shamans to a remote island to live with puffins.

I LOST THINGS. I never flew or heard voices. I didn't try to read people; they seemed opaque and I didn't care what anyone was feeling anyway. The sense of being followed was gone and the world did not give me signs. I felt like the spirits *had* agreed to take back my powers, in spite of what Calvin said. Maybe just by doubting it, the *qilya* went away on its own. Life was normal: empty, like the landscape. I scraped skins, washed clothes, chopped ice, cooked. I was normal and modern, the way Abe wanted.

After the letter, though, the morning star appeared and the sun grew stronger. She clambered up from the sea ice, red from her terrible wounds and misshapen, but healing. Women stood outside their houses to watch her climb higher and take proper form. They held their babies up to her and cleaned their homes from top to bottom to honor her. Flo let me do the cleaning.

Polly announced her pregnancy, though it was pretty obvious - the baby was due in March. The father was a Nome Yup'ik active in Native rights. She flew to Nome to be with him, but soon returned with no explanation and in a bad mood. Then Abe couldn't pee one morning and had to fly out for treatment, staying with relatives. While he was gone Willy didn't hunt, so any fresh meat we ate was a gift or what I shot with the .22, a hare or ptarmigan. A few times I took the 12-gauge in case some bigger animal crossed my path but nothing ever wanted to. Flo missed Abe, and Willy drank again. He didn't do any carving, he just tuned his guitar.

Then it was spring, very cold still, when the sun surprises you one day with her power and brilliance against the pebbly snow, and how unwillingly she goes under. Hunters or travelers were burned dark and blinded by glare. I was glad to have good biologist sunglasses for I went dogteaming a lot, even to the mainland to check my owl snares. Like a man I shot the *kakik* out of my nostril on the run. I tomcodded on the lagoon ice though it was so hard to just stand there in the cold; if he wasn't using them I took Willy's thermal underwear and sno-go gear. I couldn't bear to be inside anymore. Women teased me that I was turning into a *taqsivak*, my hands and face were so dark, but what was wrong with it? They said it made a man more handsome. Was it because that meant he was a hunter? Someone who could provide.

One late night when Abe was still away I heard someone stealing into the house, and doing a poor job of it. No one had locks except the store and the naluagmiut. The fumes of alcohol reached me, and the tilted shuffling of someone off balance. Though it was ragged and heavy, I knew Willy's breathing. He stumbled to my curtain, and sat on my bed, crushing my feet with his full weight. He whiffled and sighed strong odors for awhile, a black shadow, and I held my breath and hoped he'd leave before the others heard him. He mumbled something about a wolf, how they used to raise one and kill it before a hunt, for sacred luck. Then he lurched to his feet and got caught in the blanket. He fought with it, pawing like a blind puppy for a teat. "Shhhit!"

I felt Flo wake up and lie rigid, listening and praying silently. But Willy made no trouble before he staggered out. Maybe he realized that with Abe gone we were afraid, like we'd been visited by a demon in the night, and it shamed him. Usually shame was the first control to give way to the liquor. Then anger and sorrow rushed in, the bad dogs, set free from where they waited and watched all those years chained up. I got out of bed to shut the door.

In the morning I marched to Willy's and shook him awake. He slowly re-entered the world of bright snow: hunting weather. But here he was. He blinked bleary-eyed at me and pulled the blanket over his head. "Pataq," I pleaded, "just tell me why you go and do that. What are you doing? You came over at night and woke us up."

"Mom? Is it?" He dropped his arms with the blanket, revealing his hung-over, wincing face. "Let me sleep."

"No, tell me what you wanted."

He rolled his head from side to side with his eyes closed. "Can't remember. Maybe...oh yeah." He swallowed thickly. "I was gonna ask if you wanted to, you know, drink with me. Because Stanley went home - he didn't want to drink with me."

"Drink with you."

"Yeah, because you're very very sad, and so was I."

"Why?" I whispered.

"I don't know. I know why *you* are. At first it's real good but I drink more and get so down I hear things in the wind. I don't know..."

I didn't like that *I don't know*. What did it mean, exactly? "Don't have anymore then. Just don't start, okay?"

He groaned, flopping onto his stomach. "I promise."

Then he was snoring, one arm hanging over the side of the bed. Gently I moved it to a comfortable place. His limp hand felt heavy and warm. It had the best trigger finger in town, a hand that could carve magic, a hand I knew would love someone if he gave it a chance. If someone else - not me - gave it the chance. Everywhere women adored Willy. I wondered how his courting was going with Renee. Not good, it seemed. When I went in back to harness up the team and run out to the *ini*, my heart stopped, as frozen as what I saw lying before me. His lead dog. Her four legs were sticking up, her back twisted on bloody ice, and her eyes were frozen white. Just like a tom-cod. The wind had been strong, so no one heard the shot through her brain.

This is what he had meant, about the sacrifice. Only there would be no hunt.

Pataq, what are you saying to the world? To me.

BOOK SIX

"I Have Searched the Darkness"

Sleepless, he looks down
upon the sleeping senses
Having taken to himself Light,
he has returned to his own place:
the Golden Man, the Lone Wild Gander
THE UPANISHAD (ANCIENT VEDIC)

Who are those maidens of wisdom
seen flying over the waters?

(ANCIENT NORSE)

Moving swiftly as the raven's wing
I rise up to meet the day...
My face is turned from the dark of night
toward the whitening dawn
AUA (ANGAKOK PRAYER)

To cry aloud to the grey birds, and dreams,
That have had dreams for father, live in us
W.B. YEATS

CHAPTER 30

They say that on your barren mountain ridge
You have measured out the road that the soul treads
When it has vanished from our natural eyes;
That you have talked with apparitions
W.B. YEATS

Earth, see this pile of white bones in the wind!
PADLOQ'S PRAYER (IGLULIK)

ENTRY. SEATTLE. EQUINOX. Here trees are blossoming, but the Bering and Chukchi Seas wait beneath three feet of ice. People go on about the My Lai trials or the pathetic new "Earth Day", and I want to scream, "I'm in love with an angootcock who won't have me, and nothing you say means anything!" Dungeness Spit with the Flyway stopovers would help, the cyclone of flocks resting up before the last leg, but it's too early, and I'm tethered to campus doing penance. I should go on a pilgrimage before it is too late; the new refinery and the tankers destined for the Puget Sound seal its doom, the inexorable spill. Big Oil has to plunder the loveliest and most delicate regions on this planet. Up in B.C. some friends are planning to fight for the Mother with civil disobedience and asked me to join their cause, but I'd be denounced as a traitor because I won't point the finger at Native hunters.

Master said, "Your work is just shit; you've lost the drive it takes to be a field man." He said I've been derailed, like I'm some kind of train chugging along bearing his cargo. "What the hell were you doing up there?" (I've told him nothing about my descent into Hades, etc.). He asked when I'll write a book of my "wintry adventures". I said, "The stoic but fun-loving natives and their uncanny sense of the hunt?" He added hatefully, "And their tittering maidens. By the way, have you read Houston's 'White Dawn?' Apropos?" Fucking ignorant; it's not the 1800s. He just feels abandoned, and suspects treachery to academia.

I have been thinking about G's calling. Shamans were accused of being psychotic, but what about thinktanks researching better ways for their stockholders to profit from mass murder? They are the criminally insane. The drum opens up the deep brain that allows visions and a feeling of unity with life and seeing where life is out of balance. Maybe poets get there too, and isn't that also where love originates? All world leaders should have soul retrievals and watch for bird signs. "Not a whit we defy augury; there's a special providence in the fall of the sparrow". Science won't save us, we can't solve a problem with the same mind set that created it. The deep brain can also be roused to bloodlust by torchlight parades and a twisted occult, but didn't old societies always know there were good and bad wizards?

Itiak weighs on me heavily, all its complex forces culminating in Gretchen. I ponder the equation trying to calculate my chances but can't, no more than the invisible workings of the salt marsh or anything else in life. Last night when I threw the coins in an agony, it answered: "The maiden marries; accept the subordinate role", and portended great future happiness. Like a wino, I cast and recast until it scolded me with "youthful folly." Well, the Vikings said happiness was not seeing very far into the future...

Entry. A bad dream, it seemed so real. I saw myself dead on the tundra. Birds wheeled over me: hawks, jaegars, ravens. A wolf skirted near, a male with dirty white fur. Not the affable Farley Mowat kind, more from Little Red Riding Hood, but I felt a kinship. It looked like I had fallen from a great height, with splintered bones. There were even maggots (why not? They get to the salmon and oogrook in a day). My eyes had been taken by a raven. All I could think as I hovered over myself was, Oh, I am just carrion, I am just more bones, but at least it isn't in the jungle where you rot so fast; here I can sort of mummify. I tried to find some nobility in it and finally found it: my acquiescence to be dead and nourish the creatures and become part of the great land.

I woke and didn't feel too afraid. Maybe I would desiccate if the wolf let me, like a dryfish on a rack. I could be an exhibit in a millennium: Salt Marsh Man. But actually I was afraid. Maybe it's the recent developments with the draft, the "old grey Widow-maker". I am leery of asking even the coins about my prospects in Nam. They halved the induction rate to appease us and try massive bombing instead, but fat lot of good for such a low number as mine. Nixon aims for re-election and he needs to be at war. With no deferrals C.O. quotas are filled instantly by competitors. My latest appeal under the stricter criteria didn't go over, I intuit (and I was too flippant, and there were mouth-foaming patriots and a death camp survivor from the "just war", a mutilated Nuliajuk type; you would think he would realize about the babies, but no), so waiting now for when things come down. All this self-preservation takes wile but I can't concentrate.

Master is worried about losing his assistant. Could I convince them with his help, if I lick ass hard, that my oil work is important to National Security? No oil, no war. No country. They know that studies can assuage the environmentalists so drilling isn't delayed (I have no delusion that if the results show bad news for geese it won't be swept under the conference table). But such work is not acceptable replacement for shooting pregnant women who may be communists: Equal Disruption of Life. Should I defect now, or just go to jail? But then I would never see her. "Evening must usher night, night urge the morrow, month follow month with woe, and year wake year to sorrow."

ON A BRIGHT March night Soola's daughter pelted into the house and shouted "Gretchen Ugungoraseok, real long distance!" I had never had a call before - first a letter, and now this. But it was no surprise; I had felt him trying to contact me before he dialed. It was how people called in the old days when they were separated on journeys, in trouble or just lonely. It was how the animals phoned. Shyness overtook me at Soola's, making me clumsy so the receiver fell and dangled. I held it in the crook of my neck like a rifle and ended up gripping it with both hands.

"Hi, it's you," came his voice, a million miles off. "You can run fast."

"Yeah." My voice strangled as I tried to laugh, and to catch my breath.

"Oh that's right, you win the women's foot-race every year."

A long channel of silence flowed, where our feelings were icebergs sailing by, most of their giant selves underwater. Without a body his speech sounded even more *naluagmiusak*, magnified in its strangeness as it bounced through space. Maybe it had changed while he lived in Itiak and was back to the old way now. But the voice was his, and it made the small hairs of my face stand up, wanting to be stroked. I wanted to tell him about Willy, and how the team fell apart now, bickering and tangling in the lines every few yards because their leader was shot. It was hard to use them hunting. I felt so responsible, feeding everyone, but I was not a great hunter. I wanted to whine to Leif and have him say I was doing a great job, I was a survivor and...beautiful. I started to tremble and turned away from the room. People were trying to sleep but still had their ears pricked and I imagined they could listen in on his words.

"I didn't win this year," I murmured.

Just as I started to tell him I didn't run at all, he said "I love you, you know," and our words interrupted each other. I ducked my head, smiling, and forgot that on a phone there were no faces to convey. Suddenly I knew why he'd called out of the blue: his emotions crackled through the line more clearly than words.

"They came again," I said.

A long silence was filled with roars like distant surf. "What?" His voice was muffled like under a blanket.

"What did it look like?"

"Um...what did?"

"Spirit," I whispered.

"Sorry, I can't hear you!" He didn't believe in them. Maybe they came in dreams and he forgot by morning. "God, say something more! I want to hear your voice! I just felt like I *had* to...had to hear your voice, you know...even if we never see each other again..." he trailed off.

"But -" I swallowed. It was so strange saying this into a chunk of black plastic tethered to a wall. "But I want to see you again." My eyes were blinking fast and then everything was *kakik* and saltwater. "I *do*."

His voice became rough as if a hand clenched his throat, the mate to one gripping my own. "Then I'll be there."

"When?"

"When? When! The grant won't be processed until May and I don't have plane fare -" he laughed crazily - "but I'll get it. I'll get it! I'll panhandle or tie fisherman knots and sell them at the docks. Or my body. I'll sell my hair to the wig maker!"

"*Saglu*."

"Ya, but seriously, the professor has some dirty work he can pay for. Oh god, I'm so -" He was laughing again and then I was too, with everyone listening.

"But *when* will you come?"

"Another month? That's an eternity!" It was; a day was too long. "I'll just bicycle up - no, I'll thumb it! I can pay the fare from Anchorage. I'll send the equipment and head up the Al-Can!"

The phone throbbed in my hand. It was my pulse, shaking my bones. "What's the Al-can?"

HE WAS COMING BACK and I was tipsy with the idea of it, and suddenly little buntings, ravens and lemmings were busy leaving tracks everywhere like the world was getting ready for our reunion. But I was assaulted with worries. Hitchhiking would put him at the mercy of strange whitemen in trucks who hated longhaired birdmen. He would be a target in an unknown land of forest and bears. Spirits would be drawn to such a place. In such a hurry he would not be careful. And his voice, though he was not aware of it, had indeed carried a fear. For the long months of winter my doubts had covered me like snow and the angutkoq in me had seemed dead, as broken as the drum and Leif's heart. But it had only been in hibernation. He needed my *qilya* again and so it returned, along with my own heart.

I repaired the drum with extra walrus stomach, of which there was so much. I would be staying at the *ini*, I told Flo, and though I took the food she offered I didn't plan on eating it. I would take only Willy's small poke to melt snow against my stomach for water. Flo sensed what I was up to, and I felt caught by an invisible rope of accusation as she studied me.

"Kayuq, I pray for you," she said at last. "And I include someone else in my prayers since his father passed on. When he was hurt we all prayed for him." I looked down, thinking how wrong I had been, and how transparent. It would be a lie to answer *I pray for you too*. For years I had helped Flo, but it was not out of the kindness of my heart. It was repayment, or because that is all girls could do, take orders, and I had thought she fed me out of charity. But suddenly I saw it as...love.

"You are a good person," she went on carefully, as if afraid of losing me, like I was Willy with his secret bottle. "The Lord will take you into his kingdom too, you and Tingmiaq, no matter what you believe. That is *my* belief. Do you understand?" With stinging eyes I looked at the floorboards, and raised my brows high enough for her to see. I *did* understand. It was Flo's benediction, blessing me in what I was about to do. "So go with Jesus," she said, "He will keep you safe, *panik.*"

Panik, she said, my daughter. That was a first too, I think.

At midnight when the sky gave up its light to a herring gray I went by dogteam to the *ini*. They were more cooperative this time - maybe they felt my urgency and felt important now, racing me to something more important than food. I played the drum until the dry voice of the skin merged with the beat of my heart and I saw my little *turnaq* running ahead on a trackless white plain, showing me the way. We reached the portal, and I slipped through easily, a lemming down a hole.

After that it was not easy...

Mothers in the long night of their first labor learn this, as do seals surfacing to find the harpoon, those who leave their bodies to escape pain, drunks and scientists when they hit bottom, those who fall in love, and all who finally die. We learn that to move through the great fear, the throes of the self that wants to keep hanging on, we give up the part that cries *No*, or *Why*, and we meet it with arms open in a *Yes, all right, have your way with me*. The baby is born, the seal takes its final drink, the girl returns to her body and lets it feel, the drunks and thinkers give up their beliefs, the lover confesses, the soul leaves forever. In this way we are all neophyte angutkoq, accepting the mastery of the universe over us and stepping through to the other side.

Lay down your drum, a voice told me, *Leave this house and go further, far from humans and human thought. Become as the nursing bear.*

I mushed the dogs south over the frozen channel to the string of sand islands where no one lived and hunters never traveled. I cut blocks of packed snow and built a hut such as Willy had shown me in case I got lost or caught in a storm. Not surprised at all, the dogs watched me. It did not matter to them where they slept, as long as they were fed. But they would have to eat snow for water.

As the sun rose I pulled the last block into place, sealing me off from the world. The hut was tiny, with only room for me to curl like a dog. My blood warmed me just enough. It was hushed in there and never dark. Light seeped through the cracks, turning the snow walls pink and gold and lilac, and even when the sun was under I saw my hands cast in purple and dark blue, in a dreamy beauty. This was how bears felt in their dens with no water or food. In dreams they gave birth to their mouse-sized cubs and gave them milk. Seals had their pups too in ice dens like this.

After a long while, the third day maybe, I heard and tasted the colors and the air was humming and clicking as if northern lights had entered the hut. They used to do that, carrying off people. I saw through my parka to my skeleton, which glowed like a blacklight poster. The white bones showed in my hands, moving ghost-like as I opened my fingers.

It is time to go out.

The land is black rubble. Not even lichen grows here; it is as barren as the moon - it may *be* the moon. White-capped mountains surround me, very close, and they seem to be inching closer. The gleaming bones of my legs and feet move me. Thirst torments me. I wade a river that spills and roars over a slope, but I do not drink its strange green water. When I am very weak, nearly crawling, a silent shadow falls upon me and I dare to look up. The spirit is waiting. It stands on its hind legs, twelve feet tall, its claws curved and as long as fingers. Its eyes are beady small and red and near-sighted, but seeing into me. Its breath is carrion. It will scatter me like firewood on these black rocks and all I can do is whimper, quaking like a blade of beach grass until my bones rattle.

Kayuqtuq, are you ready? I have come for you.

I cannot speak but in my mind I form the thought that must be thought: *Yes. Thy will be done.*

And like a bad sewing I am ripped apart and re-formed.

Now I am in a green meadow full of blossoms and my mother's spirit rises from the underworld. She speaks in her language and birdsong but I understand perfectly, for my ears are new. It is my oldest wish come true. From the Land of the Dead, our mothers and grandmothers tell us how to live on the earth.

Daughter, she sings, *he was sent to help you, never to harm you. Your differences are just of the body. You have met him before and you will meet him again, in different forms each time, but the spirit is always the same and you will recognize him...Now go, for there is little time...*

And before I can ask her anything at all, like what she meant by that, she is gone again, sinking down through the green grass.

I am back in the *ini* with my drum, ready now for the dark, long-distance flight. Above the earth I speed, with my *turnaq* and his, tracing the line of coast south until we are over open water where whales sound, hemmed by dark trees thick as a wolf's mane and volcanoes with heads of snow. All is in shadow, with the moon ruling the clouded sky. Below me scatter pricks of light, then rivers of lights that are gold in one current and red in the opposite in a rushing, insane flow.

A city. It is immense with black arms pulsing with lights, writhing through grids of stars on black towers that glitter with a million spider eyes. The same channel rushes on, connecting this monster with another, like a blood vessel. They are part of each other, feeding off the same prey, and their prey is the earth. It races on, the crazy surge of colored energy. So, this is why they need all that oil from Alaska. Great airplanes scream above and below me with rows of star-like lights, carrying entire villages of people who peer out with scared pale faces. There are so many people a giant murre flock is nothing in comparison, those birds with no souls because they are too plentiful. I can see why Leif does not believe in reincarnation, for really, where did all these human souls come from?

Another city. This one is his. A pack-ice of gray stretches like a frozen sea but it is sterile of life with no animals beneath it living their rich secrets, there is no recycling in and out of the mortal plane. Buildings stretch from the mountains to the shore, devouring the resting sites of birds along their ancient sky path to the North. I have seen such things in movies but this is real, it is frightening, and I am glad to be flying high above it.

Down we must soar in the black, rain falls through us, we smell mud and algae, tide flats, exhaust and chemicals in the humid air. We hear the wail of a cop car, a little dog yapping, wind in the giant trees and the gabble of Canada geese flying low and heedless - they have grown lazy and stay in the city to fatten on bread. Beneath it all roars the river of lights, thinning as night deepens, but the city is only drowsing, it never sleeps. Even in the night the people are working and making money. But I see many lost ones down in the streets full of pain with bottles in their hands, clawing at people rushing by. They do not understand their purpose. I hear them crying out, wondering why they were ever born, I see them lying dead in the dark leads between buildings. If they had a *turnaq* to guide them away, if they had someone to love they could want to live again...

Back and forth we fly over that giant nest of humanity until I find him. There is the flowering tree from the photo, the house with a peaked roof dripping with rain. We ride the silver moonlight into his room. He lies with his arms flung out, frowning as he sleeps. I drift down but do not wake him as he had asked in the letter - we just watch over him awhile. I could flow into his dreams and rearrange them into something sweet, but I will not. His internal plane will stay foreign, alluring, a little scary, like the moon above us rolling across the night. The cloud bank parts and closes again, allowing us only glimpses of its mysterious face, and never its shadowed side. No, I will remain separate, so that I can continue to look on him and just wonder.

I make my presence known to the *inua* waiting on the other side. They know I am defending the mortal here and that the *turnaq* will travel with him; they withdraw like scolded dogs with their ears laid back. I kiss Leif with my lipless lips and he sighs, he turns on his side and the trouble departs his face. And I fly back to the North, never losing my way.

THE NEXT MORNING I sat at the table heartily eating pancakes. Everyone was watching me like I was an enjoyable sight. The others glanced at each other knowingly. They had heard about my phone call.

"*Eeee,*" said Abe, sighing, "Spring is coming, alright, and all the birds will be flying back." He and Flo shared smiles. Polly was fondling her taut belly and gazing into the middle distance. In a few days she would fly out and wait for the birth at the hospital.

"I'm going to live in Nome with Eddie," she announced. "He says he and that girl aren't together anymore." Flo looked doubtful at the news.

"Then who will be the health aide?" I asked, "That *kuangazuk* Judith?" Everything seemed to change so fast, the drum on a different beat. Polly told us once his training was done in a year, she would bring Eddie to Itiak. He would be a teacher's aide. We sat, pondering her decision and the firm angle of her chin. A Yup'ik, in our village?

Abe picked his teeth with an ivory sliver and I thought he would forbid her choice. He wanted to have another little baby around; he didn't want to wait a year to hold one. But he let it pass. "Going out to reindeer corral," he said suddenly. "Gotta help Winona and Joab; that boy Peanuk don't want to go."

He was talking about the spring roundup when the reindeer were driven in from the hills for slaughter. It lay far inland near an ancient site where angutkoq once traveled, a gathering place for spirits and ravens. The great black rocks were the highest there, for the portals, and even in winter scalding water bubbled out of the ground into a bath where Abe liked to soak. It was his fountain of youth. Abe had an obligation to help, since he was related to Itiak's reindeering clan. Usually he sent Willy, but Willy had gone to another village for something. Now Abe cracked a grin at me with his toothpick at an angle.

Funny old man, I thought, smiling back uncertainly. I couldn't read him. Getting reborn in the spiritworld didn't make me a god: I still ate pancakes, things still embarrassed and confounded me.

"*Eee*, Kayuqtuq's coming too," Abe told the others offhand. "Girls getting tougher than boys these days, they even run faster."

Flo raised her eyebrows in agreement. A happy blush rose in my cheeks as Abe's words sunk in. He never wanted to take me anywhere, and now I was going to reindeer camp to chase the deer in the corral and wrestle them to the ground for the knife! Finally I would see the mythical stones and jump in the hot springs. As long as I could remember I had wanted to go.

The old people's hints of the birdman's return, their benevolent smiles and this new faith in me - had I changed or had *everyone* changed?

CHAPTER 31

O tell her, Swallow, thou that knowest each
That bright and fierce and fickle is the South
And dark and true and tender is the North
TENNYSON

Bone of my bone thou art
MILTON

ENTRY. IF THERE IS a heaven on Earth it must be reindeer camp, though it looked more like outer Mongolia. If this is the cult of love, even if it is the biggest hoax ever played by natural selection I'll press the bar in an orgiastic frenzy until I shortcircuit. It's a different universe, a near-death escape in which all is suffused with an unworldly light and all flaws and doubts disappear. Even the reindeer exult on their way down the burlap chute to the moon. We're entrained particles in an arctic grokking and if she reverts to darkness I'll go with her, I am the sorcerer's apprentice. She can fall in a seizure and turn loose all she concocts in the febrile cauldron of her imagination that becomes my imagination in this alternate reality with no boundaries: crab-eyed half-humans drowning in the waters of my dura mater, ursine monsters come to gut my world view...it's all right. Can't we just as easily co-create a world of ecstasy?

(She seems happy now, anyway. Her grin was beatific as she fleetly chased the deer and her braids flew behind her like fetching black ropes under a red ski-cap. As her girlish peals of laughter echoed up the basin of the hills, the men were smoking and watching as if she had shapeshifted into a different species. They gave me measured looks, probably wondering about my role in this phenomenon. But her sparkly-eyed red-cheeked gaiety was infectious and everyone started joking around with the deer, though it was serious business).

Abe allowed not even mild surprise when I pulled up with Fred on his sno-go, miles and miles inland. He pointed out his white-wall tent, inviting me to sleep there. He was spending the night, "Kayooktook too." Strange for him to be so explicit on his heretofore ineffable or metaphysical comings and goings. Was it a hint in case I planned some nuptial activity with his ward? Then, oh joy, I realized it was permission.

I WAS WARMING my feet at the stove when Leif appeared at the door. The travel frost was heavy on his whiskers. When he took off the goggles his eyes were those of an animal that sneaks into a tent to steal supplies and is caught - it stares as the human as it decides what to do. I closed the distance between us fast, and without thinking pulled off his mitts - it was such a wifely act.

The *turnaq* had brought him thousands of miles, but he just stood there watching me with unwavering eyes, maybe remembering Tuguk's dogyard. I took his icy hand and rested it on my warm cheek, thinking, *Touch me, do touch me again*. His thumb caught my cheekbone and the chilly wolverine stare began to thaw. The wind and snow glare had chapped his lips. With his sleeve he wiped off the droplets from the frost already melted from his *umik*. He seemed older, different. It was still him though.

He cleared his throat. "There's warble fly infestation in those reindeer."

"Is it?" I didn't know what else to say. He was right; the reindeer were dead now so it wouldn't matter, but if they lived, the grubs living on the underside of the living hides would burrow their way out and riddle the reindeer with holes and drive them crazy. That was a funny thing for him to think about now, but of course he was still a biologist. I thought of something to say. "People used to eat those worms, in the famines."

"Oh! Well...they're probably nutritious."

"Should I get you one? You must be hungry."

"Ha." He snorted but his attempt at a smile didn't work so well. "Pass." After a long silence he dropped his voice low. "I heard a goose when we stopped for a break. It was flying really high up...but isn't it way too early?"

"Yes." I smiled to myself. "Did you see a red fox too?"

"Ya, in the willows outside camp. Why?"

"It's just a good sign. They're happy you came back." Outside a raven called its relatives for a free meal and a reindeer coughed, a young man shouted. "Me too," I said, wishing there were better words for it. "I needed you." As I uttered this, the round black entries in his eyes pooled out like India ink. A lead had closed between us and one of us could hop over - I wanted it to be him. But he closed his eyes and took in a ragged breath.

"Was your trip good?"

"I don't remember," he whispered.

"It's too hot to wear this in here." I tugged the hem of his parka. "Take it off now. And those sno-go pants too, and mukluks."

He laughed a little. "Okay, Mom." But he still just stood there. As I pulled the parka over his head and took the straps off his shoulders I discovered his heart was racing under the layers of canvas and fur and polyester and wool, and I laid my hand over his breastbone to soothe it. I had broken it, but it seemed like it would mend; it was almost mended. We looked at each other.

Swiftly he grabbed me close, hard so I couldn't breathe, but then gentle. He bent his head down next to mine, allowing me to pet the softest curls on the back of his neck under the guard hairs. Our breathing had settled into the same rhythm.

"How's the drum," he said after a while, muffled in my shoulder.

"Fixed. But it's not important; it's just skin and some wood."

"It *is* important."

"Only what you use it for."

"You sound like a wisewoman. Was I gone that long? Like Rip van Winkle."

"You didn't break it. It broke because I hit you. I'll never hit you again."

"I didn't feel it." We breathed together as I continued to pet him until I felt all the pent-up tension had melted, gone the way of the travel frost. "You never wrote back to me," he murmured.

"Your letter was too long."

"Sorry. The night was too long."

"*Really* long," I agreed softly.

Just then the snow crunched sharply as a man walked by the tent, and Leif released me fast and stepped back. I'd trained him too well! He pulled a face of dismay, then both of us were laughing. I really didn't care if anyone saw; the whole village could troop past us and have a look at our embrace. But we sank to the floor to sit knee-to-knee like we were going to just play cards. His eyes had warmed into that color of alder dye hit by sunlight and he was looking all over my face and even behind my head - not studying or

351

searching but in a kind of reverence, like he wanted to absorb my light through his eyes. But I didn't think I had a halo.

"Is a man supposed to be pretty?" I asked. "Because you are." He smiled, the kind that denies. "No, you *are*," I insisted.

"Does that mean we're friends?"

"What I said before...I didn't mean it."

He took my hand and worked his thumb over the hill of my palm, looking down at it. The moons of his fingernails were just like that, pale little half-moons. "Do you think people in Itiak are mean?" I asked, not knowing why.

"Hm? No...They're the nicest I've ever met, not that I'm a world traveler. But I've been thinking I might have to be one."

"I was mean."

"No..."

"I was afraid."

Still looking sad and held back, not recovered yet, he gazed down at my hand. The body can forget fast in its simplicity, but the mind lags behind. Or was it the other way around?

"But what were you afraid of? I mean really?" he asked.

"Life, maybe. But I'm not anymore. I'm not afraid of being with you, the only thing I'm afraid of in the world is *not* being with you."

It was amazing how good it felt for such words to tumble out. Once they would have made me scorn myself for their weakness, like tears. I saw Leif's throat work and something dark lift from his shoulders. I saw hope settle in its featherlike way all over his body. I asked, as carefully as testing milk for a newborn's bottle, "You talked about how there are no spirits. You're...cynic."

He brought his head up. "But I'm *not* anymore." I looked back in his serious eyes, wondering if he was joking.

"You believe in bad spirits now?"

"Only good ones. Not the spirit that denies. And there is a god after all."

I smiled, not quite sure I understood. He kept looking at me, steadily, as a new look crept into his eyes. "Um...you don't want a ring or something like that, do you?" he asked. I stared at him. "Because I don't have any. But I have something better." From his shirt pocket he took out a dried lemming and dangled it by a paw. I remembered his lecture about owls, *ukpik* and their funny mating habits. Going along with his joke I took the offering and put it into my pocket with a *hoo hoo* owl voice, rounding my eyes. Leif was watching me, stockstill, and finally I realized he had really proposed.

And I had accepted.

"Oh," I whispered.

"So are we officially mated now?"

"Like birds."

"In the eyes of all of Itiak?"

"Maybe. But not like naluagmiut in the movies, always holding hands, hanging onto each other in public and saying 'I love you I love you,' on the phone."

He smiled ruefully. "Uhuh. In Soola's living room. So we have to be discreet." He pretended to think. "Like undressing me when I came in? Very discreet." Feeling joyful and foolish, I laughed.

He brought out a necklace from his pocket then - an old woman gave it to him as he passed through Indian country, and he had told her about us. He should give me something besides a dried lemming, the *aka* scolded him. He put it around my neck. I turned the pendant, captivated by its loveliness so different from Itiak beadwork, dense with roses and other flowers in pink and green and copper and backed by moose leather that smelled of smoke.

"It's Athabaskan," Leif said.

IN THE GRAY LIGHT of early morning when the old man slumbers, the bride goes to her man's bed and they wrap themselves in that cocoon, they are wrapped together never wanting to let go. Both of them make some noise, I think, that kind of moan that sounds like pain.

The hunter has awoken because he is an old man who has hunted all his life and can sleep lightly while still dreaming, tuned to both worlds. He studies the couple from under half-closed lids and smiles to himself. When the woman turns her head he snaps his eyes shut, pretending sleep.

CHAPTER 32

Life-joy streams from all things
The smallest as from the greatest star
GOETHE

All is more beautiful, all is more beautiful
and life is thankfulness
TAQURNAOQ (AKA. IGLULIK)

THERE IS NOTHING like the end of an arctic winter back then, when the
sea froze for so long and we nearly forgot it was there under the ice. When
the ice broke up we thought the earth was fracturing. Our minds broke
apart too from its dark, frozen patterns, and things were hopeful and bountiful and life was enough. Everything was new. The birds poured in from all
over the world: the geese, swans and sea-diving ducks and marsh ducks, shorebirds, loons, gulls and terns, and songbirds skinny and spent from their long
trips but ready to start over, ready for love. We heard the cracks of the little
boys' rifles as they shot longspurs for their *akas*' kettles. The highschoolers lit
like noisy cranes, smoking too much, casting around uneasily, trying to figure
out where they fit in.

As the drifts melted the land grew patches of brown like a reindeer hide,
and over it blew winds rich with the stink of life and death thawing out. The
breezes seemed warm and kids played coatless, but it was really only just
above freezing. New grass sprouted on the roof of the *ini*. The old sod house
began to leak. And strange activity went on in the currents. Even if we didn't
know about it, on the sea floor herds of crabs swiftly marched on their tiptoes
from continent to continent, and walrus dove headlong into the sand to
uproot clams. Whales passed by singing their epics and left trails of bubbles
for the other whales to come, marking the ancient route. A raven flew with
a goose despite the goose's warning that there would be no land, that he
would tire, and so he plunged into the waves. A skeleton of a woman was

found drifting by a lonely hunter, who breathed life into her and married her. The Orphan took pity and stirred her cauldron down there, and more life was born.

There was no real night but we tried to sleep, and on one of those nightless nights, startled awake by cracking and groaning, we looked out to see the rotten pack-ice had broken off and moved somewhere. All that was left were chunks of berg and pans which children made a dangerous game of, hopping floe to floe or punting along the shore until the burning sky turned pale.

Next day the pack had stolen in again.

ENTRY. MININH HUDINYAAGHE, the moon when everything grows. The gear arrived so it's time to set up birdcamp for the first landings and get out of the dank den. But I have no ambition. Some dense flocks of Stellar's eider just thundered past. Oldsquaws settled last night in the off-shore lead, still riotously chortling at their private joke. As for Tallin's, zip.

My favorite rare bird comes out most nights, the endless sunsets on the beach. I get to look in her eyes as much as I want. She lets me into their onyx depths, and we talk about everything now and are both succored. She walks boldly back to town without taking some absurd route. I am getting used to her just up and leaving: I'll be getting water, I come back, she's gone, but it doesn't mean she's mad (though it could...). Probably reporting to me or letting me in on the independent-minded decisions of the Gatherer would make her feel trapped. Or like "funny white couple."

She reads the poetry books, notably the Inuit. She does not like one poem and recites it in a simpering voice, "O I am just little woman, How glad I am to be use! Gladly do I wander picking willow leaves!" I showed her the oracle and it's comment about us: "Wooing. A broken vessel's two halves join." She was intrigued that its roots are in witchcraft (I didn't show her the "Copulation" teaser that alters to "you are hurt, whipped and punished; moving camp").

Entry. Dolores invited me to their "migration party". Bill wanted to make up for the scene at Thanksgiving. Dory asked if I had a "hunting partner" to bring, but I couldn't see G enjoying such aberrant white behavior, and look what happened last time I mingled with eskooltee. "No booze," said Dory, reading my mind. "Bill's on the wagon. Anyway, other Natives are coming. You are still with the Ugungoraseok girl, aren't you?" Seeing the teacher's base curiosity and skepticism, I knew it would be difficult to figure our union out. We aren't seen together any more often than mated owls. But G imagines everyone in Itiak constantly discussing us as if there aren't newer liaisons in town to entertain, some with public scenes enhanced by drink.

Alcohol seems to be infiltrating, taking over. Was it always so? Was I blinded by the puritan Ugungoraseok clan? Even Willy. G mentioned his "bad" behavior. Some scholars think bingeing was a factor in the famines; the whites had outlawed the escapism of drum seances, but supplied booze. At least the drumming orgies were free and left you ready to face the elements the next day (no hangover). A Victorian writes: "The sway of alcohol is due to its power to stimulate the mystical faculties usually crushed to Earth by the cold fact and dry criticisms of the sober hour. It unites. It is the greatest exciter of the 'Yes' function. It brings man from the chill periphery of things to the radiant core." But the Hindus who used it for worship thought wine in excess makes us bestial sinners. Fahr had this drive for obliteration. He wasn't finding God. I don't need it. Intoxicated by life, why would I?

Later. G refused to go to the party, alarmed at the idea. So I went alone, but it was mellow. No indigenous guest showed up. The Sterns suspected it was because they were too "gloomy". L'il Mick was leaving forever, with the ghost cat yowling in a cage. The teachers kvetched about paperwork, more reports than the LAPD just for this tiny village. They'll get jobs down south after they go backpacking in Afghanistan, etc., and hope Itiak is fated to get a good replacement. I feel sorry for the village having to break in a new set of greenhorns with wild agendas, and sorry for the Sterns, footsore in the desert, still "gloomy". What's with them? Perhaps their version of the whiteman's burden has grown too heavy.

Bill gave me a bottle of Jack Daniel's with a caution to "watch out for the Pinkertons". The label evokes an explosion on my skull. I drank one capful and poured one in the sea for Fahr libation. In Viking times I'd drink it from his skull; I'd hang his skull up and ask it for advice. Maybe he'd advise me to empty it and rid myself of this pretty amber liquid that did in my childhood. But he's a modern dead father and is silent.

Entry. Dream: An ice floe, Willy is stranded on it, his boat drifts away. He's kneeling, reaching out for it, desperate. A white shadow stalks behind him, polar bear. In the dark open water streaks a black-and-white killer-whale, who can tilt the edge of a floe until the prey slides down into the toothed jaws. Danger behind, peril before. Willy kneels frozen. An iceberg sails by, Bill perched on its tip with legs crossed and pipe lit, reading a book. He holds a bottle aloft to Willy. I can't hear what he says. Avast there, mates.

Entry. G and I were on the main path and she'd narrowed her personal perimeter so it was almost like we're a couple. Then an aka I'd never seen turned down the bank, and G stiffened and got a look of naked loathing; I thought I'd seen all her negative emotions, but they were just ghosts of this true enmity. But the Enemy was just a tiny old dame shuffling pigeon-toed, head down to watch her step. Dowdy, gray hair set in dippety-doo curls.

When she looked up she double-taked and her spectacled eyes shot away, seeking escape from the angootcock's obsidian, murderous stare. I knew her alarm had nothing to do with me, a lumbering, hairy white advancing on her. My alien silhouette didn't even register; she saw only Gretchen. It had to be the old foster mother! This slight, down-at-the-mukluk aka was the evil nemesis? How do you terrorize with such a washed-out spirit, and so unformidable? (But G had been a captive little child). She hardly struck fear in me, not even rage or revulsion but rather a sadness, like when I read of wars or deforestation so long ago it's too late to act.

After she was past I asked who it was. G shot me a dark look, for she always knows when I'm being mendacious. I didn't comment and she seemed to appreciate my silence. When we reached her house she hinted that she might go willow picking later. But she's been taking her time. She is up to something.

Now that my oily sward is thawing I find that results are not as expected. Capricious experiments. Terns from Tierra del Fuego arrived at midnight, beautiful black and white but they like to divebomb my head even though I got here first.

I UNDERSTOOD Leif's puzzlement. How could such a lemming in glasses have had so much power over me? Nine years later I still avoided her part of town. The family was keeping a little boy, a Malemiut Eskimo from up north. That day I decided I would visit, but I didn't want Leif along as if I needed him to guard me. I prepared myself. Hadn't I faced worse, in the Otherworld? She was taking down laundry from the line and when she saw me coming she scurried inside.

Their names were Ruthie and Gilead. They lived in the same low-lying shack banked with sod. Their dogs were sharp-ribbed with tails molded to their rears and the *kanichak* smelled rotten. Inside I heard Ruthie saying the name they used for me, *Elliraq* - it meant "Orphan". I opened the door and stood in it, letting the slush off my boots melt on the floor I had cleaned so often. It was a dirty floor now. Ruthie sat on the floor out of breath, with her thick glasses making her eyes seem to bulge in fright. She hadn't had time to put on the old slave mask. Gilead was there too but the son was long gone; we heard he was living on Fourth Avenue in Anchorage. The old couple looked so faded and helpless now with last year's dry *ugzruk* on the table. They were poor, with no hunter to provide. I guessed they needed the foster child money.

As they peered anxiously at me I looked around, trying to picture myself there as a little girl. Though it was cluttered with the things of living, it felt barren. It was not a home but just a place to wait until death. A swarm of flies buzzed at the window. There was the corner where I used to sit silently if my work was ever done. It was occupied now by a tiny boy squatting on a chamber pot. His skull was too small and shaped like a hummock that sloped to a narrow peak. That is what a night on the town can do to a baby forming inside you, people know now.

Gilead was standing on his crooked old man's legs in tattered, greasy pants. It was hard to believe those thighs had pried mine apart. I could beat him up now. "Have you eaten?" he asked roughly, but I ignored him.

I walked to the child and knelt. The pot was a kind of prison, trapping his rear. "How old are you?" I asked, but he didn't answer - it was doubtful he could talk. His eyes were crossed and *kakik* slid endlessly from his nostrils. How could they use this boy? There could be no possible chore for him but to feed their hunger for the suffering of others.

"He is five," said Gilead, but the boy looked two. I wished I had brought candy to give him. I stood, fighting the need to flee the place, but not from fear. I thought I would weep.

My words came out unplanned. "I want to know the name of her village. And *her* name. Tell me and I'll go." The old couple glanced at each other, each waiting for the other to speak.

"Your mother was Adams," said Ruthie. A naluagmiut name. But there were many families like that, Indian especially, and it didn't mean a white ancestor, just that a missionary had named his flock. "We don't know her Christian name. Her village I forget the name. Is it on Koyukuk River? I don't know...Lot of people passed away from measles. But your mother, maybe she passed away from TB."

A ghost town. I was leaving when Ruthie's voice stopped me. I had never heard it cordial like now, nearly sweet. "Gretchen, you sure have grown. We seen you all these years, growing up. We did not know if you would live, with your brain sickness."

I turned and looked at her hard. Never had I looked into her eyes for a second - I knew their glitter behind the mask, but not their soul. I sent the husband the look too. "I am angutkoq," I said. The news seemed to glaze their eyes as they stared. I felt a delicious tremor of power, but I didn't need it. I didn't need to be angutkoq to stand against them, it just took growing up.

Then Ruthie said faintly, "You were *elliraq* but you lived good. My parents were orphans too, no one to raise them but the mission. They lived not so well as you, they were such bad times..." And she said a phrase in Inupiaq that I knew meant "*the Great Death*".

"How much did the government send for me?" I asked. "As much as for this boy?"

Gilead answered. "Not as much...long time ago."

They were so willing to answer, even eager. I could take command, even enslave them in their needy old age. They were so fearful of angutkoq, or maybe of everyone except little children. "It didn't make you rich," I said.

Gilead half smiled. "*Eee*, sure did not make us rich..."

I tried to recall what he'd been like before that night. He had let his wife be the vicious one; it was from him I had learned to not trust a smile. He had been sober when he gave the command and I obeyed, like he had just told me to fetch ice. I fought only the drunk wild boys.

"Were you my first foster family?" I asked.

"Maybe not," he murmured. "Naluagmiut keep you a while...*eskuulkti*."

Once their eyes had been four small holes in the ice, frightening, for there was no bottom and you found nothing there even if you dared look, but now they were just the eyes of sad old people who needed help and no one would give it, because they had been cruel and selfish when they were younger, when they'd had their chance to earn the love of others. It was fair, but it didn't seem right.

I headed south on the beach toward the cliffs. I needed to get out of town, where the sea and wind could clear the confusion in my head. Maybe I had been wrong in how I viewed events, the story I told myself about myself over and over until it became epic, with me as the poor *elliraq* hero raised by villains. I did suffer - the part that was wrong was that only *I* had suffered.

When I was born Alaska was just a territory, we were all just possessions. My foster parents had a disease as strong as measles that they caught when they were orphan slaves in a mission. They used me to carry their pain for them in the secret, rancid dark of their cabin. They didn't need me just for the money. Maybe no doctor or angutkoq could cure them. Would they have been so cruel if born to a different fate? I didn't know. But finally I knew that whatever they had passed down to me, as their gift, I could give it back. I could leave it.

I nearly staggered, bearing a sorrow as heavy as a sack of bones. All my life I had bent under that old sack and I would cave in someday, my spine warping so I'd be like Aka, unable to look at the face of the moon, a skein of geese, a tall lover. Then I'd have nothing at all but that poke of bitterness. There was once a hunter who, every time he turned around, that same raven was looking at him. It was his own fate and he couldn't escape it, because he kept looking for it. I had to stop turning around and finding evil everywhere.

I walked south on the *nali*, the south beach, the direction of the sun and the souls of animals and the path orphans once took in search of visions. On the edge of the cliff I faced the open water with its returning life. *Let me throw it away!* I thought. I didn't want it, I didn't! I never wanted to hate again, or fear anything, even the Outside waiting to eat us up like the terrible worm. Like the seal bones Flo gave back to the waves to be reborn, I hurled those feelings and all the unshed tears of myself, my parents, Leif's parents, and the foster parents and their dead parents, everyone, all the way back, over the edge to be washed in the sea.

When I was young Flo had told me of an entire village that vanished when everyone, young and old, were playing ball on a frozen lagoon and it cracked open like an eggshell and poured everyone into the water, then closed again over their heads. I had switched towns in my mind so Itiak was swallowed up in a Judgment Day with only me left on the shore...me and Flo's family. How could I have wished that? Most people were good, they cared but they made mistakes, no different from any animal looking out for their own.

In a daze I made my way to the birdcamp. It was the middle of the night, the sky was the color of buttercups. Leif was sitting by the rusty rectangles of last-year's oil slick, watching tiny sprouts poke through the black crude. Funny, wasn't the oil supposed to smother the grass? Maybe it would realize that soon. When he saw me Leif jumped up; he knew something was different.

"I talked to them," I said. He searched my face.

"Oh, good," he said, nothing more.

I dove into his arms to kiss him wildly and we toppled together, bending his field book. Birds circled in the evening sky, calling. The world was dear and I wanted to live forever with this man taking great joy in my strange joy, this strange man who had come to save the geese from being ravished and instead saved me and let me save him. I wanted the weight of him alive on me, the ground beneath me, the smell of him and of the dead grass sending up brave new shoots through the oil. Everything operated on birth and death, a human life not much longer than that of a tiny bird, and with no promise we'd ever return. That was part of the joy, the uncertainty, and why it stabbed the heart.

How was I to know how long life could be? I didn't know about all the chances we get - most of us - to find the beauty in things. Or that the human heart was like the old women's lamps lit again and again to burn through an interminable winter. I thought if Leif were gone all this beauty would perish too, for I would be blind to it. How was I to know?

CHAPTER 33

Eternal Woman draws us upward
GOETHE

*What can we do? We were born
with the great unrest*
(CARIBOU INUIT)

LEIF ASKED ABOUT IT but my time out at school was hard to describe. It had also been against my will; it had also felt like being ripped into, in public. High school was hard even for those who wanted to go, who'd been seduced or lured like fish. Maybe it was hard for white kids too, though they were prepared like children betrothed at birth, always knowing when they turned fourteen they would marry an awful old man. For someone with the heart of an angutkoq it was worse.

When I was too young to go I desperately wanted to; I imagined it would be my prison break. My only work would be reading books and I'd make friends from villages nicer than Itiak. Once we found out what really happened and we refused to get on the plane the next year, officials would come and spirit us away. "Like getting drafted," I told Leif, "to the war."

"Ah. And coming home in a body bag. Oops, I didn't mean - " He pretended to sew his lips together, always forgetting the taboo.

"No, I know what you mean. Like someone was killed. But not really," I hastened to add; Leif had warned me to not take him "literally" all the time.

His smile of appreciation made me wonder how often he felt misunderstood: whenever he opened his mouth? *I* understood him more as I lived with him on the beach that spring. He told me school was a "forcing bed" invented to change the Europeans back when they were wilder, living on the land, and the masters wanted to make them work in boring factories. To follow the bells and be on time was very important, but it was hard for people who followed the cycles of nature. It was even harder to go every day no matter what was happening: bird migrations, good weather, berries ripening. It was true; the *eskuulkti* got upset when families pulled kids out early to go camping, or if an aide took off on a hunting trip. The teachers didn't know you *had* to leave when it was time.

It was strange to learn that all people had once felt like I did. For myself though, the worst part was being told great parts of the world - the most important parts, such as the Otherworld - did not exist. So *I* did not exist. The teachers meant well, but their plan was to remold me. Education was re-education. They promised it was a hunting license in the Outside, yet I sensed their hopelessness. Their ideal was someone like Leif: a man who took notes and could argue fast....but with a master. If I could become that, their guilt would end. Maybe they viewed us as wolf-dogs chained up behind the house - useless, expensive and breeding. They couldn't hunt us down anymore so they trained us to walk on leashes on schedule like dogs in movies. And tried to sterilize us, as Polly warned us about.

Leif chuckled at my leash idea; he said they could carry baggies for when we *anaq* ed, like in Seattle. He said not so long ago the government executed Indians who tried to read, they even killed whites for teaching Indians to read, and now look: "coerced reading". But then he asked anxiously, "Do you think I'm such a good dog down there?" I studied him as he lay beside me in the tent. By then I knew my opinions were important to him, so I was more careful. There was some Indian in his face and manner, sure, but how much had been snuffed out in his soul? He was very punctual, he said, *so* on time it bugged even whites who weren't Norwegian. Even though he was contrary, he was a scientist and could make it in society if he wanted, he could pass. Couldn't he? But he had turned up his nose like a wolf who sees the fat in the trap is just a trick. He gets away, but not without leaving his mark. I tried to explain.

"That's kind of you," Leif said. "Hmm. But I didn't leave a mark."

Shyly, because he did look wolfish and on the verge of anger, I asked, "Who are your people, anyway?"

His eyes candled. "*You* are." My heart jumped like a wolf had sprung at me, but it was a glad jump. Yes, jump at me! *Ameguq* mated forever and did everything together, hunting and playing and raising pups. A couple could begin a whole pack. The first human man married a wolf and from them all people were created. In another story the wolf-woman ate him first then vomited him back, to make him powerful. I didn't tell Leif that story.

"Were you a good student?" I asked.

He snorted. "I argued. It's from those French ancestors who brought philosophy books into the forest and married Indians. Whom they argued with."

"You know...Pataq was good at school."

"He's good at everything." Leif's expression darkened. He was also troubled by the new, lost Willy who was the old, secret Willy just letting himself show.

"He's not so good at life these days," I said, and Leif shook his head.

"I really want to drink pop," I commanded him one day; it was costly and I never had it much. "That stuff is rot gut!" he said, but when I was quiet, his expression changed from superiority to one I had never seen. Later I woke from a nap to find a sixpack beside me. Orange pop, that's all they had, he apologized. Secretly I was tickled at this show of devotion. I swigged a few cans straight down and made my head spin from the sugar while he watched in amazement. At first, when he stood looking down at the empties I had tossed near our log, it seemed like he was unhappy I had drunk the pop, after all. Would he rather have me drink beer? "Do you have to - " he started, then cut off the rest, biting his lip. The cans were gone later, though. *That* is what had bothered him: I was a "litterbug."

I told him picking up after me the instant trash fell from my hand was really bugging too, as well as strange. We agreed to disagree on that point. "Gee, we *are* married, aren't we?" I said.

"Guess so."

He started to stroll around camp leaving a trail of trash after him, even into the tent. To get even I waited until he was eating a cracker and when a crumb fell, I'd leap up to sweep it from the log with a ptarmigan wing and race it to his garbage bag. We laughed so hard it hurt. We laughed a lot that spring, even at the serious business of lovemaking, like when we tried unfamiliar positions that reminded us of the fingerpull contest or we got tangled up and it was *kuangazuk*. He would make me laugh helplessly with his corny Ballard songs, "*Who hid da halibut on da poop deck?*" It was a good thing we were at camp: if we lived close to people we'd never do those things.

Another day a spider ran across our legs in the tent and I warned Leif not to kill it. He frowned. "I don't kill spiders."

"Why not? Because they are gods?"

He smiled. "Because there's no reason to. And they're so important in the web of life. Why don't *you* kill them?"

"Because -" I tried to remember " - they're good luck."

"Ah. Not like little green worms."

We chuckled and there was nothing we had to agree to disagree on about spiders.

We found we agreed a lot, and he tried to learn from me as much as I did from him. He would ask me, "What do you call this in Human?" and he'd hold up an object - a stone, an egg. Or he'd touch parts of me. Once I started bleeding right before we made love, and he saw it on his fingers; he looked so surprised. I watched him, scared he would be offended like a bear, like a man. They used to make women wear blindfolds and stay in lonely huts, and not eat anything worth eating. If they looked at or touched anything of a man's, it was the end of the world, everyone would starve then. But after just a small hesitation Leif smiled and said it was okay, he wasn't a vegetarian anymore. Then he tasted it, which made me cover my mouth in shock.

It was his hobby, shocking me, maybe to get even for how I had shocked him with matters of the spiritworld. We talked about things I didn't even know you could have a conversation about. Sometimes I would have to run my hand between his shirt buttons and tickle his ribs to stop him. He'd snap like a dog, making me yelp, then blow horrible *niliq* noises on my stomach until I screamed with laughter. Scrambling out of his clutches I sprinted, my knees weak from play-fear. He never quite reached me, pawing the backs of my thighs as I raced around the tent. Why did we play such games - weren't we adults now? He had tried to explain it in biological terms.

When he caught me in the tent we wrestled. I was strong but he was stronger. It was unfair - didn't I do more work, while he "accumulated data"? Why did I like that in him? He pinned me, laying his full length on me. Once I would have resented and feared that, if he'd dared try it. But now I sought it. In lovemaking I'd let him plunge from above like a seal into the ice, and I didn't let go of him after he came so he fell asleep while still on me, with his hair in my mouth and his life-force safe inside me. Now he looked down on me, his eyes so close I saw three of them, and they were silly at first but grew somber. He rolled off and we lay together out of breath, looking at each other. I wondered what he was thinking.

"I don't need anything else besides you," Leif said. "Well, besides some food. And if I died..."

I stopped his lips with my finger. Maybe all men thought that way when they were draft age. Hunters did. Just as we all worry about losing what we hold most dear, like mothers who wake in the night and fear their baby is dead, though it's still breathing. Just faintly, the skin cool from sleep. The fact is, we always do lose everything.

"Don't worry, we'll grow ancient together, right?" his lips said through my fingers. Old together. What would he be like: thin or fat in a rocking chair, long white hair and beard, listening to bird tapes from his youth? I wondered what happened to desire when a couple grew old, if once they had been beautiful. I knew I would want Leif still. But I couldn't envision him, I saw nothing at all.

He went on unperturbed, "It's this light I'll remember, in that mythical moment when your whole life passes by." We looked out to sea, then he was watching me instead. "But what is best is the light reflected in your eyes, right now."

"I'm just part of it," I whispered, "the world."

"I know, the best part."

"You're my light too," I said, around the knot in my throat.

Once I asked him, "Whitemen don't believe in ghosts, is it? Even if they make movies about them."

He gave me a curious look. "They do see them in Norway. My dad said the women hear their fishermen come home. You know, walking into the house, hanging up their coats, but not really there yet? And you see your own...um...like your double. It kind of protects you, or sends a warning. There's a word for it but I forget."

"But they're not ghosts. Because they're still alive."

"Oh. Hm. Well, they see the other kind too." Leif frowned. "Why do you ask?"

"I don't know."

I did know though, I just didn't want to say it: how some people could become ghosts while they were still alive, the ghost of who they were once or who they wished they had become. Shadows, as if you could pass your hand right through them. Like Willy.

And Leif knew better than to bring up how I was under Flo's thumb during the days. And Abe's. Everyone knew where I went nights but I was not treated like a woman with a man. I knew I should just stay in birdcamp and they'd get the idea, but I saw how Flo was slowing down. When the grandchildren ran in to report that the boat was returning, riding low, she still hustled to the beach with her *ulu,* but her knees hurt. She fell once. Her hands were getting so swollen it hurt to pull needles, and her eyes were bad so I had to split dental floss and thread it for her. As paperwork got more complicated she relied on me to figure it out, and to do the math on orders. The grandkids were still little. Polly was gone, and Willy hadn't brought a woman home who could take my place. Flo really only had me.

We never discussed the war either, how Leif was waiting for the Army's decision, and what would happen if he couldn't prove his conscience. Even if he ran away from it, his world could track him down and chew him up and spit him out. Just imagining all the other obstacles of life together was bad enough.

Then things changed. Leif was going out hunting with Abe and the Freds, the old foursome, only he was taking Willy's place. I asked him how he could hunt without shooting. "I have to learn," he said. "We can't live off the old guys forever...or do you want to just eat whiteman food?" He made his voice scary. "Like yay-toast."

I made a face. His mother had sent a carepackage with crackers that tasted like dry grass and cut your mouth, and inedible blocks of stuff made from goat milk. Still, I wasn't sure I wanted him hunting for better food. The boat could overturn, walrus bulls could stab them while they floundered. Leif could swim like a seal, but the limbs and the organs lock up, a person dies of cold before the water even gets into the lungs.

The week before, Abe and Nelson were nearly lost. They had pulled the boat to the edge of the pack to get to open water. The wind reversed and they raced, but the pack had already split off and was heading out with them on it - they could be carried past Barrow and into the uncharted sea above Siberia where cannibals lived! But the distance was narrow enough to attempt a leap on their snowmachines. First they uncoupled the sled and put it in the boat, which they launched. Nelson nearly didn't make it across and he got wet and was rigid by the time they got home. Willy had to go recover Abe's boat with his boat. The old men were in a great mood, cracking up as they told about their misadventure, how Abe had nearly *qoqed* his trousers. They didn't worry me; they seemed invincible.

It was Leif who was ignorant and absent-minded, his thoughts roaming to cloud formations. He might get tangled in a rope and be pulled under. "We don't need to eat," I protested. But he went.

They were out in the treacherous water for what seemed a week though it was only a few days. I fretted. I stopped my worries, as Flo had taught me, she who had spent most of her life waiting for the return of hunters. We got busy, and if we had to think of the men, we prayed. If they were in real trouble, we would sense it anyhow, wouldn't we? Toward evening the men re-turned, joking as hunters did. Abe was teasing Fred Sr. for his silly harpoon strike; the head had barely entered the *ugzruk*'s neck and had tangled in the esophagus. Blood still trickled from its nostrils. Abe also chided Amezuk for his poor steering; an ice pan had hit the gunwale just as Abe took aim. Abe had killed the walrus and planned to give one tusk to Fred Sr., as well as the long *usik* penis shaft. The old men were carrying on with tired old *usik* jokes and ribbing Leif, for he had sighted the *ugzruk* and let his pride show.

But Abe was also proud of him. He told Leif if he shot one he'd have to give it to an elder; "Not me," he chuckled, "some man who never hunts no more." Then Leif would be a real hunter and could take over for Pataq. Abe's voice was jokey but I knew he was troubled by Willy's absence from that hunt - from many hunts. He could no longer scold Willy for his laziness. Maybe he was afraid his son might get revenge when he drank.

At the house Flo saw that Leif was dog-tired and told him to sleep over in Polly's empty bed. "It will save Kayuq a trip too." As he and I looked at each other the smiles of the old people lengthened like sunrays in a way I hadn't seen for a time, not since they had become afraid of Pataq. This was it, this was how they used to marry; it only took three nights. But Leif and I were already wed - eloped I guess, at reindeer camp.

After that hunt the old people spoke differently to me, for in their eyes I belonged to another man now. It was up to me now to decide what I did or didn't do for them and they had to ask nicely, though they sometimes forgot. Maybe they thought Leif should command me now. I didn't care; I knew he never would, and if anyone bossed it was me.

It slowly dawned on me that I was free. As free as anyone could be.

ABE AND THE MELFYATOWIT gang took me "boating", the euphemism for hunting at sea (is it to fool the animals, or to prevent loss of face if they return empty-handed?). They were joking they didn't want to leave me in town with all the women.

Hunting is ninety percent brute endurance. You get chilled if you work up a sweat, good thing these guys barely sweat, yet hunting is intense labor, dragging the skiff to the edge of the shore-ice and launching, scrambling over ice to a distant snoozer, butchering walrus (they haul seals whole back to the women). Mostly it's tedium, gliding through the broken-up bergs, scanning the featureless white for a dot of black, a subtle permutation that could turn out to be a seal, or the nose of a polar bear. Sometimes all the guys seem to be in a collective trance, or silently praying. There's an unrelieved sense of peril, the need to stay alert even in the monotony. You constantly gauge the shifting weather and currents. You sniff the wind for the reek of a walrus herd. You continue until something happens, camping on shore-ice when too tired.

The sea and ice scape is a tabula rasa for the imagination. I kept getting disturbing images of polar bears swimming underwater, and once I flashed on the dead merman, but I tried to focus on the Now, its white nothingness. Abe says that's best for hunting since "they can tell" if you're thinking about them. He warned me to not stare as we approached, since they feel the predatory gaze. Abe liked taking me out better last summer, when I had no plan to kill. At first I was spooking the seals on this hunt, wanting so badly to prove myself. The women help from afar by praying for the men's safety, and luring the game with mental praises. (I thought they gave themselves up voluntarily, so why do you have to trick or stalk them? Why do they struggle? And does the pact apply to human prey as well? If you're a murderer or a soldier and you kill someone, did they "offer" themselves to you? I think too much).

Further misery: the boring chill tent on the ice, the smoking and farting of old men. Not liking the satanic quality of card-playing, they tell epic stories designed to kill long stretches of time, in Inupiak. Are they really discussing how "kwangazook" I am as I carry out their orders? They sense my need to please; they chuckle, they get off on having a nalockmew as their sherpa, their minion, the tides turned. It seems to ingratiate me to the patriarch (my real reason for hunting).

There were moments of primal terror. We were checked out briefly by killer whales; they swam under us. The men called out softly, "We like you; we are friends," for these whales are vengeful and will wait for years for the right moment to drown you. They can single out your boat. A walrus tried to climb into our boat, thinking it was ice, and we beat it back with oars and rifle butts but we didn't shoot it. Don't know why. We stayed far away from one walrus herd when Fred Sr. thought he saw a walrus-dog. It looks like the head of a swimming dog, but it's really a sea serpent enclosing the herd to protect it. We encountered another herd we had to cajole; the bulls were corralling us away from the panicky cows and calves. The men pleaded to be allowed to pass, and it was granted even though we'd slain one of their brothers. Once acceptable prey is spotted there's an exciting chase, the shooting and (hopeful) retrieval. Then, the connection as the seal emerges quietly from the black-green depths with liquid eyes and scrabbling flippers. Blood bubbling, wounds steaming. The men gaff it into the boat, pull back the head to snap the spinal cord. (A revived half-ton oogrook can wreak havoc. Fred Sr. told how one clawed his grandfather's back to ribbons as he frantically paddled his kayak to shore).

The coup d'grace is carried out in a reverent hush. If it's walrus Abe offers it a final drink of fresh water before decapitation on the ice. If a seal, Flo will do this at home. Abe said, "I do this so her spirit forgives me and she comes back." The head must be cut off just in case it is still angry, like the ancient Irish. Or it frees the soul. Something. The beast will report to its clan that it got good treatment from Abe, so they'll want to offer themselves to him too. And it seems to work: he rarely returns empty-handed. The ritual doesn't seem to bother the old Lutheran with contradiction. Paradoxes seem okay, the old animistic layer showing when Abe murmurs "Praise-God-all-creatures", melded into one word.

This altruism is really like buying insurance. Once you no longer believe the seal has a spirit that hangs out tattling to its family - or to the forever-unmentioned dark goddess, who's really in control - then the libation disappears, or any further shows of respect to other species. Abe says Willy only gives the final drink when "old men" are watching. Lip service. Abe frowns on Willy's headhunting (of course he found out, how can you do anything on the sly here?) and seeing his freshwater genuflection, I can dig how he'd be apprehensive, for waste is sin here, like robbery.

For lunch we ate the steaming clam-shrimp rumen of the walrus's small intestines. I swallowed as much as I could without barfing under the watchful eye of Abe, and he nodded, pleased.

Entry Willy visited camp. Not good. At first it was cool, I felt honored because he so rarely comes now and in town he's withdrawn. Anyway, he showed up, and I gave him a mammoth tusk I found in the eroding cliff. He seemed pleased, and I launched into an unfortunate lecture on mastodon diet, how they ate dandelions. According to Gretchen the tusks were from monsters that shamans drove underground. And Willy asked pointblank if I had any liquor. I pretended not to be surprised. I reminded him I didn't drink, because of my old man. Then I remembered the bottle.

"My father drank," said Willy slowly, as if tasting the words, feeling them out. I must have looked startled. "Not him," he muttered, "my real dad. And my mother." I wondered from his dark look whether that had any bearing on his parents' premature deaths. Or on him wanting to get wasted instead of just enjoying the midnight sun. "So you got any?" he pressed. It was odd. He is usually so indirect. His visit was merely a prelude, a set-up. I've seen that look before, an intensity of need as strong as Dracula for blood, an animal in heat. He started rummaging through camp. At last I asked if he was looking for anything in particular. He glanced up with a profoundly shocking look, it seemed of dislike. Of me.

"In particular?" he asked, mocking my nalockmyoot tone. His grin was just a wide stretch of the mouth. "I know you got whiskey somewhere, brother." He tried to lighten things up with a kinder smile. "Little bird told me."

The kids! I had it carelessly out in the open when I moved to camp. G had seen it too. I vowed it was not for me, that I would pour it all in the sea for my dad's spirit. But why would she tell Willy? "Is that what you're here for?" I asked. My voice sounded churlish.

"Yup. Whole goddamn town's dry, but I been thinking about the draft, you know. I want to take my mind off it."

I asked him why he couldn't just sign up for the Eskimo Scouts and patrol the ice and tundra as "the eyes and ears of the North". Abe did it in WWII, it's plenty honorable though you don't have to kill anyone or be killed and I wish I could do it for my alternative, but Willy muttered "too late". He was going into Nome for another medical; they wanted to check something. It sounds like he really might be going to Nam. Jesus.

"Well, what's mine is yours," I capitulated. I couldn't not give him the bottle or I'd break a serious rule of the collective, of brotherhood. I smiled and he returned it, more at ease.

"That's cool, man. 'What's mine is yours'. Sounds like the old way, ah? You like the old ways, Leif Trygvesen?" I felt he was only half-disparaging, still mocking, but also truly curious. What could I say? When I said sure, he said, "Good, you can have 'em! You and Abraham." He hesitated and looked out to sea, then dared to ask, "Hey, why do you like me? Because I'm Eskimo? You think I'm a likable Eskimo..."

"No! No way, man. I mean, yeah, you're likable, but – " I struggled for an answer. Why did he bring up race? He never does (refreshingly) but now I wondered if he always thinks of it. Like I always must think of it in Itiak, my subhuman status. He feels that way in the world? It made me paranoid and sad. I finally said, "Chemistry?" But I thought, maybe it is the affable Eskimo Willy I like. And maybe his cheer is just a front, and I don't know what is under it. Then I asked the unthinkable: "How about me; do you like me?"

"Sure. I do."

"Well, is it because I'm white?"

Willy laughed. "No. Maybe because you're not really."

"Because I'm part Indian?" I couldn't keep that damned testiness from my voice.

"Nope. Traditional enemies, right?"

"Like Gretchen?"

His grin lost a millimeter. "Don't talk about her, okay?"

"Why not? She's my wife." I explained when he blinked, "We're sort of betrothed. I gave her a lemming, which she accepted."

He looked askance like I'd gone crazy then laughed, forcedly. Waiting. Finally, through the fog of hurt feelings I realized what for. I handed the bottle over. What had he meant, I could have the old ways? I thought he longed for them with a romantic nostalgia. Willy half-smiled, studying the broken seal. "Let's drink it together," he said, the umbrage lifted. After I begged off he hung around a while just to be nice, the edge of junkie-urgency dulled some-what, then he split on a private itinerary. G says he drinks alone if he can't find another miscreant. I can't run and tattle to Abe, and he's powerless to stop it. Not a whit could Mom's pleas keep Fahr from snorting the aquavit, his "mind-stealing heron."

I'm still pissed; what the fuck.

CHAPTER 34

When that Angel of the darker drink
At last shall find you by the river edge
and offering his cup, invite your Soul...
AL-KHAYYAM

I think the guardian spirits
are gone from you forever
(ANCIENT NORSE)

WILLY'S DOGS were starving. They looked like Tuguk's boneyard dogs; it hit me one day when I passed by his cabin and saw them huddled and cold on such a warm day. Their mangy fur was blowing out in tufts. Quickly I gave them drinks from the barrel, which was almost dry. It had been so long since I had noticed them, though I was the one who gave them names and they liked me best. With their sad eyes they seemed to ask me why I'd gone away. Willy was dozing inside, his dirty clothes and open cans and dishes strewn around. He had not been eating at the main house. "Your dogs are so hungry!" I scolded. "And thirsty!"

He gave me a none-of-your-business look. "*You* feed 'em, then."

"With *what*?"

"Stink walrus down near the school. But maybe you should leave it for when they come back next fall." His lips shifted into some kind of smile. I stared at him. Willy always accused *me* of being the mean one.

"They aren't *coming* back."

"I don't blame 'em. What's the use." He rolled over onto his stomach to shut out the sight of me, like I was a nag and he was in the right. I hurried out into the fresh air, past his dogs, feeling all their hopeful eyes on me. On my way to birdcamp.

ENTRY. THE OIL is <u>helping</u> the grass grow, I'm certain now: it's six inches! It's got to be the heat absorption. Is the universe thumbing its nose at me? Am I affecting the results? But I don't want the oil to be positive! My intent seems futile anyway; if our minds do cause change in the great Field they must be minuscule, or our fear has a stronger effect than our desire.

Had another nightmare. First, an enormous white bird. It cast a shadow as it flew and then it stood over me while I slept, and it was not a raptor but there was a menace about it. Couldn't identify the species. Then, the floe again. Willy's still stranded. I'm naked and swimming but not cold because I have flippers and a layer of adipose. I swim toward Willy to help, but he is waving to someone behind me. It's G on another floe, her hair a raven banner. She's beating her drum urgently as if doing CPR. The floes rapidly move apart, caught in a powerful rip. Willy sees me and takes fright. It's me, I want to say, but I can only bark, seal-like. I've turned into that "Selkie" from neolithic Scotland, a human-pinniped that mates with humans, always to both species' woe.

When I scrabble onto the floe, Willy backs up shaking his head but I proceed, flopping along like a seal. G pounds the drum harder, faster with a demonic energy. She's trying to drum back the current, drum back time itself, reverse the spiral of the galaxy widdershins. A dot fast approaches on the sea: a kayak. It's Abe with a determined visage, paddling in tempo with G's drum. He pulls alongside the floe, and jumping on with his archaic harpoon, cries out in Inupiak, an admonishment? I flop to the edge and dive into the sea and it's bloody, clogged with slain animals. The merman floats past with hair fanned out like black algae. And Abe draws back his mighty arm. The harpoon is speeding to my heart, so I sound, down, down...

LEIF WAS UPSET when I got to camp. "It's a disaster!" he cried as he paced around the experiment. He'd expected zero-state biomass, and now look. He might have to "fudge" the results. On the other hand, the oil company would be darkly thrilled in a twisted "Earth abides" way. He laughed his kind of dark laugh with no merriment - the "cynical" laugh - then stopped pacing and dropped to the sand. "I just got an article by some herpetologists. Frog people. Frogs are starting to disappear and no one knows why. We're talking every frog system on the planet."

He was squatting like a frog, looking up under his brows at me. I had never seen such creatures except in pictures. "Frogs are god in some places!" he said sternly. "They're the symbol of life itself, of regeneration! They can live for years under the mud waiting for rain, and they live in eighty below under the tree bark in Fairbanks." I was spellbound by the misery in his eyes; was he going to cry now about slimy little animals? "And some geese depend on frog voices to fly at night. How will they know where the marshes are if that croaking is silenced? They'll get off course! They won't make it here!"

"Could they follow the stars?" I asked meekly.

"What fucking stars? You can't see the stars down there!" He said it like it was my fault, which made my stomach hurt. He wiped his eyes furiously and stared down at his experiment and his voice grew kinder. "You know, there was a powerful witch in ancient Norway - really a shaman, I guess. She prophesied from the grave. She said the earth would come to an end after three winters with no summer, and people would turn on each other in great wars, father against son. And massive flooding when the ice melted in a burning heat, but there was nothing anyone could do to stop it. It was preordained. So you just waited passively and hoped Ragnarok wasn't in your life...or your child's."

It sounded like the Eskimo belief, Calvin's beloved End of the World. "How can there be freezing and melting at the same time?" I asked.

"Uhuh, right. But the thing is, that's exactly what science is debating now, which way we'll go: ice or fire."

"Why are you talking like this? Aren't you happy with me?"

He looked startled. "It's *because* I love you. And I love the Earth like I love you, so I want to protect it. Or is that arrogant? It can take care of itself, so don't worry or think too much." He said this hotly.

"If they get too mad they will punish everyone," I murmured. I wasn't fighting his ideas; his "Ragnarok" was probably the way the spirits would take care of things. I asked him if the world would come back in the witch's vision. Yes, and eagles would catch fish in waterfalls like DDT had never been invented. Leif didn't say if there would be people. Eventually he calmed down, though he kept brooding. By then I knew a lot of talk was medicine for him. We lay on our stomachs in the tent with our heads at the entrance, watching the dark blue sea. Almost all the ice was gone. Soon we'd go to summer camp, and I had known Leif a year.

He told me Willy had come by that day. "Was he drunk?" I demanded.

"Well...no..." He slid his eyes sideways and looked guilty; what a poor liar he made. So, it was Willy, not the vanishing of frogs.

"He *was* drunk."

"No! He was just very...unhappy, like a man in the wrong time. But he's not alone; it's a symptom of the whole rotting whale of a system. Maybe we should defect with him to Russia. We'll fix an *umiaq* and cross over. I'll row - you don't have to." I laughed. But his profile was like nightfall, he was thinking darkness and his bare foot was limp when I tried to play footsie. Usually I could cheer him up if we played seagull: one of us would be the parent and the chick would try to peck the red spot to get the "regurgitation response". It always made us giggle, but not now.

"An individual can't move the dead whale," he said. You just have to breathe in the stench. Malcolm X called it that 'old pale thing.'" He snickered. When I told him you could bury a dead whale or even burn it, he shook his head. "I mean *society*. But you're right, you can burn that too."

"You mean...Itiak?"

"Itiak?" He laughed grimly. "It's just the little village downwind." He was being difficult. He started in on television, one of his favorite gripes, and made me vow to the ocean - "to Nuliajuk" - that I wouldn't watch it when TV came. The true domination of reality. There were 250 million sets in the world in 1972 (Leif was keeping track, I guess). Even if you never watched, it was impossible to escape. It was "herd think". I was baffled by his talk of the enslaved housewife witch and the hypocrite half-breed alien with his "pointy-eared creed of infinite diversity", and the fake half-breed Chinese priest with fake wisdom. I had once seen a TV in Nome and it just seemed silly, though the ads were bossy. Leif was too hostile, but wary of his need to fight, I didn't contradict.

He told me Itiak was being watched by anthropologists and policy makers because we were a "transition culture", an experiment to see what happened to people who changed too fast. That was something I had always suspected but it was awful to hear it, even when Leif said every culture in the world was one. Man, no one knows what's coming down, he warned me. The planet will be one boring monocrop of white bread and rats. I said I liked white bread if I could get my hands on it, and if it wasn't moldy, then I got more of that ominous laughter colored with so many levels. I appreciated that about him, but it was annoying.

I waited for him to tell me the whole story of Willy. I poked him in the cheek with a grass and plucked the single white hair from his temple, but he was far off in thought. "It must be the heat absorption," he murmured. "But it can't last..."

"Hey, tell me about God," I said; it seemed like he believed in one now, or so he'd said. He shot me a look, and thought awhile.

"*You're* God. Unless it's a frog." I blushed, a little appalled though I had thought the same about him. What would Flo think? "Why not?" he said softly. "It's better than seeing life as the perpetuation of genes with no higher purpose than replication and mutation. That's so...industrial. Think of all the different things people see when they die, coming to lead them away -" I kissed his lips before they could say more, and he sighed, closing his eyes. "Sorry."

The orange of the sky had deepened and kittiwakes sailed by. A jaeger tiptoed near the supply crate, cocking its head, aware of us in there. "I worship *you*," whispered Leif in my ear. At last we moved together and were happy. It was like that - we held off sometimes as long as we could.

LATER. IN MY DREAM I was flailing at the bottom of the sea and I cried out. Maybe I barked like a seal too. G looked scared when I woke in a cold sweat, and made me tell the nightmare. I was hoping she wouldn't interpret it as a dire eenooa message, but was kind of hoping she would, since if they were from outside forces I wouldn't be responsible for those images (which seem almost Oedipal. Is it because Abe's my new father figure?) So I let her turn it into things angootkock.

And I was into humoring her, especially after she endured that sociopolitical trip I laid on her. I watched the dark currents in her eyes as she tried out hypotheses, discarded them. "I don't know what it means," she said at last, but I suspected she did know. Well, I wouldn't tell her the full truth about Willy, so we're even. Silent, she watched me fix breakfast and check the experiment again to make sure I didn't hallucinate that Puccinellia. "We should go see Calvin," she said suddenly.

"Are you pregnant?" I asked just as suddenly. I don't know where that came from, her abdomen being flat as ever. I realized my question was hopeful, as if it would solve every problem and we wouldn't be fraught with new anxieties. A baby: cold hard reality of the matrix in a warm, wiggly form. Babies are worshipped here. There is an optimism, a faith that Earth will always provide. I don't really know how G feels about offspring, though she wants me to spill inside, nay, forces me with limbs of steel. And I surrender gladly, insanely.

But no, not pregnant. So, we went to Calvin. I'd never met the beady-eyed bone doctor; he hides out. He spoke only to Gretchen, as irate as an M.D. with a Christian Scientist. Did "the nalockmew" still think it was all bullshit? G consulted him before about my spirit problem, and apparently the prognosis had been bad then. He had me lie on a skin, and bending over me like a creepy raven-Freud, he said I must try to think of what important "rules" I'd broken to make spirits plague me. Why were they warning me of danger?

All I could think of was stealing away Abe's daughter like Nuliajuk's bird-dogman. I asked him if he could name me some local taboos so I could check them off my list. Maybe I was sarcastic, but there I was lying on the floor while this bizarre cat laid on hands, probing, with repulsive sniffing and sucking noises like he was tasting the air around me. And I didn't like how he seemed so dismissive of G, and wanted to just pay the fifty dollars and leave. I must have said something: he hissed at G, "Someone should know always try talk while shaman is working is breaking rules."

Next he beat his impressively large drum in a therapeutic warm-up that went on far too long. I think he's a fundamentalist angootkock and I prefer G's maverick neo-reformist style. When I asked if we were done yet Calvin laid down his drum and gave G a sour look. Maybe the laws didn't apply to whitemen, he said. They seemed to get away with evil without punishment, though "they sure got a lot of mental problems". He went off on a tangent of a headhunter who was drowned by the relatives of the dead walrus, for being so cavalier. I noticed he had malodorous breath.

"But Leif doesn't kill any animals," Gretchen interrupted. "Not yet." When the mighty shaman frowned at her, she decided we were leaving. He just shrugged, lit a cigarette. He'd broken into a sweat from his exercise. We watched him a minute as if to make sure he wasn't too offended. He blew out smoke with the delicacy of a courtesan while the old man in the dark corner said something in soft Inupiak. The son answered curtly. We left.

After we'd hiked in silence a long way, G blurted, "It's because he likes you, but he hates whitemen, and he can't have you." Confusingly, she was smiling, ticked off but also glad he couldn't help, though it was her idea to see him. "He has no power and he knows it!" She squeezed my hand. "Sometimes a dream is really only a dream, ah? So don't worry."

Well, I'm not the one so anxious; it's just weltschmertz. G hasn't done anything more witch-wise, as if she's lost her need to be in control of everything.

Entry. When the Ugungoraseoks go out to the Iron, I'll go too and spend the season at Bird-camp Two, see if the results are different; permafrost is so variable. And Tallin's just might be hiding along that coast. I dreamed I found their nest, with two incandescent green eggs.

Polly and her baby Albert flew in unannounced. Prodigal Niviak. She didn't say why she's returned, but she has some new ideas to replace her old health warnings: don't drink from unknown ponds, she warns us. Children are dying; the military's dump sites are leaching into the tundra as the drums corrode. A village up the coast is part of a secret test of radio-active waste in the marine food chain. In Greenland the women's milk is poisoned by indus-try far to the south. (They have not tested Alaskans; who knows?) I wish we could go back to just washing our hands to avoid hepatitis, in the age of innocence.

The village is gladdened that Polly has returned to work with Albert riding piggyback. I got to hold him; he activated a surge of parental hormones. Willy usually adores infants, but he seemed indifferent. He did play a perfunctory peekaboo with his tiny nephew. (He's saving my whiskey, for I haven't heard any reports. It must be hard to be depressed in town where everyone is watching. At least I can skulk in the marsh alone). He left right away and Polly looked upset. I made it up to her by asking to try on her umuck parkee. It's roomy and heavy with fur, with a curdy smell. The women belted Albert on me but the strap kept slip-ping, no breast shelf. They had a good laugh. Abe said gruffly, but smiling, "Yep, those Yupiks always do that at a festival, men put on girl clothes. But not here." Ja, too Lutheran. Albert didn't weigh anything at all. Flo said I looked like an uckluck - a grizzly bear - inside a mit-ten. I felt marsupial.

Later. I was dozing outside, and G was gone. Willy woke me, just standing there blocking the sun. Drunk. He asked for a drink and I said he'd taken it all. He was weaving, fuzzy-eyed. "They called me up for induck...induck whatever," he said, "but when I go to Nome they play find a hole in my heart!"

"A hole in your heart," I repeated stupidly.

"Leif!" he was shouting the way drunks do, "Leif Trigger... trygevevesonny... sonny boy! I did see that bird of yours, that goose!" He said he was sugloo-ing before, he'd never seen Tallin's at all. "But I saw them today at the old village on the mainland. They were back of there in a nest!" I had a hideous confusion of reactions: pain that he'd lied before, like I was just some asshole whiteman. Pain that it might be another lie from a drunk craving attention.

Relief he wasn't going to Vietnam; excitement that he might be telling the truth. (Pain seems to override). Willy waved aimlessly northeast. "I saw it, Leif!"

"I believe you."

"I saw it, Leif!"

I touched his shoulder. God, he has such dense muscles. "I believe you, man."

"I got a hole in my heart...this big -" he stretched his arms like a kid, encompassing the entire horizon.

I never met that kind of drunkenness before. Not mean or maudlin, but disconsolate. G told me people got worse in the spring, with breakup and all the birds. Like the world is going on without you, or you're in a witch's insidious spell. "Why are you so sad, Willy?" I asked. I thought with him so wasted it was safe to ask.

He shook his head as if tormented by mosquitoes. "I don't know...I don't know." I offered him food but he said, "No, I just came to tell you about that liglick. You can find it now." I said okay. He held my gaze a few seconds, trying to focus. His eyes looked so young and bleak beneath the inhuman fuzzing alcohol brings on. He shuffled up the beach, listing every three steps, and each time I thought he'd keel over. If you followed those tracks you'd think he was a maimed creature.

The Japanese word is a-wa-re, the note of a lone bird flying over the last marsh on Earth. What's the Inupiak word? Surely there is one.

BOOK SEVEN

"I Will Go To Where the Birds Live"

Heaven and Earth do not act from any wish
to be kind, but deal with all things
as the sacrificial dogs of grass

(ANCIENT CHINESE)

And, little town, thy streets forevermore
Will silent be; and not a soul to tell
Why thou art desolate, can e'er return

KEATS

What has happened to the Cuckoo
once the Cuckoo bringing gladness
in the morning, in the evening?
What has stilled the Cuckoo's singing?

THE KALEVALA

I am filled with joy
whenever the dawn rises over the earth
and the great sun
glides up in the heavens
but at other times I lie
in horror and dread...
in fear I lie remembering
Say, was it so beautiful on this earth?

(DEAD MAN, IN A DREAM, UMINGMAQTORTIUT)

CHAPTER 35

Whatever hope is yours
Was my life also; I went hunting wild
After the wildest beauty in the world...
OWEN (WAR POET. *NALUAGMIUT*)

Falling tears, falling tears
(PIUVLIQ WOMAN'S SONG)

A SPRING STORM blew for twenty-four hours, clear by morning. Leif had a
sudden bad headache that woke him early. As he walked me back into town,
in no hurry to part, we decided to visit Willy. The biggest flock of cranes I'd
ever seen flew over in a current that darkened the sun, not in an arrow but
swirling, their voices in a clamor, and there seemed no end to them. Leif
stopped to watch with a funny expression as they kept coming. "The immor-
tals ride on their backs," he murmured, "in China..." He tripped when he
started walking again, as though blinded by the great flock.

At Willy's the huskies near the door were quiet at my approach, curled
tight in balls like they didn't want food anymore. It made me hesitate. Leif
went in first. The stale smells of alcohol and smoke wafted out. And blood,
thick like someone had cut up a seal in there. I was still in the *kanichak* when
Leif made a strange sound and came back out with all the color gone from
his face. His lips formed words but there was no voice. When I looked around
his shoulder he moved to stand in my way. I pushed past him. The room was
dim from a blanket tacked over the window so Willy could sleep. Brilliant
gold shot through cracks. One of the fiery stripes divided the face of the man
on the bed. It was a man with Willy's features, a bad copy of his face. But
those weren't Willy's eyes, those half-open, dull things. That was not his
mouth; nothing really was his. Yet it was him.

I had seen a lot of remains - slain was how we women saw most animals.

Gore splattered the wall behind the bed, the clots blackened and hardened, some still dripping. A hole opened the wall in a jagged star. Out of habit I noted the entry of the bullet, its path through skull, and on through wood and into the light. I did not understand. Who hated Pataq like that, to spray his thoughts and feelings in such a mess? He sprawled across the bed like fallen game not even retrieved by the hunter, just an unwanted scavenger. I couldn't think of an animal no one wanted the fur of, so useless. Then I thought of his lead dog.

Leif was leaning against the door jam. He had already known, he had felt it in the pain of his own head, while I had sensed nothing. Outside the cranes still flew and flew and it seemed the world was speaking through their creaking voices, but what was it saying? "Who shot him?" I asked thinly, then my own legs gave way and I fell. The intense pain belonged to someone else's kneecaps. I scrambled up, not wanting to be near that body, but I fell again and a dark rush of wings beat through my head and my vision faded. A vast hurrying storm of birds, big like tundra swans, white...

When I came to Leif was crouched near me with dazed eyes. I had forgotten, but the smell made me remember, and in the corner of my vision jutted a stiff and gray hand. "Aah! Who killed him?" I screamed with more power now, "Run! Tell someone!" I tried to get up; the killer might be on the loose, drunk, tracking down everyone he was mad at. "Hurry!" I shrieked.

"It was Willy," said Leif. I was shouting something and he held my shoulders like a vice as if to keep me from coming unglued, and repeated that it was Willy, Willy killed Willy. No, don't pronounce his name, do not say the name! I made myself look over there, my head reluctant to turn. Leif had covered him with the blanket. On the floor near the bed lay the .30-06 *ugzruk* rifle. I didn't understand. Why did no one hear the shot? His dogs would have told the whole village of his passing; someone would have come. Then I remembered the high wind of the night, which would cover a shot and the special terrible cry of dogs, the lament they reserved for their masters. They had cried, alright, cried themselves to sleep. And then the smell of old alcohol leaked in again to my brain, insisting on its sly and ugly point.

I shook Leif's hands off and hunted the room, overturning a chair, clumsy. I didn't know why I hurried. But I had to find the killer, and I did, the bottle in the corner. My insides howled when I saw the label. "It's yours!" I whispered to Leif, but he just stared like he'd never seen a bottle nor even knew what whiskey was.

"Did you *give* it to him?" I flung the bottle down - it rolled, unbroken. Though Leif didn't answer, I knew by the anguish in his eyes. I had warned him, he never listened. How could he give this evil gift? That night near Tuguk's I had seen him as a messenger of death, the carrier. Hadn't I seen it? "I have to tell them. I have to go," I said. The voice was far-off; another woman had spoken behind me, someone old. Silently Leif began to move to the door. "No! You don't come. You stay with him," I said.

I could not go very far up the trail before my feet slowed, stumbling with heaviness. The cranes still flew; their wings blocked the sun and darkened the world in an eclipse of birds. Everything was gray and trapped and closed in. Sounds were muffled, children and puppy voices, crane voices. I thought I would have to crawl as if against a fearsome wind to bring the news to Abe and Flo of their beloved son. I was hardly aware of Leif when he came up beside me, carefully measuring his longer steps with mine like I was an *aka*. People in the road stared at us, trying to figure out something. When we were at the door I stopped, unable to go in. I took a breath that became a sob.

"*I'll* tell them," said Leif. Gray, he looked so gray. "I'll tell them," he repeated. Grief haunted his voice, thickening it.

"It wasn't you," I said. "It was *his* fault." Then I did know, exactly, for I saw Willy manipulating the bottle from Leif, using their tie of friendship and Leif's *kuangazuk* ignorance.

"It's not his fault," said Leif. "Why does it have to be someone's *fault?*" He pressed his forehead against the frame of the door, closing his eyes. "There's no big plan, there's no *reason* for everything."

But I knew he really blamed himself. Abe would accuse him too, maybe not Flo. This was the end of our time together, of everything as I knew it. The world had split apart. Weeping, I stumbled in through the *kanichak*. Abe and Flo sat drinking coffee, Polly was nursing her baby, camping gear was piled in the room, everyone getting ready for the new day. How could they not sense disaster, how would they carry on?

They looked at me as I tried to tell them, but all I could do was gasp in the open door, "Pataq! Pataq!" I still saw his poor body lying before me like a tomcod on the ice. He would always lie there. The others already knew. They'd been preparing for this in the way one readies for an imminent storm, feels the change in the wind. They had seen the signs build slowly, the stars shivering the night before a gale, animals digging in. And their hearts had known. They saw Leif at the end of the dark tunnel of *kanichak* where he stood under a river of cranes. *Stop that*! I wanted to warn him, don't look so guilty!

Abe pushed past me for his boots in the stormshed; he pushed past Leif. With a wordless cry Polly shoved the baby into Flo's arms and snatched up her medical kit to run after him. Leif followed them down the bank. Too late. I bent over, trying to get air. Too late. Willy's blasted face...*ayii*, no, that alive and happy face, the old seagull cry that was glad, relentlessly teasing me out of my bad moods until I had to give in and laugh. And no one did that for him.

WILLY'S DEAD. I can't sleep so I write. We wrapped him in a tarp and carried him to Nelson's sled. Abe found the bottle right away; he just looked at it, turning it over and over. A lot of elders, council men, came to the cabin. They examined the bottle but didn't refer to it; no one spoke at all. They seemed wracked with pain but it was inward and unexpressed. Later, Francis called the State Troopers, but no one thinks it was foul play; they look and at once they understand. Meanwhile the cranes flew over to Siberia. Two hours of flock, two hours of immortality.

Abe and Flo laid him out on their bed. I finally dared looked at his face as Flo began to wash off his head, the front part that was intact. She was half-singing in Inupiak, keening. She had trouble closing his mouth. The sight of his teeth, a cavity in his bicuspid. I was demented to be thinking about that. Abe didn't cry when he went to the cabin, neither did Polly. Or me. He had rigor mortis and it was too awful to feel the full brunt; you just feel sick and mad. Blank. But they did cry when he was there on his parent's bed and the joints had softened up again, when Flo washed his hand and it was relaxed like he could be alive.

Relatives and neighbors passed through. Nobody tried to shield the children from it. The preacher came. Around midday Abe began talking. He kept his eyes on Willy with no expression though his voice quavered. He spoke in English for the young people there, maybe even me, but drifted now and then into Inupiak. Never using Willy's name, he explained something we hadn't known. Willy's father had been drunk and had killed the mother, who was also drinking. Then he shot himself in the same manner as Willy, through the palate. And Willy, who was five, watched him do it. Polly was next door. "But I remember the blood," said Polly softly.

A great silence followed her words, and nobody looked at her. Abe said, "People may say they sinned against the Lord and their own children. But no one does this in their right mind. It is a sickness, and God forgives." He said he and Flo had tried very hard to make Willy's life good so that he could heal and forget these memories, and later, so they could heal too from the loss of their first son. But they had not succeeded. They had never talked about it and hoped Willy forgot but he didn't, and he fell into drinking until the drinking had control over him and became a pain itself. Abe had failed to help him; he had failed to be a good father. But they would meet again in the hereafter and it would be better.

The old man wept openly.

I wondered about coffins. And the stupidest banal things, like how to dig the grave in the permafrost, how long would he lie in that warm room with people crowded around? And more important things, like is this what he wanted, for us to feel this way? Or was it just to erase himself when booze wasn't enough? Wasn't he afraid? How did he do the coordinated act of blowing his own skull away when totally plastered? Would he have had enough courage without my whiskey? Where is he now, is there anything left of him anywhere? And my dad; did their energy just dissipate like heat into space? Are the bonds of the spirit semi-loose like water molecules, or does the soul sort of keep together in a cohesion so it can re-incarnate? In Itiak the spirit stays near the body for three days, and then leaves but the "atka" - the name - stays on. Lucy told me. A child is given the name, and then the atka-soul lives on in the child. I want to believe that very much.

I didn't cry in front of people. Last night though, in camp in my solitude, the whole abject dark-less beautiful glowing night. This morning Gretchen came out and left right away. She didn't come very close. Willy has rended us, I don't know, there's a rift and it is widening but we can't talk of it. We can't talk. Abe wants me to report to him "pretty soon." He has things to discuss. G didn't say what that was, yet I can guess. I feel a shameful dread and can't help but remember Abe in that dream, the eye-for-an-eye patriarch, but it comes not even close to the dread when I first entered that doorway. It seems I already knew what I'd find. And what is this prescience? An interesting word, "before science". Willy must have passed me a message I couldn't let myself grasp. I'll admit everything to Abe though. I really didn't know.

MY LEGS MOVED along the sand, carrying me from one bad task to another. At birdcamp I saw Leif had been mourning as heavily as anyone. People knew he and Willy had been close, and hunting partners, but only *I* understood his nature. He gave the whiskey not out of neglect or stupidity or a teasing whiteman spite, and not in exchange for anything. He simply couldn't refuse; he owed Willy and he feared a stingy white reputation. And he didn't know we killed ourselves so much, so young, and drunk.

As I trudged back to the village I thought about Abe's tone when he ordered me to "go fetch that naluagmiu." There was such a lack of fondness. I halted in my tracks, so still a party of sandpipers raced by my feet not even noticing. Abe also blamed *me*. I saw it when he commanded me out here: under the old layers of sorrow in his face lay a hard, chill surface, bay-ice under water. I had killed his Pataq.

A hum, deadened and from a great distance, was approaching from the sea. As it neared I recognized it as a spirit sound. It grew into a voice from the Otherworld, a whisper. *Iqsiii, fear, it is frightening*! *Watch out!* The fear I had cast into the waves forever had been reborn, but worse, stronger. Maybe the messenger was evil and trying to mislead me and confuse me by laying false traps, turning my world upside down, inside out, turning me against myself. *What if*? an old doubt howled in, what if I was the start of it? Wasn't Willy happy until the North Star arrived? After his entry into my driftwood body, my *saglu* arms, he began slipping away from the world. *You-u-u*...another *inua* voice whispered. *It was you-u*...

Ayii, I was not to blame, Willy killed Willy! *I* was not the bad influence, it was far bigger, it was named despair, and it reached from the past. "Get away from me!" I shouted. I ran. I had to get to my drum. I needed to protect Leif, and help Willy's soul if I could, but where did I leave my drum? How could I have mislaid it?

Running, pressing my hands to my ears, I tried to think. Where, oh where? Abe or Flo may have burned it in secret. On the edge of my vision up on the cliff a shadow loped, keeping up with me. I didn't dare turn my head, but from the corner of my eye I saw its misshapen dog-like form, legs all different lengths so it limped along, but fast. Somehow it reminded me of the lead dog. I had to throw it off! Such an *inua* messed with your mind, it crippled you with panic.

My drum was at Willy's.

I forced myself to go back in there, to the room dank and painted with his darkening blood, the nightmare bed. Willy had placed my drum on a ledge out of harm's way. I sat on the floor and beat it until a peace came over me, and the terrible bed was just a lonely cot. I heard a distant yip, the sharp bark of a fox, and it came closer.

I have come, the *turnaq* called, *What is your bidding this time?*

I begged it to chase away the *inua;* I asked it to help Willy over to the other side, if it knew the way. And my *turnaq* agreed. I drummed for it, speeding its way until I fell backward and was over the earth, flying. I could see whoever was coming and going, in and out of houses, getting ready for camps. Boats traveled up the coast, tiny silvery minnows on blue. When I saw Flo and Abe depart for the Iron I knew I was seeing the future. Willy was not there, but life kept going. Flo went on picking berries, Polly's baby rode on her back, Abe kept hunting, often alone.

And in the south I saw the marsh, its living cacophony of birds. There was no little green tent. Yet even if a biologist never studied them, those birds would return. Even if one species failed, somebody would keep living - seagulls maybe, shithawks. New kinds of bird might arise if the world got colder or warmer. People would wear more clothes or none at all like in the beginning of time, and again move to higher ground if floods came. And after I died everything would just continue to alter...

"*He leadeth me beside the still waters, he restoreth my soul,*" a woman's voice murmured. The crane bone was still in my hand. My legs had been straightened out, my head pillowed. Flo sat near me, watching over me. She was not afraid, just many kinds of sad. She nodded to my drum.

"I heard you," she said gently, "when I came to clean up here, so I stayed outside." She dabbed her eyes. "All this reminds me of another time, when he died, and I went through his things to decide what to do with them." She meant her first son, the true one. "I never knew what to do with his things, though he didn't have so much because he was young, younger than -" Her voice broke. She looked around the cabin at all the signs of Willy. "*Aanaa*, poor *aninang*, I just cannot think of what to do."

"In the old days they put it in the grave," I said.

"*Eeee*, you have to get rid of everything and leave that house behind... but nowadays we don't move so easy." She wiped her eyes but it was hopeless.

"I'll clean up here," I said.

"Maybe you better go home. You've been sick."

"I'm not sick."

"What is this?" Flo looked pointedly at the drum.

"I was praying." Wasn't it the truth?

Flo nodded after a time. "The almighty is in all things," she said softly in Inupiaq, then in English, "But Ihuma...my husband, he don't see things the way I do."

I understood she was warning me too, like the spirits. Flo seemed to want to say more, but she just sighed and tried to stem the flow from her eyes. I remembered she told me once it was bad to cry too much at a death - it confused the departed spirit so it didn't know which way to travel. But wouldn't Jesus show him the way? I walked to the bed and pulled the mattress off, turning it to hide the great stain.

WILLY WAS TAKEN to the church to wait for the grave. Abe was out very late, visiting other old men. By then I was convinced it was really me that Abe was going to chastise at his meeting with Leif. If he was going to punish me I would not let him do it by hurting Leif. Let him try to hurt me directly, with Flo there, and Polly to help me!

For breakfast we ate hotcakes cooked by Rita. Silent, no one ate much. Abe pushed back his plate and muttered, "Wonder where that naluagmiu is..."

I hiked out to the birdcamp. Leif looked as if he had no intention of going into town. You *had* to go when the elders called - he knew that. I hoped he remembered how to act when scolded. The elders would warn someone several times; they always gave a few chances as long as you were humble. Though they might scold forever and a day, taking turns, you couldn't show impatience or glare, but just look down, and even if you knew they were in the wrong you didn't want to defend yourself, not how naluagmiut children are trained to do like little lawyers. Did Leif remember that from his grandad, if Indians were that way?

"We'd better go now," I said. "I'll be with you." He looked at me standing several paces away. I didn't dare go nearer. He had to get ready. I never knew exactly what work he was doing that spring; he wasn't writing in the bird book or using the equipment. *Anaq*s lay uncounted, his collection jars were empty and he never dissected any geese though he was supposed to. It seemed like he could only watch grass growing for so long. Maybe he just pretended to be studying birds, but was really watching them in wonder. Sometimes he read from his poetry books. He sat a lot on hills like...well, not like a scientist. He had not brushed his hair since Pataq, and he stood with his hands limp at his sides in the unselfconscious manner of a little boy. His eyes were bloodshot and reflected the light of the sky.

"Let's go," I said. He breathed a long space so I thought he hadn't heard. "Do you want to brush your hair or something?" He shrugged. "You look pretty wild," I said doubtfully, and he smiled.

"You make it sound like a last supper."

"I remember something," I told him. "Before Itiak...when I was Indian. My mother scared me with a story about a...a Bush Man."

"Like in the Kalahari?" He looked surprised, interested finally.

"No, out in the woods. He lived out there and never fixed his hair and he had a big beard like a caveman. He kidnapped children maybe to eat them...but he was kind to poor families. He shared."

"How paradoxical," he said after a silence. "A Robin Hood bogeyman." He looked at me.

"Do you know what he really was? A crazy whiteman!"

"That's what I inferred. So what are you saying? You want me to comb my hair?"

"It might help." These words grieved me, for I loved his hair even wild and tangled, maybe especially that way, untamed. Like the feel of weeds and rocks on the soles of my bare feet, somehow his hair kept me on the earth instead of flying around in the lonely spiritworld. "They don't really like hippies, the old people."

"Oh right," said Leif, "like Abe will suddenly notice I need a haircut after an entire year?" I shouldn't have mentioned this topic. "And why don't you comb your own goddamn hair? Okay, I'll fix it." He pulled a jackknife from his coat, opened a blade and hacked off a hank. He let the wind take it, watching me, the knife held to another lock. That is what they used to do in the old days, and cut their fingers off too when they lost someone they couldn't stand to lose. How did they hunt or sew *then*? Pataq, I thought, did you even know you had such a good friend?

"Don't do that," I said softly. "It's okay, let's just go and hear him, what he has to say."

Leif's eyes weren't crazed, just full of loss and a fear of more loss that we couldn't talk about, that we couldn't even think about. He dropped his knife hand with a sigh. We walked north side by side, without speaking. Our bodies did not touch, not even accidentally, for we knew if they did we would run from Itiak until we fell onto the tundra, touching all the way.

CHAPTER 36

Happy are they, happy are they
who will never hear the Bird again
Now that the Hound has died from us
I am carried away like a branch on the stream
I will not bind up my hair today

(WOMAN. ANCIENT IRISH)

ABE WAS NOT THERE. Polly and Flo had nothing much to say. Leif kept his boots and coat on as if foreseeing the need to leave fast, and we all sat on the floor at the table not looking at each other. We just watched Polly's baby, who wasn't smiling that day. He had a shock of hair sticking up that - with his faint eyebrows and button eyes - made him always look surprised. He was sturdy too, with enough of Willy to pull tears out of my lashes, but I sucked them back in.

Aka lay on my bed, getting older and weaker. I wasn't sure she was aware of a death, but she had seen so many that maybe it made no difference. A rank smell crept across the room from a fox skin, a *kayuqtuq* that Flo had left in the corner half-finished when she stopped all her chores after Willy died. I didn't want to finish scraping it either, or even touch it.

When Abe came in and saw his meeting was at hand, he made careful mental preparation, slowly hanging up his parka. Finally he sat with a long sigh. He looked at Leif, who met the old eyes steadily and unhappily for a few moments, a little too long, before dropping his own. "Maybe a man likes to talk to another man alone, without a lot of women around," Abe hinted. But we made no move; if he wanted to talk man-to-man, why didn't he take Leif hunting? The house was where women *were*!

In the next long silence, Leif fidgeted and was about to speak first so I nudged his knee under the table. Abe offered no tea or food to him, nor did Flo fetch any. The old man talked a bit about camp and asked about the research. Leif answered tersely, looking uncertain. Finally Abe said thoughtfully, "*Eeee,* maybe they should drill for oil out there, just forget about the problems they think might happen, or maybe won't happen. Then the young men here could work. And if the animals die off, we'll have a way."

Leif studied his thumbnails. We were all thinking about one young man in particular. Abe said, "Once my son had a plan to go to the pipeline to work. Welder." I hadn't known that! Abe narrowed his eyes to regard Leif in a way only older men were allowed. He seemed to be thinking of what to say next but I knew he had everything rehearsed. "If someone has to choose between a bird and a man, which one do you choose?" he asked. "Do you take care of a bird...or your brother?"

Leif looked up to stare at him. Slowly, like a cloudbank, his face closed. "Of course a good man will choose his brother," Abe continued, his voice rising into that driving tone elders used for their declarations, "Or even if that man is his enemy. And he will shoot the goose to feed the man. Every animal is the same; we follow the same rule of God, to look after our own kind first. That is the way the Lord made us, and He made us men hunt, just as He created the wolf to hunt. But *you*...I know you since last spring, and I did love you like an uncle, I believed you were good, though we got different opinions. But now I don't know. Maybe some people feel a goose is more important than a man."

Though he had been warned, Leif's eyes had grown wide, he was not even breathing. Abe had stepped from his dream and successfully driven that harpoon into him. And tears shot into his eyes. He rubbed away the wetness and glared at the old man openly, with not even play-respect. "How can you believe that?" he asked with difficulty.

Abe wore his snow-glare mask with just the slit for seeing. His voice climbed higher. "I believe, because of what I see you and your government do! You are very careful to save a goose from the oil and from Eskimo hunters. Two years you come up here to *unga* a goose we do not even see. But you were careless with my son's life. Careless with all my people, you and your agencies!"

He was speaking so forcefully that foam gathered in the corners of his mouth. "I met with the other men. We talk about how you give my boy that alcohol, against the law we make to protect our children. You are like that whitemen you fight. That surprise us that you attack them, but it was for a good reason. We were willing to let you stay. But you had no good reason to keep whiskey, except you believe you are above the law. And we don't know why you give it to him!"

The old man sighed in a moan. Leif seemed to be in a trance brought on by the loud drum of the words. He said in a far-off voice, "I don't know why either."

"Then let me tell you why!" I spoke up so sharply Abe's head jerked back. "I'll tell you! Pataq made him give it, and he couldn't say no, because they were friends and you know it!" I cast my eyes at Flo and Polly for help as I broke tradition, saying that name and defying Abe. Why shouldn't I break it? It was not mine, and I'd already broken everything else. But the women and even the baby were staring at me with eyes empty of solidarity. They weren't going to back me up, because Willy was dead and that was all they could think about.

Abe did not even look at me; I could have been a fly buzzing on the sill. There was an old belief that if a hunter really looks into a woman's eyes he would no longer be able to spot game or aim a weapon. Why were women so powerful, to destroy a man just with our eyes and our blood, and yet so powerless, not even supposed to talk?

Abe said in a quieter tone to Leif, "So we agree you must leave Itiak. You are no longer welcome. It is my job to tell you, for you been living here like family, and I first spoke to let you live in the *ini*. They trusted me and I am ashamed."

"No!" I yelled, standing up. All eyes followed me, Leif's in a dumb incomprehension. He was not going to get the second chance. "The principal brought that whiskey here!"

"And she also left this village," Abe said. Flo touched her throat, attracting my vision, and when I met her eyes they were sorrowful. For me. For *me*!

"But he has to do his research," I said to her, begging - even my hands were pleading, clasped like in prayer. "They'll fire him, he'll get drafted!" But Flo just took in a long breath and averted her eyes to the rotting fox skin in the corner. "What about the *gun* Pataq used?" I asked, spinning back to Abe, "You gave it to him! Why did you give it to him?"

"Do not use that name," Abe snapped. "Show respect!"

Leif made a noise and sprang to his feet next to me. "All right! Okay! I'm going," he said, looking only at Abe. He was trying to tell me something, mind to mind, but I couldn't get it. His face was like that of the dolls Flo made for sale, with a sewn-on mouth. If he looked at me he would fall apart in front of everyone, I knew that. He strode past me to the door as if a plane was waiting out there in the yard.

But when his hand reached for the doorknob, "Tingmiaq," said Abe sharply, "you never let me finish." And Leif turned back, halfway, so we saw only his angular nose and cast-down eye. "Tingmiaq, there are plenty of birds on the mainland. You can go there. That marsh is not under city laws; it belongs to no family. Go there if someone will take you. But we don't want to see you, do not visit our camp, because we...will remember bad things."

Leif said nothing.

"You can come here to get a plane in the fall." It was Flo. Her face had set into a stubbornness. Her word would never exactly contradict Abe, but it would be final. The grandkids burst into the house, halting short when they saw us. They stared at Leif and trampled back outside in great haste.

Abe tilted up his chin. "Maybe he can do that." When his expression altered, it looked for a moment like he would come to his senses and change his mind. But he didn't. Polly held her face against the baby. Head down, Leif hesitated, then he opened the door and was gone.

I stood in the center of the room. "Why don't you just kick *every* naluagmiu out of town forever?" I said harshly. "They all have whiskey and they drink it every night!"

"They are not part of us." Abe spoke directly to me now. "But we took that one in. A long time ago there was a family that took in a bear because she seemed so human, like she could understand people -"

"And I am that animal!" I snarled, my hair flying back. We didn't need to hear how the story finished when the man killed the bear-wife, like Abe was killing me right then. "You'll never see *me* again either, I'll never forgive you!" Then I was gasping, honking like a goose, and streams of bitter saltwater poured down me, *kakik* from my nose.

"Kayuqtuq. Gretchen -" came Flo's soothing voice.

"I'm the one you blame, I'm the one you want to leave here, but you can't say it!"

"Kayuqtuq, this is not his home..."

"But *I* am here!" I howled. "He'll get lost without me, he'll turn into a wild Bush Man! A wild birdman!" If the Draft Board didn't find him, if he didn't freeze. He would not return to Seattle or have any human connection left. I saw him: wide-eyed, loping over the tundra, feeding chicks and flapping his arms, left behind each season by the great flocks. His hair would grow to the ground, filled with lichen. What would he eat? Larvae in the summer, lemmings in winter. Dressed in a shaggy bearskin. But others didn't care about his future; they were too worried about their own. Polly was scared the little boy she held might become the next Willy. How could I blame them?

"I am not going to live here," I said.

"Then go," said Abe. "And you will not stop her," he commanded Flo and Polly, "a woman who cares for *nal*...outsider more than her own people." He turned his back so that I saw his grizzled neck, his leathery hide that the harshest elements could not pierce.

"You are not my people," I said, crying. The baby began to cry too, throwing out his arms and legs. "No one is my people." I left there, not even gathering up my things.

LEIF WAS FAR PAST Tuguk's, marching fast like he had a new mission, another experiment. He didn't look back; he didn't sense me coming after him, though I had just given up my life for him. When I arrived at birdcamp he had already ripped out the sheet-metal walls of the oil spill and rolled them up. He was in the tent hurling everything out, then he collapsed the nylon with too much force. He backed out, not seeming to notice me. I watched him destroy the rest of camp, dumping his notes in a box, not even bothering to chase down loose data that ran away in the wind. Then he saw me and seemed surprised. Well, where else would I be?

He pushed back the hair in his eyes with a forearm. "You were right," he panted, "I should have cut it."

With great concentration, the coiled energy of a bear, he began to stomp flat the rolled bales of aluminum. In a camp with no doors to shut in someone's face, no entrances and exits, you must turn away and get busy. A flock of wheatears darted in from the sea - the little thrushes came all the way from Saudi Arabia just to mate near Itiak, Leif had said. But he didn't even glance up. After a long time he brought a crate over and set it at my feet. He sat down with it and sighed, tired out.

"What is that?" I asked.

"Books. I'll carry them to the *ini* if you want them there."

"What? Why are they always trying to give me books? I don't *want* them!" I cried, but I looked into the box. It was the poems, the best part of the old worlds, he'd said. Even in the whiteman poems the feelings and nature were still there, hiding out. The feminine.

Leif looked up in my face like a man in a kayak who is memorizing a new coastline and its landmarks for his return, his return to a place he had found beautiful. "Maybe you'll want them someday."

Quickly I started rolling up the sleeping bag. "You don't have to go into town again. I'll ask Lucy if they can let us go there in their boat today. I'll buy supplies if you give me money." He looked at me like he was deaf, trying to read my lips. "Flo will let us keep these reindeer skins," I said. My meaning seemed to hit many seconds later.

"Gretchen...Gretchen..."

"That's me."

"You can't come. No...no, don't come with me."

"Why does everyone tell me what to do?" I jammed the bag into its duffel. "It's a free country!"

"You're a little behind the times."

I didn't know what he was talking about; he was just trying to confuse me, or *he* was confused. "I'm going too!"

"You can't! Don't cut off your whole future!" My fingers stilled on the drawstring of the bag. I looked up and saw in his brown eyes a resolution under the pain. He said more quietly, "A lot of people love you here though you won't admit it. What would you do if you came with me? I'm not sure where I'll go after nesting season. There's Canada..." His eyes shifted as he planned ways to leave me. "Through Whitehorse. I can look up my relatives on the Reserve."

I could do that with him. Wasn't I Indian? He crawled to me and took my limp hand to pet my knuckles with his thumb. "Let me just go, okay? First I'll try to salvage this geese thing; I owe it to them." He let tears course, looking at my hand. "All this study hasn't done me much good, has it. How can I understand another species when I don't even understand mine? I screwed up when I..."

"When *what?*" I demanded. Did he mean when he got involved with humans, with me? He laid my hand down and stood up, wiping his face.

"You have to stay. The Outside's a bad scene, you don't know, you thought Nome was bad, try thousands of square miles of pavement and millions of alienated whites. And I hate to say it but you'd get hurt there, there's people who just...You'd get hurt."

"I know, I went there," I reminded him. "And it's not so great here. Why do you think Pa -" I cut off the name, then said it anyway - "Why did Pataq do that if it's so great?" He shook his head. "There's an old story about a man, he wandered into a village where their eyes were strange and they were mean. He thought they might be Satan's people but they promised they weren't! But they *were.*"

Leif frowned, unsure what I was getting at. "I'll go to Seattle with you," I said, scrambling to my feet like he was leaving me behind that instant. My heart was racing; I felt nauseous, I was going to pass out. "I'll go to Canada. Are you going to walk there like a caribou? Let's start now before winter!"

We stared at each other, neither smiling at my ridiculous words. "Will you go to Vietnam with me too, or prison?" he asked. "If you cut yourself off from people here, what will happen to you if the man catches up to me?"

"What *man?*" I asked furiously.

"How would you live?" he insisted. "You'd have to come back here."

"You know the future, I guess; you're angutkoq."

He threw out his hands, startling me. "*You* be angutkoq! You used to be so clairvoyant! What do you see for us? You were smart to keep away from me, self preservation, you had the right idea."

"You forget, I came to visit you *first,* and you didn't even want to know me. I read it in your book, I was bugging. I was your unwanted guest." He was so selfish; he was going to run away and hide to lick his wounds, he was the only one hurting. Didn't he know Abe was getting at me through him? "So many ways to say you don't want to be with me," I said.

"That's not what I'm saying!"

"Just say it! Say 'I don't want to be with you'. Because now you are free again. You can go back to your own culture and you won't feel guilty, because Abe let you."

He shut his eyes a second. "I'm not going to say that, because I want to be with you but I can't! And I don't care about cultures, they're *all* fucked. I only came up here to help an ecosystem."

"But I'm part of the ecosystem. I'm *part* of it. So don't...leave me." My voice quavered, the voice of a kid abandoned in a dark, snowy forest. He wasn't going to be the goose, who would never fly away from his mate.

"No, no...little fox, I'm not leaving *you,*" he said softly. "I'm still yours." He took me in his arms. He kissed my dry lips, breathed in the smell of my hair, touched his forehead to mine. I remained as stiff as a hide staked to dry. Then he pulled back to look in my eyes, intently. "I'll contact you." At my puzzlement he explained, "The old way, like the animals. Like wolves. Okay?"

"You mean howl?" He had already turned into the Bushman.

He smiled a little. "No, farther. Remote cognition." He tried to look longer in my eyes to secure my understanding, my agreement in this exile plan. But I wouldn't let him. I looked at my boots, unable to think. He was still mine but he would be...remote. I wouldn't smell him nor take his breath into my own lungs, and like stars our bodies would not touch again.

I COULDN'T WATCH him finish breaking camp. But after he was gone I came back. Not like a normal person, he'd picked up every bit of my trash and raked the sand with a branch. There was no sign he once lived at the channel. But for those patches of black oil sprouted green, and but for his impact on the village and on me, he really did leave no mark.

CHAPTER 37

Far, far will I go, far away
beyond the high hills,
where the birds live
Two mighty rocks barred the way
that opened and closed like jaws
and two bears barred the way
but I must go between them...
ANGAKOK SONG (IGLULIK)

The wild goose draws nigh to the grave
Seek help from the ancestors;
soon you will be liberated
I-CHING

I HEARD he got a ride with Fred Senior that evening. The village seemed in shock. No one had been banished since the old days, and if Itiak had real criminals, they didn't just leave because the old men said; they were taken away in handcuffs! Hoping to hear more news, I visited Lucy - naluagmiut liked to reveal plans no one even wanted to know. Lucy said he'd arranged with Fred for a ride back on September first to catch the mail plane; he couldn't afford a charter to land on the mainland beach.

Lucy fed me and gave me meat to bring back to Willy's, where I had decided to stay. Food was going to be a problem, I realized when I was thinking straight. You could slowly starve from no fat if you tried to live on hares and tomcods. There was my small government check, but I had decided to let Flo have it, like always. I'd need fuel and kerosene. And in order to carve or sew for cash I still needed a hunter for the materials. As if reading my mind, Fred Junior looked at me across the room with his broad and sweet smile. Amezuk. His eyes were kind too, with early crowsfeet, and he held his hands shyly between his thighs as he sat. Since when did *he* like me so much? Wasn't he one of the boys who had cut my lip with ice-balls and teased Willy for lik-

404

ing me? But it was so long ago.

I turned away.

Calvin came to the funeral. I wanted to ask him if he could help Willy in case the soul was lost somewhere, but Calvin wouldn't talk to me. He just chainsmoked. Only a few days later Isaiah died. I heard Calvin tried to bring him back, but not in the angutkoq way; he gave his dad mouth-to-mouth for hours until someone came by and made him stop. And Calvin cried and cried "*Ataata*". It seemed so...normal. I wondered if the old man had really passed on his most powerful secrets. Calvin left town for San Francisco then, and I was the only angutkoq left, the last one in all history. I didn't want to be one.

Polly's baby would be named Pataq. The dead Pataq's *atka* would dwell in him, and though it wasn't Christian the old people didn't care - anything to help their son. Polly visited, bringing me my things, but Abe looked the other way if he saw me in the village. Polly said he had shot the rest of Willy's team, with the explanation that once a dog is used to running it gets "very sad" when it can't run anymore. He did not mention the unmentionable, that Willy had let them starve. He'd gathered all of Willy's guns, even the .22 I used, and smashed them. Once I saw Flo shuffling to church, looking so sad I wanted to run to her and tell her she was like a mother, I didn't mean it. But she was probably just thinking of Willy.

They left for the Iron with all the grandchildren. Soon the Meleyatowits boated to their camp across the inlet. One by one, nearly every family left for the places their ancestors had summered, just like the birds, and I was left in the empty village. Me and the old, old ones and unruly teenagers trying to get high on anything.

That was when Willy visited. He had lingered outside the cabin in the empty dogyard as if afraid to go in. Part of him, anyway. He...it...waited until I was lying down with the blackout curtain drawn and then came to my bedside, not as a visible ghost, just the kind you hear breathing. I squeezed my eyes shut and prayed silently for him to go away. But he moved to the wall and was looking for something. The guitar case made the familiar snapping sound as the latches opened, though Flo had placed the guitar in the grave. When I heard a whisper of steel as a finger brushed a string I was unable to bear it.

"Pataq," I whispered, "Go to sleep now, don't play; it's late." My command would help him settle down, I hoped. "And don't smoke inside." Like he used to, he softly moved to his own bed - the bare cot with no mattress - and lay down with a creak and a sigh and seemed content. He was just resting after a hunt; I'd feed him in the morning. It angered me. Why had he left this world if he was just going to try to come back? He had been so afraid of being killed in the war but he did it to him*self*, in his own war. He shouldn't try to come back.

That is not how it is with the dead though; we have so many *inua* in us, so many souls, and one part can still love being alive and will stay behind to see the earth go through the seasons. Or one part can want revenge, or even to listen to people crying over them. I was just glad this visitor was the friendly Willy who didn't seem to need anything, not even an apology. The land was full of such harmless shades. There was no way I could stay in the cabin with him, though. I took his old whitewall tent and moved to the channel, and he didn't follow. Birds and flowers were my only company there.

Though the calls of songbirds were sweet I soon began to long for the sound of a voice, or even the whine of a dog. At night, as the low sun reached through my eyelids, I thought of Leif. The desires seemed equally hopeless. Picking *surra*, finding eggs, drinking from ponds, I hiked in great circles and began to doubt I really existed, that I'd ever been born. It was like sleepwalking, or wandering in a trance where you learn nothing. Maybe I was in the Otherworld and didn't realize.

I was by the channel after what seemed days of this when suddenly the small hairs rose on the back of my neck. Behind me I heard the voice of the woman, that same voice in the wind when I was a little girl on the beach before the storm. It was Sila, I knew that now. I did not turn around.

"Is *this* what you wanted?" I said aloud, when I was able to speak. "Because if it is, then okay. But just tell me if this is what you wanted." I was thinking about that bargain I had made in exchange for Leif's soul. There was no answer, none at all. A curlew called, its voice plaintive, and the tide rippled on the shore, but I didn't think that was an answer. Leif was right in his letter: She, it, God, universe, whatever Sila was, did not care. She was the opposite of a god who regretted when every little bird fell. She *wanted* us to fall. She wanted Indians to fall, mothers, and geese. Norwegian fishermen, Vietnamese...Eskimo hunters. In the old days she would use the wind to whisper in a person's ear, gently coaxing, "Just do it, *ki*, there's only a little pain and then it's all over and you belong to me..." And people would do it, it wasn't a sin back then, and they thought they could return.

It was more likely that she just did not care. She was not ever going to answer.

I IGNORED the changes in my body, until I dreamed I gave birth to puppies. Then I knew I did indeed exist, and a baby would prove it by the next spring. If I drank tea of the s*agrik* growing nearby that would be the end of it. It was Leif's baby though, and she surely wanted to live very badly to come to Earth at a time like this. And I had wanted her; I *still* wanted her.

Aka had told me of women who survived famines living alone on unpeopled coasts, staying clear of strange villages for fear of cannibals. They ate fish. I could do that: I could repair an old net found on the beach, build a weir for char and salmon and start my future, my child's future. It wasn't so crazy. Even with no gun I could use a bola to bring geese down, and run after molting ducks and wring their necks and string them up to dry and sew their downy skins into warm parka liners. In winter I'd capture a reindeer to draw my sled and it could eat lichen. In summer, salvage an old boat and from seal hide make a sail, and rope to climb the rock cliffs for eggs. The main problem for a woman, as it always had been, was how to get hides and oil for the lamp. Could I net seals? Suddenly I knew the answer as if the little baby in me had spoken up: people would trade for angutkoq things! I'd heal their families and I could tell hunters where the animals were! I jumped up, wanting to start at once.

But I sank back down, already weary. Every good fishing place along the coast had been claimed for centuries. It felt like the entire Iron belonged to Abe, even at the mouth. I would have to stay clear of the Iron. The stretch of marsh near the haunted village where Leif went was an old winter site with no good fish river, the reason why no one camped there. But I would not beg some other family to share their land. And soon I would be hardly able to waddle; I wasn't going to run behind a reindeer or climb any cliff. It was not the old days - people would go to Polly for medicine. They'd sooner get work on the pipeline than help from an *itkiliq* witch up the coast. It was true that pregnant women get strange and desperate ideas.

ENTRY. I ENVY the geese their acute mission, how nothing will divert them. The Taoist asked, cannot man proceed without any purpose, "like the unthinking female bird"? but how do we know they don't plan? They were given so many back-up systems to navigate, even iron particles in their brains. Their love affair with the earth and each other is unequaled, so uncomplicated. I long for such a tiny, perfect brain. If they had a neo-cortex maybe they would just get drunk. The oracle says there is an influx of energy, but in a wasteland. Ahead lies a river I must cross alone, accepting hardship. Two foxes came close to camp bouncing in rigid-legged lemming-kill postures. When I laughed they seemed offended. I didn't feel like laughing though. Howl, maybe. What's the physiology of heartbreak, what precisely is hurting? The world reflects my inner state, everything, even a clutch of duck eggs I boiled. The ducklings came out well-formed in a northern delicacy but could not be choked down. I think if a grizzly trucked up the beach, I would just say hi, bear, well met.

Entry. It must be July: mosquito clouds and waterfowl molting. They get so paranoid without their primaries. I got lost yesterday watching scared pintails on the oxbow lakes racing back and forth unable to fly. Foxes and ravens waited nearby, lured in by the predatory radar (imagine the mournful oboe in Peter and the Wolf). Made a slingshot and stunned a humpy in the shallows of a creek, an unbelievably ugly Quasimodo fish that turned into a gross gelatinous mess, massive steroid damage. I ate him though. If the Board searched my camp the slingshot would be a problem. On the gauge of suffering it's a far cry from searing babies with gasoline jelly, but so what. With my pathetic slingshot I hardly feel a member of the species so imperiling Nature; rather, I feel imperiled by It. And if the Goliath fell to my pebble, more oil gargantuas wait beyond the hills to fill the same niche. Why pretend? I did look for Tallin's for awhile though, kept a tally of geese, then gave up and now I can't find my log, it's disappeared...

Entry. Things are altering, strange. In a pond's reflection I thought I saw my own self looking over my shoulder. That self seemed to be trying to communicate something, pretty disconcerting. I saw another boat struggling up the coast filled with people, dogs and an unimaginable amount of gear. It was too far out to identify the family, though a local would know from the women's cusspucks. Someone waved and I waved back, blinded with anguish.

Off course again, I staggered into quagmires until I came across the old village, the ancient shadow of Itiak. Willy said he sighted Tallin's there but how can I believe that? I collapsed on top of an eenee. The sky spiraled hugely, cirrus clouds sailed by in a time lapse. A mosquito landed on my face, drowning there. I wondered what our lives would have been like if we lived here long ago, whether she'd have had both of us. I would try to share, but I don't think she'd want you, bro. I'm not positive of my state of mind, but it wasn't fully conscious, I couldn't differentiate between my pulse and lungs and the surf, or my mad grief sloshing up against my ribs, my reef. I was dreaming while awake.

It was getting toward the evening aspect. The periphery of my vision had narrowed and I felt like a tin-man. I had the odd conviction the village had stolen my heart and was buried down in one of the eenee, beating away like a drum. I had to get it back. The ruins seemed to undulate, breathing with me. I felt as if the sprite "eezheeguck" were playing tricks. Jaegers nesting in the grass roofs were dive-bombing me. And rage hit, limbic; I was a grizzly ripping the burrows of squirrels. I wanted to uproot the roof, the rib-cage, to find my vital organ they had pilfered. I reared up roaring and as tall as a giant but all that came out was the thin yell of a hopeless human male. A savage emptiness of landscape exploded, terrain hemorrhaged from my brain, charging out and flooding to a vast horizon. And I was a midge frozen on a grass blade in the center of the flood. The drumming was loud and mighty, reverberating the world. Things were spinning around me as if I'd whirled for hours the ways dervishes and kids spin to fall out of control.

Then I was lying on a sod roof, horribly aware of each vessel in my body, the capillaries in my retinas like spider webs overlaying the sky, and my surging blood, the same salty brew as the ocean and loess. I was madder than any acid-head or goldpanner with too much mercury on the brain. And lucid. I'd broken through the barrier and reached some kind of angootcock-ic Joan of Arc grace, only I didn't feel graceful but succumbed, knocked flat. All around me birds, birds, birds, my spirit melded with theirs, I saw no otherworld, no visions of guardian angels or grails, just me alone and schizophrenic. And I didn't mind, though my face ran for what seemed hours, leaching me of self. I thought of Willy's fable of a man who was punished by a jaeger for wantonly killing her chicks: she made his children be born with harelips. Willy seemed struck by that. Why, why did he lose that belief, that even unpopular life forms belong here?

Later I over-analyzed the experience as byproducts of neurochemicals, blah, blah, but I know it is the state sought by mystics. Maybe science has killed any archetypes in me, so rather than visions of a Great Speckled Bird or the Virgin or a burning bush, I just saw a planet rampant with life. What Earth really is. But I must agree with Hardy that "the Will had woven with an absent heed, since Life was; and ever so will weave".

Later: Heard twin engines flying low and saw a plane land near the old site. It had to be whites up to no good. In Itiak no one had mentioned a scientific party due there. As I came from the east across a stretch of tundra, I saw two men. They spotted me when I was half a kilometer away (too intent on what they were doing). Which was plundering the ruins with pickaxes for artifacts. I felt their eyes and knew they couldn't tell what make of human I was yet. I waved and and they relaxed, falling to again. Friendly Eskimo duck hunter. But as I got closer, one man looked up, sensing my hostility. It was Waldo. I knew the moment he identified me as a whiteman, and then, which one. I should have backtracked right then. But I didn't flee; he's not the Lord of the Land, kimosabe. And I felt no fear, only a calm anger refreshing after all this walkabout stuff.

But then I saw the artifacts on their tarp: dolls, weapons, pottery, even skulls. How much of a commission was Waldo taking, the sonuvabitch grave robber, and how did he know about this place? Someone from Itiak must have told him in Nome, over drinks. Willy maybe. No, it couldn't be. But the possibility was high. Would relics matter to a man about to murder himself? The past had betrayed him. God, my insides. Everything tilted, and my brain went molten, envisioning what the pickax could do to a living skull. Berserker genes. Tomahawk.

The agent was your average outdoorsman in his fifties and glasses. A real Pizarro. A rifle that looked like it meant business was propped up against an eenee, who knows what make. Bear gun. I said hi, well met, and Waldo was suddenly play-friendly, offering me a shot from a bottle, joking that now we were out of town limits we could relax. I said, "You don't have permission to be taking these." Waldo just chuckled, rolling his eyes for the benefit of the agent. I was a touched scientist out in the boonies too long. I'd been "whopped over the head too hard". I said I was going to report to Itiak so they could call in the State Troopers and the FBI, and cited recent (and bogus) legislation: "Indigenous Cultural Site Protection Act", a felony if broken. A doubt, a worry, gestated in Waldo's squint. After I left, the chopping ensued. Later they flew up and down the coast before leaving: in a reconnaissance, surely. My camp.

It was deranged to interfere, maybe sanctimonious but I don't fucking care. I think of Gretchen. Grandpere, Sutton Hoo, Willy, the Inuit father stuffed and kept in a museum, anyone who was ever chopped at and lined up in pieces, violated, exposed but never understood. Let them all be laid to rest, even the birds I have taken apart, and their old homes they once loved when I was a "Philosopher, a fingering slave, One who would peep and botanize upon his mother's grave".

I FLEW AGAIN, not knowing what else I could do, besides yearn. I found myself at the mouth of the Iron, which had pulled me to it like I was a salmon who had to spawn in its waters and no other. Far below I saw last summer's experiment, looking very green inside those polluted squares. And there was Abe returning from the sea in the boat, chugging around a bend. He was slumped weakly over the rudder like a very old man. I passed many times over fishcamp, the two white tents and the bright *kaspaq*s of Flo and Betsy moving across the land as they collected Eskimo celery. They seemed okay.

Beyond the old ghost village I searched for a pup tent, a scientist in the reeds. Just to see if he was okay too, I told myself. I found him on top of a hill, facing Gyulnyev with his eyes closed and stockstill as if listening to something faint. As I passed over he glanced up. For a long time he had been standing there like one of the boulders. He was trying to send a message to me. He was in trouble, or trouble would come, he just didn't know it yet. And the direction of the peril was not clear - I thought it was the spiritworld again.

But there was more in his message. He'd changed his mind. He knew we were joined by a shimmering cord invisible in the everyday plane, yet we needed to hold each other with our *real* arms, not with remote cognition arms. He was my home, my nest and I was his, and he knew we couldn't live apart even if we hadn't figured out a way to live.

CHAPTER 38

My cup runneth over
Surely goodness and mercy shall follow me
All the days of my life
(ANCIENT SEMITIC PRAYER)

But an old age, serene and bright
And lovely as a Lapland night,
Shall lead thee to thy grave
WORDSWORTH

AMEZUK TOOK ME to him. Leif carried me in from the boat and we were kissing and laughing through the kissing as if nothing was wrong in the world. We didn't even notice Amezuk leaving. "You're in danger," I told him later in the tent with the sleeping bag pulled up; the wind had risen from the sea.

"We're all in danger," he said, but he meant ecologically. He told me about Waldo and "flipping out". Though I wanted to scold him for going to the haunted place, I was relieved that the trouble I sensed might be just the women's spirits, complaining. They could be placated. And artifacts didn't matter; there was so much more to care about in the living world. Let strangers put the old things on their mantles or behind glass if they liked them so much. Surely the dead were used to loss.

When I guided Leif's hand to my belly to let him feel the life we had created, he took in a deep sigh and forgot all about the old village. It was joy in his eyes, alright, but also the same fear that lay in me, directly over the baby. Did the birds and other animals feel so uneasy when they realized they were going to bring a helpless family into the world?

"You're not going to the war, I know you are not," I told him, "so don't think about that." And suddenly I was sure of it. Everything was good, even the awful, cold humpy Leif served me in bed. Pregnant women weren't supposed to tie any knots, but I was going to fix the old net I'd brought and see that we got some proper salmon. I'd set it out from the beach and get silvers as they swam north to the Iron. We finally slept in the low sun, his body enveloping me like a warm reindeer-skin liner.

The drone of a distant airplane woke us. It was Waldo and the agent returning to the old village. Leif promised he wouldn't go pester them. Happily he dragged the net up from the shore and was helping me tie. Its rope had frayed nearly to the breaking point, but he spliced it neatly. I kept watching his nimble fingers, thinking, he can do that after every storm, mend and splice and untangle our problems so our worn hearts are even stronger than before.

But the trouble I had put aside grew until I knew I had just blinded myself. I put down the net and said, "They're going to come here." My voice was shaking. Leif stared at me, thinking, then burst into action. He took everything of mine lying around - the drum, my woman's *ulu*, *kaspaq*, hairbrush - and hid them in an old foxhole at the edge of the marsh. He told me to take the fish knife and lie in the tent, pulling the bag and clothes over me. I did this. Then he thought I had better not be in the tent but in the foxhole. He was going on my own angutkoq instincts, wasn't he, so how could I argue? The baby inside me, small and unformed though she was, made me want to hide. Though neither of us had said it, Leif and I both knew what could happen to me out there with no one but us against them. And no gun.

An angutkoq should not be afraid, I thought as I curled in the hole and peeked out through the tall grass. I should call up a spirit, a bear they couldn't shoot, and make them wet themselves. But I had never gotten a hook into Waldo's soul, and wasn't sure he had one. He seemed possessed, or like an evil spirit himself. He was human but his type had killed the Indians, had chased the women down and enjoyed it. He had a wife and children somewhere, he loved and pitied them and was kind to them, maybe, but we were not part of that world. I felt pregnant and weak and foolish. I had kidded myself that I had powers. True power was a bear gun. Angutkoq things took time. There was no time.

Like I was a poke being emptied out, I felt a terrible loss of energy. Leif sat near the foxhole reassuring me. "Don't worry, I'll apologize and invite them for tea and say I was only joking. I'll say I just needed to talk to someone, I was getting too lonely." He tried to see my eyes through the grass. "Think we have time for a quicky?"

"No room," I said, but I couldn't laugh. "I feel funny hiding in here. Maybe they aren't coming. Sometimes I think I just imagine things."

We were silent; Leif was hesitating about something. "Speaking of imagining things," he said in a low voice, "I might have seen a few Tallin's yesterday. I heard their call; it was for locating. And then I saw them. But I could have conjured them up like a...it was only a flash and then they were gone..."

His voice seemed to hold a plea in it, that I would vouch that the birds were flesh and feathers, not spirits. If only I had said, That *was* them! You found them at last! But too distraught, I said nothing, listening for that airplane. Time stretched out, and "Maybe they aren't coming," Leif said, but a second later we heard the approaching Cessna. He reached into the hole to touch my trembling shoulder. "It'll be all right," he said, but I could only tremble harder. After journeying the Otherworld I thought I would never be afraid of anything again, but a mortal, animal fear paralyzed me now.

They landed on our strip of beach. As they roared along the gravel and came to a halt, Leif pretended to putter around camp. I heard only the wind and birds for a time, his play-cheerful whistling. As the two naluagmiut walked into camp he greeted them. He offered tea, and after their "fuck no", apologized for his poor taste in jokes. There was no law, and Eskimos didn't care if some old "implements" were taken no one could use; after all, they had joined the modern world. I wished fervently he would shut up and not get carried away - the sarcasm in his tone would take over and rouse their suspicion. Their mood hit me like dark electricity and I knew they were still offended; they had come to warn him to back off. And they had been drinking.

Leif said heartily, "Well, men, I was just on my way out to the marsh for some research, but you're welcome to hang out if you want." And he strolled out of camp. What was he doing? I couldn't see him.

I heard the men laughing derisively, entertained. "Gone off the deep end," Waldo was saying. I couldn't bear it and crept a little out of the hole to look in the marsh. Leif was crouching and hopping in the hummocks, peering with his binoculars. He flapped his arms and made a bird call. At first I thought he really was crazy studying birds at a time like this; that is how the biologists tricked them, to get them to display. But on closer look it seemed a play-act of his real style, and I realized that he had learned a lot from the birds. He was a plover mother with a fake broken wing, luring a predator away from her nest. The drunk naluagmiut were mesmerized like foxes. Foxes standing at the edge of camp with guns.

Waldo was encouraging the agent to do something. It turned to a goading, until the agent sighted down his rifle. His arms wavered from drink or lack of skill, or both. The gun blasted and I smothered a scream and near Leif's feet a hummock blew apart, splattering his pants with mud. He froze. Three black brant geese burst into the air, fleeing to the sea. Waldo laughed. He lifted his shotgun in a careless move. The explosion ripped my ears as another hummock burst into clods on the other side of Leif. Leif started, stumbling, then righted himself and seemed to be thinking of what to do next. As the two men paused to throw back a drink in great merriment, he signaled to me with his hand to stay down, no matter what.

I saw what was about to happen, I saw that the naluagmiut were just tools. I understood this is what she really wanted, that Sila, all the while. It wasn't even Pataq. It was just a little time we'd had, Leif and me: I had bought us a little time. Had I thought I was tricking the old spirit that held the universe together, offering what I didn't care about that much, in exchange for something so dear? I began to pray. I was praying like Calvin said people did when in foxholes, praying as I climbed out and walked toward the men. They could take me instead and forget about Leif and the artifacts, and while they were taking me he would come up behind them and get their guns. From the marsh Leif cast me a look of shock, no longer pretending anything. He saw my plan.

The agent had already raised his gun to shoot another teasing bullet, just as I prepared to call out in my woman's voice and make them turn, just as Waldo swatted him on the back in a gusty whiteman's gesture. The jolt caused the agent to fire before he aimed and Leif flew off the ground backward with his arms out. He landed halfway in a pond.

"Jesus Christ you hit him!" Waldo yelled, starting into the marsh. The artifact hunter dropped his rifle. They both broke into a run, but once they arrived at the pond they just stood and stared a minute with great fear in their bodies. Waldo dragged Leif out of the pond. I saw Leif's hand move like a broken wing while the two men bickered, panicked. They came to a decision and started for their plane on the beach, grabbing up their rifles on the way. They never even saw me. I was invisible to them.

THE MUD SUCKED at my boots and made my feet heavy in the way of a dream. I fell and ran again, drenched in pond scum. Leif was still alive when I got to him but I saw why the naluagmiut were so afraid. It was a high-power-er gun for big game. He would die soon and they were murderers as well as robbers. There was so much blood. I untangled the binocular cord from his neck. The bullet had slammed through him under his collarbone. His shoulder blade was shattered, I knew. He was looking up at the sky.

I knelt into his vision. "You're shot," I tried to say, but only a kind of whine came out. "You're shot," I whispered close to his ear.

"Mm," he murmured in agreement. His eyes seemed to focus on a cloud. He had a dreamy expression, like we'd just made love and he was resting beside me. Too much blood. He was draining, melting. I was afraid to press on his chest, for then he couldn't breath, or I'd tear something completely, an artery. His clothes were wet, the ends of his hair dripping. His hand was red because he had tried to stop the flow, but the blood pumped out mixing into the water, thinning.

"You look like a goose for dinner!" I said, my voice strangely harsh. I wasn't mad at him but it came out that way. His lips moved with no sound. He was drifting off. Why was he smiling to himself, as if in a private joke? "What's so funny?" I wailed, "You're so hurt! You're bleeding so much!" I pressed hard then. His coat was soggy under my hands, hot. "I can't stop it!" I cried. "Does it hurt? Leif! Does it hurt?"

"Mm....dorphins.."

"What?" My face was flooding tears. "They ran away, those men! They just left you here!"

Around us dark wings were sailing, folding, the wings of the geese returning to their nests. Unafraid now, they stretched their black necks tall, as silent witnesses. "Help him!" I cried, "He tried to help you, didn't he? Do something, *please!*" Even if Sila had turned her back on him. But the birds stood there, powerless. I knew they didn't care anyway, but only wanted us to leave. I thought the marsh grass growing thick and green around us could return a favor; hadn't Leif tried to save it too from the oil spills? I tried to rip some up with one hand and press it into his wound, but it only cut me. My *turnaq* would come if I tried to call it. Maybe it felt betrayed, since I had said it wasn't real, but I could apologize, or maybe my mother could help, she had approved of Leif...

I was whimpering in my futility.

"Okay..." Leif murmured, and laid his cold hand over mine. It slid off a moment later. "It's...okay..." he whispered. His head had fallen sideways and he was watching the geese back with a funny look. Through my palms I felt his heart weakening. The drum, I thought, if I beat it, his heart won't fail! But I did not move. It was the end we both had seen coming and even a mighty angutkoq knew when to give in.

So I took my hands off and lay beside him, petting his forehead, and his breathing seemed to bubble. The moment hung there, long, when I had a chance to say goodbye, truly, not like the other times. It didn't seem right though, or necessary. I told him what he had always wondered about deep down, no matter if I ran in bad weather out to the *ini* or his camp and proved it, and what I always wondered about him, even if he'd already voiced it, in the way you wake each morning uncertain if you still have a warm place to sleep. I held his dimming eyes and told him I loved him with all my heart.

All of it, my angutkoq heart. I should have told you that more, not just those words, I should have showed you, should have turned myself inside out to show you. I'm not ready, I don't want to meet you again next time in another form. I want you in *this* one, this beautiful form, *this* life.

The plane was returning. They had changed their minds and circled ar ound; they were going to bring him to Kotzebue and try to save him. "They're coming back," I told Leif, touching his cheek. But he closed his eyes in a no.

"Hide," his lips formed, and his hand fumbled for mine. His fingers worked their way through mine and squeezed. I knew what he meant. Waldo remembered he had a connection to Itiak. They had seen Flo's camp from the air and knew that their flight was seen, that the land was not as empty as whitemen imagined. They would be caught.

I thought I would go with Leif, wherever he was going. I had told him I would go with him when Abe drove him out of the village, and he had argued then but he couldn't argue now. Into the Land of the Dead, or Flo's heaven or his own scientific nothingness, I would travel with him.

He collected all his remaining energy to raise his head and gasp, "Run!" And he sank down, a bubbly red on his lips, some pink foam at his nose, like when a wave pulls back from rocks. He had no words left, the man who couldn't shut up to save his life. I saw a white cloud reflected in his open eyes; he was taking in the light of the world. I kissed him through the blood and my jagged sobs, then I ran because it was too late for anything else.

When the men got to him, they were surprised to find him still alive. All the birds had fallen silent. Waldo paced a few times, thinking. In jerky motions he lit a cigarette and blew smoke over his keen features while he looked south to Gyulnyev then turned to look past Troll Mountain. He studied the fang-like peaks inland that no one ever climbed. Angutkoq used to, Eskimo men searching for copper and flint, gold miners...no more.

"You know I was in Nam?" Waldo asked. "Chopper pilot." The other man's eyebrows were twisted up as he stared down at Leif. He looked at the guide blankly, and I didn't understand either. "Come on, let's get the fuck outta here."

When they picked Leif up his head fell back and his hair hung down, the curls I loved to touch so. The whites in the old times used to keep a lock of hair from their lover or their baby when they died; they'd put it in a little amulet around their neck like it was a precious feather, and they did not fear it. I understand that. I never even had a photo of him, just one little strand wrapped around the match stick, the charm that didn't keep him safe.

I LAY FACE-DOWN on the blood-soaked spot. I felt his vanishing warmth with my whole body. The red slowly settled in the pond, merging with the rust-color of the bottom mud. *Loess*, he'd called it - a foreign word, so important to the marsh, and his blood had turned into it. I could not breathe, I would never breathe again. I turned onto my back as he had lain, with my arms flung out. I stared at the sky, unseeing, and the baby in me held her breath too, waiting to see her fate.

My vision was soaring with the airplane, tracking it over the flatlands shining with water: lakes, rivers and ponds like strands of gold beads. Birds drifted pale below us. Leif's spirit lingered with his body, bound to mine by the shimmering cord. I was pulled along like a hunter grasping a line, on the end of which sped a harpooned whale.

We reached the white and black of sheer mountains; we entered them. The wind swept down their sides as chilly as winter, and ravens twisted and tumbled in the currents, playing. I could have made the plane crash, and revenge would have been right. But I had no time to think it over, whether Leif would agree, for the door of the cabin fell back and he was bundled out into space.

He was falling fast, he was a dark plummeting form, a goose whose feathers are suddenly stilled. He didn't mind. He would feel nothing more, already out of his mortal frame. He was watching his empty body fall to the tundra between two mountains with a faint surprise, a tiny amusement, a fading, small sadness. He knew I was right behind him, with him, but he did not want me and our baby to follow. And he knew that I would be fine, though I could not know.

The line between us stretched to an impossible slenderness, a hair, a spider thread...

In the sky to the west his *turnaq* flew on rapid wings, calling for him to follow. I fainted into a cold blackness the high sun could not penetrate.

EPILOGUE

She sees the earth rising again
out of the waters, green once more

Was it for this the wild geese spread
The grey wing upon every tide?
W.B. YEATS

IN THE FALL when the salmon had faded into the gravel and their milted eggs, and ice lay thin on the ponds and the baby kicked like a drum, Abe cut his Evinrude and waded ashore, dragging the boat. He looked up, nodding to me as I stood on the shore.

In camp he took in my rack of dry chum, the pile of eider down blowing like snow past the tent. I should have been more careful of the feathers if I wanted to keep getting ducks. Abe didn't point that out, but just regarded me with a kind of silent apology. He looked around fruitlessly. "September one," he said at last. "I came instead of Amezuk. Tingmiaq goes back today, ah, get a plane out?" I couldn't answer. There was such forgiveness in his eyes. "Some letters waiting for him, one from Draft Board." Abe kept glancing around with an eagerness. He had hunted with Leif like a father.

"He left," I managed to say. "With that hunting guide."

Leaving all his equipment behind. It seemed unlikely, but whites do rash and unpredictable things. We had fought, maybe, or he had decided to suddenly defect to Canada. Abe blinked several times at my news, but not in disbelief. His eyes wavered to the shore, which he studied a long while.

"We hear that plane went down in the mountains," he said roughly. "They never find it."

IT IS DUSK *and the sky is dense with scudding cloud banks. The long, gray breakers are heavy with slush. All migratory birds have departed. The dogs ringing the village point their noses to the wind and hunker down in snow still too thin for shelter. Thirty miles out the pack-ice moves south and pauses, stealthy, waiting to seal the Bering Strait in white. Walrus and seal are out there riding the floes, but the men have all returned. A storm is collecting, due to hit at gales up to seventy miles an hour, nobody knows for how long. The radio doesn't know, nor the elders. Maybe the seals or spirits know, but who can ask them; who speaks their language now?*

A lone old hunter slogs home down the coast. He rides up on one aching knee so he can stabilize with a foot if the machine tries to roll. He wants to hurry, for he felt the wind change and saw mist shrouding a peak so he knows a storm is coming, but one ski is broken, held together with a tourniquet of fishing line. His eyes are failing, the terrain plays tricks, he could plunge over a ledge or break through the skin of a creek and freeze his feet or drown as the machine topples on him, the tread mangling. He draws up his hood in the bitter wind and goes slowly. At home his cache is nearly empty. The hunter is growing too feeble; it was sudden, this loss of vision and strength. He did not expect to become this at the end of his life, the only provider.

At last he spies lights from the village, merged at this distance into a fragile line, the eye of a child drowsing near a lamp. It kindles his weakening heart. He does not know this village will be gone before his grandson becomes a man. It is good he does not know, for he has seen enough pass away. A young woman cranes into the great dark where the light of his snowmachine flickers like a beacon. There is an urgency in the little star so slowly making its way out of the wilderness. She knows already the old man has no game. But for her baby swimming restlessly beneath her heart and the dog watching with eyes narrowed against the wind, the young woman is alone. The door of the stormshed bangs open and an old woman hurls a scrap to the dog, who bolts it down and throws itself on its chain for more. The old one would never give the bones of seal - she tenderly saves them for burial at sea so the owners return, again and again.

The hunter arrives. He sees the woman in the shadow of the cache and stands a moment in the strange, bent-over posture of a man who has done wrong, he who had always been right. He limps inside and when he comes out again the old woman follows. They shuffle to the sled where they confer softly in the old language. The young woman understands well their glance. She approaches, preparing to set her thoughts free into the sky, remove them to a distance. She hears the falling cry of dogs. Light clings to the sky, reflected in the dusting of snow. Over the sea, now a dark gray with ghostly white caps, a band of fire narrows in the black of the approaching fury.

The old hunter does not want to touch the bundle again, so the old woman works the rope and pulls back the blood-stained tarp. She closes her eyes in prayer for she has revealed white bones, loose like pieces of sled before it is put together. They could be of a reindeer, a young bear. They are already bleached from lying a summer on the tundra, gnawed and scattered by wolf, fox, raven, wolverine and then lemming.

A tatter of hair clings like umingmaq fur on a willow branch, stirring in the wind, stirring the soul. Later when the old ones aren't looking the young woman will take it, she will keep it forever in a little bag she hangs over her heart and she will not fear it. The bedraggled lock once had the power in the light of a summer sun or a winter fire to move her to a fierceness and a softness, to a joy. It had tangled with her own hair; the bones had circled hers, and the heart that had raced beneath the breastbone and slowed to hers is living now in the animals. Once inua dismembered and ate you but that was in the spirit realm, and you were allowed to keep living in this world, with more power as your reward for dying. Mortal death gives no reward. And it still does not seem fair.

The young woman is tired of the Otherworld and feels her understanding of the spirits is useless, since it could not save what was most important. But that is because she is young. In the archaic gesture she pulls her hood over her face, yet it cannot be concealed. Tears freeze on the cheeks in the Far North; they belie the appearance that all is well and you have healed or were never hurt, and people fight them, but still they must fall.

She is aware without looking how the old hunter and woman meet each other's eyes, tacit in their own longer history.

I NEVER TOLD the full truth. It's easier to take an act of God or just the way the knucklebones fell. Abe had blamed himself enough already. Yet he seemed to exile *himself* after that, going out alone on hunting trips deep into the mainland, ruining his sno-go track. I could have told him where to go but he would never ask. Before snow covered everything he found the nibbled bones of one man, identifiable through a Helly Hansen boot. People figured Leif had survived the crash and wandered away from it.

Once, when he didn't know I was listening, Abe linked the crash with the geese. Maybe "that birdman" had angered them by sneaking around their homes, bugging them, breaking the age-old contract. Yet Flo and Lucy thought the birds understood his good intention and forgave him. If anyone had been punished it was the big game hunter. God had felled *him* - the rest was fate. Or maybe Tingmiaq's father or grandfather had done a bad thing, long ago, or his baby would do something bad in the future, and their sins were now accounted for. No, said Polly, it was liquor: the pilot drank. Sometimes though, I would catch a certain wondering look from people before they quickly glanced away.

The letter from the Draft Board ordered Leif to report for duty, his appeals denied. They wanted him to be a medic and try to save a thousand men in the way I had tried to save him, in rivers of blood, or zip into their bags a thousand Willys who had already died. A few months later they froze the draft: it was like a lead in the ice closing over his head but letting the other men pass over safely. But it didn't matter.

By the next spring all the marsh grass in the experiments had died. That spurt of growth was only temporary, a trick played on Leif maybe, a kind of lesson. I tried to think of what it might be and whether he'd learned it. It seems he learned it, for hadn't he been laughing?

A year later, Tallin's goose was declared extinct in the wild. Although some were in captivity, they failed to breed.

I DON'T KNOW who had the courage to make the call - Polly maybe, after searching through his things for a phone number. When the Master came to collect the bones and the equipment I kept far away, at the *ini*. Leif never stayed on, that soul-part that drifts bewildered in the village or in the hills. When he flew, *all* of him went except for what lived on in the child. I don't know if it was because of his science; it was just how he was. We used to believe if you mourned too much a soul had trouble breaking free, but it seems that was not true for him. And I did not try to visit. I waited for a sign from him, a message carried by animals or dreams, a kind of letter sent from the Otherworld that says all is well. I heard him in every bird's call, saw him in every line of geese, every loose feather that blew into my path. I still do. He had left me but he was still mine. But there was no dream.

My mother came though, to show me more patterns woven into the spirals of grasses, and there were baskets lined up in her cabin, so many, as if there could never be enough to hold all the things she had wanted to teach me. And I had finally become a full-fledged adult. Flo and Abe called my daughter Tingmiaq - bird - and in Inupiaq would refer to her as "my son ", as they did with the new Willy. She was *unga*-ed by Polly and her *aka* Flo. Abe would have coddled her too but his heart failed on a hunt soon after he found the bones, and the Meleyatowits brought his body home instead of *ugzruk*.

I used to carry Tingmiaq to the birdcamps so she could see them. I used to read aloud to her and her father when they needed comfort; their favorite was the old poem of the man who did not worry and strive anymore and just enjoyed the best part, when the great light of dawn filled the world. I was hoping that Tingmiaq could learn to do that, as a modern girl.

WILLY AND LEIF would be amazed at how swiftly things changed soon after they left, because of the oil and television and reasons they couldn't imagine in their darkest brooding. Even the real angutkoq had not seen it when they flew two centuries ago. Everything moved north eventually, like PCBs. One thing replaced another. For some of what dwindled and then disappeared it was good riddance, but much required grief. Like when Polly left for medical school and did not return. She vowed to make it her life's work to get people to stop drinking, but she began to drink herself.

And when the ice cap began to melt. The seal and walrus changed their ancient routes and the hunters couldn't find them. The Natives in Russia had starved and froze when supplies were cut off and they could not recall their hunting lore. Don't be like them - you'd better remember the old ways, the experts warned us. Because we're running out of oil. But how were people supposed to hunt if even the animals had changed? Messages came from the Woman, arriving in the ghostly forms of stranded polar bears, and in new forms of southern birds and plants, and in the rising sea levels that ate the cliffs until the waves entered the village like the mythic floods. Itiak was evacuated forever and we were scattered to towns and cities. The *ini*, last of the old sodhouses where Leif and I lay down together, was taken by a storm. It was 2005, during the wars in the Middle East and the same year they began to drill out in the Chukchi as their last resort.

If they really are back on earth in a new form they already know all this, those who departed. But I don't believe anymore the dead are truly saddened, or insulted or joyful - that is for the living.

Maybe some things can move them though, something special to their old mortal hearts. Before we had to leave, I took the boat once more to the Iron and walked up and down the hills and coast and through the marshes. I saw them then. The messengers. A pair were flying over the old ghost village, the black V's striking on the brown feathers, undeniable.

'And now their bones are bleaching
and this tale is ended'
(INUPIAQ)

Glossary of Inupiaq in *Flight of the Goose*

ITIAK IS set in a region where Bering Strait Inupiaq was generally spoken. In the story words may come from various sub-dialects used by different villages. In the nonstandard grammar often used, verbs have only root meanings, with no Inupiaq inflection. Verbs sometimes use English inflection: for example "*papak*-ing". Plurals (*anaq*-s) use the English "s", not Inupiaq plurals. Spelling follows a system standardized after 1975 but without the phonetics that show accurate pronunciation. Words in common usage Outside (such as "mukluk") follow the old spelling that Leif tried to use, and are not here. Besides the deliberate errors, any errors in spelling, grammar or usage are the author's - no one else's.

* * *

aanaa -- exclamation of sorrow or pain

adiii -- exclamation of weariness or disappointment (used more by women)

aahaalik -- oldsquaw duck

Aka -- grandmother; term of respect for women elder

aklak -- grizzly bear

alapaa -- exclamation; "It's cold!"

ameguq -- wolf

amaq -- to carry on back (a baby); usually in a special parka

ani -- to be born; to come out of an *ini* tunnel

anaq -- excrement

angutkoq -- shaman (in Greenland and Canada, "angakok")

angukaa -- exclamation; "Wow!"

aninang -- baby, term of endearment

Ataata -- father

atka -- part of the soul lying in a name

ayii -- exclamation of denial; "No way!"

bibirak -- (or pipirak) baby

eee -- yes, that's right

elliraq -- orphan

eskuulkti -- schoolteacher

gassak -- (Yup'ik dialect) white person; from "Cossack"

ighlu -- (igloo) house, home; not necessarily of snow

Ihuma -- proper name of Abe; "reason, maturity"

iii -- exclamation of dismay, fear

Ilira -- proper name of Flo; "shy"

iqsi -- to be afraid

ini -- underground sod, bone and wood house

inua -- the spirit of a living or inanimate thing

inuk -- a person; also, a merman or mermaid

Inuit -- the Eskimo people of Canada and Greenland

Inupiaq -- one person of the Inupiat; the language of Inupiat; adjective

Inupiat -- North Alaska cultural-linguistic group; "the real people"

itkiliq -- American Indian

izhigak -- sprite, imp, fairy or elf

izhigii -- exclamation of excitement, fear

ivu -- when pack-ice surges over the shore; a disaster

kakik -- mucus

Kanoqikpin? -- "How are you?" (greeting)

kanichak -- stormshed, entryway to northern homes

kapik -- wolverine; the fur is used for frost-repellent trim

kaspaq -- (kuspuk) woman's warm weather cloth parka-dress, with hood

Kayuqtuq -- proper name of Gretchen; "red fox"

kazhgi -- traditional men's house; missionaries forbade them

ki -- "Listen!" or exclamation of encouragement: "Come on!"

kuangazuk -- clumsy, oafish

kunipiq -- kissing over and over

kupiaq -- coffee

ligliq -- goose

Malemiut -- Kotzebue-area Eskimo

mamaq -- breast

maq -- game where you try to make the other team laugh

mazu -- edible root

musuk -- oatmeal mush

--nak-- (verb) to pick, such as berries or surra

Naagarunga -- "I am fine" (greeting)

nali -- south beach

naluaq -- sealskin bleached white

naluagmiu -- white person, Caucasian (plural and adjective has "t")

naluagmiusak -- like a white

nanuq -- (nanook) polar bear

Narrsuk -- master of the weather: a male god

niliq -- fart

ninaq -- sullen, sulky

Niviak -- proper name of Polly; "cute, adorable"

Nuliajuk -- Greenland's Sedna; also the Orphan: undersea goddess

nulluk -- buttocks

oq -- blood

palrailuk -- mythological - a sea monster

papak -- get into things, rummage through

panik -- daughter

Pataq -- proper name for Willy; "marrow"

pani -- my daughter

puqik -- clever, learns quickly

qigluktuq -- sad about a loss, sorrowful

qilya -- shaman's powers

quaq -- dish; frozen tomcod cut in slivers

qoq -- urine

ququluq -- penis (childish)

sagrik -- artemisia; absinthe; wormwood; a universal medicinal herb

saglu -- to lie, to joke (sagluraata: "I am just joking!")

sauzuq -- drum

sayu -- tea

sigaaqpak -- cigarette

siksik -- ground squirrel, the fur used in dress parkas

Sila -- great spirit of the weather and everything else: the universe

surra -- new willow leaves, a food (surra-nak: to pick surra)

taqsivak -- African or black person

taimmani -- once upon a time; in the old days

Tingmiaq -- proper name of Leif ; "bird"

tingun -- airplane

tulgaq -- raven

Tulunigraq -- Raven-man, Creator and Trickster god

tunghat -- animal master, dwells on the moon

tunuq -- reindeer or caribou tallow

turnaq -- guardian spirit for a shaman

tuttu -- caribou

ugzruk -- (oogrook) bearded seal; weighs up to a thousand pounds

uiliaqtaq -- virgin witch-shaman

ukpik -- (ookpik) snowy owl

ulu -- woman's half-circle knife

umiaq -- (oomiak) large walrus-skin boat

umik -- beard, whiskers

umingmaq -- musk-ox; the soft, fine wool is used for gloves

unga -- to indulge, as with a baby; to seek affection like a baby

unipkaaq -- old stories

ushak -- fermented walrus flipper, a delicacy

ushavak -- cooked ushak

usik -- penis bone of walrus

uulik -- shiver from cold

uvva -- "Here you go" (offering something)

vaaa -- exclamation; "Oh my!"

Yup'ik -- (Yupik) singular of Yupiit, Eskimo cultural-linguistic group

* * *

ABOUT THE AUTHOR

Lesley Thomas grew up in rural communities in the Alaskan Arctic, on a fishing boat (troller) in Southeast Alaska, and on a small farm on the Puget Sound prior to its development. Her families of birth and of intermarriage branch from cultures all over the Earth and include hunters and gatherers, scientists and healers. Her interest in shamanism and birds began early. Once she studied arctic ecology and researched the effects of oil spills on a Chukchi coast salt marsh. Although she now lives in Seattle, she returns to the Arctic to visit family, go to fishcamp, pick berries, watch birds and climb hills.